About the Author

Barbara is a senior, a retired registered nurse who lives a quiet lifestyle in Victoria BC, Canada. This is her first novel. She has always been fascinated with British history and literature. She took up writing as a hobby when widowed ten years ago and is currently working on another novel.

Barbara A. Fayter

Best regards Olive

from Barb

Last Breath

Barbara Payton

Last Breath

Olympia Publishers
London

www.olympiapublishers.com
OLYMPIA PAPERBACK EDITION

A CIP catalogue record for this title is
available from the British Library.

ISBN: 978-1-78830-154-1

This is a work of fiction.
Places are real; the names, characters, and incidents portrayed in it, while based on
historical events, are from the writer's imagination. Any resemblance to actual
persons, living or dead, is purely coincidental.

First Published in 2019

Olympia Publishers
60 Cannon Street
London
EC4N 6NP

Printed in Great Britain

Dedication

For Trevor

Prologue

On a frigid January day in the very early hours of the morning, Bev awoke to the sound of frantic pounding on the wall. She automatically tapped her touch lamp and as her brain registered the time 6 am, her feet hit the floor running.

He was sitting on the side of his bed frantically choking for air.

"Oh God, I can't breathe," he gasped. She almost carried him to the window seat and flung open the window, grabbing up his inhaler and the phone in one motion. She quickly dialled 999 as he fumbled with the inhaler.

"My husband is in acute respiratory distress," she wailed. "Please send an ambulance and hurry." She gave details of the address and as she put down the phone... "Oh, dear God!" He had already lost consciousness and slumped in the chair, his arms and head resting on the table.

She kicked into nurse mode and within seconds, and with all the strength she could muster, she lowered him to the floor in position for resuscitation. In her anguish, her mouth was as dry as sawdust but she put all she had into breathing into his mouth with negligible effect. As he remained unresponsive to her efforts, she cried out...

"Oh God, Ted! No! Please don't take him now." But the last of his reserve air escaped in a sigh and she knew he had gone.

The intercom buzzed; she rushed to the door to let in the paramedics and ushered them into the room where Ted lay. She left them to their work and paced back and forth in the hallway, silently praying that he could be revived. The old tabby cat, with eyes wide and fearful, slunk past her into her bedroom.

She could hear the voices of the paramedics as they worked over him and after twenty minutes or so had passed she spoke to them through a crack in the door, asking if there was any response. With their negative reply, she asked that they please leave him be.

"What quality of life would he have after this?"

They covered him as she had asked, for she could not bear to look upon his face in death. They closed the door and joined her in the kitchen.

She answered questions while they filled out the required forms and she caught a glimpse of the ECG printout reading flat line.

After his body was taken away, she stood in the tiny kitchen and like a robot, made herself a cup of coffee. She could think of nothing other than crawling back to bed. She hid under the duvet hoping it was all a bad dream.

But it was true. Ted <u>was</u> dead and she now had the horrible task of phoning the children with the bad news. Her old tabby cat huddled at her feet, trying to give some comfort. She reached to stroke him and as he rubbed his wet nose to her face, the tears came in a flood.

In the days leading up to the funeral and after, it was the comfort of old routine activities that seemed to bear her forward. She would have the same thing for breakfast, eat, clean up and walk out, placing one foot in front of the other, just to get through the long day. She felt so alone. How very much she missed the cadence of his deep voice and rumbling laughter. Not only had she lost her husband but her friend and comforter.

On a morning some weeks after, walking slowly home with her bag of groceries, feeling as low as she could possibly get, she saw laying on the pavement ahead of her, two playing cards face down. She picked them up to reveal the ace of spades and the king of diamonds. To her, this was surely a message from Ted.

He had left so suddenly without a chance to say goodbye and she took this as a sign that he was still near.

Spring came as it always does. With the renewal of life in bird activity, warmer days forcing the grass to green and the flowers to blossom, there was an acceptance of her loss. She heard a robin's cheerful singing high in amongst the heavy pink blossoms of an ornamental cherry tree. She stopped her walking and gazed up through the blooms and spotted the red-breasted little bird, his throat vibrating in song, and she suddenly felt uplifted.

As she resumed her walk, there at her feet lay a single playing card, again face down. She picked it up and turned over the nine of spades. She took it as another message from Ted. This time she knew in a flash what she must do.

She was an old woman now, with plenty of time on her hands to ponder the memories of their life together. And of his past life, there were things to be told. She best write it all down before it was lost in a haze of dementia, or worse still, become incapacitated with a stroke. Her last gift to him would be the telling of his story, for he had kept the secret, to his last breath.

PART ONE

Grey, green. Grey, green.
It always turns out green.

An optimist

The Execution of King Charles I

I don't want to die. Tomorrow I will be dead. My every heartbeat, my every breath, my every memory is precious to me now, knowing that I will not be here this time tomorrow. Father in heaven, forgive me my sins, accept me into thy kingdom. Amen

Imprisoned and cut off from his wife and sons, King Charles spent the last evening of his life in quiet reflection in preparation to meet his maker. He had heard that just before death one's life flashes before one, but he had all the long night hours to ponder his own. He remembered his wedding day, his coronation, the birth of his children, the bloody battles he had led in civil war and many other things he had long forgotten. But a very poignant childhood memory had surfaced, one he had repressed all his life. He was perhaps four years old. He had escaped the stuffy nursery whilst his tutor was preoccupied and was in the walled garden playing with a ball. He was intent on tossing it as high as he could up into the branches of an apple tree when a commotion caught his attention.

The gardener held a noisily squawking cockerel by its feet with one hand and in the other he gripped a newly sharpened axe. He had watched in fascination as the chicken's head was held over the wooden block and with one swift motion, the squawking ceased. The head lay still beside the block but the carcass had been flung to the ground where it flopped about, spraying blood. He had been drawn like a magnet to the gruesome scene, surprising the gardener with his presence.

He bent over the lifeless head then picked it up from the ground and cradled it in his hands. Its blue-lidded eyes were closed and already the bright comb had turned a dull shade of mauve. It was the first time he had seen blood and was in awe of the sticky metallic-smelling red that covered his hands. All absorbed, he scarcely noticed the gardener as he spoke. The gardener, though, feared that his position was in jeopardy.

"Beg pardon, Master Charles. Did'na know ye was there. I would'na done this had'a known. We best bury that under rose bush." He took it from the child's blood-stained hands and led him to the rain barrel to wash. "But this," he held the chicken by the legs, "goes to the kitchen for Cook to prepare for thy supper."

Charles snapped from his reverie with a start at the stark realization that tomorrow he would die in the same manner as that cockerel.

***

London, January 30, 1649

Dawn broke through a leaden sky, upon a grey city, grey people, grey everything. A freezing mist rose up from the foul-smelling Thames and shrouded the scene. It crept to every corner of the city and to the very bones. For the King, it would have been best had the dawn not come at all.

This grey London morning was his last. It was his execution day and the weather reflected his doom.

A trial before Parliament had found him guilty of treason and he was sentenced to a public beheading. No monarch before him had been killed in this fashion. But he had set himself up as a King anointed by God and in his mind, he could do no wrong. He ruled by Divine Right.

Over the city, the atmosphere was heavy with morbid excitement. Shoulder to shoulder they waited, as the freezing mist descended over their unwashed, odorous bodies. For most, it was the first time they had felt so much a part of something important, something to take them away from the grim reality of everyday life. It wasn't every day that a King was killed.

The scaffold had been erected outside the banqueting hall at Whitechapel and people jostled for a better view of the black draped structure. Some scrabbled beneath in hope of collecting on scraps of torn cloth, his life blood, lest it should drip through the cracks in the rough-hewn planking. A souvenir of his blood would fetch a high price, no doubt, when it was believed that even a touch from the King could cure sickness.

The gentry, merchants, doctors, those of higher station, waited from more lofty heights on horseback or in carriages, they too becoming increasingly restless. They were not pleased to be kept waiting.

Two young men, sitting on huge black stallions, observed the rabble in haughty Royalist fashion. Michael, the younger, sat his mount restlessly and motioned to his brother Philip to catch a glimpse of the poor wretches milling about near their horse's hooves. He pointed to an old crone, her rheumy eyes imbedded in a dried apple-like face. She munched with noisy pleasure on a greasy pie. Scraggily age-yellowed hair hung about her stooped shoulders. As he watched her consume the last morsels of her feast, unseen, a slow-moving louse crept up her wrinkled neck toward an earlobe. Her hand, blue with cold, reached up and scratched at the intruder.

"Move old woman, lest ye be trampled," he shouted above the din.

"Mind yer mouth." She glared up at him and then pushed her way through the pressing throng, disappearing in the rabble. Had she given him the evil eye? Michael crossed his thumb and forefinger, in the sign against witchcraft just in case she had.

A fractious child, the gender of which was questionable, sat upon its mother's shoulders for a better view. The child's chapped cheeks glowed like red apples and a rivulet of green snot trickled slowly from its nose to chapped lips. In a flash, a pink tongue came out and licked away the annoyance. Philip turned his head away in disgust. The sight made his stomach lurch.

Weary from watching, weary from waiting, the crowd grew more and more restless and noisy. There was a shout from the front... "Bring 'im out, let's 'ave it done wif." It came from a drunken, unkempt, scrawny lout, reeking of cider.

Then, as though on cue, the door opened and out stepped the

guards followed by the executioners, looking fearsome in black disuise.

Lastly, the King stepped out, appearing much smaller than anyone had ever imagined. His head was bare, showing shoulder-length auburn hair and a short-trimmed goatee beard which exaggerated his already pale face. He had put on an extra shirt so that he would not shiver with the cold and *appear* to be frightened. Quietly resigned to his death, he walked forward with courage and dignity. He handed the garter he wore to the chaplain, requesting him to deliver it to his son, Charles, with the word *Remember*.

After a few words to the waiting crowd, he raised his eyes to heaven, praying in silence, then turned, slipped off his cloak, stepped forward and prostrate, laid his head upon the block.

The executioner, his menacing axe glistening in the half-light, stepped forward and moved the King's hair to expose his neck.

The King asked for him to await the sign that he was ready.

The crowd was quiet now, save for a phlegmy cough somewhere near the back, and a child's stifled cry. The troops were still. All held their breath.

Within seconds the King gave his sign, stretched out his hands, at which the executioner to the doleful roll of drums, stood over him and with one swift blow of the axe, cleanly severed his head from his body. Blood spewed in every direction, splattering the faces of those nearest the scaffold.

A collective groan rose over the city, a sound so mournful, those present would remember till their dying day.

As the executioner retrieved the King's head, lifting it forth by the hair for all to see, Philip turned to his brother Michael.

"Alas brother, enough evil this day has brought, come let us be going home. On this day of days, after this despicable deed, we can only give thanks that his son and heir is safe in France. "God save the King," he whispered.

With that, the brothers turned their horse's heads and rode from the stinking grey city. Their journey would be a long one, as they had come up to London from the West Country town of Sherborne, on the edge of the Blackmore Vale. There the undulating hills were green even in the dead of winter and the air was pure and sweet smelling.

Charles II - The Fugitive

Poor Charles. When he heard the news of his father, he broke down in bitter tears. He had tried to send a letter to Parliament pleading for his father, but whether the letter was received or not, it made no difference.

The deed had been done and now as always when a parent dies, he found himself in the dark forward line. For Charles, it was an even darker line as he had the weight of grief and the crown of England upon his young head.

He was in the Netherlands when he received the news, but prior to that had taken refuge with his mother, Henrietta Maria, at the French court in Paris. She was the late King Louis XlII sister and enjoyed the company of the Queen Regent and nephew Louis XIV. Charles now needed to comfort his mother, brother James and his little sisters.

Charles would not take all this lying down. Oliver Cromwell had set himself up as Lord Protector following the killing of his father. He heard that he was living in lavish quarters, wearing the Royal purple, all things he had despised about the Monarchy, while still declaring himself Puritan.

The people of England now paid the price for all that had come to pass. There was little joy in their already sorry lives.

Almost two years later, Charles was offered the Scottish throne. He was advised that once there and crowned, that he could muster a Scottish army against Cromwell.

He accepted, travelled to Scotland and on New Year's Day, 1651, was crowned at Scone. It was a morally difficult thing for Charles to accept the crown as he was asked to renounce the sins of his parents, who he was very loyal to, but he had his start, albeit in a protestant Presbyterian Kirk in a very humble manner. It was a New Year's day he would not forget.

By early May, the Scots had grouped together an army, many of them Royalists who had fled England after the execution, fearing retribution for their loyalty.

Over the course of several months, a number of skirmishes took place. But in the end, Cromwell's army gained the upper hand.

At the final battle of <u>Worcester</u> on the morning of September 3, all who fought with Charles remembered his confidence and courage. But his army was sadly outnumbered and although they put up a brave fight, it was not enough, and resulted in the death of almost the entire Royalist army.

Charles and two of his loyal leaders got away. One of these men, Lord Henry Wilmot, had after Charles I was executed, become 'a gentleman of the bedchamber' and was greatly trusted by Charles. Now that he was a fugitive on the run, he greatly needed someone loyal and trustworthy to help him.

The tall dark-haired dishevelled young King, even though battle weary, hoped that he might ride to London and take a ship to France. But it was already late in the day and his other companion, the Earl of Derby advised him against it.

They rode hard across wood and hill and finally at nightfall found shelter near Stourbridge, north of <u>Worcester</u>.

In the endeavour to get him out of the country at Bristol, many kind and loyal people helped to shelter and feed the King. He'd found shelter in an oak tree, a hayloft and a priest's hole. The latter could be found in Catholic households which had served as a hiding place for monks during Queen Elizabeth I rule.

He had adopted any number of disguises. His long dark hair had been roughly cropped in the style of a Roundhead, anything to further change his looks. Already handbills were being circulated claiming a reward of £1,000 to be paid to anyone handing over the fugitive to the Roundhead army.

At one place of hiding, Abbottsleigh near Bristol, he waited for two days pretending to be ill, sitting in a chimney corner, being waited on by the maids.

When all efforts to find a sailing vessel from Bristol were in vain, it was decided that he should head for Trent near Sherborne, where he would be housed in comfort at the home of a faithful Royalist, Colonel Francis Wyndham. He was the brother-in-law of Charles's old nurse.

After again setting out on horseback and almost two weeks after the battle, they arrived at the peaceful little hamlet of Trent. There were two manor houses, but the Wyndham's was the larger of the two and very near to the Church of St. Andrews. Across the road from the church was a tavern, and a number of stone houses and surrounding farms. All lay peacefully quiet in the early morning sunshine.

The little party approached the manor house by way of the back of the property to arrive as quietly and unnoticed as possible. The occupants of the smaller manor were known supporters of Parliament.

***

Charles was greeted warmly by Wyndham and his wife Ann. No servants were allowed to witness the arrival and after bowing low before him, he was ushered into one of the upper rooms, dark panelled and having a priest's hole.

"Your Majesty's safety and comfort is of the utmost importance to us, we will try to provide whatever you wish," stated Francis.

"Your hospitality is greatly appreciated, I am so very weary," sighed Charles, sprawling out on a settle by the fire.

He was made most comfortable. He could rest in a proper bed, plumped with feather pillows and warm blankets. A bath was set up in the room and buckets of warm water carried from downstairs. He was able to shed the sweat and grime of weeks. His feet were in a sorry state with blisters and it felt good to shed his boots. Ann brought him balm and bandages to help the healing. The food and drink, which was sent to the room above from the kitchen by a rope through the chimney, was properly prepared and most delicious after the meagre rations he had endured.

His identity was known only to his host and hostess, and their little cousin, Juliana. The maids knew only that there was a gentleman staying. He spent the long hours reading, playing cards and plotting with Wyndham and Wilmot for his next attempt to leave the country. Leave he must, for only a few days after his arrival, a troop of cavalry was seen on the Sherborne road.

Not only was word out that the manor house had a guest staying, but also that the Parliamentarians of the hamlet were planning a raid to see who the guest might be. To divert attention to this possibility, Lord Wilmot dressed in disguise, attended church service with the Wyndham's pretending to be a relative, thus averting the raid. It was imperative that Charles leave very soon.

Wyndham finally made arrangements for a boat he chartered for 'two Royalist gentlemen' to France, from the little coastal village of Charmouth. But they would need to travel as inconspicuously as possible. The ride by horseback would take a good day, and they would need a place to stay for the night.

It was thought that a young couple riding together on horseback would go unnoticed. They would approach Juliana with the plan.

Juliana was summoned from her needlework and asked to an upstairs room. She glanced around at the faces in the room.

"But I can't!" she stammered.

"Of course you can, Juliana, you must, it's his only chance," Ann stated firmly.

She was tempted to run from the room in fear, but her courage returned. She had wanted some excitement and had resented the boredom of endless days of tedium. Well, her prayers had been answered; this would be quite the adventure. Besides, for her King, and for him alone, she was prepared to risk everything. Slowly, she nodded her assent.

"Yes, my Lord, I will do as you wish."

"Good, Juliana, you may now meet him."

Wyndham's patronizing approval left her quite pleased with herself. Two red spots glowing in her cheeks in an otherwise pallid face, belied the stress she was feeling, now that she had agreed. She followed him through to the room where the young man was seated. She hastily curtsied before the King.

The next morning very early, they set out riding the Dorset downs by way of Over Compton and Berwick. It was a beautiful crisp October morning with the mist giving way gradually to warm sunshine.

Juliana rode pillion behind Charles and found comfort in his closeness. She enjoyed the friendly banter between him and Wyndham, who acted as guide and chaperon. Wilmot and a servant, Peters, followed behind at a safe distance. Near noon time they stopped near a natural spring and took refreshment, allowing their horses a much-needed rest. Juliana was already very weary. This activity was a far cry from sitting near her fire and doing needlework.

Night time found them in the hills above Charmouth; as the sky darkened they rode down the steep hill to the town. Wyndham had previously, by messenger, booked a room for Charles and Juliana, telling the landlady, to avert any suspicion, that a gentleman had stolen away a lady and married her and needed lodging.

The Queen's Arms Inn was full of guests. Following the evening meal, Wilmot and Peters left for the beach to await the boat that was due to arrive. Charles, Wyndham and Juliana remained at the inn. After many hours of waiting, Wyndham went out to investigate and after many more hours, returned with the news that the boat had not come.

Much upset with this uneventful fiasco, Charles with Wyndham and Juliana set out for Bridport, leaving in their wake people at the inn who had become much intrigued with them. Wilmot and Peters were to join them later when they had found out what had been the trouble with the expected boat. But Wilmot's horse needed a shoe refit, so Peters went on without him. The farrier became suspicious of a horseshoe that had been cast in the Midlands and attempted to seek help from the local Minister. After much deliberation, word was given to the Roundhead militia, of the suspicious nature of Wilmot, and. troops were soon galloping in hot pursuit.

The threesome had already arrived in Bridport which was milling with troops. There were troops on the road and troops in the town, shouting out orders and their torches flaring. Charles was truly frightened that he might be discovered.

After a few close calls, they departed the town and headed back up the London road then by way of rough countryside to eventually make their way back to Trent. Any further attempt to leave the country at this time was absolutely out of the question. Every port along the coast would be closely watched for the King's attempt to flee.

On the long journey back to Trent, through rain and lashing wind off the sea, the little party was a picture of despair and desolation. Each travelled quietly in their own thoughts. At times, Wilmot would try to cheer Charles onward by recalling some of the adventures which he thought amusing. How provident it was that the young woman following the troops had gone into labour, causing so much upset at the inn, that they went unnoticed.

Francis Wyndham ruminated over the day and became increasingly more troubled as they approached his home. It was a home that he could lose as well as his head if he were caught aiding and abetting the young King. By the time they reached the manor house in the dark late hour, he had made up his mind and would put his plan to work on the morrow.

Once the forlorn party had been fed and settled for the night, Francis whispered to his wife that they were in grave danger sheltering the King under their roof. She wholeheartedly agreed after hearing of the fiasco in Charmouth and this was already his second attempt at leaving. Between them, they decided that although Charles could remain in the manor house seeking the safety of the priest's hole if necessary, the family and all servants must leave for a week. Wilmot must go away and make further plans for Charles' departure.

In the morning when they put the plan to Charles and Wilmot, they both agreed. Ann stated that she would have the maids lay out food and drink so that he would not go hungry. Charles nodded that this would be most acceptable and that he would be fine. He hated that he had put the family to so much trouble.

Francis was much relieved. He had one errand to make, but advised that the household be ready to depart upon his return. He must ride to Sherborne.

***

One hour later, he returned with the news that the Canton brothers from Sherborne would look in on Charles. If need be they could take him over to the Sandford Orcas manor house where they were frequent visitors. They were trusted men, loyal to the Crown and good friends of the family. Charles said he looked forward to meeting them and advised Francis to make haste his planned journey.

By late afternoon, the family and all members of the household were packed up and ready to make their way to Bath. Wilmot had left earlier making his way towards Kent, where he hoped to secure another craft for the King. Word was left with the vicar of the church that the family and all household would be away for possibly a fortnight.

Two laden carriages and all horses trotted down the driveway bordering on church grounds and out onto the road. People in their houses peered through windows to see the party leave.

All was silent at the manor house now. Charles gave a deep sigh and stretched out on a lounge in the upstairs room and fell into a deep sleep.

***

Charles woke with a start as day was dawning. The fire had died down and was now mostly ash, but a few embers amongst readily combusted with the dry kindling he gingerly fed it. Then, realizing that the smoke rising from any of the chimneys might alert someone that perhaps all the household had not left, that someone was indeed in residence, he put it out.

Ann had been true to her word. An earthenware jug of brew, a round of cheese and a loaf of bread was laid out on the table. He poured himself some beer, tore off a chunk of bread and spread it with rich butter, sliced a thick slab of cheese and sat back to enjoy his little repast. The house was so quiet, that his chewing and swallowing seemed noisy to his ears. He ate heartily though and felt fortified again. Left now with just his thoughts.

He walked across the room and peered furtively out the front leaded windows over the shrubs and trees to the church spire. All seemed very still. Then in the distance he heard the bawling of cattle and awakening sounds from a nearby farm. His eyes were drawn to a spider that had spun a web on the outside of the window and was making a meal of a fly it had trapped. He hoped it was not a bad omen.

He felt so alone. He grabbed up the rough cloak and hat of his disguise and set off out the back door to take a walk over the hills. There he could survey again, his location. He wanted to take it all in, to never forget these days. Francis had said that the Canton brothers would be coming by in the afternoon.

He looked forward to meeting them, he hoped they would arrive unnoticed.

The Virginia creeper covering the back garden wall glowed crimson in the early morning sunlight. Birdsong filled the air. It was peaceful.

Several knotted old apple trees overhung the outer wall. From one of the nearest branches he picked several of the late russet apples and pushed them into his pocket. He took a less-travelled path over stubble fields and the steep rising hills beyond.

As expected, when he reached the upper most hill, the view across the vale was breathtaking. Just the tops of trees and hills and church spires could be seen rising above the autumn mist. The sun gave out more warmth now and there was a promise of a warm October day. He came upon a copse of trees, mainly copper beech. The leaves fell about his feet in a sudden breeze. Near the middle of the grove rose a huge and ancient oak, the trunk of which was hollow. He gazed up into the branches reminding himself of taking refuge in one half the size, during his early flight from the battle.

He sat down at the base and leaned back against it, his head resting on the rough bark. He pulled from his pocket one of the apples and took a big bite. It was sweet and delicious, the juice ran down his chin. Oh, if only his life could be as serene and uncomplicated as this. He hoped that this place would always be imprinted on his memory and he vowed that when his kingdom was won, he would return here. With this quieting thought in mind, he relaxed in the warmth of the sun and dozed.

***

A mist rose up from somewhere deep within the earth, swirling around and engulfing him where he sat. Within the mist stood a beautiful goddess, clothed from head to toe in a flowing pale green gossamer gown. Her face, white as a lily, was serene and glowing with life. She spoke to him in a voice as melodious as birdsong and addressed him as 'The Hope of Britain'.

"Come and I will show you Arthur's world, unseen behind the mist. It lies hidden from all but the faithful and the chosen." She took his hand and led him over the hills to the Isle of Avalon. There he could see the ancient Tor of Glastonbury and the temple dedicated to the Angel Michael by the early Christians. She showed him the blossoming thorn tree where Joseph of Arimathea had struck his staff to the holy ground on which the great monastery had been built. She told him that during the time of the ancient Druids who had worshipped there, that Christ had been brought there to be schooled in their ways. In those days, Christian and Druid worshipped the one God. When the Romans arrived enforcing their laws, killing the Druids and destroying their sacred groves, by an act of powerful magic, they removed their refuge to a misty place unseen by mankind.

"It still exists and I will show you when the time is right. But now come and drink from the magical spring. It has been flowing since the beginning of time and will flow forever."

Charles got down on his knees and bent over the bubbling pool, He dipped in his hands, scooping up and drinking the metallic tasting clear water. It seemed to leave a rusty appearance to the surrounding rocks. The cool clear water quenched his thirst of body and soul.

"You have been chosen to lead the people of Britain, you have the blessing of the Goddess." When he looked up, she had disappeared.

Well over an hour later, for he now heard the church bells toll the noon hour, he awoke from a pleasant dream. But it seemed so real, was it a dream? It had left him feeling refreshed as never before, hopeful and almost happy. He then realized he must get back to the manor before the Canton brothers arrived.

The Canton Brothers

Sherborne, situated within the Blackmore Vale, was one of the most beautiful market towns in all of England. Nearly all the buildings were constructed of the honey-coloured ham hill stone. Overlooking the lower part of the town rose the abbey, surrounded by almshouses, market cross and boy's school. The Sherborne School had been educating boys since the 8th century.

The newer castle, built on the fringe of the town, was built during the reign of Elizabeth I and owned by Sir Walter Raleigh. The older castle, in ruins since the plundering by King Henry VIII remained as a monument to the destruction.

This town was home to the Canton brothers, the only sons of a wealthy squire who had been a wool merchant. The family home was situated very near the abbey and school. It was an impressive building of the light stone and was graced with courtyard and mews. The family boasted the ownership of six black stallions, with a groom and stable hand to care for them.

Philip and Michael were former pupils, 'old Sherburians' of the boy's school. They were well educated, spoke the King's English and were fluent in the French language. They, as most people in Sherborne, were staunch Royalists.

The young men wanted for nothing. They dressed well, ate well, rode well and led a relatively leisurely life style. Their father died at an early age, leaving Philip the elder son, his entire fortune. Their mother, a lady of impeccable bearing, lived with them still. She loved her sons and left them to their own devices.

Both were well thought of in social circles and were frequent visitors to the manor houses in the area, namely Sandford Orcas and Trent.

Philip was tall, dark haired and well built. He had a deep

resonating voice and his green eyes shadowed by dark brows, had a way of penetrating his listener. His manner of dress was impeccable. He was clean shaven, his hair long and tied back. He wore a tricorn hat, well-cut coat, riding breeches and highly-polished black leather boots to complete his attire. He was arrogant, opinionated but jovial for the most part. He enjoyed strong drink, good company, playing at cards, and though unmarried, quite enjoyed female closeness. He was known to meet a certain lady in a bluebell wood on the fringe of the town, while her horse stood tethered to a tree.

Michael was 21 years old, two years younger than his older brother. He was also tall, well built with dark hair and dark eyes that danced mischievously. He was fun loving and liked to joke. His manner of dress was very similar to his brother but he preferred to wear a long cloak and brown leather boots with his riding breeches. He was an excellent horseman and was often seen riding full gallop across meadows and the Dorset downs as far away as Maiden Castle.

He was also an excellent dancer and card player, less of a drinker than Philip.

Michael tended to look after his brother even though he was younger. Women paid him much attention as he was always the life of the party. He was quite proud of his reputation for bedding the ladies; if they were married, all the better.

***

When Francis Wyndham arrived unexpectedly at the Canton home at such an early hour, they feared he might be bringing bad news. The rumour amongst Royalist circles was that it was probably the young King as guest at the manor house, so they were not surprised at his request. For them to keep him company and see to his needs would be an honour.

It quite suited, as the Lord and Lady of Sanford Orcas manor had asked that they might come by and stay for a few days there, as they were off to Salisbury to attend a funeral, taking the servants with them. The yeoman farmer who resided in the courtyard cottage would oversee the grounds and could stable their horses when they arrived.

So it was agreed on a handshake that they would give honourable service to the King, and that Wyndham could leave with a clear conscience.

Shortly after the abbey bells tolled the noon hour, they said goodbye to their mother and made haste for the ride to Trent. They knew a shortcut over the hills, and could enter the manor grounds by way of the back entrance unnoticed.

Charles Meets the Brothers

Charles entered the manor by way of the servants' entrance and through to the spacious kitchen. He realized that he was ravenous. A large tankard of cool beer was beckoning. He helped himself to the beer, a slab of cheese, bread and chicken legs and carried his meal to the upper room. It was quite chilly even though a slant of sunlight lit up a square of floor near the centre.

He sat with his feet on a low stool and watched the dust motes making a lazy pattern in the sunlight. Munching and drinking down his meal, he soon felt fortified and looking forward to meeting the brothers.

Moments later, he wandered over to a back window which overlooked the courtyard. As he watched, he noticed two men walking their large black stallions in through the back gate, then to the stables where they settled them.

Soon, footsteps were heard on the staircase and then a light knock on the door of his room.

"Enter," summoned Charles. The door opened and in walked the men. Philip was the first to greet the King and with a bow, introduced himself. Then Michael stepped forward and bowing, held the King's gaze. Neither could believe their uncanny likeness to one another, and Charles fairly gasped, he was so astounded.

"We could pass as twins if it were not for this mess of shorn hair."

"Well, certainly as brothers," mused Philip. "We are at your service, your Majesty." And after this introduction the three men fell into easy conversation, quite relaxed in each other's' company.

Philip stated that the Lady of Sanford Orcas manor, knowing that they would come while she was away, would have a meal laid out for them. A cold meal it would be, but there would be plenty to eat and drink. He suggested to Charles that they make their way to Sandford

Orcas by way of the back fields, but he should return at dark. They had heard that Trent manor might be raided by troops but it was unlikely that it would be done in darkness especially now it was thought to be vacated.

Charles was willing to do as they suggested. He had hidden in so many places and so far had been lucky. But for how long his luck would hold out, he'd rather not think about it.

Sometime later, the three rode into the Sandford Orcas courtyard by way of the back entrance. Charles had ridden with Philip as his own horse had been taken with the Wyndham's entourage.

Farmer John was busy filling the stone water trough near the stables and looked up from his work as they dismounted. He was dressed in the rough linen smock of his labour, smeared with mud and clinging straw. He called out a greeting in his broad Dorset drawl and tugged at his forelock in servitude towards the brothers who he recognized. He did not, however, know the third man who he felt was rather commonly dressed to be associated with them, nor was he introduced. He took the horses' reigns and led them to the stable as the threesome headed through the walled garden gate and through the entrance of the manor house.

The large sitting room gave welcoming warmth as a fire still glowed in the massive fireplace. The logs were of such a size that it would burn for hours. The promised meal had been laid out on a side table; a generous joint of lamb, loaves of bread, rich country butter and cheese, a plate of apples, pears and figs, a fruitcake and a cask of good Somerset cider. They loaded up pewter plates with the fare and sprawled on divans near the fire, and commenced to eat, drink and chat.

Tongues loosened after a few tankards of cider and Michael blurted out that they had been in attendance at the execution of Charles' father. The young man insisted on all the details, sitting on the edge of his seat with eyes wide and attentive. He broke down and wept pitifully, not caring of his audience. It felt good to let go of his bottled-up feelings of grief. He had been so swept up in the aftermath of that day, his subsequent travelling to Scotland to be crowned, to raise an army, to do battle and run that he had had little time to grieve. When his tears were spent, he smiled broadly and thanked the brothers for their loyalty to his father and now to him.

"God save the King!" The brothers raised their tankards in a toast to him.

Over more cider, Charles now regaled them with everything that had happened to him in detail, laughing heartily at times over some of the mishaps. Telling them of the places he had slept, disguises he had worn, his sore feet, poor food and fear of being captured, absolutely everything he had endured.

He did not know how the next days would fare; only that it had been left with Lord Wilmot to find a craft near Shoreham in Kent. There were trusted allies who knew where he took refuge and would help him to get to Shoreham where he would meet Wilmot. He had been advised to wear the disguise of a merchant seaman. These clothes, Wyndham had provided.

Through the course of the long afternoon with much smoking, drinking and laughter, Philip asked Charles if he might like to play a hand of cards. To this invitation, Charles jovially accepted and the men took the staircase to the upper floor, laughing and stumbling to enter the games room. Candles were lit all round the seating area as evening was drawing in and the room was dim. Charles was pleased to see the handsome card table. It was large, octagonal in shape, finely polished with pictograms of the higher card suits. He grabbed up the playing cards, shuffled the deck and dealt the first hand.

They continued to laugh, play and talk. Charles appeared to be fairly intoxicated with a slight slur to his voice. Little had he known that for anyone not used to the Somerset cider it could have that effect.

He never thought he would, certainly would not have sober, tell anyone of his experience in the mist of the other realm. But he had uttered the words and could not retract them now. He watched the men as disbelief registered on their faces.

Philip and Michael exchanged knowing glances at each other; they couldn't believe what they had heard from the King's mouth. Whether Charles was aware of the shock he had caused or not, he stood up from his chair, said that he needed to relieve himself. He stumbled, knocking over the chair and left the room. When he was out of earshot...

"Surely he must be addled, a goddess if you please! What manner of King might he be?" whispered Philip.

"To be truthful Philip, I fear he is not right in his mind. All this talk about an underworld, another realm through the vale. I too have wandered through the forests of the Blackmore vale and all over this West Country, but all this can only be his imagination. He sounds a bit like the old crone, Hattie of Nether Compton; she swears she sees the little folk in the morning mists, frolics and dances with them to wild abandon. The villagers have witnessed her antics. At other times she seems quite sane, growing and preparing herbs and potions and helping those who come to her for cures and advice. She may even be a witch!"

"But the King, this just can't be right," suggested Philip close to his brother's ear. "We really must do something or this country will be truly lost, never mind about Cromwell. What say we try to get him talking again, perhaps it will become clearer what he's on about?"

"I am truly worried, if and when he gains the crown of England, what damage can he do? moaned Michael. "We must think on this brother, everything we have could be in jeopardy."

Heads together, they whispered, conspiring what they should do.

"Many circumstances have been decided on the turn of a card," whispered Michael. "When he returns we will each draw a card. If you or I draw a higher card than he, we have the upper hand and must act. But if he should draw a higher card, we must let fate have her way."

"Agreed," said Philip, rising to go and pour more drinks as they could hear him stumbling up the stairs. "It's getting late and he is already worse for the cider, we must soon leave for Trent."

Charles weaved back into the room and both men stood and bowed to him. He sat heavily on the chair that had been retrieved from the floor, saying, "Sit, sit, and let us play on."

"Shall we draw cards to see who will deal the next hand?" queried Michael.

"Certainly," replied Charles as he reached to draw a card from the shuffled deck. Charles drew the nine of spades; Philip drew the king of diamonds, and Michael the ace of spades.

"You have the upper card, Michael," slurred Charles. "So deal the hand and let us play the game."

Philip and Michael again exchanged a conspiratorial look as the King drained his tankard and noisily slammed it on the table.

"One more hand, your Majesty, and then we must make tracks before it is too dark to see."

A short while later, they left the manor house and Philip summoned the farmer, knocking loudly at his door. John jumped up from his disturbed supper and got the horses from the stable.

As the King was quite drunk, Philip asked John to come with them to Trent. John helped Charles up on his large mare and being of heavy build and muscle, rode with the King sitting in front and holding him securely lest he fall.

It was a chilly clear night. From the light of a full moon, they were able to see quite clearly as they made their way over the hills behind the Sandford Orcas manor to the back entrance of the Trent manor. It was well that they had enlisted the help of the farmer as by the time they had arrived, Charles was sound asleep.

John literally carried him up the stairs. Philip led, holding a candle to light the way. The King was hoisted onto a settle and was by now beginning to snore loudly. The brothers walked over to the window with their backs to the sleeping Charles. John stood near turning his straw hat in his hands, and nervously awaited the next request. They gazed out the window on to the moonlit courtyard below.

"Go now, John, thank you for your help" said Philip. "But be around in the morning, we may need you again." Michael took up a candle and showed the man out.

When Michael returned to the room, Philip sat smoking, deep in thought, watching the snoring King. Then he got up with a candle, went to the adjacent room. Hidden behind a heavy tapestry, was the door to the priest's hiding place. Michael followed. It truly was very small and close. It had no window. The only contents were a straw-filled bed, rough wool blanket, a chamber pot, small stool, and candleholder with two extra candles. There was little space to move.

"He really is safer in this little concealed room for the night, in case the place is raided, and until we decide what to do," said Michael.

Philip agreed, so between them they carried the sleeping Charles from the room to the hiding place. Seeing the plate with chicken leg and apple, they placed it beside him, should he awake hungry.

With that, the strong oak door was closed and the tapestry pulled over to conceal it. They were ignorant of the fact that the door could not be opened from the inside. They were weary and had the ride ahead of them back to Sandford Orcas. They had much to discuss this night.

Priest Hole

The priest's hole was a hiding place which had been built into many of the great Catholic homes of England during the time of Queen Elisabeth I when Catholics were persecuted by the law. The law was severely enforced on seminary priests. They were not allowed to celebrate the rites of the faith and could be imprisoned for life if found to be guilty of a third offence. All those who refused to take the Oath of Supremacy (the Queen as head of the Anglican church) were guilty of high treason which was punishable by death.

To protect their priests, it was common for the castles and great country manor houses to be prepared in the event that a raid should take place, to have a place of concealment which was so well hidden it could not be found. They often took the form of a small chapel or tiny room in secluded parts of the house. Mass could be celebrated in privacy and safety. It was a place where the priest could slip into in a moment's notice or where vestments, sacred vessels and altar pieces could be stored.

Priest hunters or 'pursuivants' would search suspected homes, sometimes bringing with them skilled carpenters and masons to pull away boards or masonry and were known to stay for days or even weeks in their quest to find a hiding place. These raids could cause a hiding priest to be cramped up and half-starved or even die of suffocation from lack of oxygen by the time the search party gave up.

Many of the hiding places were designed and built by a Jesuit lay brother, Nicholas Owen, who devoted most of his life to protect the priests from persecution. He built the entrances disguised to make them most unlike what they really were. The ones he built, he kept a secret and would never disclose the hiding place of a priest to any other person. He alone was architect and builder.

How many he made in his lifetime, no one knows. Some may still be undiscovered. In the end, for his duplicity, he was taken to the Tower of London and tortured to death on the rack. He was later declared a Saint by the Roman Catholic church.

The Hiding Place

Charles awoke to absolute blackness. His head throbbed severely and his gut spun. He was freezing cold and in that nether region between sleep and wakefulness, he had no idea where he was. He pushed his brain to think back to his last conscious moments as to where he might be. In a fuzzy haze, he remembered two men and a manor house. He had no recollection of what had transpired. Had he been captured and thrown in this prison cell? He felt around him on the floor, felt the straw of his sleeping place and his fingers stumbled on what felt like a candle. He had his little tinder box given him by his father and pulled it from his inner pocket. He could only feel the contents; the tinder and two sulphur matches. He struck the steel with the flint several times bringing a spark which ignited the tinder and then his match. Quickly he lit the candle and as the room brightened, he gazed around and realized where he was.

The quiet was frightening. He tried to push open the door which would not budge. He knocked as hard as he could and listened. Nothing. He called out as loudly as he could, "Help, help!" Nothing. Then realizing his situation, ice cold fingers of fear clutched at his chest in a vice-like grip. This was perdition, his worst nightmare come true. He was locked in.

He consciously made himself take a few deep breaths to try to calm him, but his guts heaved and he dry retched for some minutes. Oh, how that made his head hurt, and then he realized he needed to relieve himself and urinated in the chamber pot. There was nothing to drink. He looked absently at the chicken leg and it made his gut heave again. He picked up the apple and took a bite. It helped to clear the sour taste in his mouth and as he chewed he tried to remember. Something about a card game came to mind. Yes, the Canton brothers, they would know he was here and would come and let him out. They had mentioned that troops were around, and he was here for his safety, that was it. He felt a flicker of hope now.

One candle burned down so he lit the second with it. He'd try to stay calm; he could do nothing but wait and think about things. He had his little leather-bound prayer book in his cloak. He'd just sit and read for a while.

Time passed very slowly, he couldn't quite remember what day it was. He thought he might have heard church bells tolling, but hadn't bothered to count the time. He had no idea if it were day or night. The thick stone walls seemed to muffle all sound; they were icy cold to touch and quite damp from the condensation of his breath.

As the second candle burned down, he questioned whether he should light the third and last one. But if he let it go out, he might not be as lucky starting his last match. Someone must surely come soon.

Then he got up and banged on the door again. Silence. He examined the door more closely, holding the candle flame nearer. It was absolutely solid, not even a crack around or underneath. It must be bolted on the outside, he thought.

Now as the last candle burned slowly down, and he had lost all track of time, he felt disoriented, his head crashed, he was so thirsty. His anxiety about his situation grew with each breath.

In the corner, the pot now overflowed with putrid smelling urine. Without ventilation, he was unable to get away from the odour of his own body, his smelly feet, for he had removed his boots, and the sourness of the sweat he felt trickling down his armpits and back.

The candle flame guttered out. He was again in total pitch blackness. He was freezing cold and began to shiver, as much from fear as the cold. In his panic, he tried to stand and so hard were his legs trembling that his knees knocked together. His heart pounded in his chest, his feet, palms and armpits oozed sweat. He heard a low moaning sound like that of an animal caught in a trap, then realized that the sound was coming from himself.

He was breathing more and more rapidly now, trying to take in huge gulps of stagnant air. Now he felt totally confused. He began to feel a tingling sensation in his fingertips and light-headedness.

"I can't breathe, I can't get any air. How could this happen to a King?" he moaned.

"Oh, God!" There before him stood his father, as real as he had ever looked in life. He was smiling and extending his arms to him.

Charles reached out for him, and as he clasped both hands, his father said... "Come, my son. Death is a nice warm place to be."

Still trying to take his last breaths, he succumbed to unconsciousness, slumped forward and died there in that little room. He had suffocated.

***

The brothers had had a very late night indeed. They sat up until the wee hours, smoking and drinking and discussing possible options and outcomes.

They woke in the very late afternoon with tight heads and the realization that they had left the king on his own in the little room. Philip knocked on John's cottage door.

"Come, John, we will need your help today, as the man you helped last night was sick after you left and the room needs cleaning, not something for your wife to tackle."

"Right, Sire," John replied and headed out to the stable block to fetch the horses. He grumbled to himself as he did so. What next would be asked of him?

They arrived at the manor house and entered through a back door, taking the stairs to the upper room. Upon entering the room, a nasty smell assaulted their nostrils and John feared what he would have to clean up.

Philip lifted the tapestry and knocked on the door. Silence. He knocked louder and when there was not an answer, he opened the heavy door. The smell of death leached out into the room. They looked inside to see the man leaning against the wall with his head on his chest and unresponsive. He was long dead.

"My Gawd, what 'ave we 'ere!" exclaimed John in disbelief.

"Not for you to say John," Michael replied, somehow covering his shock. "He must have died in his sleep; he was known to have the coughing sickness."

"Hurry now!" said Philip. John felt ill as he picked up the putrid chamber pot and headed down the stairs to clean it. While he was out of the room, the brothers pulled the dead man from the room, laying him out on the floor. They removed his personal belongings and ruby ring from his toe. Michael put the ring in his pocket. Then they wrapped his dead body in a blanket for John to carry to his horse.

As they made their way back to the Sandford Orcas manor house, Philip explained to John what they wished him to do. When they reached the manor house it was quite late. Michael went into the stable and found a spade while John carried the body over his shoulder, led by Philip holding a candle. They manoeuvred down the cellar stairs. John proceeded to pry up a heavy flagstone from the floor and began to dig a burial spot as the brothers watched anxiously.

When a deep enough hole was dug, he lowered the body, covered it with the soil and then the heavy flagstone. He was almost in tears, thinking to himself that no one deserved such a rude burial. Why must he be hidden? he wondered.

When the task was done, Philip grabbed a jug from the collection in a far corner of the cellar. They climbed the stairs back up to the parlour and he poured them all a tot of brandy. "Thank you for your help, John. You must say nothing to no one about this." And he withdrew a pouch of coins from his pocket and slapped it in John's hand.

"Right, Sire," replied John who belted back his brandy and took his leave. He opened the door to his cottage to darkness, save for a small fire still burning in the grate. His wife had left his supper out on the table, but he had no appetite. He poured a tankard of cider and sat by the fire, silently drinking and thinking. His wife and small son were fast asleep. John was so upset. He was a God fearing man, no one should have been asked to do what he had been forced to do, and now to remain silent. He sat for some time and then knew with absolute conviction what he must do.

He got up, walked to the fireplace, took down the small jar that his wife concealed in the chimney and put the coin-filled pouch inside. Then he replaced it. Had he been able to write, he would have left her a note, but he could not.

He looked in again on the sleeping faces of his family for the last time and left the cottage, pulling the door closed silently behind him and made his way to the stable. He led his faithful old mare out of her stall and into the courtyard and stopped under the archway. Climbing on her back, he threw a strong rope over the heavy oak beam and knotted it skillfully around his neck.

"May God forgive me!" he prayed as silent tears ran down his cheeks.

And then with a slap to his old mare's flank, he flung himself off her back. She ran down the driveway and out into the road where she grazed on the verge for a while until she was drawn back to the comfort of her stable. She stopped beneath the archway and nuzzled her master's feet as he dangled there, his white smock lit up by moonlight. Philip and Michael slept soundly, peacefully unaware.

But when they awoke and were leaving for home they were horrified to see him hanging there. Michael jumped off his horse and ran for a tool to cut him down before his wife caught sight of his dangling form.

When the sheriff from Sherborne was called, the farmer's death was deemed to be a suicide. His wife crying pitifully stated that she knew of no reason that her husband would take his life. She knew that he had been out with the Canton brothers but kept her silence on the matter, for she knew her voice would be pointless in the scheme of things. It was much later that she found the money he had stashed and even then could not believe that it had been ill gotten. She was grateful for the coins, for she was ruthlessly evicted from the cottage. Without a husband to do the labour on the manor farm, she was of no consequence.

***

The Canton brothers were now unencumbered to enact their plan.

They returned home to Sherborne as the Wyndham's were not expected home for almost a week. It would give them plenty of time.

Five days later, Michael set himself up in the Trent manor house and began his disguise. Philip had accompanied him so that they could hone the details of their duplicity. He knew that the Wyndham's would not question his being there keeping the King company without his brother.

Michael cropped his hair as Charles had. He had been unshaven for a few days already so that by the time they were due to arrive, he had a full beard to further disguise himself. Philip took Michael's horse with saddle to a far distant place in the hills behind the manor and left it to graze.

When the Wyndham's arrived they were oblivious to any change in the King. Michael wore his hat low over his eyes and feigned a sore throat. Ann hurried about, having a potion prepared for him.

"We heard the noise of cheering people and church bells chiming. What was that about?" Michael asked as he accepted the drink.

"The villagers apparently heard a rumour that you had been killed and they made a bonfire and were celebrating," she explained.

He laughed at that and made light of it but wondered to himself if there had been a witch among them who had the sight. With the farmer dead, no one but he and his brother knew that the King truly was dead.

Philip, in a moment alone with him, bade him goodbye. "Safe journey, Your Majesty, he said with a look of conspiracy.

"Thank you, Philip." He grasped his hand in his and seemed reluctant to let go his grip. "Adieu." Philip then made his way back to Sherborne to wait.

On the evening of October 5, a trusted companion by the name of Colonel Robin Phelipps arrived to act as guide for the remainder of the journey. The next morning, they left the manor house, biding the Wyndham's goodbye. Michael thanked them profusely for all their kindness and help.

"Thank you, faithful servants, when my kingdom is won you shall be greatly rewarded." At that, he and Phelipps mounted their horses and rode away. They rode by Sandford Orcas and he looked down on the manor house remembering all that had come to pass there. Then on to Wincanton and much later they stopped at Stonehenge on the Salisbury plain. He walked around between the great standing monoliths in awe of the place though he had been there many times. They sat on one of the fallen stones to rest. It was another long journey before they arrived at a place where they met up with the trusted friend, Wilmot, who planned to board ship with the King. He greeted the King with a bow, showing no outward sign that he was suspicious of his identity. Even if he was, how could he question or say, "You are not the King," for fear of losing something. When the day finally came to board the ship for France, it was not lost on either of them that the name of the ship was *The Surprise*.

On Thursday October 16, he landed on French soil where the queen mother Henrietta met him. As she took his hand in greeting, she hardly recognised the man before her. Her son had left two years earlier and now there was nothing of the lad he had been. He was tall, broad of chest with shorn hair and a full beard. His features had coarsened, his expression grown reckless. He greeted her in fluent French, and even his voice had changed.

But there appeared to be a sadness beneath his outward cheerfulness, because his heart was still in England. He already missed the green rolling hills of his native Dorset. It would be many years before he returned.

Michael was Missing

It was not unusual for Michael to be away from home for days at a time. Philip waited until a good time had lapsed and he knew Michael would be at his destination before he raised the alarm.

A search party had set out from Sherborne scanning the surrounding hills for a number of days to no avail. His horse was found unharmed but there was no trace of Michael. The men recounted a tale about a cart with occupants and horses that just disappeared on the hillsides around Trent, never appearing again. It was known that there were deep underground caves below the landscape in that area, etched out by the underground rivers well below the earth's crust. They feared he may have fallen through somewhere. But of this, there was no sign. The rough turf of the hillsides gave nothing up, not even horses hoof prints.

About a month later, when he still had not come home, a candlelight vigil was held for him in his favourite little parish church at Goathill. Many people came to honour his memory for he was a very popular person from a renowned family. They remarked about how kind he was and how he would be missed. Philip, with a stony face, accompanied his mother who broke down and wept pitifully for her son. She was devastated. Michael was her darling boy. He had been so good to her. She recalled how he would bring her the full blown white roses of summer, knowing how pleased she would be. Now the petals gathered dust in a potpourri bowl in the dim parlour. How she missed him. Philip was a pillar of strength to her to be sure, showing his concern and giving comfort. He hid his guilt well. Oh, what sacrifices he had made. How devious he had to be, how dedicated to the Royalist cause.

After long years of hoping and waiting she finally had all of Michael's clothing and belongings placed in a large wooden trunk at the foot of her bed. Each day upon rising, she would lovingly touch the corner so that by the time of her death years later, an impression of her hand print was worn in the wood.

Philip missed his brother terribly, but he alone knew where Michael was and that he was safe. He remained steadfast.

His dreams haunted him though. One night he had a dream which felt more like a visitation than a dream. It was of a lady dressed from head to toe in a pale green gown. In his mind, he thought of her as 'the green goddess'. She did not speak but he sensed she was imprinting on his brain, 'the abbey'. He awoke trying to shrug it off as a nightmare, but he couldn't help thinking about it.

The quiet of the morning was disturbed by the tapping of hammers on stone. He hurriedly dressed and went out to investigate only to see that the stone masons were at work, making some repairs on the front outer wall of the abbey.

It took only a moment to decide what he must do. Returning home, he took the stairs two at a time to his study where he put quill to parchment and wrote down as follows:

King Charles Stuart II
Dyed October 4th 1651 His bodye lyeth in
The Sandford Orcas manor

This document he sealed and hurried back to the abbey where the masons were about to replace a stone. They agreed, after receiving a generous sum, to place the parchment in the wall, concealing it with the new stone. Philip watched the process and when he was satisfied that this had been done, he felt a huge weight shift from his soul.

He felt compelled each evening as the setting sun lit up the west wall of the abbey, high to the right of the front door, to gaze up at the lighter-hued stone and know that the King's death would not be forgotten in the eyes of God. One day the stones would cry out.

***

The years following Michael's disappearance were indeed emotionally difficult for Philip. But daily life continued as usual with visits to his local haunt 'The Plume of Feathers' where he met for bawdy entertainment and the local brew.

He could be seen riding hell bent for leather down the Sherborne road to 'The Mitre Inn' or over to Trent to take a meal at 'The Rose and Crown'. He was frequently invited to Sandford Orcas manor and the Trent manor house for soirees and card games where the Royalist cause was discussed amongst his peers.

Each and every time he entered either of the places he felt guilt and was plagued with the memory of the dead king and his resting place beneath the stones of that cold cellar. The inhabitants remained oblivious.

Contact with his brother was non-existent. It could not be otherwise and remain a secret. Not one person could be trusted.
He regularly attended services at the abbey. Each Sunday he sat in the family pew gazing at the elegies carved in the flagstones, remembering the dead king. He knew in his heart that the droning prayers and hymns of praise could never give him absolution. But he silently prayed that the monarchy would be restored.

***

Neither did Michael have an easy time of it. He had to endure that insufferable boat trip to France huddled in rags against the lashing rain and then with trepidation, meet the King's family.

He had been away for so long that any change in him that they may have noticed was fobbed off. Here stood the man, not the youth who had left before.

Furthermore, who would have had the audacity to question? So he duped all.

Yes, he felt guilt at first, but unlike Philip, he was far away from the scene of the crime and was swept up in a new lifestyle.

This was his lifetime commitment for the crown of England and he would carry it off very well. He was after all 'the great pretender'.

Charles 11 Restoration

Almost ten years later

In the Spring of the year 1660, the Great Pretender sailed from France. When the invitation from Parliament had come he was elated. This was the one day he had hoped for. This was the reason for his risk taking.

As he stood near the helm of the ship that carried him across the channel, he could see the white cliffs in the distance. His heart lept for joy at the sight, *England my England.* Then as the craft arrived at Dover on that memorable spring day, he was filled with gratitude for a safe crossing. Finally, he was on English soil again. As he disembarked he was met by loyal subjects who joined him on a journey to Canterbury. Here, he spent a few nights and worshiped at the great cathedral. He prayed and gave thanks that all had gone so well.

Then as he travelled to London, he was met with joy and jubilation all along his journey. Bonfires blazed, trumpets blared and people cheered "long live the King". Now, after ten long years of rule under Oliver Cromwell, the citizens of England were well and truly ready for a restored monarchy. They were weary of the drab Puritan lifestyle; no ringing of church bells, no singing of hymns, even mince pies at Christmas was outlawed.

He was crowned King of England on April 23, 1661 at the age of thirty. After receiving the crown with all the pomp and ceremony and taking the oath, he held his breath when it was proclaimed three times that if anyone could show reason why he should not be King, to come forward and speak out. His brother sat at the back of the abbey, he breathed a sigh of relief when none came forward.

In the evening of the Coronation day after all had been done, a violent thunder and lightning storm raged over the city. One so harsh had not been seen in years. Some people took it as a sign of a blessing from God, and others were convinced it was a sign of evil. Some were reminded of the earthquake that occurred during the Coronation of King Charles I, and his reign had ended in doom. The King peered out from his rain-lashed window and hoped that all would be well, that he had not been cursed. But the thought vanished like vapour as he was caught up in the splendorous celebration of the day.

One of his first acts to show to the people that he was who they expected him to be, was to have the already decayed body of Oliver Cromwell exhumed from his grave, his head severed and placed on a pike on Tower Bridge for all the citizens to see. Others who had been loyal to Cromwell were executed. It was a callous and defiant show of retribution for the execution of King Charles I.

But he proved to be a very merry and jovial monarch. His court was very showy and flamboyant with much laughter and dancing and masque. He dressed in fine silks and satins of the French fashion, wore a curly black long wig and sat for the artists of the period. He loved the theatre with the colourful actresses and music. Here he could abandon his duties and be carefree for the moment.

In May of 1662, he was married to Catherine of Braganza, a Portuguese princess. She spoke neither French nor English. She had been raised in a nunnery and was very plain and virtuous. But he could overlook her shortcomings as she had brought to the marriage a dowry of much wealth and lands. She proved to be a barren woman and never produced an heir.

He was a rogue in the truest sense of the word, having many women to slake his lust. His most famous mistress, Barbara Villiers, who was a married woman, he gave the title Countess and Duchess. With her he sired a few bastards, the most notorious son was the Duke of Monmouth.

His other mistresses were actresses, Nell Gwyn and Moll Davis, also a maid of honour to the Queen, Winifred Wells. His lust was insatiable. He fathered and acknowledged fourteen of his illegitimate children from various mistresses giving those earldoms and dukedoms.

Those persons who were said to have helped him during his fugitive escapades were awarded various gifts, annuities and coats of arms. Colonel Francis Wyndham was among these and was rewarded financially and given the title Baronet.

**

During the early years of his reign, London was besieged with an outbreak of bubonic plague or *black death*. It had spread from Europe from the ships carrying supplies to England. Rats carried the fleas that carried the contagion to human hosts.

It hit the poor first, those living in already squalid conditions hadn't a chance of escape. The disease sickened a person very rapidly with acute headache, ague and the appearance of a rose petal-like rash that turned black. Huge acutely-painful buboes like boils appeared in the neck armpits and groin. If ruptured or lanced, the purulent discharge was highly infectious. Homes were quarantined so that entire families sickened and died with no one to care for them in their misery.

People died in the thousands each day which overwhelmed the city. Church bells tolled continuously for the deaths and burials. Carts were dispatched to collect the corpses which were carried from the city to mass graves beyond.

The physicians refused to visit the sick. They wore long beak-like masks filled with herbs to protect them. But in the end, fled the city like many others.

The King with his court fled the city to the west country, far away from the contagion. In the beautiful Cathedral town of Salisbury, he breathed in the pure clean air and enjoyed the comfort of a lavish manor house. He strutted about the grounds in the morning and hunted in the afternoon. It felt wonderful to be back. He would make the most of his time away from London, reflect on his life.

A musical soiree was planned for a warm summer evening. Some of his long-time friends were invited to attend. Among those who had received an invitation were the Wyndham's of Trent manor and the Lord and Lady of Sandford orcas. But there were two people in particular he wished to see most; Philip Canton and his mother, Mary of Sherborne.

When the invitation arrived at the Canton home, Mary was beside herself with excitement. In a flurry of preparation for the big event, she had her maid bring out her best gown to make ready. The prospect of meeting the King made her feel quite giddy. Philip hoped all would go well.

It was a beautiful warm summer evening and the doors to the ballroom stood open. The first strain of the orchestra could be heard from within. Guests dressed in their finest apparel arrived in carriages.

The King sat on a dais at the back of the room to welcome his guests as they were announced.

"Philip Canton and mother Mary!" proclaimed the master of ceremony.

Philip escorted his mother on his arm and slowly walked to the dais. He bowed low to the King. Mary curtsied so low and felt so giddy. The King could see that she was overwhelmed and stood quickly and grasped her hand. With her hand in his firm grasp, she bent her knee and looked up into the dark eyes of her son. "Michael!" she breathed and then slumped to the floor in a swoon.

The King was visibly shaken but called for a physician to be summoned. There was a whispering from all those who had witnessed the occurrence... "Could it be the plague?" Everyone was fearful.

Philip swept her up in his strong arms, carried her to an adjacent room and laid her on a chaise lounge. The physician entered the room and assessed her condition. Her speech was gone and her entire side paralysed; she had suffered a stroke. When he made the announcement there was a collective sigh of relief that it was not the plague after all. The party continued.

Philip took his dear mother home. She died only days later, but peacefully because she had finally seen her missing son. Her body was interred in Sherborne abbey.

The King had been quite shaken by seeing her again and secretly mourned her passing. Months later, as word came from London that the plague was abating, he moved his court to Oxford.

***

The King really began to wonder if his reign had been cursed when in September of 1666, only a year after the great plague, fire broke out in London.

It started in a bakeshop in Pudding Lane. The maid had forgotten to douse the fire for the ovens that fateful night and a spark caught and engulfed the shop, taking her life with it. The buildings of London were mostly of wood structure and very close together. The fire easily spread from place to place and an easterly wind fanned the flames until the entire city was ablaze. The people once again had to flee for safety.

The King could see the red glow in the night sky from his windows in Whitehall palace. He paced about becoming more and more restless. In the end, he became fed up with the sketchy reports he was receiving and decided to get involved. He summoned a horse and companion and rode into the heart of the action. There were men shouting, women screaming and children weeping. There was the crackle and snapping of flaming timbers and acrid smoke filled the air. From the upstairs window of a burning building, he saw the face of a small child appear at a window. In a flash, he threw himself off his horse and ran taking the already engulfed stairs to the top. He grabbed up the child and then through the heat waves and smoke, he could make out the form of a woman. He shook her, thinking her already dead but she roused and he hauled her to her feet and pushed her down the stairs in front of him. They made it to safety and cheers from the onlookers. People seemed to be staying in their houses until they were forced out by smoke and flames. But there were few casualties.

The King took charge of the operation of creating fire-breaks and that, with the dying down of the wind, helped the fire to finally burn out. It had burned out the slums, destroying the filthy streets associated with the plague. It had burned down many churches including Saint Paul's Cathedral.

After the fire, the city of London was rebuilt using brick in place of wood; perhaps the fire had been providence after all.

The people looked upon the King in a new light. Some had felt let down that he fled the city during the plague, but he had proved that he was brave and courageous by staying to help fight the fire.

The jolly monarch reigned for almost thirty-six years.

The Death of the King

The day was February 4th, 1685. The King had taken to his bed for the last time. He lay dying. He was attended by physicians and surgeons of extraordinary knowledge for the time. They had studied for fourteen years to attain their status. They purged and cupped and bled him numerous times to no avail. All this treatment served only to make him weaker. He complained of severe pain in his side, and great difficulty breathing.

On the afternoon of February 5th, a gentleman from the west county town of Sherborne arrived at Whitehall. He had been summoned for an audience with the King. Philip Canton entered the King's death chamber and bowed. He was immaculately dressed from his velveteen tricorne hat which he held in his hand to his well-cut clothes and shiny knee-high black boots. He sat as suggested next to the high bed.

Philip, upon entering, had taken in the assaulting atmosphere of illness and foreboding death. The air was a stale mixture of fetid breath, sweat and camphor. A bowl of congealed blood sat on a table, where the surgeon had bled him. It was a shock to the senses to see this man laid so low, made so humble in his last hours of life.

With gasping breath and in a weak voice the King dismissed all from the room, ordering that none remain within hearing distance of conversation with his guest. When he was certain that they were alone, he reached out a cool moist hand and clasped Philip's strong one.

"You look well, Philip. Thank you for coming as I had asked, dear man. You alone know of the torment I am going through," he rasped.

Philip nodded in understanding and held the hand more firmly. He had long ago realized the depth and breadth of the treachery that had been done.

"Come close, brother, so my words will not be overheard."

Philip leaned in closer to the pale oedematous face and put his ear to the King's mouth now noisily gasping for breath. Between gasps, he said...

"Should our deed be known, it could change everything, so pray let it die with me," he pleaded. He slowly and with difficulty removed the ruby ring from his finger and folded it in Philip's hand. "Something to remember me by."

Philip kissed the pale hand of his brother, 'the King'.

"You have my word," he whispered and reluctantly turned to leave the room, the dying man caught his hand again, asking that he send in the priest on his way out. Philip nodded his head and left the room, his face belied his true feelings. He had seen his brother for the last time in his life.

For the King, keeping the secret had eaten away at his soul like a slow-growing cancer and though he would not be able to utter the truth of his sins to the priest, just the act of absolution would be a comfort in his dying hours. He realized he would ultimately have to face judgement when he finally met his maker.

In the early hours of the morning of the next day, the King gasped his last breath and gave up the ghost. He was fifty-four years old, in the thirty-sixth year of his reign.

On this day in London, the church bells tolled the knell of his death. The bells of all the churches in all the land, as well as those of Sherborne Abbey, the Church of St. Andrew's in Trent and the Church of St. Nicholas in Sandford Orcas, tolled in unison. He had died with the secret intact and left no heir. His body was interred in Westminster Abbey without pomp and ceremony.

James Stuart, the brother of the legitimate Charles, ascended the throne.

PART TWO

All that we see and seem
Is but a dream within a dream

Edgar Allan Poe

Edward (Ted)

Margate Kent England 1946

With a few feeble gasps, followed by a sharp intake of breath of the seaside air, a baby boy came into this life. His weary mother rested back on her pillows, in a state of quiet disbelief that she had actually delivered a healthy child, as she had been told she would never be able to conceive. She heard his lusty wail as the nurse carried him off to the nursery.

His father had been away for nearly six long years during the war, fighting the Germans in North Africa and Italy. This birth for them was a blessed event. This child was destined for much more than he could ever live up to.

Baby Ted was named for his grandfather, Edward Piercy, a retired Regimental Sergeant Major in the British army serving in India during the Raj. At his christening in the old church of St. Paul, family, friends and godparents agreed that he would likely follow a military life like his father and grandfather before him. But that was not to be.

***

He was a bonny tow-haired blue-eyed baby, laughing more than he cried, and brought joy to all around him. His parents were proprietors of a busy guest house in Cliftonville which was prospering well after the war. Few people could afford holidays abroad during the years of rationing. It was as well that he was a contented child as his busy parents had little time for him. Until he was walking, he could be found on most days sitting in his highchair, in the hankie-size front garden, contented to watch the comings and goings of the street. He had been known to fall asleep with his face in a bowl of apples and custard until he was rescued and cared for by the Irish maid.

His grandparents were regular visitors, also his Godparents, Robert and Jane. They would take it in turn for walks on the promenade and to the beach. He loved the excitement of the place in summer when so many people came for holidays. There were donkey rides on the beach, Punch and Judy shows, ice cream vendors and penny arcades.

Ted started school at an early age, to be out of his busy parents' way. He was enrolled in a private school within walking distance of home. His grandfather taught him how to tie a Windsor knot, as his school uniform was very proper; grey flannel shorts, knee socks, white shirt, school tie, blazer and cap with the school crest. This outfit was usually in a state of dust and grass stains by the time he returned home.

At about the age of nine, he became rather delinquent. His mother was so busy preparing three meals a day for guests and his father in his carpet store, that Ted easily played truant from school. Many days when they thought him safely at school, he would be playing in the rubble of bomb sites from the war. The broken bricks and mortar, bits of pottery, shards of glass, sometimes bits of torn clothing and old photos were just so interesting for a child to explore.

He would try to seek his parents' attention in any way he knew possible, even though his punishment for misbehaviour was going without supper or banishment to the chalet in the back garden.

On one such occasion when sent to the chalet, a fierce thunder and lightning storm hit. He was terrified and wanted out some way, so he threw a flower pot, breaking the window and at the same time set light to the curtains. When the flames threatened to engulf the hut, his mother, along with the fire department, came to rescue him. He tried to convince them that a lightning bolt had struck the chalet. But they knew better.

The golden sands along the beach by the sea was his most favourite place to be. Overlooked by tall chalk cliffs, he rambled the beach collecting seashells, paddled in the rolling waves, gazed in tidal pools for tiny sea creatures and explored the many caves in the chalk. He was often joined by another boy about his own age, who was very quiet, never spoke and would enjoy the companionship, then almost as mysteriously as he arrived, he would disappear. It would leave Ted wondering who he might be, as he had never met him at school or in the community. Only on the beach. This he kept to himself.

His school bag was crammed with thermos, snacks and comic books to keep him happy until he felt it was time to go home. He had it timed most accurately to when he was expected home from school. He was eventually found out.

***

Godparents Robert and Jane were unable to have children; Ted was their special little darling. They were frequent visitors and took him to places his parents were not the least bit interested in. He especially loved the Pirate caves and the Shell Grotto which were mysterious and fuelled his young imagination.

Another favourite place to visit was Dreamland, with its circus-like atmosphere, rollercoaster and other fun rides.

At Christmas, he was taken to the elaborate pantomimes at the local theatre. He loved the colourful costumes, music and happy banter of the crowd joining in on cue. His home, the B&B, was filled with guests and they never failed to include Ted in gift giving and fun.

His grandparents often had him stay with them at their huge and elaborately-furnished home on the outskirts of London. Ted was in awe of the carved mahogany and brass Indian furniture, the tiger skin rugs and baby grand piano. Grandmother would have him sit on the stool beside her as she played for him. She told him that he was a very special little boy, that he had a 'gift', not the wrapped up kind, but one he would find out about in later life, when the time was right. When he would question her about it, she would not elaborate.

She would also regale him with stories of her life in India, the luxury, the servants and social life of the military elite. She had a beautiful voice and had sung to entertain in India. She found it very difficult to return to England and adjust to the English way of life. Ted's father was the eldest child born in India and at the age of fourteen when they returned, he found it even more difficult to adjust. Something very mysterious happened with his grandfather. It was all hushed and whispered about behind closed doors. Now instead of Ted visiting them at their home near London, they lived just up the road in a very small bungalow. He could even walk there by himself. There was no piano and nice furniture, his grandmother was always sad. He couldn't understand what had happened but from snippets of things he had heard, his grandfather was in disgrace, had perhaps taken for himself some of the spoils of India that were destined for the King, had dishonoured his regiment. Now he pled poverty and was supported by the goodwill of his sons. It was all very secret to be sure.

He loved his grandparents even more, he was too young to understand. He was contented.

***

An idyllic childhood soon came to an end at the age of ten. His parents sold the guest house, packed up and emigrated to Canada. They thought it would be a better place to raise their son. His father left in December, going ahead to begin work and find a home. Ted and his mother stayed with an aunt until their departure in February. He would forever remember his grandmother arriving to say goodbye, and slapping his mother's face.

He was borne away by ship on the angry waters of the Atlantic. The rolling waves and ice-covered decks he found exciting at first, but like so many others, he gave in to the inevitable seasickness. For many days the *Ivernia* was tossed upon the boiling waters, until finally they disembarked at Halifax, greeted by his father.

He remembered vividly how forlorn and homesick he felt when he first encountered the frigid Canadian winter. Everything looked and was so foreign to him. He missed the seaside town, missed his home, friends and relatives.

It took him a long while to adjust to the Canadian way of life. At school he was teased and mocked for his accent and different way of dressing.

Eventually though he won over many friends and teachers with his wit and charming smile. Not a fighter, he would diplomatically ease his way out of most confrontations.

His English schooling had put him well ahead of his peers in subjects of English language and history. Even though he had played truant, he had absorbed much knowledge. He had gone on many school trips in England to museums and historical sites. He was interested in the monarchy, battles and the war, and came top of his class in History. He had been to London, Dover, castles and bombed-out buildings. He lived with the war stories of his father and grandfather. His school mates were fascinated with them.

***

In high school, he was one of the first of his friends to own a car, and pass his driver's license. This attracted many friends, boys as well as girls.

The girls were attracted by his blue eyes and charming personality. When one in particular showed more than a little interest, their parents pushed them into an early marriage.

This was a disastrous move and after only a few years, ended in divorce. Now he was single, unencumbered by family and free for once to make his own choices.

He knew exactly where he was headed. He had always thought it would be exciting to travel by train across the vast expanse of Canada to the west, and that is exactly what he decided to do. He travelled the Canadian Pacific rail from Toronto, arriving in Vancouver in mid-January.

Beverley

Pick a day, almost any day, and she could be found sitting on a favourite mossy log, communing with nature, her faithful cocker spaniel panting at her side. Pixie would look up at her with brown loving eyes. How she adored him.

The thick sword ferns of the rain forest, overhanging branches of towering maples, their leaves the size of dinner plates, alder, fir, spruce and birch, she loved them all. She was adept at climbing the huge maples and found nothing quite as exhilarating as swinging from a branch high above the ground.

Set upon the surface of a huge mossy stump, a 'fairyland' had been made with the help of her older sisters. Little pieces of broken mirror made perfect ponds, tiny wild flowers for gardens, all things to lure the fairies to play. She never saw one, not once. But she knew they would come when she wasn't around. They were elusive little people.

"You have the faith of a mustard seed, child," her mother would say. She also knew that her grandmother wasn't really dead but resting on top of the huge billowy cotton clouds forming on the distant mountains, and looking down on her at play.

She had been sick, very sick indeed, for she heard her mother weeping upon their return from the doctor. Something about rheumatic fever, the doctor had said. Yes, she knew she had tummy aches and achy knees and even some pain in her chest but it wasn't all that bad that she needed so many days in bed, she had thought. Although she had been five years old, it was fun at first to rest in the old crib placed in the kitchen during the day and watching her mother prepare meals. Then the crib would be wheeled to her parent's bedroom for the night so she could be near. She could remember waking up from a frightening dream and have her daddy's big warm calloused hand hold hers until she would fall back to sleep. The memory never left her.

Now that she was well, she'd spend as much time out of doors as she could to make up for those lost days.

One thing she did gain from that experience was that she wanted to, no, needed to become a nurse when she grew up. The crisp starched white uniform and neat cap of the nurse in the doctor's office, the smells of disinfectant, medicines in glass-fronted cupboards, bookshelves lined with medical texts, the stern but kindly face of the man with the spectacles and stethoscope around his neck, all made such a huge impression on her young mind.

Right there, right then, in that wood surrounded by nature, the child's fate was sealed.

Her life unfolded in a small west coastal settlement of Canada, as far away as her British forebears could have imagined.

Her maternal side of the family could be traced back to the reign of Elizabeth I. That very great-grandfather had sailed in 'the *Mayflower*' from Plymouth, Devon England to America in 1633.

Her father's forebears could be traced to Ireland, that very great-grandfather fleeing the potato famine.

So her parents insisted she believe that she came from 'good stock' and this was true for they had survived wars, plague, smallpox, famine, sailing vessels, revolution, natives, and pioneer life homesteading in the wilds.

***

She would need all this family backbone in preparing her for nursing school. It was dorm life with so many girls, each with a personal vision. It was three years of grinding study put into practice on the patients in the long old wards of a hospital initially started by Queen Victoria's Royal Engineers.

Bev was now firmly implanted in a lifestyle of waking to a jangling alarm clock, night shifts, bedpans, blood, sweat, birth, death and yes, tears. But after all that, she was better prepared for anything life had to offer.

Her first real test of commitment and resolve was when she fell in love with and married a young man who she knew from the start, was not well. He had been stricken with a chronic kidney disease gradually progressing over a period of six years. Her mother, when she heard that they were to marry, said to her...

"But you can't marry him, dear; he is very ill and may never recover."

"But I love him; I'd marry him if he was on his death bed."

During the first three years of their marriage, things went reasonably well. They were able to go on holidays, entertain friends and family.

He studied a course in real estate and she worked full time to support them. But the illness progressed and the last three years of his life, he was dependent upon a kidney machine at home. Then there was no chance of getting away for more than a few days at a time.

His parents were indifferent to his illness at first, thinking him lazy when he tired easily. Then when he really needed them most, they moved away.

It was a difficult time for both of them. Friends were having babies, and that was not in the cards for them. He felt too ill to have dinner guests or go on outings. Bev watched him slowly deteriorate until he became only a shell of his former self, and she suffered along with him. They didn't talk about dying, just tried to believe it would not happen. He was not a religious person and could not appreciate that some of the other people he knew in the same predicament, turned to their Bibles for comfort.

It was at this time that she began to question life after death. She just knew there should be an explanation for such suffering. How fair was it that one was only able to live for such a short time, not to be able to accomplish anything or enjoy life, then just die? What was it all about?

She had faith in God, yes, but Christian religions did not recognize reincarnation. Thus she went to the books of Edgar Cayce 'the sleeping prophet' and here she gleaned the information and explanation she needed. Karma, the law of cause and effect, was the only logical answer. She began to understand then that we live many lives and that we are the result of all the learning of our past lives. The soul does not die, but goes on to another level of understanding. We shed the old body like a husk, are free as a butterfly until the time is right for a return to a new body as a baby with the first intake of breath.

Though she thought she was prepared for his inevitable death, it did not make it any easier when the time came. He did not recover from a necessary surgery and she got the call in the wee hours of the morning. She wished that she could have been with him, but circumstances prevented it. She took a modicum of comfort from the fact that she had always been there for him, and remembered him saying, "How good you are to me." She waited until she knew his parents would be up and about and then made that upsetting call. Her life was over too, she thought. But that was not her destiny. She had been so busy caring for him and working at the same time, so used to being needed that she found it difficult to get out of that mind space.

Bev was still young and attractive and after some months of grieving and sleepless nights, she began to come out of her cocoon. She changed her hairstyle, took a few long holidays, spent money on fashions and generally did as she pleased. But she needed to be needed, she needed to be loved.

Almost a year after her husband's death, she met a young man who had come, firstly from another country, and then from one side of the country to the other, and they met when each needed the other most.

Summer 1972

Across the floor of a crowded nightclub, their eyes met and instant chemistry sparked between them. Even in the dim lit room she could see that he was attractive, probably in his late twenties, longish blond hair and blue eyes that bore into her own. She was with friends and him likewise, but when she got up to go to the ladies' room, he followed. As she walked away, he touched her on the shoulder.

"I couldn't help but notice you, would you consider going out with me sometime?" he tentatively asked.

"Are you married?" she queried, looking directly in his blue eyes.

"Well, no, not any longer. Here is my business card, and may I have your phone number?"

Bev glanced at the card; saw that his name was Ted Piercy. She was quite taken in by his smooth English accent and forthright manner. Then without further delay and before she knew what she was saying, it was out of her mouth.

"I'd like to see you again, Ted. I'm Beverley and here is my number." She penned it on the back of his business card and handed it back. "But not until Friday, mind, I'll be starting the night shift, we nurses work graveyard hours you see." He opened his mouth to say something else but she had turned away and slipped into the ladies' room.

When she returned to the club scene, he and his buddies were gone. She was disappointed, thought perhaps he might have asked her to dance. She would later find out that he was so much in shock and awe of her that he was afraid that the magic would end if he saw her again that evening.

They saw a great deal of each other over the course of several months, and then realizing that they were very much in love, life totally changed. Bev enjoyed showing him the places she had known and loved since childhood. He met her friends and family and escorted her to her sister's wedding. Her parents approved of him and were so happy that she had met someone again.

Although he had his own apartment, he spent most of his time at Bev's. He worked as a car salesman in the city, hours that differed from hers. As often as not, she would arrive home to find him reclining, watching TV, with her cat on his lap. If Toby accepted him, then he was worthy, for she hated strangers. He enjoyed preparing meals she had never before tried; kippers and eggs, grilled lamb chops with mint sauce, steak and kidney pie, all English fare. He was very thoughtful she decided, when a bouquet of mauve chrysanthemums and a framed verse of *Desiderata* were left for her when he had to work on her day off. How had he known that she loved poetry? It was the most eloquent and inspirational verse she had ever read. The Latin meaning was 'desired things'.

How very fitting.

***

Travel brochures of Britain displaying bright photos of London, changing the guards, castles and picturesque scenery were laid out on the dining room table when she arrived home from work one afternoon.

"Thought you might like to browse through some of them and maybe think about a holiday, darling, I feel certain you'd love England."

"It all looks so exciting, but I've taken almost all my holiday time Ted, and it wouldn't make sense to go for just a short trip."

They sat together, sipping wine and looking through the glossy pictures, Ted elaborating on the most interesting places. It was so exciting, she couldn't resist.

Bev agreed right then and there that a lengthy holiday abroad, would be just what they both needed. It would be a time to get to know each other better and forget about the past. They would give notice at their work place and take as long as they liked. A drive across the country, taking in the sights of Canada, meeting his parents and then flying from Toronto to London was the plan. They would start afresh upon their return, finding work and a new apartment if they got on well together. She had faith that it would be so.

A month later, after packing up their apartments and putting everything in storage, they were ready to begin their adventure.

***

Ted had put together a travel plan. Mapping out the route was not difficult for there was one main road across the country, the TransCanada highway.

They began their trip mid-June, stopping first to see her parents and dropping off the cat. It would be a culture shock for Toby, she had been an apartment feline since a kitten and now she would be living outdoors. Bev hoped she would fare well, she was like a child to her and she hated saying goodbye to Toby and her parents. They enjoyed some of her mother's home cooking which fortified them for the trip ahead. Then with hugs and goodbyes they were on their way in a new VW station wagon.

To be with her new love, to be exploring her country, to be experiencing new sites, food and culture put Bev in a whirl of excitement. She almost had to pinch herself to see if it was real. With the radio blaring, they sang along to all the favourite tunes of the time and took turns at driving. Vancouver to Toronto was a very long way. Bev remembered her thoughts of cycling across the country and laughed at her ignorance.

The first night found them near Jasper National Park. They had both been in awe of Mount Robson, one of the highest peaks in the Canadian Rockies, and talked about their day over a steak dinner in a cosy lodge.

"Perhaps we could take it a little slower tomorrow love, that drive has really tired me out," she pleaded. Ted held her hand across the table and squeezed it. "Your right dear, I tend to drive endlessly and I guess I'm anxious to get there, knowing how far we have to go. I have to remember that we don't fly until July 5, so we have all the time in the world."

"Well yes, so let's lazily enjoy a liqueur after this delicious meal and head for that comfortable bed." She smiled invitingly.

Almost a week later they arrived in Toronto, booking in at the Holiday Inn. She met his parents and couldn't get over how 'English' they were. Some of the expressions they used were laughable; she hadn't a clue what they meant.

The twosome travelled all over the city, taking in some of Ted's choice places to wine and dine. Then they drove to Niagara Falls and Bev was overwhelmed at the power of that flow. She wasn't brave enough to be tempted any closer than the outer railing, where she leaned forward and took some photos.

Days followed lazy days, exploring and relaxing. But then Ted was shocked that his parents had decided to take a trip to England also. Although his mother had visited her family numerous times over the years, his father had not been back since leaving all those years ago. Why now?

Ted couldn't get his head around the fact that, no matter where he went they seemed to follow. The only place he managed to go without them was out west, no wonder he had travelled so far. He feigned excitement for them, but deep down, he was furious. He kept his feelings from Bev.

He took her to Ottawa for a few days. They took a boat ride on the Rideau Canal and he explained to her how it froze over in the winter, becoming a skating rink for all the locals. They visited the Parliament buildings, sprawling on the lawns and listening to the bands practising for the Dominion Day celebration. It was only days now before they flew.

***

Bev had never been on a jumbo jet before and looking out at the huge British Airways plane she would be flying on, gave her palpitations and butterflies in her stomach. It was also her first long haul flight.

The flight to London Heathrow from Toronto seemed like a marathon of wakefulness. Finally in their comfortable hotel room and following a short rest, the excitement of experiencing London was uncontrollable. Ted suggested they take a boat ride down the Thames to get a good view of the city from that perspective. The buildings loomed up around them. The boat glided over the water of the ancient seaway, past the Tower with its Traitor's gate and under bridges until it arrived at Greenwich. The guide elaborated on the history in his hard to understand Cockney accent. They stopped for a pint of the best ale ever, and then took the return trip back into the city. It was an enjoyable trip but jet lag caught up and they just had to go back to their hotel for a rest. They dined out late in the evening at a choice Italian eatery. Bev thought it amusing that they were eating Italian on their first night in London.

***

Now for the first time in months she really laughed, amid the flurry of wings and feathers. At Trafalgar Square the pigeons greeted them; with grey purple and green iridescent feathers puffed out they cooed and strutted about the pavement. They were greedy birds and a handful of grain attracted them from every direction, landing on shoulders, hands and head. A photographer snapped their black and white photo amid the birds. One for a keepsake.

She wore a miniskirt and platform sandals. He sported long hair, flared trousers and bright shirt. They were pictured laughing in total happiness, the lions unmoved. From there it was a short walk to the National Art Gallery and though their attention span was short, they did take in a few of the renowned artists. One could spend days in that place to see everything.

A pub lunch in one of the many establishments and Bev was introduced to a ploughman's. A huge chunk of cheddar cheese rested on a plate surrounded by slabs of crusty bread, pickled onions, and salad. She hungrily dove in, and in between sips of ale and chit chat, she managed to eat the entire meal. Ted enjoyed a steak and kidney pie with heaps of mashed potato and rich gravy and ale. Then it was back to the museums for the rest of that day. They were fascinated by the Egyptian exhibit in the British museum. The colossal-sized figures and mummified bodies, ancient paintings of the faces of the dead on the tombs and all the beautiful artefacts gave them much to talk about. Bev thought it sacrilegious to unearth the dead as such, no wonder the excavation of King Tut's tomb was said to carry a curse, she proclaimed. Ted was sceptical.

***

The following morning after a hearty full English breakfast, the city again beckoned them. It was reeking of history and Ted was anxious for Bev to enjoy it as much as he did. They took in the Houses of Parliament with Big Ben, Buckingham Palace and Pall Mall, St. James Park and the grand Whitehall where King Charles I was beheaded. To Ted who had seen it all as a child, it was as if voices of the far distant past whispered in his ear... "See us! Remember! Remember!"

Lazy summer days blended into one another. They were doing just as they pleased for once and renting the little blue Ford Escort seemed like a better way of exploring the country.

"How brave you are to consider driving here, Ted. I can't even imagine myself driving not only on the wrong side of the car, but the wrong side of the road too!" She remembered the frightening first experience of a black cab ride when they had first arrived in the city. It was a hair-rising experience with the cabbie yelling obscenities at another driver who had cut him off in busy traffic.

"Oh, it's quite easy, once you get the hang of it; just have to keep your wits about you." And with that, they headed off to Marble Arch to pick up the hire car. It was the busiest part of the day, but Ted managed with ease.

A message from his parents at the reception requesting that he get in touch with them at an aunt's place jolted Ted into another reality. His mum and dad were now in the country and they had been invited for Sunday dinner. Bev thought it would be nice to meet some of his relatives, get to know his parents better, so they accepted.

Bev had to admit it was one of the most delicious roast lamb dinners she had ever eaten, and enjoyed the easy atmosphere of his aunt's family home. His parents were heading up to Kent to visit a friend in Cliftonville where they had once owned the guest house. They asked Ted if it would be too much trouble to take them there. He couldn't refuse as he now had the car and so it was now in their itinerary to see that part of the country first. He'd rather enjoy showing Bev where he had spent his childhood, but secretly he fumed that his parents should butt in on their holiday. Bev would soon come to know what his mother was like. And she did. From Bev's observation, his mother expected him to jump when she wanted something. If they were to be together, things would have to change; it was something she would file in her brain for now, to be dealt with later. So they continued to explore some of Ted's childhood haunts, taking his parents with them.

On a day out to Canterbury, seeing the town and cathedral Bev found absolutely what she expected of this country. She felt like a pilgrim in awe of that inspiring edifice and was humbled by all the history it invoked.

From there, they drove to the little village of Chilham and enjoyed a pub meal. When Bev went to the ladies' room, Ted's mother followed.

"I'd like to thank you for being with Ted, you are just what he needs, but he is my son, and you will find that he will do as I ask," she almost hissed.

"I'm not quite sure what to say to this," Bev squeaked, but her backbone showed itself and she replied... "I'm quite certain Ted has a mind of his own and will speak for himself in that regard." And with that, she turned and left his mother with her mouth open and the realization that she was up against a formidable force.

***

"Today, we'll head down to the West country, Bev. I was up early and marked our route out on the road atlas, it should be fun." His parents were beginning to get on his nerves, so he had phoned and told them that he might be there to see them off on their flight home, but that Bev and he were continuing their own holiday as planned. He didn't wait for any negotiations on his mother's part. But to his surprise, she told him not to worry, that they would be heading down to Devon to revisit a place they had frequented in the earlier days.

"It sounds like a great plan, dear; we'll finish breakfast and then pack up to be on our way." She gave him a big grin and a hug, happy to be on the move again.

Half hour later with the little blue car packed, they began their leisurely drive towards Dover. High atop the white chalk cliffs towered the great 12th century medieval castle, the largest in England. Ted swung the car into the car park, amid Bev's squeals of excitement. This was her childhood dream come true, to see a real castle. They went on the tour of the great building, exploring the huge cold rooms and the underground tunnels and rooms used during the Second World War. Ted had been here before in his school days but was excited to be here with Bev, seeing it through her eyes. Following the tour, they wandered up a path along the cliff face that looked out over the port of Dover and beyond the sea towards France. Because it was such a clear day, the continent could be seen as a pale mauve brushstroke in the distance.

They drove a bit further, and stopped for lunch at Hastings. Over a plate of fish and chips in a snug little pub, Ted reminded her about the history of the place, namely the battle of 1066, which she confirmed she had learned about in her history lessons. They agreed to travel until late afternoon, exploring as they went and put up for the night where and whenever they felt like it.

Their next stop of interest was Brighton, another seaside resort. A wander around the gardens at the Royal Pavilion proved a relaxing retreat. The Indian design was beautiful and a look inside revealed both Indian and Chinese decor. It had been built in the late 18th century for the Prince Regent, later King George IV, who used it to entertain his mistresses. The beach at Brighton was a major one for

Londoners coming down for the weekend.

Evening was beginning to draw in and they were weary, so found a dear little guest house in nearby Worthing. They tucked into a delicious roast chicken dinner and steamed pudding. Bev had not experienced the guest house scene before and when the proprietor asked if they would like tea or coffee delivered in the morning it was a surprise to have someone just knock and enter their room with a tray. She would make certain if ever asked again she'd ask to have a tray left outside the door. The lack of decorum piqued her North American upbringing.

"At least he didn't ask if you'd like to be knocked up in the morning," Ted laughed. It wasn't lost on Bev and she gave him a playful shove.

The dining room was set up for a hearty breakfast, everything from cereal and fruit to full English; bacon, sausage, egg, grilled tomato, mushroom and fried bread. They tucked into the full breakfast with gusto. Bev found the display of toast in a rack, which was cold and unbuttered, very different from what she was used to and asked if they would mind making warm toast and buttering it for her. Ted rolled his eyes and exclaimed, "When in Rome!" Then he reached for a slice from the toast rack and slathered it thick with butter and marmalade.

These were all the little things she would have to get used to about him and his English ways. Her toast arrived and she methodically cut it into quarter triangles and daintily nibbled a slice, giving Ted an amused look. He just smiled that cheeky way she loved.

"Today I thought we should just continue on our coastal route and stop at some of the little seaside towns, but first Arundel, it looks close to here." He pointed it out on the map. She leaned close to have a look and agreed.

The Arundel castle, for Bev fit into all her expectations of a magical fairy-tale place. Here in a beautiful area of West Sussex, the majestic structure towered above the landscape. It was home to the Dukes of Norfolk for over eight hundred years. It was hard for her to fathom, having come from a country that was not yet two hundred years since settlement. They toured the castle along with all the other tourists and gaped at the splendorous furnishings and paintings it held. It was hard to imagine that people actually lived like this. Ted reminded her that there were literally hundreds of other such places and it would probably take a life time to see them all.

They stopped in the little town for a cream tea which she learned was tea served with scones that were lavish with thick clotted cream and strawberry jam. Licking her fingers, she exclaimed that she'd quite enjoy that fare daily. Ted was just pleased that she was enjoying herself. She really deserved this holiday.

Bringing out the map again, Ted suggested they make a bit of a change in plans and drive up through the Salisbury plains of Wiltshire; there was something he didn't want her to miss seeing. So they drove onward, bypassing busy Southampton and then took a smaller road cutting through the heart of Wiltshire.

There in the distance across the expanse of countryside, stood Stonehenge. The sight of it in the middle of that wide open space was awesome. At that time, it was unfenced and one could wander around within the circle of stones at will. They walked slowly around the massive blue grey menhirs, recalling what they had learned about the legend of the structure. Nothing was really known about its origin but there was evidence that the stones had come from a long distance and must have involved incredible skill to erect such massive pillars. It was thought that it was a giant calendar oriented to the rising sun of the summer solstice where perhaps the ancient Druids worshipped and made human sacrifice. It had such a magical quality about it. The quiet of the place on that warm summer day had such a healing effect on Bev. It seemed so surreal. Now seated on one of the fallen stones with her eyes closed and face to the sun, she imagined the long-robed priests, chanting and worshipping here. There was truly a spiritual feeling about the place and save for a couple walking some distance away, she and Ted were all alone.

"I'll just rest here Ted; you can pick me up on your way back." He was occupied taking photos of her and just laughed at her suggestion.

She rose up from the stone and walked over to him, and cupping his face with both hands, kissed him full on his mouth.

"I'm just so delighted that you brought me to this magical place, I've never felt so alive and happy." He just held her close and kissed her back.

They continued their drive until they spotted a pub nestled in a grove of trees and off the busy roadway. A sign 'The Highwayman' hanging above the door creaked in the breeze. Smells of food, beer and cigarette smoke greeted their entrance. All seemed unusually quiet for the time of day.

The publican welcomed them warmly and after a short exchange about where they were from, served up thirst-quenching pints of lager. After meat pies and chips, they scanned the map again to plot the next stop. Ted pulled out a pack of cigarettes, lit one, and took a long drag and squinting through a cloud of smoke, pointed to Dorset County.

"I've always been drawn to this place." He tapped his pen on Dorchester, then circled Maiden castle. Bev just nodded and finished her drink.

Feeling well fortified with food and drink they drove until late afternoon. They stopped in Shaftsbury. Walking through the town they came to Gold Hill and couldn't resist walking down the steep cobbled street, lined with ancient houses. The view of the surrounding countryside was breathtakingly beautiful. By the time they climbed back up the hill, they were both panting, realized too that they had needed the exercise.

They continued the drive into the late afternoon. Then needing to stop and stretch, they spotted a signpost pointing to 'Old Sherborne castle' and turning up this road they discovered an ancient church. The grounds were lush with rich grass and peppered with little white daisies and dandelions. Poking up through the grass at intervals were ancient gravestones, covered with lichen and ivy which almost obscured some of the epitaphs. On bending down to inspect the markers, they were shocked at the age of them, some dating in the 1600s.

Upon entering the church, the distinct smell of age assaulted the senses, matching the cold atmosphere. A monument on one wall was in memory of Sir Walter Raleigh who had worshipped there. They ambled up and down the aisles reading the flagstone epitaphs until the chill of the place forced them to leave.

Moving out of the building and into the open air, Ted laughingly said... "Thanks be to old Walter, the patron saint of tobacco, now I can enjoy my next cigarette!" They walked over to the wooden bench and sat in the sun's warmth.

A short distance from the church, a gravelled pathway led up to the ruins of the old Sherborne castle. Like Stonehenge, in those days it was not a protected site and they were able to wander the grounds at will, surrounded by huge Lebanon cedar trees sending out shadows of shade. Sheep wandered here too and beyond the remains of a wall, a gypsy camp was set up with bright painted cart and horses tethered to a post munching at the grass, while noisy children romped with a dog. The mongrel, seeing the pair, gave a warning bark, sending them racing to the car in fits of laughter.

They drove on to find a tourist information centre which supplied them with pamphlets of places to stay and dine. The previously circled Dorchester area seemed like an interesting place to stay and explore.

"Look, this book says here that it was Thomas Hardy's birthplace. He is one of my favourite authors," Bev remarked, now all enthusiastic about the place they would be staying for a while.

It was a scenic drive down the A352 through quaint little villages; one they would always remember called Godmanstone. They stopped at the 'Smith Arms' reputed to be the smallest pub in England. It truly was a dear little place with thatched roof and seating room for not more than about a dozen people, having to share tables. They sat outside at a picnic table in the garden and enjoyed the most delicious cold turkey sandwiches made with mustard greens and cucumber and washed down with Guinness. It was said that Charles II had stopped here for a drink at one time so it was an indication of how ancient it was.

***

Arriving in Dorchester, a bustling town, they booked in at the 'Kings Arms' hotel. The room met with all their expectations. It had a huge four-poster bed with luxurious bedding, deep window seat with a view over the rooftops and a deep claw-legged bathtub. Bev unpacked and decided to take a reviving bath while Ted went to the lobby to look over his travel booklets and smoke.

She lay back in the deep bath with her eyes closed and thought about what she had read about this bewitching corner of the country. Even in Hardy's time people were still very superstitious, believed in witches and little folk. He spoke of ancient lore, magic, fertility rites and the like in many of his novels. She had read them all. It certainly seemed to have a magical quality about it here and she could hardly wait to explore further. How excited she was to be here. Upon hearing Ted return to the room, she stepped out of the bath, dried herself off and dressed for the evening.

They enjoyed a marvellous evening meal in the old world dining room. It was a traditional meal of roast beef, Yorkshire pudding, gravy and vegetable medley followed by a steamed treacle pudding with custard. They were stuffed.

To walk off dinner, they explored the evening quiet streets. They looked in the shop windows, down little alleyways, in the neat little gardens of people's homes then finding a snug little pub, stopped in for a drink, and then back to the hotel. The day had been long and enjoyable, but they were still a bit jet lagged and the bed looked most inviting.

***

Having fallen soundly asleep, Ted sat suddenly upright awaking Bev.

"So sorry if I woke you, dear. I felt certain that someone was standing at the foot of the bed." The room felt very chilly for a summer evening. Even though Bev dismissed it as him being overtired, and now that she was awake it made him feel better, he had an uncanny feeling that there was still a presence in the room watching him. Bev fell back to sleep almost immediately and even though he snuggled close to her warm back with his arm around her waist, it left him feeling disturbed. He finally fell back to sleep as the pale light of dawn showed through a crack in the curtains.

Even upon waking he still felt a bit disturbed and couldn't quite shake off the memory of last night. At breakfast, he turned to her and said... "I'm really sorry about last night, kid, must have been that chat I had with the night porter. He spoke of people having seen the ghost of a lady in grey on the stairs over there."

Bev felt a shiver run through her when she heard this and at the same time felt very excited at the prospect of ghosts.

"Well, I do believe in ghosts, but I sure wouldn't want to see one." She poured their coffee and sat back to gaze at Ted. He did look a bit peaked this morning.

It didn't seem to spoil his appetite though; he polished off a hearty breakfast and was eager to explore.

"I'd like to see Maiden Castle this morning, are you game for it Bev?"

"Lead the way; I'd love to see it, too."

A short drive from Dorchester town centre and Maiden Castle came into view. Bev was a bit disappointed as it wasn't a structure at all but it loomed up before them through the windscreen like a huge terraced mound of earth. It was the largest hill fort in England and had been occupied around 2000 BC. It had been a complex arrangement of ramparts and ditches, but now was totally overgrown with short stubby grass and had a pathway leading to the top. They pulled into a parking space, got out of the car and with binoculars and camera, started their climb. Bev was anxious to scale the steep pathway; she needed this exercise and scrambled ahead. Thinking that Ted was right behind her, she looked back to speak to him and realized he was lagging far behind her. He had a rather vacant look on his face and seemed a bit dazed.

"Hey, are you coming? Are you alright?" He seemed to snap out of his reverie and haltingly replied to her ...

"Yeh, I'll tell you about it when we make it to the top." He hurried to catch up to her, and now having reached the crest, they walked about arm in arm enjoying the view. The surrounding countryside was a patchwork panorama of ripening crops and grazing sheep on the distant rolling hills. A west wind played over the fields of oats and barley, moving it like a rippling sea. Cloud shadows scudded across the landscape and the sun was obscured momentarily, dropping the temperature by degrees. Ted put his arm around her waist and held her gaze. "As we started the climb, I saw a black horse and rider moving up the side of the hill. He sat tall in the saddle and wore old-fashioned clothing and for some inexplicable reason, I thought it was me, and when I realized that couldn't be possible, in a flash he disappeared. It has left me with such a weird feeling, Bev. I really can't explain it. I hope you don't think I'm going mad."

"Not to worry, dear," stated Bev. "I'm sure there must be some explanation, maybe we should get back to the hotel for a while, have a bite to eat, and you'll feel better then."

They returned to the town and after a pub lunch, walked about and explored shops of interest that had been closed the previous evening. Bev bought a few souvenirs and stocked up on some of the yummy chocolate treats that were new to her. They fell into happy chatter and the incident of the morning was not mentioned again. Ted felt relieved that she had taken it so lightly, but he couldn't quite shake the experience.

Following drinks and dinner that evening, Ted settled in the lounge with a glass of sherry and lit a cigarette. Bev had gone up to their room to freshen up and make a phone call to her parents. He put his feet up on the footstool and rested his head back on the comfortable chaise. The lights were dim and he was alone in the room, the lazy ticking of the mantle clock was the only sound. He closed his eyes and easily drifted off into a trance-like state. He was the stranger again, looking out of his eyes, listening with his ears, unable to see his face. It was as if his soul was housed in another man's body and mind. He was the rider again. He could feel the ripple of the stallion's powerful muscles through his thighs; hear the animal's snort of protest as he urged him forward.

He snapped out of his reverie to feel Bev shaking his arm. His cigarette had turned to ash, balancing on the ashtray by the filter, his drink untouched. His only thought at this moment was that he knew without a doubt that he had lived before.

***

No further incidents occurred during their travels to the coast again. They spent a night in Beer, Devon and became ill after overindulging in clotted cream fudge. Then if that was not bad enough, they were kept awake all night long by the noisy raucous screeching of seagulls.

Then they drove on to Lyme Regis, which they found to be a pleasant little place with very steep streets and ancient buildings. They bought fish and chips served in newspaper and walked to a nearby park bench to sit and gaze out to sea as they ate. There were so many interesting shops selling everything from fossils to souvenirs. Bev bought bottles of Devon violet perfume for her sisters. She remembered how they all loved the gorgeous purple Devon violets which grew in her mother's garden back home.

The next part of their holiday found them in the Lake District and then on to Scotland. They spent several days in Edinburgh and were lucky to find a hotel room as it was the time of the St. Andrews' golf tournament and everything was booked. The weather was warm and sunny, so they were able to enjoy touring the castles and gardens and all the places on their agenda. They found the food most delicious, but were amused at how very traditional the Scots were. Ted could not get over the fact that at dinner one evening, a trolley of desserts was brought to their table, the chocolate gateaux looking most appealing. He was too full to enjoy it then but later, when he called down for room service for a piece of the same cake, he was told sorry but it could only be served for high tea. Even though the cake was still there, it was not available at that time of day. Ted burst into the song 'Tradition' from 'Fiddler on the roof.' And that would be the theme song for most of their adventure in Scotland.

From Scotland they travelled down the East coast, through Nottingham, famous for the legend of Robin Hood, and then back to

London. They saw his parents off at the airport, meeting Ted's godparents for the first time. Little did Bev know then that she would be seeing them again in the future.

Back in London, the days flowed into more lazy days and they took in some live theatre shows, 'Hair' and 'The Black and White Minstrels'; both very entertaining. London was an exciting city at night with so much to see and do.

Then on a whim they booked a mini tour of Europe, flying from Stanstead to Ostend, Belgium. By coach, they travelled to Hidleberg, Germany made famous in the movie, 'The Student Prince'. They dined and drank German red wine while students sang ballads. Ted overindulged in the wine, as the waiter just kept filling their glasses and he talked freely about his parents, his childhood, even becoming tearful. Bev just listened. She was a good listener and she knew that it did him the world of good to express his feelings.

In Amsterdam the next day, they strolled through 'the red zone' which Bev in her naivety thought was a Communist area, much to Ted's amusement. He would never let her forget it. They visited a diamond cutter, a cheese factory and rode the canal boats through tunnels aglow with lights.

They continued on to Austria, and were to visit Switzerland, Italy and France.

But on a very rainy day in Innsbruck, they realized that they were homesick. Bev looked at Ted with tears in her eyes and said she had had enough. The tour was tiring, they had to be up early every morning, and the food was not to their liking. Bev could not remember ever having cold meat and cheese for breakfast. She could kill for her own kitchen again to prepare meals. Ted agreed and they made the decision to break off the tour and return home.

But home was a long way off, and to accomplish this ahead of schedule was not an easy task. By taking the train, there was no guarantee that they could get a seat even though they had purchased tickets for the following morning. In the end, they had to take a bus to Munich, and then fly from there to London. They then travelled from London to New York with a connecting flight to Toronto. All in all, it was 24 hours of non-stop travel. They were so glad to be back on Canadian soil, they could have kissed the ground.

Yet, they were still not home. They had the long journey across country back to the west coast before being home. There was no set time in which to be back so they would take their time and camp along the way, still enjoying the summer. On a clear August morning as they drove the highway near Lake Louise, Bev could not believe what she was seeing through the windshield.

"Stop the car, Ted, pull over." Ted couldn't understand what she was on about but he quickly did as she suggested. They gazed in awe at what appeared in the clear blue sky to be a UFO. It was a glowing metallic disc-shaped object hovering in the sky. Other people pulled over to see it also. But within seconds, it left at a speed that was mind boggling and disappeared over the distant mountains. Everyone was in awe at what they had seen.

Of all the things that they had seen in their travels that summer, they would have to agree that topped them all. It left Bev with the feeling that the universe was more mysterious then she could have ever imagined. There were many unexplainable things in heaven and earth that boggled the mind. It made her feel as insignificant as a blade of grass. She could accept anything that life cared to send her way now. It renewed her faith and humbled her.

Yes, they had enjoyed their holiday. Yes, they had got along very well together indeed and yes, they would commit to each other for a lifetime together.

Bev and Ted the Early Years

It was fortunate that they had decided to return home earlier than planned as not long after their return, Bev's mother passed away after a bout of flu. She had a chronic health condition which made her vulnerable. Her death was only a year after Bev's husband and in the same month. Bev, as well as all the family, were devastated and rallied around their father. Ted was a pillar of strength to her. She could not quite fathom how her life would have gone after the death of her mother, if he had not come into her life.

They had set up a lifestyle living in the city of Vancouver in an apartment looking over English bay. There was an unobstructed view across the water to the distant mountains and only a short walk to Stanley Park. Both worked in the city, with weekends free to enjoy entertaining and short trips away. Things were going well with their relationship and when Ted asked her to marry him, it was no surprise. She had felt as though they were already. She suggested that they should wait for another year, give them the needed time to save for the big event.

In the early spring, Ted's parents decided to come for a two-week holiday and stay with them. After all they did have a guest room, and would be no trouble, they assured. They had never been out west before, so coming from Toronto still in the grip of winter, to the green and mild western climate where spring blossoms and sunshine greeted their arrival was like a dream come true.

His mother, Inez, fell in love with the place at once. She loved being near the ocean and squealed at the sight of wallflowers. She had not seen these since living in England. His dad was in his element, touring the city on his own. They were certain that they had found paradise. Ted and Bev wined and dined and took them everywhere, so that by the time they were due to fly home they were smitten with the place and keen to return.

Inez couldn't wait to brag to her friends that she had walked the entire seawall around Stanley Park, albeit that she had to have a nap when she got back to the apartment.

A phone call came to say that they were safely home. Their voices were nearly drowned out by the howl of the wind in the background. They had returned home to another blizzard.

***

October had always been Bev's favourite time of year and that year it did not disappoint. From the air, Ontario was ablaze with a mosaic of scarlet, bronze and gold foliage. The weather in Toronto was warm with bright sunshine and blue skies during the day, showing off the splendour of bright-coloured autumn leaves, and then it would turn crisp and cool at night. They had chosen to come east for their wedding and on that day, with Ted's parents and a handful of friends, they exchanged vows in a church lavishly decorated with the harvest bounty and candlelight.

As they repeated their vows, Bev could not help herself from crying, the tears streamed down her face as she repeated, "Till death do us part". It was such a moving, emotionally joyous time for her to be standing before this wonderful man who was wholeheartedly giving himself to her. Ted gallantly and with a big grin, took his hankie and dabbed at her eyes. She smiled through her tears as they exchanged rings, and then kissed most tenderly.

An informal light lunch was enjoyed at his parents' home, around the dining room table and served on dinnerware that had been a wedding gift for their wedding in England, many years earlier. As the guests toasted the couple, they felt happier than they could ever remember being. Some say the second time around is more fulfilling and they felt this to be true.

The days end found them boarding a plane back home, for a honeymoon was not in order, having spent many months away in England and Europe earlier.

***

They worked hard, saved their money and within the first year of their marriage they had bought a home. They just happened on the area while out for a Sunday drive. It was in a new subdivision, so not only were they able to have a newly-built home, but they were able to choose the carpets, paint colours and trim. They were only nicely settled in when news from his parents shocked Ted. They had sold their home in Toronto and were moving out west to be near him.

It was expected that they stay with them until they found a place of their own to live. Ted worked diligently once they arrived to make their move as smooth but as far away as possible. He didn't want to be so close that they could just drop in whenever they pleased. He knew what his mother could be like. He even went so far as to place some blame on her for the breakup of his first marriage.

It soon became apparent to Bev that she always seemed to be the one cooking meals for holidays and every other occasion. It seemed also that Ted's parents demanded a lot of Ted's time and were frequently on outings and holidays when the young couple preferred to be on their own. This Bev tolerated as best she could. She had been very close to her mum and dad, but they were never demanding of her time. Her Dad was managing fairly well on his own after her mother's passing. He had the company of Bev's cat who he had begged her to leave with him. She would have loved to have Toby back but it did not seem fair to take her from a settled life. Ted soon rectified that and bought her a Siamese kitten. A note left for her one day when she returned from work read: 'Look in the red room'. The door was closed and when she opened it, the dearest little kitten made her way across the carpet and rubbed against Bev' s legs. She fell instantly in love with Cocoa.

***

Bev was back working in the hospital setting and really enjoying it. Ted managed a car dealership, so they were both very busy.

In the autumn a year after they were married, Bev found that she was pregnant, much to their delight. She carried on working for a time, but felt so tired and morning sickness was a problem. She found that the hospital smells especially set her off. She awoke in the wee hours one night and as she put her feet to the floor, she felt a warm trickle down her legs. In horror, she found that she was bleeding and her back ached. She gingerly climbed back to bed and woke Ted. He rubbed her back till she fell back to sleep and in the morning she called work to say she would not be in and made a doctor's appointment.

She was only in the first six weeks of the pregnancy and on examination everything appeared satisfactory, but she was told that if she wanted this child, she would have to rest. That meant giving up her job, and she did just that and rested. Within a few weeks, things settled and she was doing well, the little being clung to her womb like a limpet.

***

And then it happened. They had just nicely settled to sleep one night; Ted shook Bev to wake her and whispered, "There is someone in the house!"

They both got up quickly and crept out to the doorway of the bedroom and peered down the hallway, listening and moving forward. There was not a sound; the cat was sleeping and there was no sign of an intruder.

"But I saw a lady in a long green dress standing in the hallway just outside of our bedroom, Bev. She was not looking in the room, but standing with her hands crossed in front of her and staring straight ahead." His voice was trembling. "Something woke me, I was definitely awake, and she was so real. Surely you believe me?"

"Of course, I believe you, dear. Just because I did not see her, it does not mean that she wasn't there."

They were wide awake now so put on the kettle and made a cup of tea. Sitting at the table, they sipped their tea, neither speaking for some time just trying to take it in, a lady in green.

"You know this is the first experience I've had since England,

Bev. What should we make of this?"

"I don't know, dear, but it's not something to worry about. Like a dream, it can't hurt you. Right?"

"Yes, of course, you're right, but she was so real and I know I was awake. Best go back to bed, it's almost morning."

But it was not alright. Something was definitely happening to Ted. Oh yes, he carried on with work, was doing very well in fact. But he seemed somehow distant, his mind preoccupied.

One evening after company had left and the kitchen had been cleaned up they were sitting in the lounge having a drink, chatting about conversation shared. The drapes were drawn, a fire blazed in the fireplace, the cat was asleep on the hearth rug, and all was cosy and peaceful. Bev sat with her legs curled up leaning against the cushions in the opposite couch. Ted suddenly looked over at her, and he just looked different. There was something strange about his eyes. It frightened Bev and in her mind she willed whatever was happening with him to go away. He looked straight at her saying, "He doesn't know, you know," and with his right hand he literally crushed the glass he was drinking from. Glass and sherry was over everything, but there was not a cut on him. Then suddenly he became aware of the spilled drink and shattered glass but hadn't a clue what had happened.

"My God, Bev, I'm sorry. I don't even remember doing this."

And then Bev felt real fear. "Whatever is happening, Ted, you must will it away. This pregnancy and this child coming is enough for me to deal with right now. I don't understand what's happening to you now, but it frightens me."

"For what has happened, Bev, I'm sorry. It was as though I had drifted off somewhere else, and you're right. I hope it won't happen again. I'm so sorry if I frightened you. It scares me too, but it will be alright."

The movie 'The Exorcist' was showing about this time, and Bev refused to go see it. She felt it was too believable. She'd had a nightmare about something unspeakable outside her bedroom hallway, growling and moving along on all fours. Now what was happening with Ted was totally unnerving. She didn't need it.

***

The incident seemed forgotten; at least, it was not spoken of again. But Bev, in her quiet moments wondered if her pregnancy had been a catalyst to whatever was happening with Ted.

Her pregnancy advanced well and she delivered a healthy baby girl a few weeks before her due date. They named her Tessa Mae after Bev's mother.

The first several months were hectic and tiring until they had established a routine. Bev was a good mother and enjoyed her baby. There was no going back to work like some of her friends, she wanted to enjoy every moment. She believed the first years of life to be the most important in a child's life. Her mother had always been there for her. She had waited so long for this child; she was going to do her very best. She had said to her mother-in-law that she just wanted for Tessa to grow up as a lady.

Ted adored his little daughter and spent as much time as he could with them.

It was a rarity that he ever had to change a diaper or do any of the hands on care that Bev performed. He worked long hours though and missed her first laugh and first steps. Some of her first words put together were; 'Bye bye, dada', and 'dada go way'.

Ted was so busy in fact that had he any 'happenings' again, he didn't say, but when he had to go off on a business trip for a few days, Bev had her mother-in-law, Inez, stay with her. She didn't want to be on her own and have any 'lady in green' appear to her. She did not actually say this to Ted; she thought it best to just be quiet about her fears.

When Tessa reached her first birthday, everything was about to change.

The Revelation

"I have something I'd like to tell you, Bev, and maybe before I do, you might want a large glass of sherry?" It was a Sunday evening, and they had enjoyed a roast beef dinner and then went out for a walk with Tessa. The fresh air and exercise was good for them all. She was now sleeping so they had the evening to themselves. Ted poured them both a drink and steered Bev into the sitting room, guiding her to her favourite chair and set her drink on the coffee table in front of her. He sat in the chair opposite and lit up a cigarette, taking in a long drag. He seemed to be more relaxed when he was smoking and he would need to be for what he was about to tell her. Bev took a sip of her drink, the liquid warming her as she steeled herself in anxious anticipation of what he was about to say. "From what I see of the books you read, Bev, I expect you will listen with an open mind for what I am about to tell you. But maybe we should talk first about your beliefs? I know you believe in ghosts and reincarnation because you told me so." Bev nodded in agreement.

"Yes, I do. You will remember me telling you that I had come to the conclusion that reincarnation was the only logical reasoning when my first husband was so ill and died so young. I believe that at the moment of death the soul leaves the physical body and that all deeds and everything learned is assessed and brought back with the newly-incarnated soul back to earth in another body. I believe that karma, the law of cause and effect comes into play so that misdeeds from a past life may need to be redeemed in the present one. For example, if a person committed murder in a past life, then he might be killed or suffer and pay with a dreadful disease or handicap. I remember reading that the spirits of all those who have passed from the physical level can remain about a place until their development carries them forward or until they return to life and further development here. While they remain, any may be communicated with, if one is open to it or has the gift."

"Well, how do you think they can communicate with the living?" Ted responded, taking another sip of his drink.

"I would say by making an appearance as a ghost, or through a medium, or even an Ouija board. You might remember me telling you how interested I was in an Ouija board, and threw it away when I became convinced that something otherworldly was happening. It frightened me. I wouldn't see that movie 'The Exorcist' either when you wanted to see it in the theatre. From what I saw of the preview, it was just too believable." She took a gulp of her drink and waited for his response with anxious anticipation.

"I do remember these things, my love, and how supportive you were when I had those experiences in England, and the 'green lady' episode. I suppose those things happened for a reason, perhaps to lead up to what I am about to tell you now." He took a long inhale of cigarette smoke and a large swallow of his drink and cleared his throat.

"I want you to know that I have a brother."

A shocked look crossed Bev's face. "But I always thought you were an only child, Ted. How can that be? Did either of your parents have an affair and produce another child?"

"I am an only child, Bev. This has nothing to do with this life. My brother is from a past life some three hundred years or so ago."

"Oh my God! Please, please tell me about it. This is so exciting," Bev squeaked and choked on her drink.

"Well, maybe for you it's exciting, but not much fun for me having someone who appears to me in the full dress of another era and speaks to me in my head and tells me who I was in another time. It's damned hard to come to terms with that. I only hope I'm not going mad. I'm left thinking about it when I'm trying to get on with working and living my own life. I can actually tune into places and events psychically. I guess when I saw that horse and rider at Maiden Castle that time, I really was seeing myself." He laughed. He waited; thinking that by now Bev would just get up and leave the room. But he could see that he had her full attention.

"Anyway, getting back to my brother; his name is Philip Canton. He lived in Sherborne, Dorset, England in the time of King Charles I. You might say he is a spirit guide. I was his younger brother, Michael. He tells me that my life here and now was planned in the realms of that afterlife. There are some things that I must fulfil and he can help me along the way. He says that he will never tell me what to do but will make suggestions if I am open to them. Everyone has free will." He sighed and leaned back, wearily rubbing his temples.

"I think I understand what you tell me, love, and I do believe you. It's all so exciting and hard to take in." Bev got up and went to the kitchen to pour them each another drink. She checked on Tessa, who was soundly asleep. When she returned Ted appeared to be more relaxed and was lighting another cigarette. He took a long drag and placed it in the ashtray near his drink. Bev sat back down across from him and was startled to hear him taking huge deep breaths and exhaling in a controlled deep-breathing sequence. Then suddenly, he looked across at her with a totally different look to his blue eyes. "Grey, green. Grey, green, it always comes out green." These words came from his mouth in a most eloquent deep-voiced English accent.

"Who are you?" she gasped. "Ted doesn't speak like that."

"No, of course not. But I am here now and I hope that you will listen to me. My brother is relaxed and drifts off to another place whilst we speak. Do not be alarmed... Please know that I have seen you as a child sitting in a wooded place and I have waited such a long time to speak to you. I have also known you in a past life when you were the daughter of the Italian artist, Jacopo Pontormo. He gave you art lessons. You have that gift in this lifetime? Yes?"

"Well, yes," Bev stammered, quite taken aback with what she was hearing. "How are you able to speak through him like this?"

"One must accept that there are many things in heaven and earth that can't be explained. This is where faith comes in, my dear. Read from your Bible from the book of John; chapter 14 verses 1 to 10 and that may help."

When Bev heard this she was even more certain that this could not be Ted speaking. He would never in a month of Sundays say these things.

"There is work to be done. Child. If you will be so kind as to fetch your souvenir book you brought home from England, I want to show you something."

Bev remembered the book of which he spoke and she pulled it from the bookshelf directly beside her.

"Open it to page 52 and you will see there, the most haunted house in Britain. I think you might enjoy exploring it." Bev turned to the page that he had suggested and sure enough a photo and explanation about the Sandford Orcas manor house was there in black and white.

"He tires easily and that is all I have to say for now. I really must go."

Deep breaths were taken, once, twice and then Ted was back in the present and Philip was gone.

"Did I fall asleep? God, would you look at the time and look at my cigarette. It's all ash. You shouldn't have allowed me to fall asleep, Bev. Is everything OK?"

"Yes, of course, dear," Bev replied. "Maybe this talk has tired you more than you would expect. We can talk about all this again; maybe take our time to absorb it little by little." Having said that, she got up and kneeled before him. Leaning forward, she hugged him and kissed him on the forehead. "I do believe you, Ted."

"Thank you, Bev. I really appreciate that you are a good listener. Think I'll go to bed now though, I feel achy all over, even to my very bones and cold too. Hope I'm not coming down with something. I am ever so weary."

Bev walked to the bedroom with him, and helped him to settle in, then got him a hot water bottle and tucked it around his cold feet. "How about a nice hot drink and a couple of aspirins? I'll be to bed as soon as I've made you a drink and checked on Tess."

"Sounds good, dear, you are so good to me." He sighed and pulled the covers up to his chin. He felt absolutely exhausted but relieved to have spoken about what had troubled him for some time.

By the time she returned with his drink, he was already fast asleep.

***

The next morning, Ted felt like he had been run over by a truck. His head ached as he recalled their conversation of yesterday. But there was no time for self-indulgence; he had to go to work. He kissed Bev and Tessa goodbye and was off out the door, still munching on a piece of toast.

Bev though, did have time to ponder yesterday's happenings and while Tess was having her nap, she got out her New Testament and looked up the verses that had been mentioned. There was certainly a message there, it was about the doubting Thomas, and the disciple Philip was mentioned. Also 'in my father's house there are many mansions'. But it was verse ten which had the most significance: 'Do you not believe that I am in the Father and the Father is in me? The words that I say to you I do not speak on my own initiative, but the Father abiding in me does his works.'

Then Bev took the encyclopaedia from the bookshelf and turned the pages until she came to Pontormo. Here it was, Jacopo Pontormo, 16th century Italian artist, most famous for his painting 'the birth of St. John' and many others. He had been patron to the great Medici family and had been taught some of his skills by Leonardo da Vinci. His paintings were on display in some of the famous galleries of the world including the British art gallery.

Next, she again opened the travel book to page 52 and read again about the Sandford Orcas manor house. It stated that it was the most haunted house in England and was open to the public for tours. This gave her chills up her spine. Not only was the information given through Ted correct, but she was certain that he would have no knowledge about any of it. She would have to ask him. She certainly had never heard of the artist Pontormo until now. Now, alone she had to really think about what had transpired. She would bring it up with Ted at a later date but she was almost certain that he was oblivious to his trance state.

She found her old medical texts and had a look through her books on psychology and psychiatry. She had a pretty good knowledge of the human mind and psychology through her nursing studies, but this didn't fit into any category she had known of nor was it in her texts. It was not multiple personality disorder, nor schizophrenia, nor a manic state. It was as though Philip was implanted in his head, breathing through him, speaking through him, seeing through his eyes. I know exactly what I heard. It is all so strange, yet exciting. Where will it all lead to, and why?

***

The synchronicity of events following that day and leading up to their decision to leave for England, was truly uncanny. On a gorgeous late spring afternoon, Bev was out for a walk with Tess. The lilac bushes gave off a heady fragrance; bees hummed in the flowers along the roadside and all about there was a peaceful stillness. Tess sat in her stroller reaching out for the bright dandelions she saw. Bev was overcome with a pleasant warm premonition of change. As she handed Tess a dandelion and her fat little fist clasped it, there was the unmistakable aroma of smoke from burning thatch stubble. She knew the scent for she had smelled it when on their travels in England. There was no tell-tale trace of smoke anywhere in the atmosphere, yet she was not mistaken.

"We're going to England, Tess!" She almost shouted in glee and laughingly bent to remove the dandelion petals from her baby's mouth.

That evening at supper, Ted announced that he had the okay to take a week's holiday that could be right after Tess's first birthday. They were expecting the grandparents for the celebration, so it would be right after.

"I have arranged for an RV and just us three can get away and explore some of the places I've not yet seen. It will give us some time to talk and relax around a campfire. Sound alright with you, dear?"

"I'd love that Ted, you know I would ..." And then she just blurted it out. "Let's just do it, dear, let's just sell up everything and move to England. You have every right as a UK citizen and your passport is in order. Let's just do it!"

"Well, this is a surprise!" He stared at her almost dumbfounded.

"I didn't think I would ever hear that from you. Of course I'd love to go back, but that would take some planning. What has brought this all about?"

She pushed some food around on her plate and stated frankly. "Everything has changed since your revelation. Things that I felt were so important, mostly material things, have lost priority. I just feel that a total change of lifestyle would be good for us. God knows you're fed up with your work dealing with the public, and you spend so little time at home. We need this!"

The shrill jangle of the telephone interrupted their conversation. Ted reluctantly got up and caught it on the third ring.

"Oh, hi, Dad. No, sorry, didn't have a spare minute today. Tell Mum I'm ever so sorry, I'll try tomorrow. No, don't put Mum on the phone, it won't help. We're right in the middle of dinner. I'll talk to you later. Bye now." And he hung up with a sigh.

"You're right, getting away from all this would be great."

Ted's father had retired early from the retail business in the east and they had followed him out west as soon as they learned he was settled. They had been upset with him over his divorce and never failed to remind him, mostly his mother, in whispered tones when she thought that Bev was out of hearing distance. They had never had time for him when he was a child and then pushed him into an early marriage for their freedom.

As much as he loved them and had always been devoted to his mother, he was weary of always being at their beck and call. It was one of the main reasons he had moved to the opposite side of the country and now they were trying to run his life yet again.

"Yeah, you're right Bev, let's give this some serious thought over the next while. It would do this little family good. Let's toast to that and jolly England!"

***

Later that night as Bev was preparing for bed, she peered in the mirror while brushing her teeth and negative thoughts of her mother-in-law,

Inez, came to mind. She had such irritating ways about her that could ruffle Bev no matter how many miles she was away from her. But it was the little things that bothered the most; taking home a half bottle of wine she had brought for a meal with them, or coming out of the bathroom smelling of Bev's expensive perfume, or rearranging Bev's things to suit *her* taste. There were many things she did that irritated Bev, but she thought it would seem too petty to call them to Ted's attention. No, she would not miss her in-laws.

Ted's dreams took him back to his childhood of seaside haunts, tidal pools with little sea creatures hiding beneath the shells and rocks, chill salt spray and chalk cliffs gleaming white from a distance. In his dream he was happy, carefree and grounded.

***

Around a campfire on a warm summer evening they talked more freely, and made plans to travel. Bev brought up all the things she had been told; the Bible verse, Jacopo Pontormo, the Sandford Orcas manor. Ted sat open-mouthed and found it difficult to take in. Just as Bev had expected, he had no knowledge of any of it. He would just have to accept the fact that he was different. Where all this would take them, he had no idea. But he decided that if Bev believed in him then he would accept and run with it.

As sparks from the fire snapped and crackled it was reflected in his eyes, but he was no longer present. His hand reached out and grabbed Bev's.

"I am so pleased that you have decided to visit my home, my dear. Be certain that you head to the West County of Dorchestershire. Find the place I have suggested, you will not be disappointed."

Sandford Orcas

Walk on
Down that lane
Where the great oak tree Towers to the grey sky.
The rain that touches your skin Coldness that is sorrow
Walk by,
As though you did not know
As though you had all but forgotten. The faces that peer
From the eaves Will forgive you. Walk on
Let not your eyes stray
For fear of what you might see Or recall.
The hills are still there Bleak with age
Crying out in silence Sanctity unrecognised
The belated dirges on the wind
They go unheard.
Walk by.
Pretend that you do not know Though it is not simple to forget.

By Allison Marie Payton

Summer 1976

The little family arrived in England to be welcomed to one of the hottest Julys on record and the city sweltered even though it was still early morning. Heathrow had been crazy in the heat, such hustle, bustle the likes of which they had never experienced before. It seemed that everyone travelled at that time of year, arriving from all over the world.

London sightseeing was not on the agenda this time around, certainly not with a toddler on board. After a few nights' rest in a hotel to get over jet lag, they rented a car and headed to the West Country. It was an unspoken agreement between them that it would be there that they headed first. Two steamer trunks packed with everything they needed were to be picked up at the freight terminal at Heathrow, so they could not loiter.

Bev had forgotten what it was like to be travelling on the opposite side of the road, so the busy motorway coupled with jetlag, was a hair-rising experience even though Ted was an excellent driver and had no difficulty adapting. Tess was soon lulled to sleep by the motion of the car and Bev sat back more relaxed in her seat now and took in her surroundings which seemed almost surreal to her. Bev thought to herself how her mother, who had never flown on a plane, would have thought of this. How one afternoon you could be safe in your home in another country and then in a matter of hours, be in another reality altogether. The busy built-up areas gave way to rolling countryside, ripening crops, livestock grazing on the hillsides then small hamlets tucked in behind ancient stone walls.

They passed by Stonehenge sitting out there on the wide open Salisbury plain but did not stop this time around although they remembered their first sighting and talked about it with fond memories.

By late afternoon they arrived in Sherborne in the county of Dorset. Seeing this ancient market town was a new experience, as they had only passed by on the outskirts on their previous trip. At the top of the town on the Sherborne to Yeovil road was a newly-built modern hotel 'The Post House'. They drove up the long driveway to the hotel and booked in for three nights thinking this would give them time to explore and find a more permanent location. Local papers, maps and brochures from reception would give them a good idea of what accommodation was available. The receptionist welcomed them cheerfully and made a fuss of Tessa. The porter carried their bags to the room.

While Bev attended to Tess, Ted stretched out on the bed sipping a cup of good English tea and was surrounded by newspapers and pamphlets.

"We can explore the town tomorrow, dear. We'll take Tess in her stroller and walk to the town centre, apparently it's not far. I'd like to have a look in the abbey also. Can you hear the bells? There's something nostalgic about hearing the Westminster chimes. The desk clerk says that they chime out on the hour, the half hour and the quarter."

"No I can't hear them from here, but plans for tomorrow sound great. Can't wait!" Bev called from the bathroom as she was bathing Tess.

The next morning following a full English breakfast in the dining room, they packed a bag with all the necessities, strapped the baby in her stroller and headed down the hotel driveway to the town.

They walked along the upper road and then turned down Cheap Street which snaked through the town. It was a bustling place with people going about their daily lives. Students dressed in formal school uniforms both from the boy's school and the girl's, jostled through the crowded street amongst the shoppers. Both sides of the street were lined with medieval buildings, housing, shops of every description; greengrocers, jewellers, newsagents, butchers, wool shops, banks, charity shops, pubs and much more. Bev noticed that the jeans she wore were not in style here, and she felt quite alien amongst the women wearing sundresses and carrying wicker arm baskets for their purchases. How very quaint, she thought.

They approached a toy shop with bright painted signage and a toy train in the window display. Ted took Tessa from her stroller and held her up to the window. She gurgled in excitement as they moved through the shop door. After a session of checking out all the toys, a wooden carved horse caught her eyes and so she left clutching her new prize. The shopkeeper had exclaimed how sweet a child she was and how well behaved. They were proud parents indeed.

Near the bottom of the street and a short distance from the market cross loomed the great abbey. Stone steps led up a gravelled path which was skirted on either side with well-manicured lawns and led to the great oak door of the front entrance. To the left of the abbey were the almshouses which still housed elderly people. Beyond the abbey rose the elaborate building of the Sherborne boy's school. This they would visit later.

Ted carried Tess and Bev folded up the lightweight stroller as they made their way up the pathway. They gingerly opened the creaking door and entered the cool quiet stillness of that ancient building. No service was taking place, but as they began to walk down the main aisle, someone began to play the organ, the sonorous sound resonated to the elaborate fan vaulted ceiling and sent shivers up Ted's spine. He leaned to whisper in Bev's ear. "I know it's not possible, but I feel that I have been here before."

"Well, if you believe what he has told you, you could have been in this very place in your past life," she whispered back. They walked up and down all the aisles taking in the edifices of the long dead and engravings on the flagstones hardly able to fathom how ancient they all were.

An elderly gentleman came up to them and relayed some of the history of the place. It was an opportunity to ask where they might find the Sandford Orcas manor house. Having lived here all his life he knew everything about the town and was most obliging.

"At the top of the road and to your right is the signposted Sandford Orcas Road. It is just over a mile to the hamlet, but the road is very narrow, mind. But there are places to pull over if you meet an oncoming vehicle. Good luck!"

They thanked him for his help, left the abbey and slowly strolled back to the hotel. Tess had fallen asleep which suited, as they were both in quiet reflective moods. Bev could hardly fathom the age of the town with its 1200 years of history compared to her own small town which was less than 100 years old.

Ted was deep in his own thoughts, trying to come to terms with his feelings of familiarity to this place. That realization made him feel quite dizzy. He *had* been here before. He just knew it.

The exercise, fresh air and jet lag had caught up with them once again so upon returning to the hotel, they stretched out on the bed and fell asleep.

***

The following day after a good rest and a hearty breakfast they decided to drive as far as the parking lot near the supermarket and then walk the distance to Sandford Orcas. It was another glorious day, just right for a walk. After parking the car, they bought drinks and snacks at the store where they were told there was a taxi service if they needed a ride back.

The old man's directions were accurate and seeing the signpost, they followed the narrow road past a large thatched-roofed cottage on the left. A man was at the side of the property cleaning up in a garden in which he was burning stubble, the fragrant smoke drifting across their path.

"Oh God! What dé jà vu!" exclaimed Bev. That particular smell gave her such an uncanny feeling. Then she explained to Ted how she had smelled the same smoke on that day back home and how she felt it had been a premonition of this very day. He squeezed her hand in understanding, happy that his wife had unusual experiences also. They continued past a group of houses on the right with children playing in the yard and dogs yapping as they passed. Further on, the road opened out onto sprawling fields either side, the grass was bleached golden from the sun and it was only mid-July. Further along and behind a wooden slatted fence, two donkeys rubbed against an overhanging beech tree. Ted held Tessa up to the fence and she patted the shaggy heads, giggling in delight. The road led near a golf course and beyond. Both sides were banked with hedgerows in a jumble of hawthorn, blackberry vines, hart's tongue ferns and nettles. Birds darted back and forth within the foliage, twittering and feeding on the ripe berries. The air was heavy with the fragrance of new-mown hay and ripening fruit. The only sounds were the lowing of farm animals, the drone of bees and birdsong.

Around another bend and at the top of a fairly steep rise, the idyllic little hamlet came into view. On their right, a massive maiden oak rose to a great height. Ivy entwined the trunk and its great branches overhung the roadway. It offered welcome shade for a rest, so they sat for a time in a spot farthest from the road. Ted picked up an acorn and showed it to Tess.

"Just look at that knarred bark, Bev, this tree has got to be hundreds of years old. I read somewhere that it takes three hundred years for an oak to reach maturity, three hundred years of life and then another three-hundred-year process for it to die. Isn't that incredible? Just imagine how many people have passed under these branches; it truly boggles the mind."

"I love how the sunlight filters down through the leaves and how cool its shade," cooed Bev. "I could just fall asleep here, but we wouldn't see the village if we did that." So they got up and continued their walk. A little stream followed the road into the village; it was only a trickle in the summer heat. As they moved past solidly built stone houses, the lace curtains of a window moved slightly, as though someone watched their every move. A marmalade cat sat atop a stone wall lazily sunning itself and gave them only a cursory golden-eyed glance then stretched and yawned widely.

"It's so quiet here, and oh, look straight ahead at that gorgeous old pub, 'The Mitre Inn', exclaimed Ted.

It was a two-story building with shuttered windows and a low thatched roofed porch entrance. Window boxes held a profusion of summer flowers. There were cars in the parking place and a few brown hens scratched and picked about on the grass slope. At the top were picnic tables sat on the level. Beyond lay a lush garden, ripe with summer vegetables and berries.

"It must be open for lunch, let's give it a try?" Bev enthusiastically suggested. They entered the cool atmosphere heavy with the aroma of food and beer.

Within moments Bev was seated, Tess was asleep in her stroller and Ted went up to the bar. The publican greeted him warmly, suggesting some cool draught ale when Ted told him they had walked all the way from Sherborne. He was interested to learn that they were newly arrived from Canada and quite blown away by the coincidence that he and his wife had lived in Victoria before buying the pub. John and Julie had gone into partnership with his brother and wife, buying the freehold property as a joint venture, only for the couple to split up and leave them in the lurch to run the place.

"We're married to this place, seven days a week with only a break in the afternoon when we close for a few hours."

After taking a large swig of his ale, Ted exclaimed in sympathy for his plight. "We're really interested in seeing the manor house; we read that it's haunted."

John rolled his eyes. "Some say so, but I don't believe in such stories. To me it's just an ancient pile. It's just a short walk from here though and if you want to view the inside, you're in luck as it's shown between 1and 3pm."

They were delighted to hear this news. Following a delicious lunch of deep fried prawns, salad and fresh-baked bread, they were refreshed for the walk to the manor. John suggested that they come back to the pub to call for a taxi.

The sun was almost directly overhead and beat down on their bare heads. They ambled along, admiring the roses blooming around ancient doorways, the neat verdant gardens and the general old world atmosphere of a place that seemed to be from a fairy tale.

Just beyond the centre of the village on a rise to their right and behind a stone wall, loomed the ancient manor house. Rising on the left of the driveway stood the church of St. Nicholas. Both had been built in Tudor times.

They passed under the archway which connected the main building to a small gate house. Leaded windows overlooked the courtyard. Menacing looking gargoyles stared down from several locations near the rooftop. Against a background of clear blue sky, they seemed to lose some of their power. More large gabled mullioned windows reflected the sky and though the general appearance of the building was rather ominous, there seemed such peacefulness about the place at that hour of the day.

A door at the garden wall bore a sign about visiting times. But before entering they walked around the gravelled courtyard taking in the mews and coach house cottage. A fig tree bearing sticky fruit overhung the stone wall. Beyond the wall was a view of the back portion of the church and surrounding gravestones.

As the day was so hot, the door to the manor house stood open; the large wrought-iron knocker summoned a small grey-haired lady in casual dress. She welcomed them warmly, introducing herself as the caretaker. She said that she and her husband, a retired colonel, were caring for the place while the owner was away in London. She ushered them through the entrance hall, on the walls of which hung armour and other relics of a past age.

They were guided through to a spacious living room that was panelled in dark wood. A fireplace large enough to roast an entire venison was piled with logs laid ready for a cool day. The oak-board floors were covered in places with old and worn Persian carpets, their faded patterns amplified by the sunlight filtering through the high mullioned windows. Heavy dark velvet curtains pulled back with tasselled cords draped the windows. The walls were hung with ornately framed portraits of past family members painted by the renowned artist Gainsborough. The eyes seemed to follow them as they moved about the room.

Ornately carved tables and a grand piano displayed antique vases and bowls of pot pourri. There was a pervasive smell of old dust and memories of a past age. Ted shivered.

The little lady escorted them through the upstairs bedrooms and games room, keeping up a commentary about the ghostly sightings and happenings from the past. She said that the ghost of a yeoman farmer wearing a white smock of the trade appeared at random. He was reputed to have hanged himself from the archway. She said that her husband awoke one night feeling as though he was being smothered. There was said to have been a priest who had smothered a guest with his cloak. On occasion, a lady in white appeared on the stairs and a little dog ran through the place.

Some guests who had visited stated that they had heard screams of madness, scraping noises, the sound of metal chains dragging and low growling. On hearing this, hairs on Bev's neck stood up and she noted that Ted had turned quite pale. The woman also showed them photos sent to her from others who had viewed the place, and these could back up her claims. In one photo taken of the courtyard, in the background was what appeared to be the filmy image of a man wearing a white smock. Another taken on the stairway showed the image of a lady, her hourglass figure in a billowing dress of a much earlier era. Another was the image of a face with goatee beard peering from the leaded window pane over the archway. One could use one's imagination, but a camera does not lie. "I'd show you the room over the archway but the poltergeists don't like children, they have been known to throw sand and make quite a mess of things."

"Well, thank you for showing us through, Madam. Perhaps we'll come back another time." Ted cleared his throat to signal Bev that it was time to leave. He couldn't wait to get out of there.

They came out into the warmth of the sun, shivering with cold. Or was it with fear?

"God, Bev, I don't think I'm too anxious to go back in there again. And what the hell is a poltergeist?"

Bev could hardly keep from laughing at the look on his face. "I think it's the word for a noisy disruptive spirit," she laughed.

"Well, you may laugh, but I have such an overpowering feeling that I have been in that place before, especially when I saw that card table in the games room."

"I did notice that you ran your hand over the table and the card icons, especially resting on the ace of spades," Bev remarked.

"Yes, dear, and the other horrible feeling that came over me was that there are human bones buried in the cellar. I would not have dared to ask to see the cellar, but I'm quite certain it too would be off limits."

They wandered for a while in the formal garden and then around and into the church, trying to absorb their experience. The quiet sanctity of the church was in stark contrast to the manor house. They made only a brief tour as Tess was becoming fussy. They walked over to an old wooden bench in between some headstones and Bev brought out a drink and lunch for her.

Directly across the road from the church stood a little cottage that appeared to be vacant. It was well back from the road, with a gravelled drive leading to it.

"That's a nice little place," remarked Ted, taking out a cigarette and lighting it. "I think I'll ask when we get back to the pub to see who owns it."

They quite enjoyed cool ale when they arrived back at the pub. John was able to tell them that the small cottage was owed by a retired major living in the large stone house adjacent and that it was sometimes rented out as a B&B.

"His name would be in the phone book under Holmes. You're welcome to call from here if you like," John replied. "If you are able to rent the place it sure would be nice to hire you on as help here for the summer. It's so busy with the American serviceman from the Yeovilton air base coming most weekends."

"Well, that's very kind of you and food for thought, but right now I'll just call a taxi. We really need to get back as the baby is fussy." Ted called the taxi and when it pulled up they left, biding John goodbye and thanked him for his help.

"I'm sure you'll be seeing more of us this summer if all works out."

They were all very weary when they arrived back at the hotel. It would take a while for them to absorb all that they had experienced that day; the walk to the village, the pub and the great food, the walk to the manor house and tour through amidst the stories of ghosts, the feelings they had evoked, the church and little cottage. Both were in a state of awe. But tomorrow was another day. It was so exciting to anticipate what it might bring.

But the more Ted thought about the place, the more fearful he became. He was almost certain that he had been there before and that something horrible had happened there. Why ever did he agree to come here?

During the evening after Tess slept he divulged his fears to Bev. She was very concerned as she had never seen him so fearful. She called room service and had a bottle of sherry delivered. They sat and sipped at their drinks and Ted smoked.

"I don't think we should try to stay in that cottage, Bev. It's too close to the manor. I don't think I can do it," he whispered. Before she could reply, he got up from his chair to head for the bathroom, but collapsed in a heap at her feet. Alarmed now, she kneeled down beside him. His breathing was normal but she realized that he was in another trance state. She sat quietly beside him holding his hand, a hand that suddenly gripped hers with fierce strength.

"He is in my domain now, my dear. You must convince him that he must stay and fulfil his quest, for if he will not, one day I will take his breath." His mentor had spoken and this time she had no reply. She was shocked. She sat with Ted for a few moments after and he finally seemed to be more aware. She helped him to a chair and when he snapped out of his swoon, he no longer spoke in a negative manner about the manor house. He seemed quite exhausted though.

Every time it happened, it seemed to sap every bit of strength he had and chilled him to the bone. She helped him undress and climb into bed where he pulled the covers up to his neck even though the night was warm.

As Ted slept, Bev lay awake for some time trying to absorb what had been said to her. Was she fearful? Perhaps so, but she also had an overwhelming sense of intrigue. If Ted needed convincing, she felt she could do just that.

***

The next morning Ted woke up with a more positive attitude and although he had found the phone number for the owner of the cottage, he felt it might be better to just show up at his home rather than be denied over the phone. Appearances have far more impact than a voice over the phone he thought. Bev agreed that it was a good plan so before lunch they drove this time to the village.

Luck was on their side as they met only one vehicle on the narrow road, a tractor. It was driven by a very considerate farmer who squeezed well over into the hedgerow to let them pass, and even then the doors of their car were very close indeed. They drove past the pub, past the manor house and church and up the lane to the large stone house. A friendly black Labrador barked in greeting, summoning the housekeeper to the door.

"Lie down Laddie! Oh! How may I help you?" She was quite surprised to have a Canadian couple with child in tow come unannounced.

"It's the little cottage next door we are interested in," stated Ted. "We are hoping Major Holmes might allow us to rent it for the summer."

The elderly lady scrutinized the couple with an air of suspicion, but agreed to ask if the gentleman would see them. She left them standing in the hallway but within moments she was back and ushered them into the sitting room.

It was a spacious dimly-lit room with the aroma of well-cured tobacco. The old gent sat smoking a pipe near the window, a Pekinese dog on his lap. He was white haired and appeared to be well in his eighties. His face crinkled into a smile when they introduced themselves.

"Well you've certainly come a long way to find this remote little hamlet. Perhaps it might be nice having neighbours for the summer, you look like a strapping lad perhaps you could sort out my pond while you're here. Since this warm weather it's not doing so well. Josie here will show you the cottage. I'd like £30 weekly, mind."

"That sounds reasonable," said Ted. "We would love to view the cottage. And yes, I'd be happy to have a look at your pond."

With that, the woman called Josie left the room and returned with a set of keys. "We'll make our way by the little path, shall we?"

They followed the woman and dog through a gate in the fence and down a narrow path to the cottage. The stream that snaked through the village ran its course behind the cottage. Here it was overhung with high branches giving shade and a pleasant sense of coolness.

They entered through the front door which led to a fairly small sitting room and hallway leading to two bedrooms. There was a small bathroom with tub but no shower. The kitchen was tiny but adequate. It was only sparsely furnished but would suit their needs. Agreeing that it would be adequate, they followed the housekeeper back to the house to make payment.

"We're staying in Sherborne for now but would like to move in tomorrow, if that's okay?" Ted explained.

"That would be just fine," said the Major. "Give them the keys Josie. You can move in at your leisure."

They left feeling more than a little surprised at their luck.

"Isn't this exciting?" she squealed. "And it's right across from the manor house." She watched his face expecting a sign of hesitance, but there was none. "You're right dear, and it's only a short walk to the pub. We'll stop by for lunch and tell John he'll be having a bartender after all."

John was well pleased at the news and treated them to drinks and lunch on the house. Turkey sandwiches and ale just hit the spot.

***

The trunks had been unpacked, clothing hung up, familiar items of books and toys placed about, and then the little cottage had a more homely feeling to it. Without television, telephone or radio they would awake to the chorus of birdsong just as folks did centuries before, and retire late in the evening when the darkness refused to settle. It was the change and peace they had longed for and it truly seemed as though their wish had come true.

Twice weekly there was service to the door by a man with a van selling dairy products and vegetables. Other things had to be purchased in Sherborne as there were no shops in the village. Julie at the pub kindly sent supper home with Ted when he finished work and they would enjoy the meal late at night when Tess was asleep.

One evening as they sat with a glass of wine enjoying the meal of ham, chips and salad they reflected on their move, how things had just fallen into place for them and how lucky they had been to find this place. The life they had lived back home was already becoming a distant memory.

Bev told Ted that she and Tess had walked over to the churchyard and explored through the gravestones. They had sat on the bench making daisy chains. She found it so relaxing and from that vantage point she could watch the comings and goings of the major and his housekeeper. Later in the afternoon they had wandered up behind the manor house and climbed the hill overlooking it. From there she could view the beautiful countryside as well as the manor house and gardens. It really was a dominating structure and in the bright sunlight appeared less foreboding.

Ted still could not shake the feeling that something rather sinister hid behind the façade of tranquillity and he wasn't sure if he was brave enough to find out.

As they sipped their wine, he became relaxed and quite suddenly began a deep breathing rhythm, seemingly to slump in his chair. In the space of seconds, the voice came through him, the candlelight revealing the difference in his eyes.

"Bev, do you love this man?"

Hesitantly, as she was suspicious still, she said, "I do."

"Well, you are a very brave woman, my dear. Stay with him always and you will be rewarded one hundred fold. One day you will bear a son, but that will be some time from now. His name will be Philip. Your life will be a very rocky road, you need to be strong." Then with a few deep breaths he was gone as quickly as he had come.

Ted came to his senses with a start. "You let me fall asleep here? We should be getting to bed."

As Ted slept, she lay in the darkness and tried to make sense of what she had heard. Having another child was the farthest thing from her mind. She had a difficult birth with Tessa. No, absolutely no plans for another child, I'll pass on that one she thought. I won't even mention this to Ted.

***

The long summer days stretched out before them like a strand of beads, each different from another. The weather stayed warm and dry with no rain in the long-term forecast. They took long walks, drives to the surrounding villages and towns and went shopping on market days. On one such day, they walked to a nearby farm for a viewing of a huge sow and her many babies. Tess laughed in delight at the sight of the squirming piglets.

They thought the farmer's rich Dorset accent charming and he found theirs equally so. Upon enquiring about the countryside, he told them that if they were to climb the hill behind the manor, on a clear day one could see Camelot.

"Do you mean the Camelot of King Arthur?" Bev wondered.

"Aye, the same," he replied. "It's at South Cadbury, not far from here, might be a nice day out for you."

They were indeed intrigued at the thought and later at home Ted looked up the place on his road atlas. It was only five miles from Sherborne. Bev wanted to go and see it right away and began packing a picnic lunch. She was so excited.

They could stop in Sherborne on the way home for grocery shopping.

They found the ancient hill fort rising above the pretty little village. There was a path leading to the summit and they picked their way through the overgrowth of trees and shrubs. Earthwork ditches surrounded the place but it was flat surfaced at the top where cattle grazed peacefully, paying no attention to their intrusion. A welcome breeze stirred the air, heavy with the smell of wild garlic and nettle. The view of the surrounding countryside was spectacular in every direction. There truly was a magical quality about the place and one could almost imagine it to be the place of King Arthur's court.

They had worked up an appetite with the exercise of climbing to the top, and then slowly made their way to the little parish church at the bottom. Bev spread a blanket on the grass and set out the picnic lunch she had prepared. They ate, talked and laughed at Tess trying to catch a butterfly. It was a wonderful relaxing way to spend an afternoon.

***

Late one night as Ted walked home from the pub, he had only just arrived near the manor house when he heard the distant pounding of horse's hooves.

Suddenly the sound was very near so he moved as close to the wall as possible to avoid being trampled. Then the sound stopped as horse and rider were directly beside him. He leaned still closer to the wall. They were so very near, so near in fact that he could feel the warmth of sweat and breath. Though it was so dark he could scarcely see, he heard creaking leather and sensed the rider lean from his saddle. Suddenly he felt a smart slap of leather to his cheek, and he raised his hand to his face to ward off a further attack. The horseman said not a word but seemed to straighten in his saddle and then in the blink of an eye, horse and rider just were not there. Ted was truly shocked; he could not believe what had happened to him. His cheek stung. Had he been struck with a whip or a glove perhaps? Had it been a challenge? This sort of thing had been done in the bygone eras. Bev will never believe this he thought, but she did, at the sight of his stricken face and the red welt on his cheek.

***

The headache came crashing through his skull like a bulldozer through a brick wall. It was all consuming and felt as though his brain would explode. He tried to sleep but when he closed his eyes he could see apparitions of long dead souls, as real as they had been in life. When he opened his eyes they seemed to surround his bed, all of them queuing to be heard; spirits of relatives who had passed and one tall dark haired young man in rough clothing claimed to be King Charles II and was most insistent to be heard. His huge ruby ring glowed blood red in the dark. It was the only thing that could justify his claim to noble birth. There was an all-pervasive smell of rotting apples or dead flowers. Was he truly going mad? He had to be. He covered his head with a pillow and willed it all to go away. He tried to pray. 'Our father who art in heaven...'

He must have slept, for when he awoke, daylight showed through the dark curtain. Bev had long been awake and up, for her side of the bed was cold. His head ached behind his eyes as though he was hung over from a booze up, but that was not the case. He had no recall of what had happened to him the previous night.

Bev scrutinized his face and could see no trace of the welt from the previous night, so she thought it best to be silent. Ted complained only of a dull headache.

Then almost every day for the next week, he continued to have a headache that would ease somewhat when she massaged his neck and temples with her skillful hands. But by the time he was due to go to work, he was almost incapacitated.

At night when he tried to sleep, he fearfully anticipated the sudden appearance of a ghost lurking in the dark recesses of the room. He would keep his eyes tight shut and will for nothing to come to him. He slept fitfully.

"If this keeps up, I'll be forced to pay a visit to the doctor," he moaned. "You should try to drink more water, dear; you could be dehydrated in this heat. Why don't we drive to Weymouth today, the seaside air will do you good." She lovingly rubbed his shoulders and neck as he sat at the table sipping coffee and picking at his bacon and eggs.

"That feels so good, mmm ... it does help. I'd love to go there; the cooler air would be wonderful. Just getting away from here would be nice."

The day at Weymouth was just as he imagined it would be. The air was cooler, there was an on-shore breeze, and the tide was way out, exposing a wide pebble beach. There was a carnival atmosphere of happy holidaying people with bright beach umbrellas and wind breaks. There were kiosks selling everything from A- Z and donkey rides on the beach. Tess was delighted to sit on the back of a shaggy animal which was slowly led by a much-tanned young lad in bright clothing.

It was seeing her laughing face that took Ted back to his happy childhood memories of a Kent coast with golden sands and he realized then that he longed to see it again.

***

It was late evening by the time they turned down the Sandford Orcas road. The lights of the Mitre Inn were lit and cars crowded the little parking lot, a confirmation that John would be very busy and probably missed his help. Just as they approached the manor house, he felt a sharp stab of pain in his right temple. By the time they arrived at the cottage, another full blown headache consumed him. He had never been troubled with headaches before, why now?

Bev settled Tess to bed after a bath and joined him in the sitting room bearing ice cold drinks of gin and tonic and handed a frosty glass to him.

"Take these aspirin tablets dear, maybe with the drink, your headache will ease." Ted did as she suggested and held his iced drink to his forehead.

"I can't understand it Bev, I was fine all day until we got back here." His face looked truly troubled. "I almost get the feeling that someone or something doesn't want me to be here. We can try and explain it away all we like, but I've never in my life had headaches this powerful. You have to admit things are a bit strange here, are they not?" She slowly nodded in agreement and he continued.

"My dreams too are tortured but I can't remember when I wake and I am left with a feeling of great anxiety, my heart is racing and I feel breathless."

"Well dear, maybe we should think about moving on. We've been here for over a month in this unrelenting heat. Perhaps being nearer the water would help. You mentioned Margate today, maybe we could go there, and you could look up some of your old friends?" Ted sighed loudly.

"You're right you know. Just the thought of getting right away from here makes me feel better all ready." He got up from his chair and sat near her feet, anticipating a shoulder massage. She ran her hand through his hair, squeezed his neck and kissed the top of his head then whispered close to his ear.

"We'll start making plans tomorrow. I'm sure if John advertizes he should be able to find help with the pub." He already seemed more relaxed and they talked about the old major and his pond and how it would all be fine when the rains came again. They had climbed the hill behind his place to take in the view towards Camelot, but the heat haze was too dense, it was beautiful still.

"There's definitely something here alright!" Ted sighed. "It whispers on the wind, it's in the hills and hollows of the ancient oaks. It's as though it's holding its breath just waiting to be discovered. If you put your ear to the earth you might even hear its low hum."

"Well, aren't you sounding lyrical!" Bev exclaimed. Ted laughed and sipped his drink. His headache had eased already.
"Don't really know where that came from, dear, but I'm sure it's true."

**

The following day they drove to Sherborne for supplies they would need for their trip. Ted had already begun to feel a detachment from the place knowing that they would soon be leaving. He looked at the town and the people in a new mindset now. But he felt more relaxed than he had been since arriving there.

On the return drive, they had only just started down the Sandford Orcas road when ahead they could see that on both sides of the road, the grass was ablaze. They lined up behind all the other stationary vehicles stopped by the fire brigade. It was speculated that with everything so tinder dry that a carelessly thrown cigarette or even a piece of glass magnifying the sun's rays could have started it. Acrid smoke, flames and heat waves rose in the already hot atmosphere. There was nothing to do but patiently wait for the all clear.

On his right where the land became steeper, Ted could make out through the haze of heat waves and smoke, the figure of a man sitting a large black stallion. It was too distant to see him clearly, but he appeared to be wearing a long dark cloak, tricorne hat and tall black boots. It was a though once he knew he had Ted's full attention, he lifted his hand in a wave. He heard in his head the powerful voice of his mentor ... "I concede that you will need time to find what you need to discover about this place. But the time is not right for you. You will return time and time again until one day you will find what you are seeking. Until then, my brother, adieu, have a safe journey." Then in the blink of an eye he had disappeared. Ted made no comment; he just kept it to himself. He did not even feel shaken in this instance, but more than anything a sense of relief.

He had been given a challenge to discover something and it might take his lifetime before the answer came, but he would get to the bottom of it one day. But not now. He definitely felt a connection and a drawing to this place but he had to think of his little family and what was best for them all.

He jumped with a start as Bev jostled him to start the engine as the fire was now out and they were expected to drive on.

He enjoyed the drive back to the little village this time. He savoured all the sights along the way knowing in his heart that it would be a long while before he made this trip to Sandford Orcas again.

Bev had been so happy here. She had spent such quality time with Tess and Ted. She would really miss this place. Maybe one day they would return.

Summer '76 Margate, Kent

The following weeks spent in Ted's birthplace were enjoyable indeed. Thankfully there was no reoccurrence of the headaches he had suffered from earlier in the West Country. Being here gave him a sense of continuity to have his own child playing on the beach where he had spent so much time in his childhood. It really hadn't changed much. The fact was that the entire place was much the same as he remembered; Dreamland was still there and the old roller coaster, the side streets were still lined with operating B&B's, Northdown Road was still a busy street with many of the businesses that he had known in his childhood. They were all likely owed by strangers or relatives of people he had known in the past.

The hot dry weather continued unabated until the first part of September. On one such day they were on a walk along the promanade overlooking the sea at Cliftonville, when they saw in the distance across the water, dark ominous looking thunderheads forming. The atmosphere was hot, humid and threatening. Darkness gathered far across the water and then dark sheets of rain could be seen coming from the black clouds. A strong wind picked up within moments, scattering bits of paper and other debris in every direction. With it came the rain; a light pitter patter at first and then it came down in a deluge.

They ran for shelter to a nearby band stand on the green. Tess giggled in delight as the rain hit her face. They were laughing and running like children. They sat on a bench under cover and watched the steam rise as the rain hit the warm pavement and quenched the dry and thirsty earth. How refreshing it felt after the long months of hot dry weather. Bev felt like dancing in it as she had done as a child after a lengthy hot spell. They sat for what seemed like hours until the downpour decreased to just a sprinkle, then made their way back to the B&B.

They were staying at the very B&B that his parents had owned and where he had spent his childhood. The present owners were very friendly and interested in what Ted remembered of its history. Although much renovation had been done, the structure and general layout of the rooms was unchanged. Ted had asked if the room that had been his bedroom was empty, and luckily it was, so this is where they stayed. The decor of the 50s had been kept in place so for Ted it was like stepping back in time. A small table and chairs sat by the French doors opening onto a small balcony overhung with grape vine. There was a double-canopied bed and side tables with lamps of that era. A cot had been set up for Tessa in the alcove. The only modern addition it could boast was an en suite bathroom.

The proprietors served three meals per day, as Ted's mother had done. So following the evening meal of rich meat pie and vegetables, they went walking again to the beach. They held Tess by her hands between them as she now hated to be in her stroller, having learned to walk on her sturdy little legs.

The rain had stopped leaving a fresh earthy smell on the breeze, mixed with the scent of seaweed. They discussed at length the weird episode of itching that Ted had experienced a few nights after they had arrived. There was no evidence of a rash or hives to indicate an allergic reaction to anything, he had just felt itchy. It lasted for only a short while and then was gone. Ted had spoken to his mother on the phone and happened to mention the episode. She remarked how strange it was as that was the very room that he had been in with a bout of measles.

"Well, that's as good an explanation as any, in view of all the other strange things that have happened," Bev remarked. "Houses probably hold a memory bank of all the happenings that take place within the walls."

She had felt compelled to walk around the room after that phone call, touching the old wallpaper and running her hand along the banister of the outside balcony that overlooked the front of the building. She could almost picture Ted as a child propped up in bed, his face covered in the red wheals feeling sorry for himself, but enjoying the parental attention that his sickness had brought.

"You could be right, Bev, probably the explanation for haunted houses too."

***

One afternoon as Tess slept, Ted was sprawled out on the bed; his head reclined on the pillows. Bev sat across the room at the table looking through a magazine and sipping a cup of tea. She glanced across at Ted who was staring at her. His blue eyes held a gleam that was not his own. She recognised at once that it was his brother staring back at her. How could she explain it? There was a certain depth to the eyes that were just... different.

"I will never leave him, you know. One day you shall return to my home." Bev didn't know quite what to say or why she did so but she crossed the room and gave him a light kiss on the forehead, like greeting a friend.

"You can kiss my lips, my dear." She leaned forward and brushed her lips to his. A spark ignited somewhere deep inside her, a spark of intense lust and he smirked in amusement. "I'll be with you later," he said and in an instant he was gone and Ted grabbed her hand and kissed her long and lovingly. "I love you, Bev!"

"I know you do, dear, and I love you, too. I'll show you how much tonight," she teased, enjoying the thrill of anticipation.
"I'll hold you to that, you know," he said with a cheeky grin.

But they had enjoyed several glasses of wine following dinner and when bedtime came, Ted felt exceedingly weary. He gave Bev a peck on the cheek and rolled on his side away from her with a deep sigh. Within moments he was asleep. She cuddled up to his back and wrapped her arm around his waist, hoping he would wake.

"Beverley, I wish to bed you," Philip stated shamelessly. She couldn't believe what she was hearing and gingerly lifted her hand away from his waist. Grabbing back her hand, he slowly stroked her palm with his forefinger in a most suggestive manner. Her whole body tingled.

"It is permitted. I am in my brother and he is in me and I must know you as he does." Turning to her then he began a slow and sensuous seduction, more exciting than she had ever known before which culminated in a powerful explosion of orgasmic pleasure, and a cataclysmic union of souls.

Then, as swiftly and without comment, he turned from her. Again Ted slept quietly, his breathing deep and satisfied. Bev lay in a blush of sensuous afterglow, reliving each tender kiss and touch of the unfamiliar powerful persona that dwelled within the familiar body of her husband.

She awoke feeling very different. She tried to rationalize her encounter with 'a ghost'. True, it was her husband's body, but in no way was it Ted who had seduced her in such a pleasurable way. She and Ted had been together for more than four years now. She thought that she had a satisfied marital relationship, until now... He had awakened in her something she never knew she possessed.

It was primal, erotic, yet spiritual. Yes, a spiritual awakening. How fitting she smiled to herself Mona Lisa like, and with a ghost.

***

Ted was quiet today, walking hand in hand with Tess on the beach. Bev trailed behind seeing the sand and seaweed covered outcrops of chalk, but her mind was far far away. She idly picked up seashells and turned over rocks sending tiny grey crabs running in every direction. She longed for the night to come and a repeat of last night's performance. Ted turned to look back at her, noting her preoccupied mood.

"A penny for your thoughts, my love!" he teased playfully.

She caught up to him, hugging him in a deep embrace then swooped up Tess and spun her around until she squealed. She felt incredibly happy.

But night came and it did not happen. She thought that she could initiate his return, but in the end she made passionate love to her husband, astounding him with her sensuality. It *was* better he thought, his lips twisting in an all-knowing smile to himself. He said it would be.

There was now a fine silvery thread that tied the three together. He gave it to her and she in turn passed it back to her husband. It completed the circle and bound them forever.

***

The following days were spent in idle ramblings to places that Ted had remembered. Being there brought up many memories, some good and some bad. Some he had repressed in that repository of memories that could only be accessed in dreams. It was good to see all the old places but he didn't think he could live here.

"You know, Bev, my mother went to a fortune teller in Toronto once, and was told that her son would die in the place of his birth," he casually remarked.

"Well, who knows what the future holds, dear, I wouldn't dwell on it. It's best not to know anyway. Could you really see yourself putting down roots here?"

"No way!" Ted replied, "But it has been nice visiting here."

He had been in touch with his godparents, Jane and Robert, who lived in Essex, and they had insisted on a visit which was arranged for the following day. He had spent much time with them as a child, going there for school holidays, and while his parents took the occasional break. Bev had met them on her first trip to England and looked forward to seeing them again.

By the time they arrived at the old blue door of Number 7 Clover Road, Romford, Aunt Jane had the guest room all prepared, even a cot for Tessa borrowed from a neighbour. They were greeted with hugs and handshake, cups of tea and lunch.

They were a very lovely couple and took Ted's little family to their hearts and they got on very well together. Robert was a tall lanky man, quite athletic and enjoyed a game of golf and working in his greenhouse and garden. He worked in the city of London and commuted daily by train. He had been doing this for at least twenty years and knew the route so well that he could nod off to sleep and awake at precisely the time to get off. He likened the ritual to a herd of sheep moving together and then dispersing in all directions.

Jane was a tall raw-boned woman with dark hair and eyes and a voice that had a tendency to be almost moaning. The couple were not able to have children; consequently, Ted had been treated as their own. He could remember them coming to the guest house for Christmas and holidays every year.

There were endless cups of tea and laughter in the home. Jane served good wholesome meals, but she hated cooking and they lacked variety. As Robert said, one could count on having set meals on set days of the week; roast beef on Sunday, shepherd's pie on Monday, sausages and mash on Tuesday, chicken on Wednesday, chips beans and egg on Thursday, curry on Friday, fish and chips from the chippy on Saturday and the odd steamed pudding for dessert.

She was quite happy to let Bev prepare some of the meals so she served some of Ted's favourites; chilli con carne, escalloped potatoes, meatloaf, and much more to delight their British palates.

Robert brewed his own beer and wine, some of it good and some not so good. He would take them on excursions in the countryside picking wild sloes, blackberries, nettles and dandelions and bringing them home to brew. The front porch was crowded with bottles of every description in various stages of processing and amongst them were large plants of geranium and busy lizzie.

Tess blossomed in the love and security of the little home. She found the little room under the stairs that still hung with the childish pictures her father had made for his Auntie Jane so many years before. She played hide and seek and peek a boo with Jane, laughing joyously. The back garden was a wonderful place to explore, she loved the little fish pond that Robert had made and would watch the fish in amazement. The old potting shed and greenhouse at the back of the garden was another favourite place and she would amuse herself putting soil from one pot to another with an old spoon. She had learned to walk at nine months and now she was running on her sturdy little legs down the garden path, there was no stopping her. Ted delighted in seeing her enjoy the same things he had as a child. He had spent time in the old shed with Jane's father helping in the garden. Uncle Mac had been a greengrocer in the town. At his death, his body had been laid out in the old tradition, in the bedroom, as had his wife before him. Jane had lived her entire life in the small house. Here she had spent her childhood, continued to live there after her marriage and then after the death of both parents.

Another relative who had been there for Ted as a child was Aunt Olivia who lived in her own home just across the street. She was the epitome of the old maiden aunt. She was very plain, dressed in the most unattractive fashion, but her keen brain made up for her shortcomings. She was a draughtsperson who worked in the city of London as well and was also an interpreter. She spoke five languages fluently. She would come across to visit, bringing with her various toys and books and would entertain Tess for a Sunday afternoon. Everyone loved her and she adored children.

Within many spinsters was a life story of tragedy, sadness or betrayal and she was no exception. Although it was never spoken of, her mother had hanged herself in the stairwell of the house when Olivia was only two years old. She was raised by her father with the help of her aunt who was Jane's mother. As a teenager her father sent her off to France in the disgrace of pregnancy, the lover forbidden to marry her. The convent that took her in for her confinement made the arrangements for the child to be adopted. Olivia never laid eyes on her child. There she remained for many years after, getting the phenomenal education that now provided for her comfort. The little children of family and her church family filled the emptiness within.

***

Within a short time, Ted had found a good paying job and helped out with household expenses. As far as Robert and Jane were concerned they were happy to have the little family remain with them indefinitely. But no matter how well they all got on, Bev and Ted longed for a place of their own.

Finding housing in those days was difficult. If one was not able to buy a home, the social structure provided government-owned council houses. Young couples would generally live with parents and wait for years for a council house to become available. Although Ted and Bev were eligible, the wait was years not months. People were generally afraid to rent out properties because in those days, tenants had 'squatter's rights' and it was very difficult for a landlord to remove a tenant once they were lodged under a roof.

So when an ad for a rental property showed up in the local paper, Ted and Bev excitedly went off one evening to view it, hoping it would be suitable. But to their surprise, two dozen other couples showed up at the same time. The landlord chose the most eligible, and they were not chosen.

Now with Ted away at work every day, Bev found that she was somehow at a loss. She had helped Jane by cleaning every cupboard, baking and helping clean up the garden but it was not enough to occupy her, especially when Tess was napping. They would take long walks in the park, running through the autumn leaves, and at times such as this Bev really missed her homeland. When she gave way to her nostalgia she had to admit that there was a great deal more that she missed; stores open on Sunday, products that were not available here, her family and friends and yes, just the Canadian lifestyle. She had never been away for so long. She became moody and quiet, her spirit at ebb. Ted sensed her distance and took her out for a meal to celebrate their anniversary. It helped little.

**

Then one night, an encounter with 'his brother' happened again. It had been so long that she was taken quite by surprise and was reluctant to again be involved in that way. But he was convincing, it needed to happen he said. The act was not a sensual one as the first encounter had been; it was over before she could even become aroused. It was as though he had a mission to accomplish.

"There now, my lady, you have the seed, nurture it." Then he was gone.

She lay in the darkness listening to the quiet breathing of her child, her husband beside her and the soft snoring from the next bedroom. Then with startling clarity, she understood the profound act. Truth told, she had run out of her contraceptive pills but had planned to visit a doctor; she just hadn't got around to it. She had relied on the age old and unreliable method of contraception; avoiding the act when she felt her body to be in a fertile phase.

Ted seemed to be none the wiser the next morning, he just went off to work as usual. Bev mulled everything over in her mind and was even more convinced that she had had enough of this place; also she didn't want to wear out their welcome. When she ran this by Ted that evening he had to agree that things were beginning to grate on his nerves also. They would plan to go back soon.

November 5th found them all celebrating Guy Fawkes Night with a bonfire in the back garden. The fireworks were bright and noisy and although Tess was excited she covered her ears with mittened hands. Halloween was not celebrated here. There were no roasted wieners over the fire, nor toasted marshmallows but potatoes and sausages (bangers) and hot chocolate spiked with spirits for the adults. Bev had to admit it had been fun.

That evening after the celebration, Ted phoned his parents to tell them of their plan to return. He was not surprised to hear that they had planned a trip to England to stay with a sister for six months and would soon be on their way.

"They're following me here, too. It really is time to return."

They left England at the end of November, stopping over in Toronto where they met his parents for a brief visit before parting ways.

"Not to be rude, Ted, but I'm happy that they won't be around for a while. It'll give us time to get settled again without their input."

"You're quite right there, my love," Ted remarked as they boarded their flight.

Prediction Fulfilled

In the days following their return, Bev was too occupied with settling into a new home to pay much attention to her body. But when the nausea hit her for a third morning in a row, she knew without a doubt that she was pregnant. She avoided telling Ted right away until she could take it in and get used to the fact. Looking back, she realized that she had most probably conceived in England at the time she was *visited* by the spirit through her husband. Am I being blasphemous? she considered. Can I suppose that the Virgin Mary conceived in much the same way? It says in the Bible that an angel appeared to Joseph in a dream telling him not to be afraid to take her as his wife, because what is conceived in her is from the Holy Spirit. It has forever been disputed that she could not possibly have become pregnant without a male counterpart. What an amazing possibility, she thought.

Ted was delighted at the news when she finally did tell him.

"I can't be happier, my love, and Tess will have a playmate. We'll have to get you to a doctor for the very best care, dear girl." He kissed her lovingly.

"I will wait for a month or so before I go, as long as I'm well," she smiled.

***

Ted was happy at his work, he loved being around and selling cars and he had the gift of the gab. Tess was developing her own little personality and talking non-stop. Bev blossomed in her pregnancy. She had decided to again be in the care of an obstetrician in view of the fact that she had had a difficult birth with Tessa. All seemed well. Philip Canton remained absent.

The in-laws returned two months before her due date and in a way it was comforting to have them close by. Inez looked forward to caring for Tess when the time arrived.

Early one July morning after Ted had gone to work, Bev felt the first unmistakable pang of a contraction. She was not due for another two weeks.

She waited until she was certain that things were progressing until she called on his parents to come over. Inez fussed around her and then with towels tucked in place, should her waters break, she went on a hair-raising ride with her father-in-law to the hospital. Her contractions were becoming strong but she was so focused on his driving she had difficulty timing them. Ted was informed and came as soon as he could. Tessa was left with her grandmother.

Her labour progressed only to a certain point and after many hours it was obvious that a Caesarean would have to be performed. Bev was screaming to get the procedure underway; she was in agony, thankful that she had the expert care of her obstetrician. As the anaesthetic took effect, she lapsed into a peaceful blackness, oblivious to the birth of her son.

Ted had seen her briefly before she was whisked away to the operating room theatre, then gowned and masked he nervously paced outside the door. Though it seemed as if he had waited forever, it was only minutes before he heard the lusty cry of his newborn. Then swaddled in green towels, his son was handed to him. He looked down on the tiny face and instantly bonded with the child. He felt privileged to be the first to see him even before Bev who would be recovering for hours before she would see her baby.

She was delighted to hold her son and tears of joy welled in her eyes and spilled over. She was so emotional and cried then and for days for just any reason. Not only was she hormonally influenced but she was also recovering from major abdominal surgery. It was probably this factor that delayed the naming of the baby. They had picked out a few names for a girl as well as for a boy. It was not something parents did lightly; one lived with his name through life and it was all that remained when life was over. They had thought of the name Stephen, and Franklin, and Edwin. It was already three days since his birth when Ted sat at her bedside holding her hand.

"I think we should name him Philip Edward." His jaw was set with determination. "Philip is a fine name and Edward of course is for me, what do you think dear?"

"Of course, dear, it sounds right to me, and if you're happy we can announce the naming immediately." Bev couldn't help but feel astounded, for the prediction of a baby boy named Philip had been fulfilled. She again burst into tears. Between sobs she managed to say, "He said it would be so, he told me so when we were in the Sandford Orcas cottage that we would have a son named Philip. I just never believed it would come true." Ted held her close and whispered in her hair...

"I had no idea, my love, but had you told me then, I would have doubted it too." Ted held her thus until she stopped crying and was comforted.

***

The little family settled into a new routine. Tessa delighted in helping with the baby but she was no longer the centre of attention. It was not until he was able to sit up and giggle at her antics did they truly bond. Ted was there for most of the special moments; his first smile, first tooth, first giggle. He thought that there was nothing as joyful or heart lifting than to hear his son laugh.

One evening after the children were settled to bed, Bev and Ted sat together enjoying a glass of wine after their barbequed meal. Bev was more relaxed than she had been for quite some time. Then, to her surprise she had a visitation. It was the first since they had been in England.

"You are well, my love?" His sonorous voice came through Ted.
"Yes. Yes, I am and very happy too," Bev hesitantly replied.

"Well your duty now is to nurture your children well. They are both very special to me and you may like to check, they have matching birthmarks on their right little fingers. They will always be close, even as adults. You guard them well now; don't worry about your husband, for I will always guard his back." Then he was gone and Ted was back in the present.

"We haven't had wine for such a long time, it has made me very sleepy, guess I must have dosed off."

"Yes dear, but we also had a visitor." Bev said hesitantly. "Oh, so that's what it was. I wondered."

No more was said and they both climbed the stairs to the bedroom. Bev checked on the children sleeping peacefully in their little beds. Baby Philip was sleeping through the night now and her rest was more peaceful too.

In the morning as she was dressing Tessa, she had a look at her right little finger. She had seen the small brown mole before. Then when she bathed the baby she checked the little finger of his right hand and sure enough there too was a mole, not as distinct as Tess's but nevertheless it was as he had said.

***

By the time the baby's first birthday rolled around, Ted was becoming restless to return to England again. He didn't really talk about his feelings too much as he knew that Bev was preoccupied with the children, but his past life thing never left him. It was like an itch that he just had to scratch.

He broached the subject with Bev one evening in their quiet moments. They enjoyed having a meal when the little ones were asleep and this evening Ted was barbequing steaks. As he served up her dinner...

"How would you like to go on a nice holiday, dear? We could rent an RV cheap through my place of work and drive down the coast to California."

"Well, it sounds as if you've already given this some thought, but it's not a big surprise to me. Are you sure it's not England you'd like to be heading to?"

"Well, yes it is. But I didn't think you'd be up for it," he smiled.

Bev mused on it before she replied. Travelling with Tess had been doable and one more wouldn't be much different if they worked together. Both children were in good health and for that she was thankful.

"I think that would work, dear. Hopefully this time we can find a place to live for a while. You parents won't be pleased, though."

"Of course, they won't," replied Ted. "They are so used to us being around and in truth they haven't been that much help with the little ones. Not once have they offered to stay with them to let us get away of an evening."

"Well, I'm for a holiday," Bev agreed. "We can take a leisurely trip down the coast to California, take the children to Disneyland and then fly to England."

"Done deal, I'll start making plans and give notice at work at once. We can store our belongings with Mum and Dad and see if we are welcome with Robert and Jane for a bit."

One evening before they were due to leave, they were enjoying a quiet talk and drink. Although it had been a long time since the last visitation, Ted went into a trance state. The voice through him said to Bev...

"Go see your father before you leave, as you will never see him again."

It had shocked Bev to hear this but she was not about to dispute it. They did in fact make the trip to see her father and although he was sad that they were leaving, he was happy for them.

***

On a fine summer morning in July, they headed out. Tess and baby brother were in their car seats in the rear, giggling at each other's antics. Bev had prepared well with lots of toys, drinks, snacks, disposable diapers and the like. Having the RV would enable them to stop whenever they needed to rest, cook a meal and stay overnight. They drove through Washington state, along the Oregon coast and then the coast of California. The weather was warm and sunny, the scenery spectacular and all were in good spirits. One evening when they were camped near Santa Barbara, baby Phil got to his feet and took his first steps, then plopped down on the rug. With both parents and his sister cheering him on, he got up and did it again. It was just after his first birthday. He giggled in delight at his own accomplishment. There was no stopping him after that.

Disneyland never failed to please and although the children were very young, their first visit was no exception. The sights and sounds made such an impression on their young minds. In later years, Tess still remembered the little dolls of 'It's a small world'.

A return to England 1978

They arrived at Heathrow and took a train directly to Robert and Jane where they were once again greeted with open arms. The couple made a fuss over the new baby and Tessa, of course. She didn't remember them and was shy to their attention. Jane had made them a lovely dinner and over Robert's homemade wine they caught up on all the family news. It was not long before Aunt Olivia rang the doorbell. She sat on the carpet and entertained the children until their bedtime. When Bev settled the children to bed in the small guest room which she and Ted would share as well, she realized that their stay would have to be as short as possible.

Within a week Ted was anxious to make the trip to the West Country and Sandford Orcas. He had rung up John at the Mitre Inn and was given a hearty welcome to come for a visit. Two days later, they travelled by train and were met at the Sherborne station by Julie. On the drive from Sherborne, Julie confessed to them that she and John were having marital difficulties, probably related to the fact that they never had a day off to get away together. They were always working and even when the pub was closed for a few hours a day, the time was taken up with other tasks; cleaning and getting more supplies.

"It will be lovely having you come for a while. Perhaps John and I can get away for an afternoon, if you can run the pub for us?" she tentatively asked, keeping her eyes on the road.

"It would suit us," said Ted. "Once the children are in bed, we could handle the pub for you for an evening." He glanced at her with concerned sympathy. Bev listened in silence in the back seat of the car, bracing herself for the ride down that narrow road to Sandford Orcas. She couldn't help but feel sorry for their situation. She would hold her opinions to herself until she had made her observations. She wondered if the couple were not just tired of each other. Working together in such close quarters for all those years could test even the strongest marriage.

"John will be so pleased to have your help, it will be like old times," Julie sighed. "Oh, how lovely it would be to get away."

John was pleased to see them and escorted them to the upstairs guest rooms, one for them and the adjacent room for the children.

The children were adored and entertained. Julie allowed Tess to help her gather eggs from the back chicken coop. Tess bravely faced the disgruntled hen and tucked her small hand beneath the warm breast, and with giggles of joy brought out a warm egg. Phil watched from his stroller and grabbed for a stray hen as she left the nest cackling in fury. This made him squeal in delight. The memory of these times would linger with Tess all her life.

The little village was unchanged and seemed suspended in time in the warm August sunshine. They took long walks with the children, passing by the manor house and churchyard. The manor house seemed to have an air of sobriety about it, probably because the owner was back in residence.

The little cottage they had stayed in two years previous was now housing some of the major's wife's relatives, for he had married his housekeeper. According to Julie, it had been the talk of the village for some time. Then only a short time later the old major died, leaving her all his estate.

As they passed by the little cottage, Bev could not help but think about how it had been foretold of their son's birth and their return. On the walk back they noticed an old wooden signpost pointing the way to Trent 1¼ miles. It was almost obscured by overhanging branches.

"Why is it that we have never been to Trent?" Bev remarked. Ted thought about it for a moment and then stated,

"I don't really know, dear. In all the time we have been here before and now this time, it never occurred to us to check it out. Now we are leaving soon and may not have the time. If not, it will have to remain a mystery until the next time." He pulled Bev close and hugged her. He was well aware of how much she loved this place and that she would be sad to leave. But he knew also that everything here would remain unchanged for centuries.

They had stayed for a week and gave John and Julie the much-needed afternoon and evening away. Ted quite enjoyed running the bar while Bev made meals for the patrons. They even served the squire of the manor house who came nightly for a meal. He had never married and spent much time away in London. Bev thought to herself, who wouldn't want to get away if one lived in that foreboding huge house all by oneself. She felt sorry for him and loaded his plate with extra food.

Nothing untoward happened on this visit and Ted felt happy that he had checked the place out once again. He did not want to live there though, not wanting to take the chance of strange happenings.

The day before they left the little village, they decided to walk the distance into Sherborne, savouring each step along the way. Ted pointed out to the children the small birds and animal life as they passed the hedgerows. Bev picked blackberries to taste and wild flowers for a nosegay. When they reached the ancient oak, they circled around to a place farthest from the roadway and sat down in its shade. They would remember this moment for all their life.

They arrived in Sherborne and checked into the Post House for one night, with plans to leave on the early train to London. Robert and Jane would be there to meet them.

***

Whilst they were away, Robert had been checking into accommodation for them and was pleased to announce his luck in finding a place.

"You may not like the area, but Jane and I have checked out the house and will take you to have a look at it tomorrow," he grinned. "It's in Leytonstone which is in the Greater London area. It's well known as the birthplace of Alfred Hitchcock, the late film director."

"Oh, how exciting," squealed Bev. "I can't wait to see it."

"Likewise," said Ted. He had been a TV fan of *'Hitchcock presents'*.

The following morning being a Sunday, they waited until Jane had her joint of beef in the oven to slow cook, and then left to view the house in Leytonstone. Apparently a key was to be left with the neighbour.

They were pleasantly surprised with the general attmosphere of the town on a Sunday morning. They drove down the High street and followed a road which led to a dead end at Bushwood Road and there found the huge early Victorian semi-detached house just around the corner. Much to their delight, it was directly opposite woods and parkland. The neighbor, a pleasant middle aged woman, gave them the key when they knocked at her door.

The house was a huge two-story red brick semi-detached. The stained glass fronted door opened onto a hallway with a staircase leading to the upper rooms, of which there were three bedrooms, a full bath and a sitting room overlooking the back garden.

Downstairs lay a front enclosed room and a large back dayroom with French doors which opened onto the back garden. A small dining room was off from the kitchen. A door lead from the kitchen which opened out to the garden. Much of the furniture had been left behind as it had been an estate sale bought up by the housing company. Each room had a fireplace either of gas or wood burning as there wasn't central heating. Ted and Bev looked at each other in agreement that the place would be perfect. The sooner they could move in, the better.

Leytonstone and After

Leytonstone is situated in the Greater East London area. The high road in ancient times was a Roman road leading from London to the Epping Forest of Essex County. The house was in a suburban area, across from woods, a small lake, golf course and a graveyard beyond. The little family soon settled into a comfortable way of life. They had explored the shopping district, the surrounding streets, school and church, but their most favourite spot of all was the wood in its quiet stillness, a refuge from the hustle bustle. Bev remembered her wonderful childhood forest haunts and to her it was a comfort. She wanted her children to appreciate the wonder of nature too.

On a day late in November, she was returning with the children having taken them to the little lake to feed the ducks. They loved this outing and laughed at the comical antics of their feathered friends, quacking and feeding with upturned bottoms. When they had set out from home it was a beautiful sunny afternoon.

A sudden wind sprung up. Dark ominous clouds formed and scudded across the sky. They were dark clouds to be sure but with them came the dark flapping blue-black wings of hundreds of crows, landing on every conceivable branch and scolding with raucous caw-cawing. Bev gripped the children's hands and moved more quickly for home. She grabbed up Philip who was not yet two and almost ran with Tess. She was truly frightened.

"They scare me, Mummy," whimpered Tess, clinging tightly to Bev's hand.

"It's OK sweetie, they are just birdies having a meeting." She tried to laugh, but thought to herself, no wonder they were collectively called a 'murder'. She wondered also if Alfred Hitchcock had experienced such a phenomenon, fuelling his imagination for his story *'The Birds'*. It felt foreboding, and as they neared home the first loud thunder rumbled overhead. A lash of wind and rain hit, just as she closed the front door.

Bev was determined to prevent the children from having bad memories of the time and set to making popcorn and hot chocolate as soon as they were in. She started a fire in the dining room fireplace and sat with a child on each side and read to them from Dr.Suess', 'The Cat in the Hat' which was a favourite.

***

Christmas came and went and during the period in January that Bev often referred to as the 'post-Christmas blahhs' Ted became despondent and moody. She felt he should see a doctor for which he was reluctant but finally he agreed. He was prescribed tranquilizers which were a big mistake for Ted's psyche.

One night she awakened to find him not in bed beside her and hearing a commotion downstairs, she crept from her warm bed. She checked in on the children who were sleeping soundly and then hurried down the staircase to the kitchen only to find Ted wielding a poker at some unseen assailant and then slamming the door from the kitchen to the outside. He clearly had a look of horror on his face and was yelling...

"It's outside now; I think I killed it. Oh, my God."

She approached him warily, took the poker from his hand and led him to a chair in the dining room.

"It's OK, it's OK," she soothed. "Whatever you saw, it was not real, not real, Ted." As she soothed, he slowly became less fearful and then wanted to explain what he had seen.

"I came downstairs to get a drink of milk, and as I passed the lounge at the end of the hallway, I could see someone there. I looked in and saw, lounging on the sofa, a naked woman with a most lascivious and sinister smile beckoning to me. I could tell that she was not of this world, because her feet were on backwards.

Then as I entered the kitchen there was this thing ... It looked like a man, but had the head of a fox. It frightened me so; I grabbed up the poker and hit it."

"Well, whatever you saw, and I do believe you, dear, it's not here now. Come we will look outside and in the lounge." She led him to both places and of course there was nothing to be seen.

"Come now; let's be off to bed, there is nothing to fear." She led him up the stairs and settled him back to bed. In the darkness as she hugged him tightly he fell back to sleep. But she lay awake for what seemed like hours, and realized that he had to come off those pills; they were causing the hallucinations, or were they real?

Ted did in fact stop the pills, but things were not much better. Tess was having night terrors, or 'wobblers' as Ted put it. She would be heard screaming in the night, and Bev would run to her to pick her up and cuddle her. She would appear to be awake, but would continue to scream, often staring over Bev's shoulder at something to them unseen. Ted would get a cool facecloth to help wake her out of her terror, it always worked,

"It's what my mother did to me when I had them as a kid," Ted confessed.

***

They had noticed a crack in the marble of the front sitting room fireplace when they had first moved in, but it appeared to have widened. Then one evening as they were sitting, a large chunk just fell off. How odd. They had done nothing to cause it. Bev got up from her chair and walked over to where the piece of marble lay. Then she peered inside the opening it had left. There, a crumpled piece of paper lay within her reach. She pulled out the soot-covered paper and slowly opened it up.

"I can't believe this!" she gasped. "It appears to be a kind of poem or riddle, Ted." She walked over to him and they read it together.

'Ten gold bells and coins are hidden. Find them now, you are bidden. Beneath the stars, but halfway to Albert.' They read it over several times trying to make sense of it. Then Ted got a torch and had a closer look in the hole. There was nothing there.

The incident had left them searching the house from top to bottom for weeks, to no avail. In the end, they gave it up as just another mystery. Who knew who had lived in the house before them, perhaps the place was haunted. The graveyard was only a short distance beyond the woods... maybe Albert had been buried there, and the treasure had been hidden in the woods. People hid all manner of things in earlier times, having little faith in the banks.

Then they moved all furnishings from the room to the back lounge and shut the door, there was no question of them trying to repair the damage. How could they explain that to the housing company?

And that was not the end of weird happenings. Ted was at the stove cooking breakfast, the bacon and eggs sizzling in the frying pan. Bev had her back to him, at the kitchen sink. She heard him say a loud, "Ouch!"

"My God, look at that, will you!" He held up his right arm where droplets of blood welled up in scratch marks on his forearm. They were long and appeared to be like a cat's claw marks. She could not believe her eyes, and reached for the first aid kit she kept handy for the children.

"No one would believe it would they?" He remarked as she cleaned the area. "I've just about had enough of all this Bev. This place is really getting to me."

Then that evening, as they sat with a glass of wine after the children were in bed, Ted looked across at her with the most sinister grin and stated in a voice that was neither his, nor Philip's ...

"I win, you lose!"

She did not reply but got up and left the room. When she returned a few minutes later, Ted was himself again. Bev felt really frightened and realized that something very evil had taken possession of her husband, over which he seemed to have no control. He lacked the power to prevent the slipping through that open window of his soul, the unwanted spirits with sinister motives. She truly felt that the only thing that might be able to help him would be a visit to a man of the cloth. Exorcism might be the only answer. She felt that Philip had let them down. Ted had to be stronger and claim his own space.

That night as they lay in bed, and after Ted seemed to be asleep, Bev felt his hand grab her neck. When she pushed his hand away, with a cruel laugh he grabbed at her crotch. She knew this was not Ted acting out like this. She was truly frightened and got up and crawled in bed with Tess. She would not sleep another night with him until something was done about it.

The final straw was when she was descending the stairs the next morning and as she neared the bottom, she felt a distinct shove at her back and she fell down the final few steps. She landed hard at the bottom and hit the back of her head on the wall. Laying there in a state of shock, she looked up to see Ted running down the stairs towards her, the children behind him, their eyes wide and fearful.

"Are you OK, love?" he called.

"Yes, of course I am, just tripped; I'm OK, just a bit shook up."

She got up, rubbing her head and smiled through her pain for the children's sake. Then as any wife and mother was likely to do, she carried on as usual but following breakfast she took Ted aside.

"Dear, I really think it would do you good to get away for the day. Go into London; maybe meet up with Robert on his lunch break." She was convinced that Ted was the catalyst for all the paranormal activity over the past while.

"You wouldn't mind me leaving you for the day? I'd really enjoy that."

"Yes, of course I'm sure, I'll take the kids out shopping and to the library, they'd like that." So it was agreed that he would have the day away.

***

The synchronicity of events that took place that day was amazingly fortunate. On the train to London, Ted sat opposite a man of the cloth. This he could tell by the cleric's collar and black attire he wore. As Ted was often to do he struck up a conversation and before he knew what he was saying he blurted out...

"Is it in your power to do exorcism?"

The man was truly taken by surprise by this, but gently folded the paper he was reading, looked over the top of his reading glasses at Ted and replied in a kindly manner.

"Are you in need of help, my friend?"

"Well. ...I will let you be the judge of that if you have time to chat?" Ted hoped. "Indeed I do, I'll be stopping for a bite of lunch when we arrive in London, and maybe you would join me?" he smiled. "That would be great, sir, that would be really great." Ted was well pleased.

***

No, he did not disclose to Bev what was said between them. He told her only that he had met a kindly Reverend of the Methodist church on the train and that they had lunch together. But Bev could tell by his whole demeanour that something wonderful had taken place.

He made the trip into London just about every week for a month and seemed so much better. In that time nothing untoward had happened again. It did not stop Bev from looking into the possibility of a move though. She felt that the house itself was haunted.

When they were given the option of a move, they made plans to pack up their belongings and get away for two weeks. It had turned from spring to a warm early summer so in June they took a holiday to Wales.

They found a lovely guest house in Swansea and visited all the tourist haunts and sampled the local food. They were a bit sceptical when the lady of the house served them a traditional oily green sauce made from seaweed called laver. It was said to be very rich in minerals and iodine. The locals ate it with everything including the bacon and eggs for breakfast. It did not appeal to them but one could get used to most things they thought.

Tess had her fifth birthday while they were away and it was celebrated at the beach. They walked far out on the hard sand and ran laughing as the tide came in and they were forced to run to make it back to the shore. Then at teatime, a cake and gifts were produced much to her delight.

The next morning both children came down with chickenpox causing them to stay a few extra days. But when they returned their new abode was ready to move in.

***

The Slade Green property was a three-bedroom maisonette with the luxury of forced air central heating. It was modern and seemed clear of any residual atmosphere, Bev felt that it would do nicely for the time being, but she was already feeling the urge to return home. They had been away almost three years. Tess started school and was soon reading silently and well above average for her age group. Philip was happy and absorbed in his little world of toys and tricycle and parental love. Ted decided that he'd like to take up writing for a hobby and purchased a state of the art portable typewriter, one he could take anywhere he wished.

"I've always wanted to write a book, this could be a good outlet for trying to understand everything that has gone on, don't you think?"

"Whatever you wish my love, you have my full support," said Bev.

So Ted did take up writing, dabbling at first until he got the feel of the typewriter and then he was turning out quite a few humorous short stories. He continued his visits to the city and met with his Reverend friend for lunches. It had done him good, she felt. At least things were quiet on the spirit side, he seemed at peace, perhaps he had just learned to live with his difference and he knew he had her acceptance. But she had plans of her own. It had been before Tess was born that she had stopped nursing. If she waited much longer all she had learned would be outdated in the fast-moving world of medical advancement. She had given the children 100% of her time and she felt that if she returned to work full time that Ted could stay at home and care for them, and write. They could work things out some way. So when she saw an ad in a London newspaper for an American company recruiting nurses to work in California, she answered it immediately. On the day that she had an appointment in the city, they took it as a family day out and while Bev went for her interview, Ted and the children walked to the zoo.

She greeted them with a big grin, for she had been told that she was just what the recruiters were looking for. She also had the advantage of being trained in North America. It would take months to get her nursing licence in order but all going as planned they could be living in California in the autumn.

Although it would only be for a year, it would be well worth it and then they could return to England if they wished to. What an exciting turn of events.

***

They spent a very pleasant summer while waiting. There were days spent on picnics, walks in parks, beach days and it all culminated into one huge celebration for the wedding of Diana and Charles. Their wedding day fell on Philip's fourth birthday so it was an added celebration. After watching the wedding on TV with Robert, Jane and Aunt Olivia, and feasting at a table laden with food, they all went to the local park where hot air balloon rides were being given. Aunt Olivia threw aside her usual reserved manner and hoisted her skirts displaying one pale skinny leg after the other to climb up into the basket, taking the children with her. Their little faces could be seen only just above the rim of the basket and with cries of glee, they rose a few feet off the ground, the basket having been secured with a rope to prevent it rising farther. That day was the highlight of the summer.

California Dreaming

The dream of California finally became reality in September 1981. The little family spent a few final days with Robert and Jane ending a glorious summer with an outing to a farm where they picked the fruits of the harvest; beans, corn and late strawberries. The children helped Auntie Jane prepare beans for the freezer, and ate their fill of strawberries. They would always remember that joyful time.

All arrangements had been made well in advance with the hospital that Bev would be employed with. Air fares were paid and they would be met at the Los Angeles airport and whisked away to a lovely two-bedroom garden apartment in the suburbs. The flight had been good and when they arrived at the airport displaying a huge American flag, they knew they had truly arrived.

It was a culture shock, having come from England to this spacious sprawl, of never-ending blue skies, warm sunny days, and a new reality. Bev had to pinch herself to believe it. She hoped it would not be too daunting to be back in the workforce of her profession. It would be a reversal of roles for them. She was excited. Ted was delighted. The children were in awe.

She had only two days to get over jet lag and then she was in full time education to become accustomed to the practice of nursing. Luckily, she was working day shift Monday to Friday with every weekend off. It was a nurse's dream come true. While she was away at work, Ted took the children everywhere. They enjoyed the great shopping malls, the parks, the beach, and zoo. But their most favourite place to visit was Disneyland. This outing was reserved for a family day when Bev was off work.

Life for them was totally changed. She had been in contact with her father in Canada and had made plans to visit him in November during the Thanksgiving weekend. He was delighted that they were back in North America. He wrote her a letter which she treasured for many years. In it he paid her the best compliment she could have ever expected from her father; 'Bev, you sure got guts!' Yes, she had to agree.

Then only a week before they were planning on seeing him, a phone call came from her sister giving the bad news of his sudden death. Bev was devastated. She just could not believe that this had happened. They made plans at once to travel up to Canada so she could attend his funeral.

They were met by Ted's parents in Bellingham and it was decided that his father would stay and visit with Ted and children whilst she and Inez would attend the funeral.

She met family and friends at the packed church on that cold November day. It was like walking through a dream it seemed so surreal. As she bent to place a kiss on her father's coffin, she remembered the prediction that she would never see him again. Another prediction had been fulfilled.

It was a long journey back to California and during this time Bev grieved the loss of her father. Looking out of the car window, she saw fields and trees through silent tears and Ted squeezed her hand in sympathy. She didn't want the children to be upset by her upset. They were too little to understand and had no memory of him.

Then it was back to work and life had to regain normality. With her mind totally on her work, it was probably the best way of coping with her loss. The warm sunny weather continued and each day they woke up to clear blue skies. Every weekend they were off exploring and enjoying all the many beeches; Playa Del Reye, Malibu, and Santa Monica. What better diversion from the blues. They were all tanned and healthy and Christmas was looming. Ted's parents planned a visit at this time; it was something to look forward to.

***

Christmas Eve found them all in Disneyland. It was hard to believe that they were in shirt sleeves on a winter day. The children were in the heights of glory, going on all the rides with their grandparents who were like big kids themselves. It was truly a day to remember. Ted's father said he had never had so much fun in his life.

On Christmas day they gathered around a traditional turkey dinner with the patio doors open to a warm sunny day. Earlier in the day they had opened gifts by the artificial Christmas tree. To Bev who had gone out with her sisters to cut a tree from their own property, it did not seem much like Christmas. She was remembering her parents especially her father at this time of year. But her little son who was already developing his own personality, never failed to make the moment precious.

"Just look what Santa has brought me, and I've been naughty all week," he blurted out, his eyes bright with excitement. There followed gales of laughter from all. In the years ahead, he would bring much joy and laughter to the little family. He had Ted's sense of humour.

Boxing Day, the in-laws flew home and they were again back to normal. They found it hard to believe that in America it was back to business as usual, when in England the whole country seemed on a holiday for weeks.

Bev was due back at work so they were all up early the next morning. It was their routine that Ted would drive her, drop her off at the hospital and return with the children to begin their day. It worked well for a time.

***

They had been concerned that Tess had reached an age where she should be in school. She had already gone to school in England, so was well ahead of her level of learning. The system in Los Angeles was to bus the children to a school that may not be close to where they lived. Ted and Bev did not want this for their child. So after much deliberation they decided to move to a place in Northern California where Bev could step into a job immediately and a small Christian school was there for the children.

The small town of Alturas sits in the upper most north east corner of California, bordering on the state of Oregon and Nevada. Just over the mountain pass sits a very small town of Cedarville in a valley. Early settlers had come upon it after traversing the Sierra Nevada desert and named it Surprise Valley, the name obvious.

Each town had a small hospital which was owned by the Catholic Church. Bev was given the option of either place and they chose to live in Cedarville. The town at that time had a population of only 800 souls, about forty of which belonged to the small Baptist church of which the school was a part. The main street was flanked by buildings with false fronts like an old western scene.

They found a place to rent immediately and Bev started work at the hospital. It was a cottage hospital in every sense of the word. The bed count when full was no more than a dozen. It had a small emergency room and X-ray, and patients were assessed accordingly and if needed were air lifted to Reno.

She was a bit nervous at first working the night shift, for there would be only one nurse and a helper on duty. If someone came through the door pushing in full labour of childbirth or injured from a gunshot wound, she would have to call in the doctor and another nurse to assist. It was rather daunting, but like anything else one soon got used to it.

It was also a concern to be leaving her little family on their own at night, but Ted was quite capable and their house was only a stone throw away. Bev quite enjoyed seeing the sunrise over the far distant Sierra Nevada Mountains, turning the sky from dark to a blaze of crimson and orange hues. It was so peaceful walking home at dawn with the owls still calling in the cotton woods.

She would arrive home to a family still warm and cosy in their beds. Ted had brought his portable typewriter with him from England and there was evidence that he had been at work. She glanced at the page still in the typewriter and what she read showed promise that he was able to write well. There was scope for writing about some of the people in the community.

The citizens of the town were very interesting people indeed. Ted said it was like stepping back in time to the old West. It was as if some had just stepped out of an old Western movie he had seen as a child. The cowboys dressed the part and roped and rode the cattle to pasture in the spring and went on roundups in the autumn. There was always a hub of activity at the general store and post office. One soon learned that most people were related so being mindful of what one said was of upmost importance. The locals said that the town was so small and that news travelled so quickly that if you wanted to know how you were, you only needed to visit the post office for an update. So news of the little family and a new nurse at the hospital spread with amazing speed. People were friendly and they soon got to know a group within Bev's work place and the little Baptist church.

The Pastor and his wife and parents were very helpful. Soon the children were enrolled in the little Christian school, run by them. Ted was invited to help supervise and this worked very well while Bev was working. He seemed quite happy and the spirit side of his psyche seemed at peace. Perhaps it was the influence of the church. They settled into an easy lifestyle, venturing further afield on Bev's days off. They took long drives out on to the dessert, ever mindful of rattle snakes when out of the car. They did not see any but were aware that they were ever present, and had been warned. Bev had never before worked in a hospital that stocked anti-snake venom serum. Even around the house and yard one had to be careful as in the hot weather the snakes would come down closer to water. There was a creek at the edge of the property so the children were not allowed to go near it.

A co-worker gave Bev a half dozen hens and a rooster as they had an out building on the property. It was a memorable experience, one that the children would always remember. Bev's parents had chickens when she was growing up so she could recall how they were to be cared for, and once they settled and began laying eggs, it was a bonus.

Summer came and went and with it came the realization that it would soon be a year since leaving England and that they would have to return. It was when Tess took ill with bronchitis and had breathing difficulties, that Bev realized their mentor, Philip, was still around. It would seem from then on that he was always near when there was a family crisis of any sort.

Tess had been diagnosed at quite a young age as having asthma tendencies, but seemed to have gotten over it. But it had reoccurred at this time. Her breathing became very difficult and it warranted a visit to the emergency room where she was given an injection of adrenalin with immediate relief. Still, they were concerned for her health.

"Be certain that you get her to a doctor soon after you return to England, or one of these times when she takes ill, her lungs will just collapse," he said very emphatically through Ted. Bev was surprised to say the least for there had been no contact since before they had left England. But she would remember what had been said. It was comforting to know that they were being watched over. She had her faith in God and that would never waver, but to have a spiritual guide and comforter was a blessing to be sure.

***

At the first of November, Bev gave her notice at the hospital. Co-workers and friends they had made were sad to hear news of their departure, but it had to be.

Mid-November they travelled up to Canada to see Ted's folks who tried to talk them into staying. But England was where they wanted to be. Truth be told, they really missed the English way of life. It would be good to get back.

During their absence, England had been at war with Argentina in the Falkland Islands. They had followed the proceedings with much interest, glued to the TV most evenings. Now it was over and England had been victorious. It was good timing to return.

On the American Thanksgiving weekend their flight left Los Angeles for London.

London Borough of Lewisham (Catford)

The huge semi-detached two-story Victorian house was built in 1906 and was typical of those of that era. It would be home to them for almost four years. Behind a wrought iron gate, a tiled path led through the hankie-sized yard and to the entrance. Upon entering the front door, a wide hallway stretched through to the back portion of the house. To the right lay a large front room with a bay window and a view of the street. As one proceeded down the hallway, another smaller sitting room was also on the right. Proceeding further, a door opened into a small kitchen and further still to a bathroom. It appeared that the latter room had been added at a much later date. Houses of that period usually had an outdoor toilet. But that had been given way to the modern plumbing. A door from the hallway opened out into a large, narrow and fenced back garden with a garage. Beyond the garage the garden continued to the property line.

Stairs led up to a landing off of which were three bedrooms and a small closet-size bathroom. It was perfect for their needs they thought, but it was badly in need of redecorating. They would paint, wallpaper and carpet throughout and make it as comfortable as possible.

The street outside bustled with traffic but when they entered the house and closed the front door, it was a quiet sanctuary, the energy of the place benign.

The back garden, enclosed with a gate that locked from the inside, was by far the best feature, for here the children could play quite safely for hours. Ted could putter on his car projects to his heart's content within the garage. At the very rear of the garden grew a huge cherry tree. There was also a plum, pear tree and a lilac bush. The children climbed and swung from the branches, preferring this to playing with toys. Tess delighted in climbing to a curved branch of the pear tree and picking pears for her little brother to catch. Bev realized that this was what she loved to do as a child and although she knew there would be occasional falls and scrapes, she was loath to stop them. She had Ted make them a swing from a branch of the old cherry tree and for her, a clothesline so she could hang washing out in the fresh air to dry.

They soon struck up a rapport with the neighbours on both sides of the fence and welcomed a hello or a chat. The children also made friends.

Within a comfortable walking distance from the home was a large public park that lay atop a hill. From this vantage point one could see as far away as the city of London with the dome of St. Paul's cathedral in the distance. The children loved this wide open space and would run and play happily under their parents' watchful eyes.

It was on one of these outings that Tessa's breathing difficulties became more evident. She became so breathless that Bev had to carry her home.

That night, what started out as a chest cold, turned into asthmatic bronchitis and in the small hours of the morning they had to call an ambulance to get her to the casualty unit. She was immediately seen by the doctor on duty who assessed her condition and admitted her to a ward.

Bev sat at her bedside listening to every laboured breath. As she held her little hand she noticed that the nail beds were bluish and at seeing this she ran to the nurse's station calling out for help. The medical team within moments had initiated more aggressive treatment to which the child responded almost immediately. Nonetheless, Bev was shaking with fright. She had been forewarned this could happen. The prediction that the child's lungs could collapse had been too close for comfort.

Ted and Philip came to the hospital later that morning, eyes wide with concern. "How is she?" Ted whispered.

"She's over the worst of it now, Ted but I have to stay with her until I know she'll be alright." He hugged her close, thankful once again that his wife was a nurse.

Several days passed and Tess improved. She was peacefully asleep one night when a nurse came to the bedside insisting that she must wake her for a new inhaler medication. Bev bristled at this knowing that if awoken, Tess would surely have one of her 'wobblers'. But the young nurse was adamant.

Sure enough, Tess woke up screaming with the mother of all 'wobblers', waking every child in the ward.

"Am I dead, Mummy?" she wailed, clutching at Bev's neck as she held her close. "It's okay, it's okay," Bev soothed and gave the nurse her most defiant glare.

It took ages to calm her down again and in the end the nurse left, unable to carry out her mission. The act of using an inhaler was a process that needed careful instruction when one was totally alert, especially for a child. Bev did not waste time in complaining to the Matron about what had happened, and she agreed. The nurse was reprimanded and thereafter gave Bev a respectfully wide space, speaking only when she had to.

Tess was home after a week, and with the medications she was given, she could breathe normally and was soon happy again.

***

Robert, Jane and Aunt Olivia were still very much a part of their lives. Visits back and forth between them continued. Jane went out of her way for the children, always preparing their favourite goodies at tea time and little treats they did not get at home. Robert took them on countryside rambles and football games. Aunt Olivia continued to entertain and help them out with school work.

They had waited several months to enrol the children in school, wanting them to be used to the change from one country to another before they were back in the school scene. It had been so different in the Christian school with almost one on one teaching. Here, they would be with hundreds of noisy robust children, in a totally different system of education, including school dinners.

Tess adapted well, as she always did in new situations, but young Philip hated school. Bev would be near tears as she left him inside the school gate. Tess held his hand until he entered the building. Either she or Ted would walk them to school. They would be waiting when school was out for the day. It was usually a noisy time with all the other parents dropping off or picking up their kids. The ice cream van would always park near the school gates and often a treat was purchased to soothe over the cares of their day.

***

One morning, Bev left Ted to get on with some wallpapering. She had walked the children to school and then went shopping on the High Street. She preferred grocery shopping by herself so that she could keep to her list without the children wanting this and that.

She returned home an hour or so later. Doing a balancing act with shopping bags at the front door, she rummaged for her key. Then with key in hand, she noticed that a wire by the front door appeared cut and dangled there. It had probably been wiring for a doorbell or telephone at one time, but was no longer in use. She opened the door to silence. She had a profound feeling that something was terribly wrong. She stepped inside holding her breath.

A loan moaning sound from the small sitting room prompted her to open the door. To her horror, Ted lay naked and prostrate on the floor, a gag in his mouth. His trousers were crumpled at his ankles and both his wrists tied with wire to the legs of the sideboard. His blue eyes were wide with pleading and distress.

In a split second, Bev had the gag from his mouth and before he could say a thing she ran to the kitchen to get the scissors and a large shot of sherry. Then, sobbing, she was at his side. She cut the wires releasing his hands and feet, then helped him to a sip of the amber liquid. He spluttered and gagged and moaned some more. Bev was near to tears.

"Who has done this to you, Ted? I'm calling the police!" she yelled.

"No, no, nooo..." he moaned. "They said they would be back if the police were called in and I believe them," he pleaded with her.

Bev, with her lips set in a tight line, helped him to get up and sit in a chair. "Tell me what has happened here," she demanded of him, taking a sip of his drink.

"There was a knock at the door and when I answered it, before I could say anything, a black fellow pointed a gun at my head, forced me into the hallway and then into this room. There were three others with him, all young women. One was a black girl, the others were white. They did to me what you saw and also the unthinkable. I'm so sorry Bev; I have never seen any of them before." He was in tears now and she cried along with him, rocking him in her arms. As she held him close, the voice of his mentor came through him.

"Do not call the police. It was a case of mistaken identity. It will not happen again. I will see that the trauma of this act will be erased from his memory and you must never mention it to him again. Get him into a hot bath and then to bed where he can sleep. I promise you he will not remember."

Bev went with her trust in his wisdom and got Ted another large drink and ran a hot bath. She helped him into the tub, bathed and dried him, got him into his robe and guided him up the stairs to bed. She sat at his side while he drank and wept. She got him a bowl of soup and wedges of buttered toast, and sat with him while he ate it. When she was satisfied that he would sleep, she tucked him in and sat there until he had drifted off. Only when he was asleep and snoring did she leave his side.

She went into the kitchen and got out all the cleaning supplies. She entered the cruel scene and began to clean with a vengeance. She vacuumed the carpet, wiped down all surfaces with disinfectant and threw open the window to the fresh air. She noticed that her leather-bound bible on a side table was lying open. On closer inspection, it became apparent that what had happened there that day was evil. Bold obscene words were written in black pen through several of the pages of her precious book. She wept anew as she tore out the desecrated pages and set them to light in the fire.

Ted still slept soundly and Bev realized it was already time to collect the children from school. She quickly prepared a casserole and put it in the oven for their supper.

As she closed the door behind her, she couldn't help but feel fearful. After all, their privacy had been invaded, her husband traumatized and she felt absolutely shattered. She had to put her trust in what had been said to her. All these things raced through her head as she walked to the school to meet the children. They were sweet faced and smiling at seeing her and ran skipping towards her for a hug. Their cheerful chatter soon had her back in the here and now and in mothering mode.

"Daddy's not feeling well so he's having a sleep. You can see him in the morning," she explained as they sat to table for supper.

Next morning when Ted awoke, there was no mention of yesterday's incident; it was as though it had never happened. It was never ever spoken of again. But it did not stop Bev from wondering if it had been an act of karma. This explanation alone gave her the ability to never speak of it again throughout their life together.

**

They both found jobs at a local nursing home, Bev as Matron and Ted did maintenance work. It was directly opposite the children's school so it worked out very well to drop them off and meet them again after school.

They enjoyed their jobs and the good income enabled them to take weekend trips to places of interest; Colchester, Ipswich, Clacton on Sea and Frinton.

A day trip to Brighton stood out in young Phil's mind for most of his life. They were rambling along one of the busy side streets when he spotted a gift shop that caught his rapt attention. There were many interesting figurines in the display window fashioned from crystal; a clown, a giraffe, a fish. The lights above the display case set them to sparkle like so many jewels. A handful of small cut-glass stones made to look like diamonds were sprinkled around the base of each figurine. "Can we go in and have a look, Mummy?" he asked politely.

"Alright, we can, but don't touch a thing," she warned.

Ted held Tess by the hand as they walked through. Phil was

captured by the allure of sparkle as he stood with his hands clasped behind his back gazing into the display case.

The young lady at the till took note of his rapt expression and approached quietly. She took his hand and placed in his palm, a collection of the sparkling stones. He looked up at her with awe... "Oh, thank you so much!"

He shared them with Tess, of course. He shared everything with her, but he treasured those stones as though they were real diamonds.

That night he had a vivid dream... He was in the kitchen of a large stone house. For some reason the old cooker was being moved ... and then he reached down to find a little bag laying there. He opened it and shook out a handful of sparkling diamonds.

***

On a visit to Cornwall, they found Molesworth Manor, a former 17th century rectory in a little village near Padstow. The place was rather derelict at the time and was up for sale. It would make a good nursing home they thought. But when they discovered that it lacked central heating and the roof leaked in places it would be a very costly project, certainly not in their budget. Nonetheless, they had a good wander through the place and were even invited to stay the night. But because of the ancient bedrooms with four poster beds, damp curtains and the pervasive smell of old, they gratefully declined. Bev was certain the place was haunted.

It was after they had left that young Philip confessed that he had taken stairs to the top room. He was there without their knowledge. The room was empty save for bundles of old magazines. On the far wall he saw a door and opened it.

There was nothing there but empty space. He could see the courtyard below and the car parked there. Had he taken a step, he would have fallen. When he was back outside he looked up to see if he could spot the door, there was only a window.

"See, Mummy, I found this on the floor beside the door." He held it in his hand, it was a small pearl-handled jack knife that looked old and worn.

"You should not have taken it, dear, but it's too far to go back there now. I'll take it for safekeeping for now," she admonished.

What could be said of it? Had he really had the experience? As far as Bev was concerned, he had not been out of her sight. It was entirely possible that he also had the ability to see things that others did not. Had not Tess also since her hospital stay, talked to an imaginary friend she called Ceecee? The hairs on Bev's neck stood up at the thought that her children might follow in the footsteps of their father. Well, as long as no harm came to them, what more could she ask?

***

He raced in from the back garden all out of breath.

"Mummy, come, Mummy. There is an old black lady sitting at the back of the garden, and she looks so sad. Hurry, Mummy!"

Bev took his hand and followed him out of doors but when they reached the back of the garden there was no such person.

"She was just there, Mummy, sitting on a bench. She had very white hair. Where did she go?"

"Well there is no one here now, dear. I believe that you saw what you saw but I do not see her." Bev realized that he had seen a ghost, for there was no one by that description living near and no way could an old woman climb over the fence to the enclosed back garden. Tess was quietly playing with dolls in the sitting room so she would not be able to back up his story.

"Don't worry, love, if you see her again, just smile, she will not harm you. Okay?" He nodded his head and hugged her waist.

"Think I'll go and play with Tess now, Mummy."

***

There is nothing quite as magical as an English wood in autumn. On this particular day they had the woods to themselves. All was very peaceful and quiet save for the occasional cooing of the wood pigeons and the scolding of grey squirrels in the upper branches. The huge ancient trees, grey and bare were well spaced, many with large limbs reached to ground level making an ideal place for the children to climb. The ground was a carpet of fallen leaves; russet, brown and gold. A damp almost musty smell welled up around them as they tramped through. The children picked up handfuls of leaves and threw them about in a euphoric state of glee. They wandered, talked and laughed for what seemed like hours until the sun dipped low in the sky casting shadows as evening was drawing in. As they wandered back to the parked car, Tess lagged behind. A faraway look was in her eyes as she finally scrambled into the back seat. Ted turned around and knew in an instant what had happened to her.

"There was a man and big grey dogs behind that old tree, and he was laughing and waving at me," she exclaimed. None had seen what she had seen.

It was in later years when she was much older and well read that she realized that she *had* seen a ghost. The manner in which the man was dressed; puffed pantaloons, long hose, short jerkin and peaked hat with feather, put him in a time period of perhaps the 15th century. The dogs were the large grey wolfhounds usually owned by noble families. Who was he? Why did he appear to her? It would remain a mystery.

***

To presume that the little family had not been happy here would be wrong, for they had indeed spent many happy hours, living life at a leisurely pace. The children learned so much with all the many outings to historic places. There were few children in the world who could boast to having stood on the meridian line at Greenwich and fewer still that had parental attention 100% of the time. But change is good at times and Bev again felt the stirrings of a need to return to her homeland. Her home province of B.C. was hosting Expo 1986 and with all the exciting coverage of it in the media they felt a longing to be a part of it.

One evening as she and Ted were relaxing with a drink discussing the possibilities of going back and what it would entail, his mentor came yet again.

"It is well that you are thinking the way you are thinking, for his father is not a well man and he prays that his son will be near in his final years. I see your plans coming to fruition, take care my dear. I must also warn you that if you do not heed my advice to be very loving to your husband, he will stray one day for a woman named Jacquie." Having said that, he was gone. Bev was in a state of shock and was given no time to reply. But she pondered it in the days ahead

***

It is after all the boredom, the sameness, the tedium, the disillusion of everyday life that prompts one of courage to move forward and out of the ordinary that drags one down. To walk away with bravado from all that is familiar; to move towards the unknown, to start again in new surroundings, a different country with children in tow takes faith and guts.

Bev looked around her little kitchen. Her eyes settled on the old gas cooker over which she had prepared so many meals. She took down the teapot from the warming grill, poured boiling water in it, sloshed it around and added two spoonfuls of loose tea leaves, poured the boiling water over the leaves and waited the three minutes before taking the strainer and filling the awaiting mugs. She mindlessly sugared and creamed the brew as she recalled how she had missed this English of rituals when they were in California, and how delighted they were to receive tea sent at Christmas by Jane and Robert. It was of course the little things that one missed and longed for.

"Cup of tea, dear?" She handed the mug to Ted who sat browsing over the Sunday newspaper.

"Here is yet another ad for Expo 86', Bev. Doesn't it make you feel homesick?"

She leaned over his shoulder staring at the colourful ad showing the Vancouver skyline with snow-capped mountains in the distance. A lump started in her throat and her eyes welled with tears. She brushed them away before he could notice.

"Yes, I guess I do miss my homeland, dear, and it takes a scene like that to make me realize just how much. I would dearly love the children to experience a world fair, maybe we can talk about it?"

***

They enjoyed a final spring there with excursions to places they had not seen, and many that they wished to see again. They enjoyed picnics and fetes, days at the beach and visits with Robert, Jane and Aunt Olivia. But by the end of May they were on a flight to Vancouver.

Home Again

Everything had changed since they had left eight years previous. Her father was no longer alive and her family was estranged. To the children it was a culture shock, for they had left the country as babies and had no memory of this place. But they were determined to make it work.

Unlike England, there was an amazing choice of places to rent, and they found one close to a school, a hospital and the grandparents. They were swept up in a flurry of activity: shopping for furniture, home wares and a car. Bev had a knack for making any dwelling place cosy and comfortable; a few plants here, pictures hung there and there and books always made it seem like home. Soon the smell of home-baked cookies spiced the air and gave a homey atmosphere. Everyone was happy and Ted had not had any psychic disturbance for quite some time.

"Maybe it's all behind me now that we are away from the source," he mused while lounging with his feet up one evening.

"Don't be so sure," replied Bev. "Perhaps you have been given a reprieve; a time to gather in your thoughts and really analyse what is expected of you."

"You may be right, Bev. I believe he knows how important the children's welfare is at this time of their lives and how they need my full attention."

The children had the entire summer ahead of them before they needed to enrol in school; it gave them a bit of time to assimilate. Ted's parents were seniors, long retired and made it clear that they did not want their routine disturbed by grandchildren dropping in without prior arrangement and would not be willing to babysit at any cost.

Bev was back in the work force almost immediately, there was always a demand for nurses. She worked evening shifts on a very busy surgical ward but was home every morning and night. She had long ago learned not to bring anything about the work place home and no matter how upset she might feel about happenings at work, it was always put behind her as she walked in the door, stepping into the role of mother and wife. She was able to be with the children, to take them out shopping, to the beach and parks and still have time for her housework. She enjoyed the freedom of driving again, as she had never felt comfortable behind the wheel in England. Ted's job was in car sales, so he was in his element once again. He was very much a people person and loved the banter of making a deal and sending away a happy customer. He worked the day shift, so this worked out well; the kids were never left on their own. They had never relied on babysitters; their children came first and had all the attention they needed. Some might say they were spoiled with affection.

The children had left England with very distinctive English accents and just as Ted had been singled out for being different, they too experienced ridicule. But unlike Ted, they both set out to change the way they spoke.

"It's water, Tess, not woota," said young Phil.

"Bonjour, ma mere, we're learning French, too," said Tess. Bev had to really think about the correct reply. She would have to brush up on her French vocabulary to be of any help to them. They were advanced for their years in English language and history, but hadn't any knowledge of French.

***

They attended Expo for one day only and never returned. After all the hype about it they had to admit disappointment, it just did not live up to their expectations. They had missed the best part, the opening ceremony with Prince Charles and Princess Diana. For the children who had been to Disneyland several times, it was a letdown. But it was the one thing that had prompted their return, so for that it was memorable.

Ted's parents did not bother to go to the fair, as his father was becoming increasingly feebler. They were, however, interested in hearing all about it over dinner. Nana was at least, but Grandpa kept interrupting the conversation with a tirade about his life in India and World War Two, until the children became so fidgety they were excused from the table.

He also brought up the fact that Ted's ex-wife and all her family had moved to the west coast as well as others of Ted's acquaintance from his past. It was difficult for Ted to accept the fact that people from his past were following him once again, no wonder he felt happier in England. They weren't able to follow him there. He knew he shouldn't let it bother him, but it rankled.

His mother still liked to get Ted aside and talk about his ex, with whom she still kept up an acquaintance, probably comparing her to me, thought Bev. She also felt piqued at some of the comments from her mother -in-law about how they were raising their children.

"You give them too many choices, dear. Just put it in front of them and make them eat it. That's what I did." Bev felt it was pointless to argue with her, so would say nothing just to keep the peace.
So when Ted confessed that he was tiring of living so near his parents again, it came as no surprise to her, and she couldn't blame him. She felt the same way.

***

Alarm bells went off in Bev's head upon being introduced to the in-laws neighbour who lived in the apartment above them.

"This is Jacquie, she and her partner live upstairs," said Inez.

"Nice to meet you," said Bev, instantly taking a disliking to the brash blond with the tobacco husky voice. Bev had always been good at judging a person's character and knew at a glance that here was a heavy drinking hussy, her hard blue eyes seeking out the attention of every man who came in contact. It was later disclosed that she had broken up a family and was now living with the man, Jack. They were said to be happy together. Surely her Ted could not possibly fall victim to someone like this. Could he? Surely not. Nevertheless, she had been warned of a woman of that very name.

Bev would give a polite nod or 'hello' when she encountered her, but did not encourage further conversation. She had been told in the past that she possessed a very cool demeanor, perhaps this was her best defence, and she did not want to become more familiar with the likes of her.

***

It was the first Christmas in Canada in years, and they spent it with the grandparents. Inez decided she would like to do dinner and they all gathered around a laden table with roast turkey and all the trimmings. She had not considered the children though, and laced her traditional English trifle with sherry, to Bev's horror. But she had to admit that they slept well that night, exhausted from the day's activities and the trifle.

Santa brought them all bicycles and from then on the four of them could be seen riding together to the parks in the area. The weather remained very mild and before long, the spring bulbs were forcing through the gardens.

With the spring came a restless feeling to be in a place where they could have a garden, with country air and peacefulness. Bev thought of the Okanagan, with its drier climate, hotter weather and abundance of fruit orchards. She could remember having spent memorable holidays there picking the fruit and asparagus that grew wild in the orchards and along the train tracks. She knew the children would enjoy the adventure, so she would approach Ted with this idea.

"They are not going to like it one bit if we move away, you know," Ted sighed. "But it's not far away, only a two-hour drive, we can come for visits, it will be okay, dear. We just have to be firm," stated Bev.

And so it was that they made their plans against the wishes of the in-laws. Inez didn't say too much about it to Bev, as she knew better but to twelve-year-old Tess she made the remark...

"You will never have a German Shepherd dog as you think, or a horse for that matter. Just wait and see."

Tess was upset with her grandmother for saying such a thing, but kept it to herself until much later. She too, would come to know this woman for the selfish person that she was, always putting herself before others.

***

Bev's research paid off and she landed a full-time position in one of the hospitals in the interior of the province and also found a large home with gardens for rent nearby.

It was just as they had imagined; a house with yard and gardens within walking distance of Okanagan Lake and the school. The summer would be one to remember. Ted was at home with the children, taking them everywhere while Bev was at work and then they would do things together on Bev' s days off. The weather did not disappoint and they woke up every day to blue skies and sunshine and heat. It had a 'California feel' about it. The orchards flourished under such conditions. Seeing the first crop of fat juicy cherries prompted Bev to talk Ted into signing the kids up for cherry picking. It would be an adventure.

"They can earn a bit of pocket money and you can go along and help them," she suggested. They were eager at first, but found the heat draining and Ted feared for them climbing ladders, so it lasted for only a short while. They did, however, enjoy eating as many of the juicy cherries as they liked as well as some for home. Now the days were filled with biking, horseback riding, playing with friends and swimming.

On a sweltering day in July, the kids were at the lake with friends. They were both good swimmers so were allowed most times to go alone as there were always other adults at the beach. Ted and Bev sat in the garden sipping on iced tea. Suddenly Ted exclaimed that they must go and check on the kids immediately. Bev was startled into action and they hurried to the beach which was only a short walk away to see that their kids were out in the middle of the lake on a raft. A wind had sprung up and they were drifting further and further away from shore. Ted called to them to sit down, not stand and he would come out to them. But before he had a chance to take off his shirt, a young man who had been sitting on the beach with his girlfriend, jumped in and swam to them, towing the raft back to shore.

Two very thankful kids waded out of the water to be greeted by two very thankful parents. Bev and Ted hugged them close, but scolded them for going on the raft and out of their comfort zone.

"Thank you, so much," exclaimed Ted, shaking the young man's hand. "You're quite welcome. I had been watching them for a while and decided to go out after them when you called out, so it was no trouble."

That evening, Ted disclosed to Bev that he had experienced a profound feeling that the children were in danger; he ached to his very core and knew that he must act immediately. He just knew it was his mentor's prodding. This would happen time and time again in the coming years, even after they had reached maturity. It prompted Bev to check to see if they still had the matching moles on their little fingers, and to her surprise, they had disappeared.

***

By July, the temperature rose to 37°C almost every day, it was sweltering hot. Bev's little garden flourished in the heat and soon they were eating their own produce as well as some from the neighbour who had an over-abundance. On trips to the coast to visit the in-laws, they took fresh veggies and fruit.

The hot dry weather dried out the countryside; the hills were scorched and craggy with sagebrush. Only the orchards remained green due to the irrigation. Then the fire season was upon them. Fires started with a lightning strike or carelessly thrown cigarettes, making the hot air even hotter. Forest fires were a natural phenomenon but still it became a concern when people's homes and businesses were threatened. Acrid smoke filled the atmosphere; cinders and ash was carried on the wind. The only place to cool off was the lake which was like stepping into a warm bath.

It was a relief when the sun went down behind the mountain so that the house could begin to cool. Then, as darkness gathered, the forest fire across the lake was more visible. They watched in awe as the fire crowned the treetops and exploded in bursts of flames. What was needed was a good rain, but it was not in the forecast.

***

Bev at least had the comfort of an air-conditioned workplace but when she would step out the door to leave for home, the heat struck her like a blast furnace. It was no wonder that Ted seemed irritable when she arrived home one evening.

"Let's take the kids to the library after dinner, at least it is air-conditioned," he sighed.

"Sure enough, dear. Are you alright? You look a little peaked." Bev gave him a closer look when he sat eating his dinner, there was something about him that she had not seen in a long while and her inner voice gave warning. He had been a bit moody of late.

They all clambered into the car and were soon off to the library. Ted selected a few books and checked his out. He came to where Bev was still scanning the shelves and said that he was going out to the car and would wait for them there.

The kids had a load of books too, and Bev helped carry them out. They headed to where the car had been parked and were surprised to see that Ted and the car were no place to be seen. "He's probably driven to the store to pick up a few things for home, kids, we'll just wait inside, okay?"

But they waited and waited and after more than an hour had passed, Bev became worried. Nonetheless, she wanted to get home and so she called a taxi. Hours later, the phone rang at home. Bev picked up the receiver to hear a profuse apology from Ted for having left them. "I can't remember when or why I left you there. I found myself way up in the hills. I'm so sorry, Bev. I will be home very soon."

"Just drive safely and get home, okay." She hung up the phone with a very uneasy mind. Things were happening again and she didn't feel she could cope with a heavy workload and worry about Ted. "Oh God, I don't need this." The kids were concerned too, and pressed her for an explanation. "Daddy will be home soon. He just needed some time on his own." They seemed satisfied with this excuse and returned to their reading.

She realized then that he probably did need some time on his own. He was with the kids on a daily basis while she was working the long hours and trying to get some sleep after the night shifts. Perhaps, as she had three days off, they should take a trip to the coast to the cooler temperatures and visit with his parents. She decided to talk to him about the possibility.

Ted returned shortly after and came through the door with a sheepish grin, bearing flowers for Bev and chocolate for the kids. After a cool shower, he seemed himself again. "Yes, I'd love to get away dear. Mum and Dad will be pleased to see us, too. I've been quite worried about Dad with his upcoming surgery," he sighed.

"We'll get an early start in the morning; I'll begin packing and get together some vegetables for them this evening." Bev turned off the TV and sat next to him on the couch. "Are you sure nothing else is bothering you, Ted?" He shook his head in denial, but she noticed a faraway look in his eyes. She glanced at the books he had selected from the library. One in particular caught her interest, 'The hidden places of England'. England always beckoned him.

***   .

His father's surgery finally took place; the surgeon assured them that it had gone well. But he had become confused after the anaesthetic. He raved about seeing camels on the desert and struck out at the nurses. Inez was not amused, declaring that he must think he's in North Africa. She had never had much patience for her husband. His recovery was slow and even though he was home from hospital, he would still need nursing care for dressing changes. He was in low spirits and wanted them to return. Inez was finding it hard to cope with his care. She told them that a large apartment was coming vacant in their building and begged them to consider taking it, if only for the winter.

If truth be told, after the relentless heat of the summer and now the prospect of a much colder winter, they were ready to return. Before Christmas they were back; the kids back in their old school, Bev back in her former job and Ted back doing what he loved most, selling cars. Ted seemed much more contented here. Perhaps it had been a mistake to move to the interior, but Bev was convinced that the experience had been a good one, especially for the children. They always adapted well and that circumstance was no different. They were soon in a circle of friends as well as making new ones.

Ironic as it seemed, the woman upstairs, Jacquie was still there, living with her partner, Jack. Their paths would cross from time to time, and Bev kept up her distant demeanour towards her. Ted was always friendly towards people, it was just his nature. Only time would tell if this was 'the woman'.

It was an interesting place for the children to be living. There were so many neighbours coming and going from the apartment building; the Polish couple in 207 who had been persecuted in their homeland and had fled in a volley of gunshot; the old German couple who lived upstairs in 308, childless and sad. The children's presence brightened their days.

One such tenant, a very nice young man, Jerry, who lived on his own in the bachelor apartment, had made a real impact on their young minds. He was perhaps in his early twenties, very good-looking, wore his hair long, very hippie-like. He went missing one cold March day. He had rented a row boat from the local dock, told the owner he would take it for just an hour. When hours later he had not returned, the man became suspicious and called the police. The boat was found with the anchor missing and Jerry's wallet and backpack still in it. Divers went down the next day and recovered his body. He had taken his life; he had tied the anchor around his waist. Then it was all the news. People asked why he had done it. Only his sister knew, for he had left her a thick envelope with his writings and a letter. He must have been a very troubled young man.

"But he can't be dead, I saw him just this morning!" Phil exclaimed in alarm. Bev, Ted and Tess listened to him attentively as he continued... "He was walking down the back lane towards me, carrying his tennis racket. I said hello, and he smiled and continued around the corner and disappeared from view."

"Are you quite sure that it was this morning you saw him?" Ted asked doubtfully.

"Yes, it was definitely this morning," he assured. It was Tess who piped up... "You saw his ghost, Phil," she said with conviction. "If he smiled at you, he must be happy." There was nothing anyone could argue with that.

It was to be the children's first experience with a death that so touched them. Ted and Bev realized then that their children definitely were sensitive to supernatural forces. It left them all with much to think about.

***

At spring break, they were on their first visit to Disneyland in many years. The trip would take their minds away from the death of young Jerry. For young Phil it was 'the one day' he was told about whenever he asked, "When are we going back to California?" He and his sister could hardly contain their excitement and Disneyland never failed to please the young and old alike. It proved to be a wonderful family holiday and they enjoyed the road trip.

England 1989

Ted held on to his British status as though it were his lifeline. Although his parents had become Canadian citizens, he had never felt the need to. He had his landed status and that was all he cared about. But for some reason, he was told he had to leave and then return to Canada, have his passport stamped to prove he had been out of the country for a given period of time. It didn't bother Ted, he just took it in stride and thought it a golden opportunity for another family holiday. It was just three years since they had left England.

In a flurry of excitement, they packed their bags and were soon on English soil. How they had missed so many things about England and now here they were careering down the motorway in a rental car headed for the West Country. The countryside was a verdant green of every hue, just as they had remembered it to be and summer furled out before them. Through a travel agent, they had found a moderately-priced self-catering place to stay which was on a working farm not far from Yeovil in Somerset. But it was too far to travel on the day of their arrival, so they put in at a comfortable lodging in Basingstoke for the night.

Following a good night's rest and full English breakfast, they set out again in anticipation of finding the place they would call home for the summer. They made a stop in Salisbury with the idea of having lunch and found themselves very near the cathedral.

"I really, really want to see inside," gushed Bev. She had recently read the novel *'Sarum'* about the building of the cathedral so many centuries earlier. Seeing the cathedral proved to be a rewarding experience, not only for the most beautiful stained glass windows in the country, but also for the Magna Carta on display in a lower room. It was carefully protected in a locked glass case.

"Now pay attention, you two, this is something you can tell your teacher. It's the foundation for all the human rights that we enjoy today," chimed Bev. But they were more concerned about their rumbling stomachs and she could see that jet lag was having an effect on their attention span. Tess, a poet in the making, was drawn to a plain glass window that was engraved with a text: *And all shall be well and all manner of thing shall be well when the tongues of flame are infolded into the crowned knot of fire, and the fire and the rose are one. T.S.E.*

"Isn't that lovely, Mum? I've got to write this down." Bev agreed with her and waited while she got out her journal and wrote down the beautiful words.

After soup and sandwiches followed by rich Dorset apple cake, they were fuelled for the trip ahead of them. Ted was already opening the car doors and anxious to move on.

"Come on, you lot, get a move on," he called.

Having left the motorway and now on smaller and less travelled roads winding through the countryside, they arrived at the farm. They were greeted cordially and shown to the guest house which was a separate building from that of the farm house. They were pleased to see that it was private and nicely furnished. Bev declared that it would be just perfect. She could cook all their meals in the small but well-appointed kitchen. There was a sitting room with TV, books, games and puzzles. The bedrooms and bathroom were on the second level and they too were comfortably furnished. From the bedroom window was a view of the stables, courtyard and out to the rolling hills beyond. It was a peaceful setting although there was a pervasive smell of farm.

Tess and Phil raced up the stairs to the second level, throwing open doors in anticipation of selecting the room that they would prefer.

"Not so fast, you two. Your mother is to get the first pick of the bedrooms' said Ted. "You know how fussy she is."

"Thank you, dear. I'll be up in a minute after I've have a better look through the kitchen cupboards." She knew she would have to get supplies for their supper, but at least the salt and pepper shakers were full and there were complimentary teabags, sugar and milk for a welcome cup of tea.

Only a short walk from the house was a little store and post office, a pub and the parish church. "Come, Tess. Let's leave the boys to do some unpacking and we'll buy the groceries."

The tinkling of bells announced their arrival as Bev and Tess opened the door of the little store. They were greeted by the clerk who eyed them with interest. Another patron looked them up and down as Bev opened her mouth with her Canadian accent. "Hello, yes, we are staying at Holgate farm for the summer."

"Yer welcome, Ma'am. Hope yer enjoy yer stay."
The shelves were well stocked with all the necessary canned and packaged goods. A glass counter displayed cold meats and cheeses, and an abundance of fruit and vegetables lined the wall outside. Bev eyed the prices and was pleasantly surprised at how reasonable they were. She selected the items they would need for the evening meal and breakfast, placing them in the wicker basket provided. How quaint she thought, no metal shopping carts here. She decided they would have to do a big shop in Yeovil the next day.

***

Every day was an adventure.

The farmer's children were in the same age group as Tess and Phil so an easy comradeship developed. They eagerly pitched in with the chores of feeding the animals and spent hours playing in the hay barns. Within days of their arrival, they had the privilege of seeing a newly born colt. The dear little animal stood sturdily only hours after birth and followed its mother around the stable yard. Tess was in her element and spoke of nothing else for days.

On a walk behind the farm across stubble fields and over stiles, they found themselves in a sheep pasture. The chorus of baaing in every different tone from lambs to rams had them in peals of laughter. A path through a meadow abundant with wild flowers and butterflies, led to another small hamlet of West Coker. They walked along the narrow streets admiring the light stone buildings and peaceful setting. In the little post office store, they purchased favourite chocolate bars to fuel the trek back. It had been a perfect day.

***

Ted insisted that they get out and about to other places he wanted to explore; Wookey Hole, Cheddar Gorge, Bath, Wells, Castle Coombe, Weston-Super-Mare; there were so many places to see and things do and he had made a list so they would miss nothing. It was the town of Glastonbury visited first that made the biggest impression on all of them.

They wandered through the grounds and old abbey ruins and looked in awe at the supposed gravesite of King Arthur and his Queen Guinevere. In 1190 A.D., it was recorded that the relics of Arthur and his queen had been discovered, exhumed and reburied in the abbey church where they remained until 1278. In that year, the tomb was opened in the presence of King Edward I and his queen. The remains were reverently placed in a tomb beneath the high altar. In the destruction of the abbey during the dissolution, the bones were probably dispersed but the gravesite on the grounds honours them still.

A well-maintained orchard still thrived from the time when the monks grew apples to make cider. The majestic Tor of Glastonbury rose behind the abbey. It could be seen from miles around and they were told that the view from the top was a breathtaking panorama of the countryside.

It was here, while browsing in the shops, that they first became aware of the crop circle phenomenon which made such a lasting impression on all of them. As early as 1972, circles had been forming in the crop fields in and around sites like Silbury Hill and Stonehenge, mostly in the county of Wiltshire. At first appeared one or two simple circles which were thought to be made by hoaxers. But for the fact that they usually occurred overnight and the complexity of them could only be fully appreciated when viewed from the air, it was suggested that they were made by an extra-terrestrial force. Ted and Bev opted for the later version as they had never forgotten the UFO they had seen in the summer of 1972; to them that theory was totally believable.

Conversation around the supper table that evening was dominated by a lively discussion about the crop circles. It gave fuel to the children's imagination; to them it was a magical, mysterious phenomenon. They declared how they would love to witness the moment of a circle formation as balls of energy darted at lightning speed across the fields. Ted suggested that one would have to be pretty naive to think mankind was the only intelligence in the universe. Bev was pleased that her children had open minds for the supernatural. One day in the future they would need those open minds to accept that their father was psychic.

***

At two in the morning, something woke Bev. She registered the time by the glowing red digits of the clock beside their bed. It was so bright outside that she rose from the bed and moved toward the open window. It was as though a white light illuminated the entire courtyard below. It was silent. She could see the white VW parked below the windows, and every detail of the surrounding buildings as though it was broad daylight. Unnerved, she made her way to the bathroom trying to make sense of what she had seen. But by the time she returned to the bedroom it was again as dark outside as it should have been. She crawled back into bed and moved as close to Ted as she could without waking him. She just could not wrap her head around that bright white light. She knew that she had been awake and that it had not been a dream. It took her hours to fall back to sleep.

In the morning with the family sitting for breakfast, she mentioned how a bright floodlight had lit up the courtyard in the night.

"There are no floodlights, dear. This is a farm in the depth of the countryside, they have no use for them," Ted remarked, stirring sugar into his coffee.

"Well, a bright light woke me last night; you know how sensitive I am to anything out of the ordinary when I am asleep." She got up and went outside to see if Ted had been correct about the lighting. It was true, there were no external lights on the building. She knew she had been wide awake; it had not been her imagination. Where could it have come from?

And then she realized that what she had witnessed was surely light from a UFO hovering over the farmyard. To her, it made as much sense as did the crop circle formations. She was reluctant to share her theory in case the kids became frightened. She would wait until they were on home territory.

She did however share her feelings with Ted, she knew he would understand.

"It's nice to know that I'm not the only one who sees things," he laughed. "But in saying that, things have been pretty quiet on that front, thank goodness."

"I've noticed though that we have not yet been to Sherborne and Sandford Orcas, Ted. Are you purposefully avoiding those places?" Bev wondered.
"There are so many other places we haven't seen, no need this time, OK?"

***

A picnic lunch was packed for an outing to Wookey Hole caves on the edge of the Mendip hills. These were limestone caves that had been carved out by the river Axe over many millennia. None had before explored underground caves so there was an air of excitement as Ted pulled the car into the gravelled parking lot and they tumbled out, the kids racing ahead. Bev followed with trepidation, she didn't like small spaces and wondered about the bats and other crawling things that might be living there, nor did she care for still, deep water.

They were ushered through the entrance into the dripping dampness by the guide who began a commentary about the discovery of the caves and the exploration of them over the years. The cool air within was in stark contrast to the summer heat. Floodlights strategically placed illuminated the beautiful limestone formations of the stalactites and stalagmites. Especially interesting to the kids was the witch of stone and her little dog which legend told had been turned that way by a Glastonbury Monk because of her curses on the village. Bev thought about the witch as she tripped along behind the others. She had an affinity for witches, they were herbalists and healers after all and had been so misunderstood and persecuted throughout history.

They gingerly walked behind the guide along a boardwalk into the very depth of the cave where an underground river was lit up to reveal the crystal blue-green waters. They were told that a large quantity of human skulls had been found at one end of one of the caverns, it had possibly been an early Iron Age cemetery. There was also reputed to be a least one ghost haunting the depths.

Having been thoroughly frightened, the children were only too keen to get out of there and into the adjoining cotton mill, the house of mirrors and the penny arcade. It had been fun to put old pennies into the slots and watch the mechanical antics of the clowns and animals; fun to see one's distorted reflection in the mirror maze.

Leaving there and following a picnic lunch, Cheddar Gorge was the next destination. The main road cut through the high cliffs of the gorge and was in stark contrast to the surrounding countryside. They noted that the place was well known for its Cheddar cheese. Apparently, the caves in that area remained the perfect temperature of fifty-two degrees, winter or summer, so afforded ideal conditions for the maturing of cheese in the early days.

The souvenir shops attracted the children's interest as they were meant to do and they came away with mementos of their visit; a shirt for Phil and earrings for Tess. Ted selected the famous cheese to enjoy later.

***

Another day trip was taken to the beautiful city of Bath. It had been a favourite place for rest and relaxation throughout history and many famous writers and poets were known to have enjoyed the healing sulphur waters of the Roman baths. They made their way through the building and were impressed by the extravagance of the architecture, the bathing pools and the sophisticated early central heating system.

"Smells to me like hard boiled eggs," said Ted and was reluctant to taste the sulphur water from a fountain.

They wandered through the city and found a park adjacent to the royal crescent where they sat for another picnic lunch. And then it was off to do some shopping in the modern stores.

It had been another interesting experience and they arrived back at the cottage, tired and hungry. Bev had found a bake shop and purchased a variety of cakes and buns to have with tea. It was a perfect ending to a perfect day, she declared.

***

All good things come to an end and so did the holiday. They had been away for nearly six weeks and the return flight from Heathrow was booked. Bev was picking out a few items at the little village store when the realization that this was their last day there really hit her. Oh, how much she would miss all this, but the children had to go back to school and she and Ted back to work. They were all reluctant; it had been such a pleasant experience. Bev dearly wished they could stay forever; she just loved the West Country and the rural life of England. But in her heart she knew they would return. It was inevitable.

They had all allowed the beauty of it, the mystery of it and the magic of it to become so deeply embedded in their souls, that it would never leave them.

It was well after the family had left England that the first sophisticated crop circle was formed at Winterbourne Stoke on August 12, 1989. It was a Swastika enclosed within a circle.

***

After a holiday it is always difficult to get back into the pace of life one had left behind, but for Ted it was especially so. It was as though a dark cloud hung over him. He found it hard to concentrate at work and was testy with Bev and the children. And then to make matters worse, he became downright depressed and would take to his bed for days at a time. His work suffered as well as the family relationships. Bev sat on the edge of his bed one morning and decided she would not leave until she had an answer from him as to why he was so in the doldrums.

"I only know that nothing here seems worthwhile anymore; it's as though I have left my soul in England. I so dearly wanted to stay there." His lips twisted with emotion. Bev hugged him close and allowed him to continue. "I have a feeling that my brother is responsible for this, it's as though he imbeds his own feelings into my psyche, and I can't seem to shake him off."

"It will be alright, Ted. I was just as reluctant to come home as you were, but you know full well that we will return," she soothed. "And so does he."

Ted did finally snap out of his depression but it took the sudden illness of his father for that to happen. His dad was taken to hospital in acute abdominal pain with subsequent surgery and was diagnosed with bowel cancer. Then to make matters worse, he had a severe stroke. Two weeks after surgery, he was dead.

Perhaps it had been expected, he had been ailing for some years. But Ted took it hard, much more so than did his mother.

The Aftermath

Bev saw her mother-in-law, Inez, in her true light during the illness of her husband and confirmed to herself that she was a stone-cold bitch of a woman. Following his surgery for bowel cancer, she visited him only once in hospital and when she was told he had had a severe stroke, she would not go again.

"But, Mum, he looks for you. It seems that he is trying to tell me something." Ted thought about how his father had desperately tried to speak, but it all came out garbled and nonsensical. "Even if he is unable to speak, he knows when people are with him. He looks for you. I can't keep making excuses for your not coming," Ted pleaded with her.

"No. Absolutely, no. I can't bring myself to see him like that," she whined. Bev tried to tell her that even though he was unable to speak, he could still hear and comprehend. He needed her. But she would have none of it. How could anyone be so cold, uncaring and self-centred she thought? Though she wanted to say these things, she bit her tongue. It was not her place to admonish Ted's mother. She could see the hurt in Ted's eyes, though, for his mother's callousness.

And so, they gave up trying. It was Ted who sat at his bedside holding his hand. It was Bev who helped the nurses with his palliative care. And it was Bev who took the phone call in the wee hours of the morning to inform them of his death. Even then, Ted was considerate of his mother and gave her the news in person rather than with a phone call. But he could not forgive her for her uncaring attitude towards his father when he had needed her most.

Even though they had been married for over fifty years, Inez hardly shed a tear. She seemed to enjoy all the attention of family and friends rallying around her in the days leading up to the funeral, especially that of her good friend, Jacquie.

Following the funeral service, Bev noted that this woman gave Ted a hug that was especially lengthy, more so than was necessary to convey her sympathy. Bev was dressed in a dove-grey suit and heels, looking elegant. As the jeans-clad woman turned to speak to her, Bev turned a cold shoulder and greeted her partner, Jack, instead who was the next person in the receiving line. Whether Ted noticed or not, he did not mention the slight. Bev just couldn't help it; she had such an aversion to this woman.

***

As always after a death in a family life must continue, and so it was for Inez. She had always been a busy woman, putting her work before her family. Her mother had died of cancer when she was only fourteen. Because her mum was ailing at home for a long while, her father had employed a young woman as a housekeeper. It was obvious, in hindsight, that her father had been carrying on an affair with the young woman while his wife was still alive, and right under her nose. The woman became pregnant and so he did the honest thing by her and married her within months of his wife's death. Inez was ordered to quit school and start a job. She was good with arithmetic so her father had her do the accounts at his printing office.

She lived at home with her new stepmother who was not very much older than herself. She watched the young woman grow steadily larger in her pregnancy and seethed within that her father could have been so blatantly carrying on. Little by little, it had hardened her heart; made her strong and of an independent nature. She married at the age of twenty-one and within months of the wedding saw her husband off to war. She filled the six years that he was away with her work. When he finally came home, she worked harder still running a guest house. She worked during her pregnancy with Ted, and after his birth. She worked until the sale of the guest house and saw her husband off to Canada to prepare a home for them. She worked as soon as they became settled. She worked throughout Ted's growing up years and after he had married.

In an era where women as a rule did not work outside the home, she had always had a job. There was always a job; in bakeries, sales, and grocery stores. And now here she was as an elderly widow and still she had a job as an apartment manager. She no longer lived on site but that was not an issue. She would just have Ted continue to collect the rents for her and she could get her friend, Jacquie, to do the cleaning for her. She could keep the job still and the income it provided. Couldn't she? In truth, she hardly missed her husband. She had a wide circle of friends who kept her active and of course, she had Ted. She had always been able to manipulate him to her will, so she thought.

***

But this became a bone of contention with Bev. She was fed up with her mother-in-law's controlling attitude towards Ted and she was having none of it. A shouting match ensued between them and for many months they were not on speaking terms. It was the first, but would not be the last time they would agree to disagree. Ted and the children continued on good terms with Inez, but Bev refused to see her. It would be many months before she relented, called and invited her to dinner. But Bev had made her point and Inez had resigned herself to a more respectful awareness of her daughter -in -law.

Paranormal activity

They had all experienced it. The tinny-sounding voices as though a radio was not quite on the station, heard at various times of the day or night. The house was too old for a North American building but it had been chosen for a number of reasons; the wide front veranda and gardens, its proximity to the beach, school and work. It was a home where Tess could have her German shepherd dog and Phil his gerbil. And as for mother-in-law, she didn't like the fact that it was on a very steep hill so never came to visit if she had to drive. That suited Bev. They would just have to put up with the unusual noises.

When the children were home alone though, it unnerved them to see Duchess with her hackles raised, appearing to be seeing something that they did not. It especially frightened them one summer evening when they were watching TV downstairs with a friend. They all heard the unmistakable footsteps overhead from the attic room which was Phil's bedroom. Tess turned off the TV and as she did so, the noise stopped and as they listened, it resumed again, a heavy-footed tread overhead. The dog gave a low throaty growl and started for the stairs.

Whoever was there had best beware. The three of them cautiously followed her, expecting to see an intruder but only the gerbil in its cage was present. The dog slunk past them with her tail between her legs and headed down the stairs.

"We all heard it, don't you guys agree?" Tess whispered. The boys nodded in agreement, their eyes wide in disbelief.

"Let's get out of here and take Duchess for a walk on the beach," said Phil.

"I second the motion," exclaimed Tess. "We don't have to be back until Dad gets home." With that they were off, locking the door behind them.

Ted just laughed and dismissed what they told him about the

footsteps. He didn't want them to be worried. He would just watch and wait, but it would seem that things were beginning to happen again. He may no longer be able to keep his secret from them much longer.

Phil especially loved his room because it was so private and the size of the entire downstairs rooms combined. He spent many hours there putting together his model cars and painting them in bright colours. All the little jars of paint he had meticulously arranged on a shelf. This particular afternoon, he sat at his desk going over a piece of homework to be ready for the following day. The radio played rap, and his gerbil was spinning on the wheel in its cage.

Having finished his writing, he stretched, reached to turn off the music and rose from his chair to leave the room. As he moved towards the stairs, one of the jars of paint hurtled across the room, hit his back and fell to the floor. He stared dumbfounded at the little blue paint jar, looked over to the vacant spot on the shelf where it had rested with the others. Then in the next heartbeat he was down the stairs in a flash, yelling, "Dad!"

***

It was a Sunday morning. While Bev busied herself in the back garden, Ted got out the hose and bucket and washed the car in the driveway. He enjoyed this activity, had always kept his car clean and shining. He paid extra attention to the windows. He polished the windshield to a high gloss until he could see his reflection. A quick movement behind his own reflection caught his eye. In a flash of recognition, his brain registered the face of Philip Canton.

Unnerved, he opened the driver's door, slid on to the seat and began to polish the dashboard. Feeling the familiar presence, he turned around to see that the man was sitting as bold as brass in the back seat.

"You will have to tell them, you know. I have waited long enough." The voice was in his head causing a stab of pain in his temples. "Okay, okay I hear you!"

Tess passed by the car on her way out to walk the dog and tapped on the window. "Are you alright, Dad? I thought I heard you talking to someone."

"No, no, must have been talking to myself." He shrugged it off with a laugh.

"See you later, dear; don't let Duchess off her leash."

Bev had relegated Phil to help her weed the back garden, so was oblivious to what Ted was experiencing. Phil was hunkered down, slowly weeding a patch of peas in quiet companionship with his mother.

"Do you believe in ghosts, Mum?" He asked, looking at her directly.

"Well, yes, I do Son. I know they exist, but I have never actually seen one and wouldn't wish to. Are you concerned, dear?"

"We have all heard noises lately and I was just wondering if maybe this house is haunted. Dad won't say much about it but I think he knows something."

"Well, we will just have to sit down and have a chat with Daddy," she replied, all too aware that the kids would have to know sooner rather than later.

Ted also realised that he could not put it off any longer, so after consulting with Bev and seeing that she was of the same mind, it was decided to call a family meeting. The kids were used to these sessions; it was usually about some change to take place or a reprimand.

Tess thought it might be to discuss her late hours. She had a boyfriend now and sometimes came in later than her curfew. She knew it couldn't be about her school work as they were out for summer holidays and she had passed with flying colours.

Phil, on the other hand, was quite certain it was to discuss what he had talked about with his mother. He sat at his father's feet in anticipation.

"We have a ghost!" Ted's opening statement came as a shock to them and the look on their faces was worth a thousand words. To hear their father actually confirm what they had all been experiencing was not what they had expected.

But what he said next really got their attention.

"His name is Philip Canton and he was my brother from a past life. Don't be afraid. He has been near you all your life and he wishes to speak to you."

At this point Bev intervened, only to reassure them that it was okay. She motioned for Phil to sit near her and she held each child's hand to dispel any fear. Ted told them that he would come to no harm as his brother's spirit spoke through him. They sat wide-eyed, holding firm to Bev's hands.

Within seconds, Ted began a sequence of deep breathing and his brother took over his voice with his deep well-spoken English accent.

"Do not fear me, children. I have been waiting for this moment for all your lives. You have grown to be the most beautiful children and I am well proud of you both. I do not intend to stay, but I want you to know that I am always near." Then in a few moments, Ted, with his eyes, closed began the deep breathing and was soon back in the present. What he said next also came as a surprise.

"I have a very strong feeling that another family holiday to England will be on the agenda in the very near future. Anyone object to that?"

Tess looked crestfallen; she had hoped to spend time with her boyfriend on the beach this summer and said as much. She also was very sceptical about what she had witnessed with her father. Phil, on the other hand, accepted it all at face value and believed in his father, thought it amazing that another soul could speak through him. He was also overjoyed and looked forward to the prospect of another adventurous holiday.

"I suggest that we give them time to take all this in, dear. Enough has been said for today," stated Bev. She gave each child a hug and sent them off to the kitchen to start a salad for supper. They were only too happy to be excused.

***

The experience left both children with much to think about. Tess believed that she had known for some time that her father was different. She had read it in his eyes from the time she was a small child. She could only describe it as a deep unspeakable sadness. She sympathised for him and felt that he should try to resist the power of another spirit over his own. She was the least able to accept what had been spoken. She would always see him in a new light from this day forward. It was not that she didn't believe in ghosts; hadn't she seen one as a child, that day in the woods peeking around the tree at her? Now that she was much older and well read, she realized that was the case. She had never forgotten the experience of that autumn afternoon of bare branches and fallen leaves and the man in medieval costume with the large wolfhounds at his side.

She would just have to observe and hope for the best.

Wembury, Plymouth Devon

A little cottage in the small south west coastal village of Wembury seemed like an idyllic place to spend the summer and early autumn. It had a well-furnished, comfortable and spacious living space and even an extra room for Tess's boyfriend when he came to stay with them. Ted had relented and agreed that Peter could come when they were settled. He was of German descent and it surprised them all that his father had, as a young lad, been a gunner in one of the planes of the German Luftwaffe bombing the city of Plymouth. The irony was not lost on them that his son would be visiting that very place in a peaceful time.

Plymouth was one of the largest ports in England, had always been through the ages and boasted of Sir Francis Drake and his defeat of the Spanish Armada. It was also the place of departure for the *'Mayflower'*, the ship that had carried the pilgrims to the new world. This especially sparked Bev's interest as her maternal side of the family was able to trace its linage back to the second sailing of that famous craft. Eight generations previously and in the reign of Elizabeth I, her very great grandfather left Scotland for America.

Wembury was only a short distance from the city, but had all the charm of a small coastal village. There was a parish church, post office, a few small shops for groceries and as so typical of every place in England, a pub. A road cut through the village and wound down through narrow stone walls. It ended at open fields and downward to the sea. High atop a steep hill sat the parish church with a view out to sea of the Mewstone, a craggy triangular shaped rock. A coastal path wound for miles giving access to explore the rugged landscape. The lads from the Royal Navy used the path for their exercise runs.

As soon as they arrived at Shippen cottage, it felt like home. The 15th century building was a converted domestic animal shelter attached to the main house. It had warm polished wood floors throughout the downstairs rooms, sitting room kitchen and bathroom. Wooden stairs rose from the sitting room to the bedrooms and bathroom above. Through railings in the hallway one could see into the sitting room were heavy beams criss-crossed far out of reach. Bev was very particular where a clean house was concerned and nothing missed her scrupulous inspection for detail. One of the high beams in view but well out of reach she noted had a thick layer of dust and cobwebs, a haven for spiders to hide? One would have to have a very long-handled duster to reach that one, she thought. But then her attention was drawn to the leaded windows through which she had a view of the courtyard below and could see Ted hauling cases from the car.

As always, it was the kitchen that captured Bev's interest. She bustled about to prepare a dinner of carefully selected food she knew they had all missed; faggots with gravy, Cornish greens, baby potatoes and ginger cake with custard for dessert. She had noticed an herb garden at the entrance and had selected a handful to flavour her cooking.

Tess unpacked her cases and arranged her books and art supplies at the small desk by the window. Hers was the largest of the rooms for which she felt justified as Phil had the biggest room at home. She especially loved the window seat with cushions where she could picture herself sitting to read.

Phil joined Ted to find a local newspaper and make a phone call to his mother. There was not a phone in the cottage so the red phone box across from the store would have to suffice. If Inez wanted to contact them she would have to leave a message with the landlord who lived in the adjacent building. Now with newspapers and books of local interest purchased, they headed back.

"Any chance you might be interested in doing some fishing son?" Ted asked. "I'd love that," gushed Phil. "Never know what you might catch out there."

"Well, we can all head into Plymouth tomorrow and sort you out with some fishing gear; I may even join you myself."

Following the evening meal, they headed out for a stroll through the village and down the winding road to the sea. The evening was pleasantly warm and a breeze heady with the smell of seaweed stirred the overhanging branches of the tree tunnel through which they walked. Tess was already taking note of plant life and making simple sketches she would later paint; dog roses, wood violets, hart's tongue ferns. Phil ran ahead as usual, always wanting to see things before everyone else, and called out for them to hurry. Bev and Ted hung back in discussion about the phone call to his mother. She was well, but missed them, when could she expect them home? Never, Bev thought to herself. She was very contented to be away from her mother-in-law.

They explored the ancient stone church and walked about the graveyard reading the epitaphs on the headstones. One in particular caught Tess's interest and she would later write a poem about it. It touched a chord in her, she felt there was something so sad about the young lad's early death and the feeling that his spirit lingered still.

They walked down to the small cove and checked out the tidal pools. The tide was coming in, creeping slowly around the rocks and they skipped from rock to rock, avoiding wet feet.

It was almost dark and darker still in the tree tunnel by the time they walked back. "I'd hate to be by myself walking through here at night," remarked Phil and to this they were all in agreement.

***

Tess shrieked, "There's a spider in my room." Both she and Bev were petrified of spiders, fearing they might end up in their bed at night. So Ted was delegated to do a spider search under the beds and in the corners. It would become a ritual every night before bedtime. He had read somewhere that an aversion to spiders was a deep-seated primordial fear. He knew for a fact that if Bev even saw a picture of a tarantula, much less the real thing, she would scream, shiver and shake and go cold inside. She just couldn't help it. He laughed as he thought of how he would either have to warn her or tear out a page of the newspaper so she wouldn't be frightened.

That first night they all seemed to be nicely settled when again

Tess called out, "There's something scratching around in the attic, come listen." Reluctantly, Bev crawled out of bed to investigate. There surely was the scratching sound.

It's probably mice, they won't hurt you, dear. Try to get some sleep now."
The next day when they saw the landlord, he explained that the sound they were hearing was of bats. They would fly in and out of the attic at night. Bats were a protected species here in England, so they would just have to get used to the sounds. Bev would make good and sure that the windows were closed but for a crack; there were no screens on the windows. It would seem that the North American concept of screens was lost on the British.

***

Through winding roads, they drove to Plymouth to spend an afternoon of exploring. They walked the length of the Hoe, a strip of parkland that cut up through the city and rose to a height that faced out to sea. They looked down to the large swimming pools below with diving boards of spectacular heights. It was a beautiful warm sunny day to stroll the walkways on down to the Barbican. Here they saw the steps that led down to where the *'Mayflower'* had sailed. Bev was delighted to finally see the place her great forefather had sailed from and hoped that the children would remember.

Other things were on their minds at this time though; Tess to find a place to buy essential oils and Phil for the promised fishing gear.

On the main thoroughfare, Ted pulled them all to a stop to take in the huge mural painted by one of the local artists. In his eyes it appeared to be a scene from Hades. "I think you might be right, dear. It certainly leaves much for the imagination. Look, it says here that the artist has a studio on the next street. Perhaps we could have a wander through on another day?"

There was just so much to see, but they could come back another time; they had all summer. All purchases made and following a lunch of fish and chips, they returned to the village.

***

That night as Phil fell soundly asleep, he was sucked into a dream that caused him to shout out for his mother. Bev responded to his call and tried to calm him. He was so fearful that she stayed with him holding his hand until he fell back to sleep. She couldn't remember him having such a nightmare since he was a small boy. As a child, she had to screen what he watched on TV before bedtime. "Whatever did you dream about, son?" she asked in the morning, frowning with honest concern. Reluctantly, he tried to tell them but the telling seemed lame in comparison to the experience. It was always the way of dreams.

"It was so real, I thought I was awake. A hooded monk stood before an open fireplace. His face was almost hidden from me but the firelight flickered on the lower portion of his face. His hands were clasped in front of him and held a large wooden cross which dangled from a cord around his neck. He said to me that the village had always been a peaceful place until 'Mad Margaret' had come and caused so much upset. I then heard someone outside, so I looked out the window into the courtyard. A barefooted woman in a long white nightdress was standing there. The hem of the dress was all muddy and wet as though she had been walking barefoot for a distance and her hair was wet and scraggly. She had a blindfold over her eyes. In her hands she held a brick and cackled in crazy laughter. When I thought she was about to throw the brick at the downstairs window, I woke up. But as I tried to go back to sleep, it felt as if I was being sucked right into the mattress and pulled back into the dream. It was really scary, Mum, I wish you would cover that window with something. I'm scared if I come downstairs in the night I will see her again."

Bev tried to reassure him that it was only a dream. Tess had a good laugh at his expense but Ted was more sympathetic. "Can't say as I blame you, son, not a very nice dream to have. I think those kind of dreams are called the 'hag syndrome' dreams. Not funny when experienced. I do sympathize."

That day, Phil and Tess took the bus to the Barbican. They were drawn to an antique shop on the main street which was crowded with old books, photos and other paraphernalia. Like a magnet, Phil was drawn to a box of old cigarette cards and as he flipped through a handful, to his shock, there was one depicting 'Mad Margaret'. Upon inquiring of the proprietor if he knew anything about it, he explained that she was apparently from an old Cornish legend about a young woman who went mad over unrequited love of a bad baronet. She had placed a witch's curse on him for his family background of persecuting witches.

The hairs on his neck prickled and his hands became all sweaty, but he took the card and paid the asking price. He was grateful to be able to make some sense of his dream. But why me? Where did it come from?

Ted checked out the card and looked across the supper table at Bev and just shook his head. He felt certain that this could be the forerunner to other strange happenings. And in that, he was correct for they all began to hear strange noises in the night of people muttering and there was no one around. Bev was awakened to the sound precisely like a gong being struck and it disturbed her sleep on more than one occasion. She would be startled awake to silence and would lay awake listening and wondering where the sound had come from. Finally, she would fall back to sleep with the duvet over her head and snuggled close to Ted who had not stirred.

One evening as the children were watching TV, Ted came into the living room bearing a plate of freshly-made chips for them to munch on. He sat the plate on the table and as he turned his back, the plate flew across the room, crashing to the floor with glass and chips scattered in every direction. They were all awestruck. There was just nothing to be said. They knew what they had seen; the plate had just hurtled across the room untouched by human hand.

On a morning after that, hand prints appeared on the dusty beam that Bev had noticed upon their arrival. None of them could possibly have reached it without a ladder. The prints were of both flat palms, probably male. It was without question that they were experiencing poltergeist activity.

"Try to not let it upset you, kids. It's not harmful; a spirit world is just letting us know it's near. Probably just testing to see if you are open to the paranormal. If you get upset or angry, it will feed on that."

The next night it was Ted who would have to question what he had seen. He found it hard to sleep and at about four in the morning went down to the kitchen to make a cup of tea. As he sat at the table sipping his tea, he could hear the distinct sound of footsteps crunching on the gravelled courtyard and then up to the door. The sound stopped. It occurred to him that perhaps it was the landlord coming with a message from his mother; he was calculating what time it would be back there and was about to open the door. The footsteps continued past. He peered out the window into the moonlit night and could make out the form of a man in a long cloak standing on the rise just beyond the house. Almost before his brain could register what he had seen, the person just disappeared. His imagination ran rampant with thoughts of long dead sailors lost at sea. They had seen a number of headstones in the churchyard with such epitaphs. As he climbed the stairs to the bedroom, he felt a hand touch his shoulder, yet there was no one there. He thought that he should be used to this by now, but it sent shivers up his spine. He knew that it was not his brother. He had said he would stay away for now and Ted knew he would not break the promise.

***

There was nothing like a hike in the open air to clear away thoughts of ghostly happenings. They packed a picnic lunch and headed to Edgecombe Park. Through fields of grain scattered with flowering red poppies they trekked. They climbed on the ramparts of ancient castle ruins with a view out to sea. All the exercise was just what they needed. Finding a pub garden to sit in, they enjoyed cool drinks and chatted about Peter's upcoming visit. Tess could hardly contain her excitement. It had been weeks since she had last seen him.

There was little time left before he arrived so it was decided to take a trip to Cornwall while they were still a foursome.

"We'll head to Newquay and then to Padstow to see if that old manor house has changed at all," suggested Ted. There were many sites to revisit that would bring back memories and that place was one.

"We can begin packing a bag tonight as I think it would be fun to stay somewhere overnight," Bev suggested. She was all for getting away from the cottage. Things were beginning to get on her nerves, and it would be all work for her when Peter came to stay, what with the extra laundry and meal preparation.

***

The drive to Cornwall was indeed pleasant. They crossed the little Saltash toll bridge into Cornwall and continued on to Newquay. Here they stayed in a guest house close to the beach and delighted in seeing the large breakers coming in from the sea. It was a popular area for surfers.

The following day, they drove on to Padstow and then to Little Petheric and the manor. As they pulled into the circular gravelled driveway, the kids gasped in awe of the place. They had remembered it from their visit years previous and were excited to see inside. It had finally been sold to a couple who spent a fortune on refurbishing it to a highest standard B&B.

They were taken on a grand tour of the place through to the large ballroom that had been converted to a guest sitting room still sporting the baby grand piano. Large windows bearing the old family crest allowed the sun to filter through and light up the stairs to the upper floor. Rooms were selected for the night and Bev was pleased to see the modern fitted bedrooms. Gone were the ancient four poster beds of the bygone years. After telling of their previous visit five years earlier, one of the first questions Ted asked of the proprietor was, "Are there any ghosts here?" The answer plain and simple was, "No, not that we know of. But in saying that, when the builders were checking the structure of the attic, they found a door that had been boarded over and then plastered. They thought perhaps it had been used in early times to haul up kegs of smuggled brandy." Though he said nothing, Ted mused ... how very interesting, as he remembered young Philip telling about a door opening to nowhere on their previous visit. Could he have seen through to the past? It was entirely possible, he concluded. Bev would be intrigued.

They spent a very comfortable night and enjoyed a beautifully laid out breakfast in the dining room. It had been a pleasant stay and they were ready to explore further to Bodmin and surrounds and then make their way back to Wembury and the cottage.

It was late evening by the time they returned. The cottage was in darkness and it was with trepidation they entered the place. Ted went ahead and switched on lights throughout while Bev put the kettle on for tea. All seemed peaceful.

Tomorrow Peter would arrive and hopefully his presence would put an end to the paranormal.

***

Tess enjoyed showing Peter all the places she had discovered and it was as exciting for her as though she was seeing it all for the first time too. He was in awe of the ancient places, and Tess had him in the open air climbing stone walls, trekking through farm fields and the like until he was exhausted. Phil accompanied them on most occasions but soon grew bored with their company.

His idea of a good day was to spend it out on the rocks in the water, casting out his fishing line. He would come home bearing fish that were unfamiliar to him and enjoyed looking them up in the book Ted had bought him. He would gut and fry them up to sample. He dearly wanted to see a conger eel.

One such day when he had been out by himself fishing, he had not paid attention to the incoming tide. He had been so absorbed in his sport that he didn't notice the deep green water and seaweed moving slowly around the rocks cutting off his way back to shore which was some distance away. And then it was too late. The water was already too deep and all that was left for him to do was to jump from rock to rock and then try to scale the steep cliff. With fishing rod and tackle box clutched in his left hand he grabbed for whatever he could with his right hand, his feet trying to find a foothold up the craggy face. He didn't know why he called out, "Dad!" as loud as he could but high above him, Ted heard.

"Come this way, Son, it will be easier going. That's right, there you're safe now." He grabbed his hand and pulled him the last few feet to safety and greeted him with a big bear hug.

"Please don't tell Mum, will you, Dad? She would be ever so upset with me."

"It could happen to anyone when not aware of the tide times. I'll pick up a book for you to have with you the next time. And I'll keep it from your mother."

What Ted did not tell him was that he had been sitting at home quietly reading the newspaper when suddenly a feeling of extreme concern for his son overwhelmed him and he just knew he had to hurry to the water and see if he was okay. He felt so grateful that he had been given that intuition or whatever it was. He remembered other times this had happened.

They walked home in quiet companionship, father and son, even closer now if that was possible. Neither could have possibly imagined how that bond would be put to the test over the next year.

***

Autumn was upon them and the time for returning home was fast approaching. They had to make the most of every day, filling it with new adventures. They took day trips to Totnes, Torquay, Abbotsbury and Weymouth. A hiking trip on the coastal path at Lullworth Cove though, was the highlight of all their outings.

Bev sat on the rocks near the beach looking out to sea. If anyone was to observe, her face was unreadable but her thoughts were foreboding and fearful for the future. She really couldn't justify why she felt that way, she just felt that a change was coming and hoped to be prepared for it. She really didn't want to return home, she was happy here in spite of all the strange happenings. She and Ted had been closer than they had been in a long while and, for this, she was grateful. But she just had her intuition that all that was about to change.

That evening after supper they all took the little path behind the property which led to Langdon Court manor house. It was one of their favourite walks as it passed through fields bordered by sweet chestnut trees, wild apple, hawthorn, blackberry and sloe. Bev had spent many hours here with her thoughts, picking the fruit for homemade jams and apple sauce.

The medieval manor house was said to have been visited by Henry VIII and other royals including Edward VII with his mistress, the actress Lily Langtry. It was set amongst well-manicured gardens with picnic tables and benches out on the front lawn where guests could sit and enjoy drinks and meals. They selected a place to sit and Ted went into the bar to order drinks and snacks. He came out with a laden tray and they sat talking and laughing until darkness forced them back to the cottage.

They had left no light on so all was in darkness. As Ted opened the door and reached for the light switch, he felt an icy cold hand on his shoulder. The others had lingered in conversation, taking their time to enter the cottage so were unaware. He shuddered at the touch but shrugged it off as his imagination playing tricks and held the door open for the others.

The next morning, Phil was the first to notice a change in his father. "What's wrong with Dad?" he queried as Bev set out the breakfast. "Nothing that I know of, dear. Although he has said nothing to me, I'm sure he's a bit anxious about our trip to Heathrow and getting us all home in one piece. I haven't noticed anything unusual."

"There's just something different about his eyes," he sighed and sat at the table spooning sugar on his bowl of cornflakes.

Ted had showered and come down to the kitchen where he poured a cup of coffee. "We have to start packing today to get an idea of how much luggage we will have, Bev."

Bev looked at him directly and agreed with him. She could not detect anything in his eyes or his manner to give cause for concern. But when Tess also asked if everything was okay with Dad, it made her wonder. I'll just watch and wait until we're on home soil, she thought to herself.

She would look back on that day as the beginning of her children's uncanny ability to detect psychic influence on their father long before she was ever aware.

From the Dark to the Light

If ever they were asked, Bev and children would say they would rather forget about the following two years of their lives, for they were the dark years.

Having returned from England, it did not take long to shift back to their old lifestyle. The children back to school for Tess's last year and back to work.

But life was just not as it should be. Ted had changed. It seemed as though he had carried along from England the burden of another's soul. He was moody and irritable with the kids, he even looked different. He seemed to have lost his joie de vivre. Slowly, day by day, the fabric of the marriage wore away and when it became threadbare, through the holes came an evil and threatening force in the guise of another woman. In his altered state, he had been vulnerable.

Ted had led them through hell with a downward spiral of lies, deceit and infidelity. He would say after the fact that he had been seduced by a woman who patiently waited like a spider for just the right moment to catch her victim, and it may have been so. It had all been so well orchestrated by his mother and her friend, Jacquie. Perhaps it was inevitable, at any rate he had succumbed.

Bev felt totally and utterly betrayed. She had always felt that their marriage was a special one and that Ted was better than most men. But he had proved her wrong, and that he was just an ordinary man after all. Bev and his mother were not on speaking terms yet again for some slight or another and it left an excuse for Ted to say he was visiting her on his own, sometimes staying overnight. But that was not the case.

On one occasion, Bev was getting ready for bed and found pinned to the sleeve of her housecoat a note saying he would be away for a few days, something had come up with his mum and he needed to take her somewhere for a few days.

He told her not to worry, that he would phone. He never did and days later came home with some lame excuse or another.

Bev tried to keep it from the children for as long as she could but they were teenagers now and could see the change in their father too. It was his lack of interest in family life and other little things that gave him away. He began to drink in secret and Bev would find whiskey bottles hidden in the garage or back cupboards. He'd say he was going out and when questioned, an argument would ensue. It was all so nasty.

Then one evening when he had not come home, Bev decided to look the woman's phone number up in the directory. She didn't think she would really lower herself to call her. But to her surprise, the entire page from the book had been torn out. And so she borrowed the neighbour's directory; wrote the number and the address down.

When he finally confessed, Bev tried to persuade him to end the affair but he would not and then he walked out.

A few days later when he had not returned, she did something she would later, always regret. She called the woman and asked if Ted was there? Surprised by the phone call, Jacquie confirmed that he was.

"Well, you can tell him that I am on my way to bring him home," Bev yelled. The phone was hung up in her ear, which infuriated her even further.

"Come, kids, we're going to get your father." They reluctantly climbed in the car. When Bev arrived at her house, her car was gone, so she knocked hard on the door. Ted came to the door, looking dishevelled and drunk. Bev railed into him insisting that he "COME HOME NOW!" When he refused, she slapped his face in front of the kids. Ted stood shocked on the doorstep and watched as Bev and children left him standing there. They cried all the way home.

That evening, Bev didn't quite know where to put herself she was so distraught. She ran a bath and submerged in the deep hot water up to her neck. Slow tears of hurt and betrayal rolled down her cheeks until it seemed that the level of the water had risen by inches. She felt so unclean, so contaminated, so ruined. She had taken her marriage vows seriously, but Ted had let her down, did the unthinkable. And then in a flash, she realized that she had been forewarned all those years ago. 'He will leave you for a woman named Jacquie.' It had happened just as his mentor had predicted. However, he had not predicted what the outcome would be. She realized that would be up to her.

They all reacted in different ways, each in their own misery.

Tess wanted nothing to do with her father. She was at the age to realize what he had done. She slammed her bedroom door and threw things about in her room. She cried bitter tears and vowed she would never forgive her father.

Phil was devastated. He would go for long walks on his own and return hours later with eyes red and swollen from weeping. Then he would lie on his bed, staring at the ceiling, not caring to speak to either Tess or Bev.

Bev felt physically sick and took to her bed for a day, going over and over the past in her mind, trying to find if she were to blame. Then realizing that she was made of stronger metal than that, she threw herself out of bed.

"Come along, kids. We're going on a little trip today to somewhere I think you might like." Like a small child, she wanted to retreat to a safe haven and the only place she knew of was that of her childhood home. She had not seen the place in years. But she had a sense that it would be a place of welcome refuge.

On a bright warm autumn day, they drove to the country town of her childhood. It was nestled in a valley surrounded by tall mountains. The air was fresh and heady with the smell of ripening corn, cut hay and cow dung. She had forgotten the country smells but it all felt so right to her. She even laughed at the kid's expressions about the smelly air. They took a stroll through the little village and then on to the lake and the hot springs. With ice cream cones in hand they walked to where the volcanically-heated water bubbled out of the ground and breathed in the healing smell of sulphur.

They fell in love with the place and all agreed that it would be a great place to live. Tess had finished high school and was anxious to find a job until she found what she really wanted to do with her life. Phil had two years of school left; he could graduate from the same school as his mother had so many years ago.

Then back in the village they entered a real estate agents and left with a rental agreement in hand for a small house near the school and shops. Bev was delighted; a new start for them here without Ted would be just what was needed. Here, they could restore a semblance of family life and heal. Without him.

***

Her decision to move was the right thing to do, and by allowing Ted to go his separate way there were no further arguments. Ted even helped them with the move to their new home. He bought his son a new mountain bike and for Tess, a rocking chair she had admired. He was obviously trying to get in their good favour. At the end of the day though, he left. They were on their own and it was okay. Peace reigned.

Bev could not remember the last time she had just sat and looked out the window. But there she sat in her old recliner looking out on a view of the mountains, fields of ripening corn and grazing Holstein cattle. The air was filled with the hum of insects and birdsong. There was a garden in the backyard to be worked. She was in her element.

They were welcomed into the little community and Bev found work in a nursing home. Some of the residents she had known since childhood.

Tess found a job she was happy with and Phil was back at school enjoying new friends and activities.
Christmas came and Ted stopped by with gifts but did not stay. It was the first Christmas the children could remember without their father. Tess's boyfriend, Peter, came for the afternoon. They had a lovely dinner and played games. Bev patted herself on the back, declaring that it had been okay. It had lacked the joviality of the usual family Christmas. But it was okay.

***

On a cold winter evening Ted arrived at their door and was invited to dinner. Tess was staying with a friend in town. Phil updated all his activities with his father, but he had plans with his friends and left soon after dinner. Ted suggested that Bev go out with him for a drink and a chat. She acquiesced. Over a drink in a quiet pub, their eyes locked and before a word could be spoken, unbidden slow tears rolled down Bev' s cheeks.

"Are you happy?" she asked, her lips quivering with emotion and her eyes cast downwards trying to avoid his scrutiny.

"No. I'm miserable," Ted confessed. "It has all been such a huge mistake and absolutely no fault of yours Bev. Never in my life have I known anyone as perfect as you. You have never ever given me cause to wander as I have. I don't honestly know why it happened and any excuse seems *so* lame. I love you and miss you and the kids terribly." He reached across and held her hand.

"Well, Ted, you made the choice. I don't know how it could work for us ever again." Bev said with dry-eyed conviction. She drew her hand away from his grasp. "I really must be getting back. I have work in the morning and you have a long drive ahead of you," she stated with firm resolve.

Ted drove her home in silence, dropped her at her door and went on his way. The following morning though the phone rang just as Phil was about to leave for school. He talked for a few minutes with his dad and then passed the phone to Bev. Ted was in tears on the other end of the phone and soon Bev, too, was crying.

"Please, Bev, I want to come home. I promise it's over, please believe me. When I saw you yesterday, I realized how much I love you and the children."

Bev relented. Eventually Ted moved back home. Phil was elated and couldn't wait to go fishing on the lakes with his dad. Tess, on the other hand, was furious with Bev for taking him back. She was spending less time at home. She was busy with her job and with friends. She had *a life*.

"You do what you want, Mum, but if it were me, there would be no coming back. He doesn't deserve you after what he's done," she was adamant.

"Well, my darling, when you love someone it is hard not to forgive and try again and you know your brother needs his father around." Bev pulled her close and hugged her. "Everyone deserves a second chance, dear. Let's try, okay?

"Well, only if I can just ignore him for a while, maybe it will be fine. He deserves to suffer just a little."

"You just keep yourself busy doing what you love best, Tess. Stay more with friends for a while. Give it time," Bev stated and to this Tess agreed.

***

And so it was that Ted returned to the fold. He was very remorseful and many nights he lay awake wishing he could change the past. Bev was pleasant enough to him but he could not blame her for keeping him from her bed. He knew full well that he was on trial with her and would have to prove himself, and that would take time. Tess had given him a reluctant hug on his return but he could tell that she was bitter under the façade. Phil, on the other hand, could not have been happier; he had felt outnumbered by his mum and sister during his father's absence.

Bev had said the words, "I forgive you", but it was the forgetting that was the hard part. She had felt at times that Philip Canton had forsaken them all. But then she remembered being asked *do you love this man?* When she had replied that she did, she was told that *it would be a rocky road.* At that time in her life she had no idea how rocky the road would be or how she would be tested. But her love for Ted and her faith had brought them through. She believed that he was still near.

***

They were all very busy. Bev worked long hours at the nursing home. Ted helped Tess with the opening of a book store. Phil was busy at school, working a part-time job on weekends and mountain biking

207

with his friend.

The garden helped immensely with the healing of hurt souls. Tess took pride in her herb garden, spending long hours there with her cats at play. Bev, too, found peace working in her vegetable garden and decided she would enter some of her produce in the annual fair. She also became very active in the community.

Life ticked along comfortably and then the love Bev and Ted had felt for each other in the beginning rekindled. It went very slowly at first, with just a look, a touch in passing, or a hug and then there came a force which seemed to bring them together, doing things neither thought they were capable of.

Bev awoke one morning to the smell of brewed coffee and the sound of Ted bustling about in the kitchen and she came to the realization that she was happy.

Change

The only discontent in the family centred on Ted's mother. It had been many months since Bev had seen her. So when Ted had suggested that he bring her for Christmas, Bev had agreed. It was after all the season for peace and goodwill. She had long ago forgiven Inez for her part in Ted's affair. To harbour upset from the past was far too stressful and unhealthy for Bev's new lifestyle. But she was not prepared for the change she saw in Inez.

She arrived for Christmas dinner, hardly able to hold her head up. She was wearing a neck support, appeared pale and malnourished. She had lost most of her teeth. Bev was shocked at her appearance. She sat at the table and toyed with her food, complaining that the turkey was too tough for her as well as other candid remarks. Tess and Phil were not amused. She was putting a damper on what would have been an otherwise happy Christmas.

"Whatever has happened to your mother?" Bev whispered to Ted in the kitchen while she was serving up the pudding.

"From what she tells me, she suffers so much from arthritic pain that she takes prescription drugs and sleeping pills throughout the day and night and sleeps most of the time. She's probably not eating properly either," Ted whispered.

"I'll talk to her this evening and see what might be done for her," Bev whispered back, putting dessert on a tray. "Let's just try and get her through this dinner." They went back to the dining room and were as cheerful as was possible.

***

"No! Absolutely, no!" Bev stated. Ted had had a conversation with his mother while driving her home the next day. She had not been in a mood to talk to Bev about her health but she did talk to her son. After hearing what she had to say, Ted felt it would be best if she were to come and live with them.

"Mother tells me that she is afraid. She said she woke up one night just recently and that standing in her bedroom was a man in a dark hooded cloak.

She was unable to see his face. He said nothing and just disappeared through the wall. The one thing that she especially noticed was that he was wearing a dark ruby ring that seemed to glow in the dark. The impression that he made on her brain was that he was *the grim reaper* who had come for her," Ted sighed.

Bev's eyes widened as she listened. She could easily dismiss it as the ravings of an old woman on too much medication, but could not, for the fact that she was Ted's mother.

"Well in view of what you tell me, dear, I can understand how she must feel and that you are worried about her. Give me time to think about it."

***

The phone call came one morning just as Ted was about to head out the door to the book store. The doctor stated that he had admitted Ted's mother to hospital for investigation into her recent lab results. Her blood platelet count was dangerously low. She could quite possibly haemorrhage.

They arrived at her hospital bed to witness a woman who looked as though she might blend right into the mattress; she seemed so withered and ill. She reached out a pale hand and grasped Ted's shirt. "I'll be okay, but make sure they give me all of my pills ... I *need* my pills."

"Your pills could be the problem, Mother," Bev spoke up. "Your doctor will do what is best for you. You're in good hands."
"Oh, whatever you say." She closed her eyes and fluttered her hand to wave them from the room. "I just want to sleep."

***

Bev had never imagined herself as a martyr in this lifetime, but she agreed to take Inez to their home and care for her. After almost a month in hospital she had improved greatly, but was advised that she would no longer be able to look after herself. She could stay in long term care and wait for a bed in a nursing home in her own community. Ted was not happy at the prospect of driving back and forth and wanted his mother with them while she waited for a care home nearby. Seeing Inez once in a while was tolerable, but to have her under their roof for twenty-four hours a day every day, for how long? Bev really didn't know how she would cope.

They had raised their children to independence. Tess had her own apartment with a girlfriend. Phil was finishing his last year of school. How fair was it to now have to care for a parent?

Nonetheless she came to stay, took to her bed and was waited on. Bev prepared special meals for her served on a tray in her room three times a day and with numerous cups of tea throughout the day. The room was large enough for her table and chairs. Bev had set up an area with kettle and tea making items so Inez could get up and make her own, but she never did.

She stayed for six long months. Bev had nursed her back to health with good care and nourishing meals. Then a place in a nursing home nearby finally became available. It had been a gruelling experience for them, never having any time to call their own. They were unable to leave her alone for fear she might fall. Bev would look in on her, and she would be sleeping soundly. Bev would just nicely be out in the garden to do some weeding and she would hear Inez calling from her room. They were never able to get away together. They were so relieved to hear this news.

The day she was moved and settled, Bev and Ted breathed sighs of relief. Neither said anything but when they arrived home they began to pack up everything she had left behind and put the house back in order. They knew that no matter what happened, she could not return to stay again.

She settled well in a room with all her things around her; her favourite chair, her TV, her telephone, her pictures and mementos. She began having meals in the dining room, making friends and was active with crafts and outings. Although she had always hated the thought of living in a care home, she was contented.

***

"What we really need is a holiday, Ted." Bev sat across the room from him. She could see that he looked drained. During his mother's stay he had had many breathless attacks. Bev thought that it was her presence that caused the occurrences. "Let's get away to the Island for a few days, the air is fresher there." She got up and crossed the room to him. She knelt before him and held his hands, then leaned in and hugged him close.

"That sounds like a splendid idea, dear. I'd really like that."

They left on a weekend, taking the ferry to the Island. Ted always loved being near water and found that his breathing was better. They enjoyed being tourists in the capital city. It felt as though they had been away for a week instead of a few days.

The next few weeks were taken up with activities for Phil's High School graduation. He had passed all his exams and they were so proud of the handsome young man he had become. He was flexing his wings for independence; had his own car, a close-knit circle of friends and a part-time job that he was now able to work full time.

***

One afternoon as Bev was pouring the jelly she had made into jars, Ted sat at the kitchen table watching her. She could see that he appeared absorbed in his thoughts. He sipped at his tea and flipped through the newspaper.

"What is it, dear? You look as though you have something on your mind? Do you want to talk about it?" She put the last lid on a jar of the blackberry jelly.

"I was wondering if you would mind if I got away by myself for a few days. I just need some time on my own. I thought I'd camp and do some fishing. Phil is too busy with his friends to join me." He leaned in the doorway studying her face; waiting for an excuse to keep him home. But to his delight, Bev agreed.

"You go dear; it would do you a world of good to have some time alone. I will quite enjoy being at home to catch up on the garden and other things I have neglected lately. I have several days off from work." She smiled at the look of surprise on his face.

He wasted no time in getting ready for his camping trip. It was not far to travel, he would set up his tent near the fast-flowing river and fish for his meals. He began by putting all his gear in the truck and Bev made him a sandwich and sorted out other supplies he would need. Within the hour, he was on his way.

Ted had found just an ideal place to put up his tent. He noticed that a middle-aged couple were camped some distance away from him; it would be quiet he thought, especially as it was a week day. Weekends were a different matter.

Ted was in his element. He had spent all afternoon fishing. Low-flying insects dipped near the surface, enticing the fish to jump here and there.

He had eaten the sandwich Bev had packed for him and he was beginning to feel the first grumblings of hunger when he felt a tug on his line. It was a catch.

After playing the fish for a while he reeled it in; it was a nice pan-sized trout, and then another catch. He had caught his supper.

While the fish sizzled in the fry pan over an open fire, he sat with a cigarette and beer and mused over the past months. He was grateful that his mum was settled. He thought about his son's graduation and how proud he was of him.

He thought about Tess and how happy she seemed with her partner, Alonzo. But mostly he thought of Bev; how she had been such a rock caring for his mother, how patient and kind she had been. He realized it had not been easy for her.

She had been kind in forgiving him for all his indiscretions and his blatant affair. She had always been there for him; was the only one who really understood and believed in him. *I have been a terrible husband. I will try to make it up to her.*

Night fell. Bright stars were visible. The camp fire had burned out. An owl hooted somewhere deep in the forest.

Ted crawled into his tent and zipped up the door flaps against insects. A huge moth fluttered at the screening, attracted to his lamp. He settled on the camp bed, stretched and yawned and closed his eyes to blackness. It had been a relaxing day, he thought.

As he began to drift into sleep, there was a humming in his head and the distinct smell of aromatic tobacco smoke. His eyes snapped open to the sight of his brother sitting at the foot of his bed as though in daylight. With legs crossed and wearing his signature shiny black boots, he nonchalantly smoked a long clay pipe. He sat for what seemed like an eternity to Ted before he spoke.

"So, she has taken you back? You rogue! You do *not* deserve her! There was nothing Ted could say to that. "Come home brother, hear again the abbey bells." And then the little tent was in darkness as before and Ted was left wide awake trying to absorb the impact of the visitation and the words which were spoken.

He stayed for another two days, pondering on the idea of returning once again to England. He knew that Bev would jump at a chance of a getaway for the two of them. He would run it by her.

***

Bev had spent a blissful few days on her own. She had walked around her garden; pulled a weed here and there and filled her basket with baby carrots, new potatoes and pea pods. She sat on the back porch shelling the peas; popping some in her mouth and enjoying the sweet flavour. She reclined on the chaise lounge with her face to the sun, savouring the peaceful time to herself. She couldn't remember the last time she had been able to just sit and relax.

Many thoughts surfaced. She thought over the many months she had been tied down with the care of Ted's mother and the things they had discussed. Inez had no contact with the woman, Jacquie. Ted had made it clear to her that contact was not an option. However, she disclosed that before she had gone into hospital, the woman had attempted to contact Ted through her. She was hurt and bitter, had even faked a suicide attempt for attention. Inez had no sympathy.

On one occasion the phone rang and when Bev had answered, there was no reply. She sensed though that it was the woman, Jacquie, on the line.

Bev wasn't sure where the words came from at the time, but they spilled from her mouth... "I win, you lose!" She was certain she heard a hiss like that of a viper and the phone was hung up in her ear with a loud clunk.

Bev laughed out loud and then the saying 'hell has no fury like that of a woman scorned' came to mind. She also remembered that she had heard the words, 'I win, you lose' spoken to her many years previous, when a sinister force had overtaken Ted. She shuddered at the memory. But now she had the conviction that she truly was the winner.

She sat for longer reflecting on so many things. It was difficult to fathom that her babies were now fledglings. Where had the years gone? They seemed to have passed in the blink of an eye; her Tess a beautiful young woman, strong willed and doing her own thing. She thought of Phil, her baby, how handsome he had become, how eager for independence. She was so proud of them.

She thought then of Ted, of how he had regained her trust. It had not been easy for either of them. She still feared the possibility of the woman harassing and stalking him. She had heard of such things. She knew of one place where she would be unable to bother their life, a place where she was unlikely to follow. That place was England.

Just then the phone rang and she jumped up to answer it. It was Ted.

"Hi, love, just want you to know that I miss you and I'll be home tomorrow by suppertime," he assured.

"I miss you too, dear. All is well here. Come home safely."

"Oh, by the way, I've got a splendid idea. We'll talk when I get home." Bev could hear the excitement in his voice.

"I look forward to that, Ted. Bye for now." She hung up the phone thinking; *I bet we're on the same wavelength.*

England, Autumn 1996

Sherborne had changed little in the years since their last visit. The ancient Tudor cottage where they stayed was only a stone throw from the abbey and to hear the bells again was so incredibly nostalgic. Ted could hardly believe that he was there. Once the decision had been made for this holiday everything just fell into place and it just felt right to have his wife all to himself.

They had planned to begin this adventure with a walk to Sandford Orcas to relive old memories. It was a gorgeous September morning, warm with the hint of a breeze as they started down the Sandford Orcas road. Nothing had changed. It seemed like a flashback to that very first day so many years ago when they had experienced it for the first time. The thatched-roofed cottage on their left was there still although the thatch had aged from golden to gray. An old gent gathered harvest from the garden and waved as they passed by. Bev recalled how she had smelled the scent of smoke on her very first visit and even now there was a hint in the air.

Further along, a horse and rider passed by. The young lady in full riding habit sat her mount proudly and gave them a friendly nod. Then around a bend, the old oak tree came in view. Bev couldn't help it; with a cry of glee she ran to the trunk and gave it a hug, as though it were an old friend. Ted laughed at the sight and snapped her picture.

They wandered past the homes on both sides of the road, admiring the gardens and apple trees laden with fruit. And then in front of them stood the old Mitre Inn, just as it had for hundreds of years. The outside appearance was as they had remembered; window boxes full of autumn blossoms and shutters brightly painted. The old oak door creaked as Ted pushed it open to be greeted by a friendly golden Labrador. It was not John who called out a welcome from behind the bar, but a new publican. John and Julie had apparently sold up, split up and moved on many years ago. The bar was in a different location to what they remembered and looking around they could see that the interior had been totally changed but in a complimentary way.

It was lunchtime and the atmosphere buzzed with friendly banter and smelled of good food and drink. They sat at a small table in the corner and gazed about at the decor and paintings while waiting for their order.

When their food and drinks arrived, Bev couldn't resist snapping a photo of Ted holding up his pint of dark ale with a jovial "Cheers!"

"I have dreamed about this moment for so long," he exclaimed with misty eyes. Then he took a big swig of the nectar and grinned.

"I know you have, dear. That's why this is so special." She reached across and squeezed his hand. Then putting her camera aside, she tucked into her chicken sandwich, and declared how yummy it was.

Following lunch, they headed out towards the church and manor house further down the road. There it loomed, just as grand and imposing as it had always been, just as they had remembered.

"This is why this country is so special," Ted exclaimed. "Nothing changes. You can go away for years and when you return, everything is just as it was, preserved for generations." Bev agreed wholeheartedly, thinking how relatively new buildings back home were just bulldozed down and new ones built in their place. She lovingly patted the ancient stone walls and smelled the roses climbing there. They walked under the arch to the gravelled courtyard. The garden door was open, welcoming visitors to the manor. They chose not to go inside. Ted did not feel ready for an onslaught of the psychic. It was enough just to be there again, enough to relive all the old memories. They walked hand in hand out under the arch and into the cool atmosphere of the church. It was quiet; none but they at this time of day and they walked the aisles inhaling the pervasive smell of old. Bev sat on a pew, gazed at the altar and said a silent prayer of thanksgiving for all her blessings. Ted walked about deep in thought and then there was a rushing in his ears and he had to sit down. His head was filled with sound: the scuffling sounds of shovelled earth as though the digging of a grave and then the stink of rotting apples... *death*. To Bev, he appeared as though in prayer sitting there with his head on his knees. She went to him and sat beside him. It was minutes later that she realized he was in trance. She grasped him gently on the shoulder and shook him from his reverie. Although he appeared a bit dazed, he admitted nothing and so she let it pass without comment. They just got up and slowly walked out and into the sunlight.

***

Ted sat in the parlour, historical books before him on the table. He hoped that by doing some research into the history of Sherborne, he might find some clue to his past life. He had total recall of the episode in the church earlier that day. He could still remember the sound of digging and the smell of death. He felt as though he had been handed a puzzle with a few pieces missing and all he had to do was find the missing pieces and he would understand all about his past life. He truly hoped so; maybe he would no longer be subjected to the dreams that haunted him. Bev would help him. He knew he could count on her.

After supper that evening, they walked out to the red telephone box across from the abbey to make phone calls to the kids and Inez. All was well with them, but Ted learned from his mother that his godfather, Robert, had been diagnosed with a malignant brain tumour and was not expected to live much longer. It occurred to Ted that maybe he had been given a premonition of impending death and it had nothing to do with his past life. He would give Jane a call in the morning.

Ted did phone Jane the next morning. She was so pleased to hear from him and that he was in the country.

"You can't go home without seeing Robert. Please come, Ted. He would love to see you and Bev... before he..." she broke down and wept over the phone.

"Why, of course we'll come. I'll talk to Bev and will call you back by this evening, okay?" She seemed satisfied with that.

"I'll tell him that you are coming, it will give him such a lift."

They sat in the little parlour, glasses of pale cream sherry in hand and talked about the man Ted had loved all his life.

"How bloody unfair is that? I can't believe that after just two years of retirement, Robert's life should end so abruptly." Ted rubbed his forehead in that way he always did when he was upset. "To think that he gave all those years to that job in the city and now this? Jane will be devastated."

"Yes, it does seem cruel, but it's not how long we live that counts, but what we have done with our lives. Robert has had a good life and touched so many people with his fun nature and goodness," Bev sighed. "We can only hope that he has a good death."

The news of Robert's illness put a damper on the plans they had had for the day so they stayed local and arranged to travel up to Essex by train the following morning. They could stay at least two days without too much interruption to their schedule. It might very well be the last time they would see him.

They arrived at the Sherborne station early and boarded a train to London where they would have to change to the Gidea Park line. They found a comfortable seat facing in the direction of travel and bought snacks from the young woman pushing a trolley down the centre aisle. Ted recalled many memories of Robert from his earliest childhood to adult life. But it was Bev who brought up something that Robert had talked about in the past. He had told about being in a train crash years earlier when he had been on his way home from work. It had happened on a damp autumn night. He recalled that it was dark outside and suddenly there was the sound of squealing brakes, a crashing grinding noise and he was tossed about along with all the other passengers. He had hit his head on something, but was able to climb through a broken window. In his confusion and shock, he had scrambled up an embankment and at the top had hailed a cab.

Jane had been anxiously waiting for his return. He was always promptly in the door the same time every night and that night he was very late. When Jane heard his key in the door she was relieved but totally unprepared for the dishevelled state his was in. There was dried blood crusted over a huge bump on his scalp. She took one look at him and after sitting him down, she rang for the doctor. He was told he had suffered a concussion and should stay home and rest for a few days. He had not gone to hospital.

"It makes me wonder if that earlier trauma to his head could have been the cause of his brain tumour," Bev pondered.

It had been a long journey but when they arrived at Gidea Park station they decided to walk. They remembered the way, even though it had been many years. They took the very route that Robert had taken all his working life and would never walk again. They headed down the little streets, past the allotment gardens, through an alleyway and then the familiar road came in sight and the old home. Then they were at the old blue door, ringing the bell with apprehension of what they would see. Jane opened the door and gave them each a warm hug.

"Prepare yourselves, he is not the Robert you saw last."

It was true; they could hardly keep from gasping at the sight of the man who sat in his favourite recliner in the sitting room. He was as a worn-out husk of his former self. He was skinny and bald from the radiation and chemotherapy, was unable to walk and had lost the use of his left arm. But his speech and thought process had not yet been affected and he greeted them with a warm smile. He had always been a smoker and enjoyed an alcoholic drink so these vices were his only pleasure. They sat with him in quiet reflective conversation until his home care workers came to put him to bed. They arrived only in the morning and then at bedtime, so Jane still did a lot of heavy lifting and running for him. It had clearly worn her out. She was getting very little sleep at night.

"He's waiting for a hospice bed," she sighed. "But it is wearing me out and I don't have the patience I should have with him."

"Well if he needs anything in the night tonight I'll see to him and you sleep," Bev said with the authority of so many years of experience.

But after one night of getting up to him at least every half hour, Bev was adamant that his doctor be called for a home visit and get him admitted to hospital. He needed more care than he was getting. Jane agreed and after a home assessment he was admitted to hospital to await the hospice bed.

They stayed just one more night and then the following day visited Robert in hospital. He was much more comfortable. Ted helped him into a wheelchair and took him to the smoking room for a 'fag' as he referred to cigarettes. It was here that they bade him farewell for the last time. They were holding back tears as they hugged him saying, "We'll see you soon." What could one say to a dying man? "Cheerio, God bless," was Robert's farewell. He waved with his good hand and Jane wheeled him back to his bed.

She bade them goodbye and then they were all in tears. Luckily their taxi was waiting to take them to the station for the return journey to Sherborne.

***

A day out in Glastonbury proved to be just what they needed to raise their spirits. It was another gorgeous day to roam the streets and enter shops of interest. They found a 'new age' shop in which to buy gifts for the kids; photos of the most recent crop circles that had formed during that summer, all of them intricate and fascinating, crystals, beads and books, the choice was endless.

All the walking and shopping had made them hungry so they sat outside in the courtyard at a table to sample the 'roots and shoots' on offer. Ted wasn't keen on such fare, but he was hungry and discovered that his sprout and chicken sandwich was tasty after all.

Following lunch, they walked to the Chalice Well Gardens to sit in the magical surroundings. One could sample the water that bubbled from a spring that never seemed to run dry. It was said to have healing properties, very high in iron which turned the rocks a rusty red.

Glastonbury Tor loomed behind them. They would have loved to make the climb to the top to view the surrounding countryside but they were weary and put it off for another time. It would be late by the time they reached Sherborne. Bev still had to shop for supper and maybe do a laundry, so they left and walked back to the bus stop in quiet reflection.

The following day they took a bus trip to Salisbury. From the height of the double-decker bus the magnificent cathedral spire came into view. Bev sucked in her breath at the sight. It never failed to overwhelm her; the tallest spire in all the country. They walked down the lanes of the water meadows and sat for a time under a huge Lebanon Cedar tree admiring the cathedral from that perspective.

The door was open and they wandered into the cool, silent atmosphere of that most holy place. Down the aisles they went, taking in the script on ancient tombs, massive pillars soaring to the elaborate ceiling and the splendorous stained-glass windows. It was the west window in all shades of blue that seemed to draw them closer and caused them to sit for a while in quiet prayer for dear Robert. With souls fed spiritually they left the place in search of food for their bodies.

On the main thoroughfare a 15th century pub, 'The New Inn', caught their attention and they entered to a busy lunch hour rush. Weaving through the crowded room they made their way to the back garden which appeared almost uninhabited. Bev sat at a table under an umbrella to gaze at the spire from another view while Ted went back to the bar to order their meal. She was deep in thought when Ted returned; it seemed he had only just left. Before long their meal arrived and Ted tucked into his stilton ploughman's with gusto.

"I could get quite used to this," he exclaimed with a mouthful of salad greens. "I agree," Bev said as she bit into her turkey sandwich.

Following lunch, they wound their way down another crowded street where a market had been set up for the day. It was a colourful and noisy place, just what Bev loved; fresh produce, bric-a-brac and clothing. Everything was a delight to the senses. They wove among the crowds picking out some fresh veggies here, and there gifts to take home. They had been absorbed in the atmosphere of the place, time flew by and it was time to catch the train back to Sherborne.

It had been a lovely day and as Bev prepared the evening meal she thought to herself, I could get used to all this, indeed.

Over the next week they visited other places they had not before seen: Exeter with its beautiful cathedral and shopping district, Exmouth, a seaside town, and Teignmouth, another seaside resort, all in the county of Devon.

They had been enjoying themselves so much that the days just sped by and then it was time to return home. Bev looked around the little cottage with a feeling of regret that she was leaving the place; it had felt so right being there.

The bags were packed, the place tidied and as they closed and locked the door, she had a feeling that they would return. From the back window of the taxi, Ted gazed at the abbey and bid a silent farewell as they were whisked off to the train station, destination Heathrow.

***

It was always good to come home, no matter if away for only an afternoon or weeks. They had missed the kids and were happy to see their smiling faces at the airport. There was much to talk about and they were exhausted by the time they reached their front door.

To Bev, it had seemed as though they had been away for much longer than two weeks and it felt weird to walk into that house. She felt like a stranger; as though she no longer belonged there. She looked around at their modern furniture and state of the art kitchen and remembered that less than a day earlier she had been comfortable in an ancient cottage in England. Bev caught Ted's eye and she could tell that he felt the same. They shared a mutual feeling that the return to Sherborne would be much sooner than later.

A Year of Death 1997

Death came knocking that summer. Ted could not help but feel that he had been given a premonition of death that day in the church of St. Andrew in Sanford Orcas last autumn. He recollected the scraping, grating sound of grave digging and the smell of death in his nostrils. It had haunted his dreams.

He was present with two other men; one man dug a grave where a huge flagstone had been moved, the other stood with him watching as the earth was flung aside in a pile. An unshrouded body of a man lay on the cold flagstones of the cellar floor. This would be his grave, in a cellar, in a manor house.

Ted woke in a sweat. He lay for what seemed like ages, trying to make some sense of his dream. It had seemed so real. He played it over and over in his mind until his thoughts turned to other things. An image of his godfather formed behind his closed eyes and he drifted back to sleep.

His beloved godfather, Robert, had died peacefully in a hospice bed only weeks after their return. Crying over the phone, Jane had expressed how grateful she was that they had come to see him; it was all he had talked about right up to the end. The funeral had gone well. She was somehow able to cope.

One of Bev' s sisters had lost her husband to lung cancer that summer and then shortly thereafter, her only brother passed suddenly. As he had not been well for some time, his death was expected, but it didn't make it any easier. Then only a month following his death, the eldest sister died of a heart attack. She had been very close to her brother, they were soul mates as children and she took his death very hard. It was supposed that the heart attack was the result of her overwhelming grief at his loss.

Bev showed tremendous strength in the face of it and was a strong support to her family. She had been through it all before; with her first husband and then one by one her parents.

***

Bev was driving home from work one August evening when she was alerted to the sound of police sirens screaming in the distance. With quick thinking, she pointed the car down a less travelled road as she sensed that there had been a car accident on the route she would normally take.

She pulled in the driveway and was getting out of the car when Ted met her at the door, his eyes wide with disbelief.

"Did you hear about the accident?"

"No, but I sensed that something was happening so I took a shortcut home. I heard the sirens," she stated.

"No, no, nothing local. It's all on the news. Princess Diana has been in a horrendous car crash in France," he exclaimed as he returned to his chair in front of the television. What a shock it was. Bev peeled off her work clothes, her attention now focused on the TV screen.

Tess and Phil flew in the door to announce what they had also just heard only to be silenced by Bev's upheld hand as she watched in disbelief.

And then the breaking news... Princess Diana has succumbed to her injuries. She had died there in France in the early hours of the morning.

Princess Diana dead? How can that be possible? These were the questions asked by everyone all over the globe. The family sat in a state of shock.

"I need a stiff drink," Bev announced as she got up from her chair, the tears streaming down her cheeks already. Tess joined her in the kitchen and they hugged and cried together. Ted and Phil sat with stiff upper lips, pushing down feelings as men will do.

The wine was poured. They sat and sipped and watched and grieved. All of Bev's feelings of grief for her lost siblings resurfaced afresh and she cried and cried and got quite drunk as well.

***

225

It was only a matter of days following Princess Diana's funeral that they received further bad news. Inez had fallen and fractured her hip.

She lay in a hospital bed looking frailer than ever, but her tongue was as sharp as a tack.

"Don't touch me!" she snapped at Bev as she tried to arrange her pillows to a more comfortable position. "Have you come to gloat over me?" she levelled at Ted. She always had a way of making him feel guilty for her pain.

"Mother, that's not called for. We know you are suffering, but once that hip is mended you'll be your old self again." He leaned down to kiss her sweaty forehead. "We'll just go have a word with the surgeon now." He gave Bev a look to say let's get out of here. "We'll see you after your surgery tomorrow, be good." They quickly took their leave with her glowering at their backs.

Her surgery went well. They came to see her on one occasion to find her already sitting up in a chair. She would be up and walking again soon.

"Have you had any visitors, Mum?" Ted wondered.

"Well I've had a man from the Houses of Parliament come to see me." She said very convincingly. "He was standing at the foot of my bed in the night."

"What do you mean, from the Houses of Parliament, Mother?" Ted laughed.

"You know, he was dressed in an old-fashioned way with a strange hat. I asked him if I was going to die. He said with a very posh English accent, 'No, not yet, Inez, you have not suffered enough,' and then he just disappeared. I rang for the nurse and she said there had been no one in, visitors weren't allowed that time of the night."

"You must have been dreaming, Mother," Ted dismissed, all the while realizing that she had had a visit from his brother. He looked across at Bev who nodded in acceptance of what she knew he was thinking.

She was back in the nursing home two weeks after surgery and seemed to manage fairly well. It was a relief for Ted and Bev to not have to drive to and from the hospital that seemed to take up so much of their time.

***

September came and went. They were all very busy. Bev had her garden to harvest, jams and jellies to be made and vegetables to put by in the freezer. One never knew what to expect with winter on the west coast. It was best to prepare. About mid-October, word came from the nursing home that Inez would again have to undergo surgery. The circulation to her toes to the previously fractured hip was very poor. Several toes had blackened and were becoming gangrenous.

She would either have to have a below the knee amputation or a procedure to improve the circulation, either option was a risk. She opted for the procedure.

The day before her surgery the family gathered around her bedside. Tess and Phil hated the hospital atmosphere of strange smells and sounds and the murky green of the walls. It was enough to make anyone sick just being there. But they put on a brave face for Nana. Although conversation was light and a laugh shared; there was somehow a feeling that this would be the last visit with her. She looked so frail and tiny in the high bed; her thin grey hair was scraped back from her face revealing hollow cheeks and making her blue eyes appear as though the light had gone out.

"We'll be here at the hospital while your surgery is taking place, Mum. Try not to worry." Ted leaned down to kiss her brow. "Love you. Be good, see you tomorrow." Then Bev and the children took it in turn to say their goodbyes.

"Love you, see you soon." Bev held her cool hand, noting how the blue veins protruded through the papery frail skin and thought to herself what a very poor surgical risk she was and would probably not fare well. But she was between a rock and a hard place and would not get better if left as she was.

***

That night after the nurses had made their rounds and the lights were dimmed, Inez lay for long hours thinking about her life. Yes, she had to admit that her childhood had been happy, but she had been forced into a cruel reality when her mother had passed away. There was no escaping her father's strict rules and her stepmother's overbearing personality until she had met her Bernard. She had waited until after her 22nd birthday to marry him. They had been exceedingly happy for the first short while of their marriage. A home was bought for them by his father and there was money to furnish it as they pleased. She had no idea that Bernard's family was so wealthy. He had even bought homes for her two sisters, said they were a tax haven. She hadn't questioned it then, had finally found out that her father-in-law's wealth was from an ill-gotten source. But then the war broke out and her husband was called for service to his country. She felt that she had made the most of the six long years that he was away. The bombing raids had been truly frightening. She remembered running for shelter at the wailing of the air raid sirens, never knowing whether the house would be there afterwards. But she had been a strong woman and had been through the London blitz and lived to tell the tale. She had been blessed with a son when she didn't think she would ever have children. But she knew she had not always been a good mother, there were so many other things she preferred to do with her time. She worked; she loved to dance and party. She realized that her smoking habit had been the cause of most of her health problems today, but that was what everyone did in her era. She felt that all in all, she had had a good life. Her husband had been a good provider; she had always had a home, had never gone hungry and she had always had holidays and trips back to her England.

She let out a deep sigh. I am about to turn eighty, I've had a good life, I miss my Bernard and I really don't want to live any longer. It's too late now to tell my son about the property in Devon or any of the other family secrets. Just as his father was unable to tell him on his deathbed, so may it be with me. It's all Piercy family business anyway. He no longer needs me and I don't wish to be any more of a burden. *God be with me,* she whispered.

***

Ted and Bev sat all the long hours while her surgery was taking place, sipping strong coffee, waiting and waiting. While they sat in a waiting room just outside of the recovery centre, they could hear the nurses talking to her. Her surgery was over.

"Breathe, Inez, breathe!" they commanded her. But she would not breathe on her own. Moments later, the surgeon appeared to announce that although the surgery went well, she had to be hooked up to a ventilator as she was not breathing on her own. Only time would tell what the outcome would be.

Ted and Bev went home and waited for news from the hospital. It came at 7am the next morning. She was doing poorly, had suffered a stroke and they were taking her for a CAT scan. They wasted no time in getting to the hospital.

They were met by the surgeon who ushered them to a waiting room. They were given the bad news that she had died on her way to the X-ray department. She had never regained consciousness. The surgeon apologised profusely for the outcome and conveyed his sincerest sympathy. Unfortunately, the surgery had been risky but necessary.

In a state of resignation to what Ted had already felt had been the inevitable, they collected her small suitcase and left the hospital. Grief would come later.

The day of her death fell on October 31: Halloween. When Tess was told of her grandmother's death she gave her dad a hug, but could only manage to squeeze out a few tears. Phil did likewise and took it like a man. Neither had been very close to their nana, she had shown little interest in their lives and was not one to show any emotion.

Tess held beliefs deep rooted in pagan culture and felt that there was significance in the fact that she had died on Halloween. It was the ancient Celtic celebration of 'Samhain,' summers end and the beginning of winter. It was an eve when the door to the otherworld opened enough for the souls of the dead to pass through.

It was a day to honour the dead; to pray and remember family members who had died. This year there were four within their family as well as dear Princess Diana who had passed beyond that veil.

Over the next few days Ted would be very busy calling family; his mother's sister in England and his father's only living brother in South Africa and also making arrangements with the funeral home. Inez had requested that no service be held, she wished to be cremated and her ashes to be interred near her husband. Everything she had owned now belonged to Ted.

He found to his surprise that his mother had very little to leave him. What had she done with it, he wondered?

***

Winter came that year with ferocity, as though to sum up an already bad year.

It was a crisp cold day with blue sky when Bev headed off to work. She had agreed to work the evening shift so that her colleagues could enjoy a pre- Christmas party. There had been no warning of inclement weather.

Thankfully all residents of the home were tucked in their beds before the storm hit. It began with a howling hurricane force wind that blew from the far reaches of the canyon and out into the valley. Freezing rain lashed at the windows and the lights flickered. In the next breath, the lights went out. Bev sat at her desk in total blackness, save for a few dim battery back-up lights.

She picked up the phone and breathed a sigh of relief that it was still connected. She quickly dialled the number of the venue where the party was being held to speak with the manager of the home. He informed her that there was a back-up generator and he would be on his way to start it. Bev sat waiting with the sound of the howling wind and lashing rain. The fifteen-minute wait seemed like an eternity. And then the generator kicked in and basic power was restored. It would be adequate until the electricity came back on.

She arrived home to total blackness, save for a fire Ted had started in the fireplace. There was no other source of heat and the water supply which used an electric pump was also cut off. She found a few fragrant candles, lit them and placed them here and there. It gave an almost festive atmosphere in the face of the dire circumstance. They sat in opposite chairs near the fire and sipped sherry to warm them. Then when the power still had not come on, they went to bed and huddled under the duvet.

The storm raged all night. But at some point Bev woke to the sound of a dog barking and realized that the wind had finally died. She got up and gingerly peered out the window. A sliver of the moon lit up the silent scene. As far as she could see there was a vast covering of ice. It shone eerily in the moonlight on every surface; the tree limbs hung in ice, icicles hung from the fencing turning it to lace. It was beautiful but terrible.

She made her way to the fireplace and threw several logs on the dying embers. The fire sprang back to life and she warmed her hands near the flames. She could hear Ted snoring lightly as she crawled back to bed. She curled up to his back and laid thinking of how she detested winter weather, especially wind.

They awoke to sunshine in the morning. The ice glistened in the sunlight and had already begun to thaw, but there was still no power.

"I hate winter!" Ted grumbled as he dug out the old camp stove. But he soon had water boiling for coffee and eggs frying in the pan.

They sat near the fireplace, sipping the strong brew and tucked into fried egg sandwiches. Tess phoned to inform them that she had power in her little place, so they were invited to visit with her until their power returned.

"If it's all right with you, Ted, I'd much rather not be here again next winter," Bev announced.

"Let's make plans for Sherborne in the spring."

"Here, here, I agree wholeheartedly," he replied.

***

Christmas came and went that year. They had celebrated a more subdued affair out of respect for Inez. New Year's Eve though would have been her birthday. Bev and Ted sat together near the fireplace, a roaring fire in the grate and shared a bottle of good port wine. Ted

231

smoked a cigarette and tossed the spent end into the fire. He reached across and fed more logs on the fire and satisfied, sat back to watch it burn. As his eyes focused on the leaping flames there came the old familiar feeling of being consumed. He closed his eyes and relaxed into it.

Bev moved to the kitchen to get them cheese and crackers, and as she turned her back the rumbling voice of Philip Canton caught her unaware.

"Beverley. Come back and sit down. I wish to speak with you."

She warily turned back to the sitting room and took up her position near the fire. Ted was off somewhere else and his brother was in command.

"The time is ripe for returning, my lady, to seek out the hidden places. Tell my brother that he must call his uncle; there are things he needs to know. Also seek out a box tucked away by his mother ..." His voice trailed off. "He grows restless, I must leave now."

Bev roused Ted from his trance state with a shoulder squeeze. "It's almost midnight, Ted, shall we toast the New Year?" He looked a bit stunned.

"Why, yes, dear. Happy New Year, love you." He stood up and enfolded her in his arms and kissed her tenderly.

"I love you too, dear. Happy new year," she murmured in his ear. "I predict it will be a very good year. Now let us get ourselves off to bed, the kids are coming for dinner and I have much to do." She led him by the hand to the bedroom, thinking, *I'll just keep to myself what was said to me until just the right time. There is so much to take in.*

Secrets Uncovered

Bev was doing a spring clean and decided it was high time to go through all of Ted's mother's belongings. It was not a job he wanted to undertake and she could sympathize. It was a difficult thing to go through a person's possessions after their passing; she had remembered drinking red wine in copious amounts to enable her to do so after her first husband had died.

She started first with the trunk of clothes. There was nothing there that she wanted to keep and she knew Tess was not interested. She packed them all in a box and labelled it for charity. Ted had already gone through her papers looking for anything of significance. He had found her will and certificates; births and marriage written in long hand and aged yellow. Also her bank book from a local bank; she had moved her account when she came to stay with them. That had been taken care of long past.

Bev sat in a chair by the window with the ornately-carved wooden jewel box in her lap. It evoked poignant memories of Inez sorting through it from time to time. She would take each old brooch and necklace out and then one by one reverently replace them; it had seemed to give her pleasure. Bev tentatively opened the box. A slanted ray of sunlight filtered through the window and fell on the collection of trinkets, making the rhinestones twinkle. A prism danced on the far wall. Bev removed each and every item; there was nothing there of value, nothing she wanted to keep but she would see if Tess wanted anything before she packed it all up in the charity box. And then, one item in particular at the bottom of the box captured her attention. A key. There was a small paper label attached to it with twine. She picked it out, held it up closer to the window to make out the spidery script... B of E safety deposit box. A burst of excitement filled her; she went through various stages of awe and elation, realizing that the key had been found in a box and belonged to a box that his mentor had foretold.

"Ted!" she called. "Ted, you must come see this, you won't believe what I've found." One could not mistake the excitement in her voice and Ted was aware that his mother's possessions were being sorted, so he hurried from the back porch where he had been putting away his fishing gear.

Bev held up the dangling key with a grin and placed it in his outstretched hand. She studied his face for a reaction and was rewarded with a huge grin.

"Well, I'll never ... I can hardly believe my eyes. She has a stash with the 'old lady of Threadneedle Street,' has she? Well, I'll be damned!" He shook his head incredulously. Bev was rapt with attention.

"What do you mean by 'the old lady of Threadneedle Street?" she wondered. "That's the old name for the Bank of England; it's in London on that street," he laughed. "Well, I wonder what she's hidden away there."

"Come sit down, Ted. There is something I need to share with you." Bev took his hand and led him to his chair near the fireplace. "I'll just get us a drink first."

Ted sat studying the key, turning it over in his hands while she bustled about in the kitchen and then joined him in the chair opposite. She waited while he had a few gulps of his sherry before she spoke.

"On New Year's Eve, I had a visit from your mentor, Philip. He told me that your mother had a box we should seek out and I could only think he may have meant her jewel box. He also said that you would speak with your dad's brother, for what reason he didn't say. He suggested too that the time was ripe for seeking out the hidden places of England. I've kept this to myself because I didn't think you were ready to start delving into the past at that time. I somehow feel that the time is right now as we have talked about returning, not spending another winter here." Bev studied his face as he absorbed what she was saying. "I hope you're not annoyed with me for not mentioning it until now." She gazed into his blue eyes for an answer.

He sat just shaking his head.

"No, love, of course I'm not annoyed with you. You were right; I would not have been ready for all that at the time. Give me a while to take it in and then we'll do some serious digging into whatever may be out there," he smiled.

As they sat there, the phone rang, just as though the powers that be had set in motion something that was preordained. Ted reached for the phone.

"Hello, Ted. Just wondered how you were fairing." It was his uncle Des phoning from South Africa.

"We're all well, thank you, Uncle. It's funny you should call. We had only just been thinking about you."

Uncle Des was never one for mincing words and got right to the point. "If you don't mind me asking ... What are you planning to do with the Devon property? I might be interested if you were selling?"

Ted was silent for some minutes. "Are you still there, Ted?"

"Yes, but I have no idea what you are talking about. I know of no property in Devon." Ted was shocked. "Tell me more, "he prompted.

"You mean your father never told you about the inn that he inherited after our father passed?"

"Dad seemed as though he was trying desperately to tell me *something* but he was unable to do so because of the stroke. Perhaps it was about this."

"As he was the eldest male in the Piercy line, it went to him. Father purchased it after the war and although he never lived there, your parents used to stay there on holiday. I can't believe you were not aware of it. Your dad arranged for a couple to oversee and run the place. He said they had done so very efficiently all those years. They must be getting on in years by now. You haven't seen the deed in amongst his things?"

"No. Mother kept all his papers; I never saw anything after his death. I had absolutely no idea, believe me, Uncle; I would have been there in a flash."

"I spoke to Bernard about a month before he died and he said then that he would tell you. Maybe he had an inkling that he was not long

235

for this world, he didn't say. And then to think that your mother never told you either. I'm truly shocked and sorry, Ted."

"No need to apologise, you had no way of knowing. This does come as a shock. I really need time to take it in. We found a key to a safety deposit box for the Bank of England. It may well be that the deed to the property is there. Mother probably thought if I knew of it, I'd be gone and she'd not see me again. Who knows what she was thinking."

"Well, I must go now, Ted. Take care and let me know how you make out. Bye for now, Son."

"Goodbye, Uncle, thank you for telling me. I'm really grateful."

Ted put the phone down and lowered himself to his chair. He felt a bit faint. Bev sat wide eyed and waiting for him to tell her all that had been said. She had heard the bit about a deed and could hardly contain her elation. After a good space of time, Ted did tell her all that his uncle had said and they chewed it all over at length.

Why had his mother been so secretive and deceptive? Why had she stowed away in a safety deposit box, in another country, anything that might be of importance to her only son? Did she really hate him so much? He recalled that over the years she had made many trips to England by herself, the last time only a year before her death. He remembered that his father had made only three trips back there since his departure; the first was in 1972 when he and Bev had taken that holiday together. Business must have been conducted on those occasions.

"There is really nothing more we can say or do, Bev. Right now it's all 'pie in the sky', absolutely nothing concrete, until we can go to London and check out this little key." Ted let out a sigh of resignation.

"Well, plans will have to be made, love, and you'll feel better once we have set a date to go there. What strikes me the most is that we may never ever have known anything if it weren't for your mentor. I could have easily just packed the entire jewellery box up and sent it to the charity shop with all her other things."

"For that, we can be thankful. Enough said for now, dear, I feel exhausted," Ted exclaimed.

***

Desmond hung up the phone. His expensive leather chair creaked as he leaned back with a snifter of brandy served to him on a silver tray by 'his man' and sat musing over his conversation with Ted.

He had done very well for himself in Port Elizabeth since leaving England all those years ago. He vividly recalled how he and his brother had come to a decision to emigrate. He had come to South Africa and Bernard to Canada. They were both concerned about how their father's dealings in India might affect their lives. They wanted no part of it.

Most certainly they had all benefited from the life in India and the wealth that had been amassed. When others had been struggling to survive after the war, they could quip that they were 'alright Jack, not short of 'a bob.' When others lived in poor housing they had all been comfortable in homes that they owned. When others went hungry on the meagre post-war rations, they dined well on 'black market' food and drink.

It was too bad that it had crumbled all around them. It was too bad their parents had lived in relative poverty; they didn't really have to, it was all a front. At least he and Bernard had had the sense to get out while the going was good.

His father, Edward, had been very shrewd in his dealings; was somehow able to buy the Devon property without a problem. He knew for a fact that a small leather pouch of cut diamonds was hidden there. It was under the stone base beneath the aga cooker in the kitchen of the inn. It was their father's idea.

He and Bernard had overseen the installation and were able to stash it there while the workmen struggled to bring in the cooker. They had looked on, satisfied that it would be safe for as long as the inn was owned by family.

It was this treasure that Desmond coveted, not the property. Ted was obviously oblivious; had not even been aware of the property, let alone the diamonds. They were still a secret that even his mother had not been aware of.

He recalled how he and Bernard had gotten their father drunk on brandy one evening after they had hidden the diamonds, and then asked him.

"Father, tell us now how you came by those diamonds?" Bernard coaxed. "Well, my two Indian men servants; low caste, no families, unable to read or write, afraid of their own shadows; I ordered them to steal for me from one of the palaces. The diamonds were among a few other valuable items. When it was all safely in my possession, I cut out their tongues. Well, I didn't trust them to keep quiet. That took care of it!" he said without remorse.

He and Bernard gasped in utter horror. They knew he had been a ruthless bugger; proud of his military status, but that candid announcement truly shocked them.

"You keep that information as well as the diamonds a secret just between the three of us. Your wives and children are never to know. Do I have your word?"

"I swear, Father," they both replied in unison.

Desmond realized it was getting late. He had taken too much brandy. As he stood to make his way to bed; a severe pain shot through the back of his head, he felt weak and dizzy, and there was numbness in his right arm and leg. In the next instant, he crumpled and fell to the floor with a loud crash, bringing the house servant running. By the time an ambulance arrived, he was stone dead.

***

About a month after Ted had had the conversation with his uncle, a letter with a South African stamp arrived in the mail. It was from his uncle's widow. She had found Ted's address in amongst some of her husband's notebooks and was writing to inform him that Desmond had died of a massive stroke. It was all very sudden; he had died at home.

Ted read the letter over several times before he realized that the day of his death coincided almost exactly to the day his uncle had phoned him, taking into consideration the time difference between Canada and South Africa. His next thought was that had his uncle not called him at that precise moment, he would not have known about his inheritance. It was sad. Although Ted had memories of him only from childhood, it was his family after all.

He had a memory as a little boy sitting and watching his uncle brushing his wife's long blond hair. She was a Swedish lady, beautiful and distant. Now she was widowed. He would send her a card of condolence; it was all he could do.

As he slowly walked to the house from the mailbox, a plan began to formulate in his head. They needed to return to England as soon as possible. Sherborne could wait. London should be first on the agenda and if what his uncle had said was true, it would be on to Devon. He would run this by Bev right away.

He vowed he would not keep all this secret from his children as his parents had done to him. They should be aware should anything unforeseen happen to him and Bev. He was aware that according to British law, his son would inherit the property.

He read the letter to Bev and she read it again before the impact of its content hit her. "It's really sad that your uncle is dead dear, I'm sorry. But had he not called you when he did, you would have no idea about that property."

"Of that I am well aware. Everything happens for a reason and this is as good an example as any. We've got to make plans to go back. But I want the kids to know everything, do you agree?"

"By all means, Ted. We can have a family meeting this evening."

***

Tess and Phil were stunned and equally excited at the news. But like everything else in their lives it would be taken in their stride. They had seen so many changes, this one would be no different, only that they were grownups now.

"Don't worry, you two, we'll be okay. Phil and I are both working and have our own places now, our own lives to lead. It will be an adventure for you," Tess exclaimed and meant it. Phil nodded in agreement.

"Well, if you miss us too much, you'll just have to come and join us. Wherever we are, there will be a place for you," Ted said with conviction.

It made it so much easier to go when they had such great children. They were adaptable by nature and mature beyond their years. But Bev and Ted had never been away from them except for the Sherborne holiday. It would be a true test for all of them.

First Stop London

London sizzled in the summer heat. They had arrived at the start of a weekend and booked into a hotel overlooking St. James's Park. They now strolled through the park hand in hand stretching their legs after the long-haul flight.

"How lovely to be here, just the two of us after all these years. Do you realize Ted that twenty-six years have passed since our first trip here together?" Bev squeezed his hand as they stopped to admire the lush gardens.

"It is hard to believe, dear, but I somehow think that the timing is right. Whatever I am meant to discover, I will this time around, I can feel it in my core," Ted replied with resolve.

On Sunday they visited the art gallery, taking in some of the famous paintings of the past and remembered other times they had been there. Bev especially wanted to see again the works of Jacopo Pontormo and so they gazed for some time at the detail and bright colours of his paintings. She got a strange feeling, knowing that she had been connected in a past life.

It seemed that many hours had gone by before they descended the gallery steps and out into Trafalgar Square. A pub just across the busy street lured them with the smell of food wafting from the open door. Bev started to step out onto the pavement and Ted grabbed her just in time; being jet lagged she had momentarily forgotten the direction that vehicles were driven in England.

"God, Ted, you saved me there!" she yelped. They were in fits of laughter as they entered the busy pub scene. A table for two near the window looked inviting and they were soon tucking into steaming roast beef dinners.

"Well, kid, tomorrow is Monday, so we've got to be at the bank as soon as it opens. No use delaying the mystery of 'the box'."

"I'll be ready," Bev replied as she finished off the last of her drink." And then if we find a deed to a property, we should make plans to leave the city the following day, agreed?"

"Yes, love, we can take a train and maybe rent a car later. We best be getting back to the hotel and catch a good night's rest Jet lag is catching up with me."

***

On Monday morning soon after the bank was open, they stood gazing up at the impressive columns and statues of the 300-year-old building. Then hand in hand, and with much anxiety they climbed the stairs and entered the front door.

It was already a busy scene. They walked over to a reception desk where a young lady sat diligently working on her computer. She looked up.

"Good morning, how may I help you?"

"We would like to see someone in regard to a safety deposit box of a deceased person," Ted stammered. He had no idea what the procedure would be.

"Not a problem, please follow me." She got up from her desk and ushered them to a room nearby. "Take a seat. Mr Jones will be with you in a moment."

They sat and within moments a tall dark-haired young man impeccably dressed in pin-striped suit entered the room and introduced himself with a very proper English accent. Ted shook his outstretched hand. "I am Edward Piercy and this is my wife, Beverley."

"How may I help you?" He sat behind the desk and picked up a fountain pen. "Well..." Ted stammered. "My parents are both deceased and we found this key..." Ted took the key from his jacket pocket and passed it across the desk.

Mr Jones picked up the key. "It is indeed one of ours, Mr Piercy. We will need some information from you. Do you have documentation?"

Ted nodded and pulled from his folder his passport and a sheaf of papers, some of them age-yellowed. "Here are my parents' birth certificates, marriage and death certificates and of course my own birth certificate." He passed them across the desk.

Mr Jones studied them for a few moments and then turned to his computer where he checked out both parents' names to confirm ownership of a safety deposit box in either of their names.

"Yes, we do indeed have your father, Bernard Piercy registered to a box. I believe we have enough evidence as to the ownership. Do you wish to view the contents?" he queried.

"Yes, please. Whatever the contents are, I will remove today and close the file," Ted stated.

"Very well, Mr Piercy. Please sign here and I will bring you the box." He left the room. Ted looked at Bev astounded and just whispered his feelings of that moment for fear it all might disappear like a dream.

The box was placed on the desk in front of them.

"I'll just leave you for now. When you have viewed the contents and are ready to leave, just open the door and I will return," said Mr Jones.

They sat staring at the metal box as though it might bite. Then Ted, with a shaking hand picked up the key and placed it in the keyhole. It fit perfectly; he turned it and then held his breath for the moment of truth. The drawer slid out easily and they stood for the first look inside. Bev gasped in amazement at the thick bundle of cash. Ted picked it up and flicked through the tied stack of £100 notes; it had to be many thousands. The only remaining item in the box was a brown envelope which he lifted out and held tightly in his trembling hands.

He gingerly opened the envelope and slid out the piece of paper inside. He hesitated for a moment and looked at Bev with tears welling in his blue eyes.

"You read it dear, please," he passed the paper to Bev.

She opened the folded paper and gasped. It truly was a deed to a property; she read out the key points; this is a deed of ownership to the freehold property of Edward House, Roundham Road, Paignton in the county seat of Devon, England.

It was signed by Bernard Piercy and witnessed July 25, 1972.

Ted took it from her to read the document for himself. Finally, after he had read it over several times, he sighed and just shook his head.

"Now we know why my father decided to visit England the summer of 1972; it was obviously to claim this property after his father's death. Well, let's get out of here, Bev; we have a lot to accomplish." He slid the paper back in the envelope and placed it in his folder and passed the bundle of money to Bev which she stuffed in her handbag and then opened the door to alert the banking officer that they were ready to conclude their business.

That accomplished they left the bank, hailed a cab and returned directly to their hotel room. It would take the remainder of the day for them to take it all in.

Ted had called room service and ordered a bottle of wine and a hearty lunch; there were phone calls to be made and he needed to be fortified. He pulled out his ordnance survey map of England for the location of Paignton. It was a place they had never been before but seeing it there on the map, it was very close to Torquay and there they had been. He pointed it out to Bev.

"Wouldn't it be funny if it was like 'Fawlty Towers?' he laughed, remembering that the sitcom starring John Cleese was based on the running of a Torquay hotel.

"Nothing would surprise me, we'll just have to wait and see," Bev remarked.

A few phone calls later, they realized that a trip to the land registry office for that area and most probably a solicitor would be necessary to validate his claim to inheritance, so they planned to leave in the morning for the West Country.

***

All business free and clear, Ted and Bev took a drive by for a first glance at the property. Edward House was indeed a working hotel in a very prime location of Paignton.

Not wanting to cause a stir by arriving unannounced they decided to tour the area and phone the proprieter later to set up an appointment for a meeting.

Paignton is a coastal town and together with Torquay and Brixam, is known as Torbay; the English Riviera. It truly is a beautiful place and well known for tourism, catering to family holidays throughout the decades. The architecture along the beachfront is of a Victorian period; elaborately designed hotels and long pier boasting a colourful arcade. The beach is of golden sand and the waters crystal azure and relatively warm for most of the year.

To their delight they discovered by driving down a small road past the hotel, that it opened out into parkland with walkways, botanical gardens, food kiosks, a pub, entertainment arcade and the Goodrington Sands. They parked their hired car and walked through the park past the pond and bird sanctuary. A graceful pair of white swans with their brood of signets glided across the still water.

It was high noon and giving in to rumbling stomachs, they entered the pub. Over a lunch of soup and salads they talked about the prospect of living in Paignton. Ted put down his chicken sandwich and gazed across at Bev who was diving into hers with gusto.

"I don't know about you, dear, but I really have no interest in running a hotel," Ted remarked. "I've never had any experience and saw first-hand as a child when my parents had the guest house, how it takes over your life. And, of course, you must remember John and Julie at the Mitre Inn in Sandford Orcas. It broke up their marriage."

"Nor me, but it might be nice to stay there from time to time," Bev agreed. "I'm hoping you will agree to go back to Sherborne for a while." Ted changed the subject. "I believe we are meant to find an answer this time."

"I'd love to do that, dear, and more than likely we can rent the same cottage, and there is plenty of room if the kids come."

They finished their meal. Then, as it was a glorious summer day, they strolled along the crescent walkways past the colourful beach huts that were typical of most English seaside towns. They looked down into the clear waters to the sea life and watched as young lads cast out fishing lines for a catch. Bev shivered at the sight of a mass of huge squirming maggots that was being used for bait. Then climbing up and up to different levels of the gardens by way of stairs they arrived at the top to find Rounham Park with a golf course and a most spectacular view of Torquay. It appeared all blue, white and shining in the summer sun, just as depicted in the holiday brochures.

They had booked into a comfortable hotel between Torquay town centre and Paignton, very near to the quaint little hamlet of Cockington. Ted had planned to make his phone call to Edward House in the morning at a time he thought would be the least busy for the proprietor. So with hours to spare before dinner, they parked the car on the outskirts of Cockington and strolled along the pathway which followed a stream through a meadow and then came upon the settlement. It was an amazing sight to behold; every building was of ancient stone and thatch. There was a forge with a blacksmith working with red hot iron and hammer just as it had been done in centuries past. A dear little teashop displaying tantalizing pasteries in a bay window drew them in and to a table for two in the back.

Cream teas were always on the menu here.

"Tea and scones would just suit me fine," Bev enthused as she gazed about her at the displays of gifts and souvenirs lining shelves and walls.

"Cream teas for two, please," Ted ordered from the matronly server wearing a frilly apron and a quick smile. Within minutes, a steaming pot of tea, warmed scones and side dishes mounded with fresh clotted cream and strawberry jam was placed before them. Bev poured the tea, creamed and sugared hers and watched as Ted mounded thick cream and jam on his scone and took the first bite with a sigh of pure delight. "My God, that's delicious; brings back so many memories, doesn't it?"

Bev mumbled a reply just nodding her head as she savoured her first bite too.

**

The manager of Edward House reacted with surprise just as Ted predicted he might. For so many years of not hearing from Ted's father, he expected this day to come; but it was still a shock when the phone call came. His parents before him had run the place until retirement and then he had taken over. He had been well prepared with courses in hotel management and had first-hand experience helping out his parents.

His reply was polite and professional... "We have a bit of a lull after the noon meal, sir, and I would be pleased to show you around the place. I look forward to meeting you."

"I know this must come as a surprise to you, but I must tell you that it has been a shock to me and my wife as well. I will assure you that we have no interest in taking over the running of the place but we will talk about that when we come," replied Ted.

"Right then, I look forward to meeting you and your wife. See you soon."

They drove into the parking area of Edward House at precisely 2 pm hoping that the lunch rush was over. Walking up to the entrance they took in the three-storey structure noting that the pale golden paint appeared fresh, the windows clean and sparkling and the grounds well cared for. The front door opened into a carpeted foyer with a table laden with tourist brochures neatly displayed. A bell somewhere on the lower floor announced their arrival.

The manager, expecting their arrival, appeared from the dining area... "Mr and Mrs Piercy, I presume. I'm Sean," and he extended his hand. "Indeed, we are." Ted replied. I'm Ted and this is my wife Bev." They both shook his hand. "We're hoping for a grand tour if you have the time?"

"Yes, certainly, follow me."

He led them into a small bright lounge just off from the foyer. It was well appointed with chintz upholstered chairs and matching curtains, a table with a bouquet of fresh flowers and books, a TV, everything required for the comfort of guests. They followed him through to the dining room, the tables neatly set for the next meal. At the back of the room was a small bar with cushioned window seats and French doors that opened out to lawns and flower gardens beyond.

There was a large kitchen next to the dining room. Bev noted that it was immaculate albeit rather old fashioned compared to North American standards, especially the cooker. A chef sporting navy and white trousers and white apron looked up from his salad preparation with a smile.

Then they climbed stairs to the next two levels and were shown into some of the rooms which were unoccupied. They appeared to be nicely furnished, not all with en suite, but the main bathroom on each floor was equipped with oval bath tub and showers. Large windows let in the sunshine.

"I'll show you a room with en suite that is vacant. Perhaps you may like to stay for a few weeks, get the feel of the place and the general area?"

"That sounds like a splendid idea," Ted enthused, and Bev had to agree.

Two hours later, having gone over all the details of the running of the place and an appointment made to meet the accountant, they left with heads in a spin.

***

Well satisfied that everything was in order and that the hotel could continue to run as it had been, they relaxed and enjoyed all that Paignton had to offer.

The weather was just right so one early afternoon they headed out for a walk along the coastal path. The view of the water and beach coves was stunning and they walked along carefree and happy. Soon they came upon a little kiosk with tables outside offering light snacks and beverages.

They sat for a while and enjoyed cool drinks and continued onward. They walked through a small park and then seeing a public footpath, decided to follow it. The path led through farm land of the rich rusty red soil of that area.

Off to their right was an age-worn gate with a sign; fresh eggs and honey for sale, and beyond it lay the farmhouse and out buildings. Bev waved to a small girl playing with a dog. Chickens picked about the yard making happy hen sounds. It had such a lovely country feel to the scene and yet so close to the town.

She would have dearly loved to buy some honey and eggs, but thought better of it, things she would have to carry not knowing where the path would take them or how long they would be. Maybe on the way back, she thought.

The path carried on through a golf course and then taking a right turn down the signposted Church road, they were in the tiny hamlet of Churston Ferrers. Next to the Parish church stood an ancient medieval building, Churston Court Inn. The wisteria-clad light pink exterior of the place lured them forward. Sun-bleached wooden benches and tables were set up outside near the ancient oak door. Bev breathed a sigh of relief as she sat on one of the benches.

Ted pushed open the door to a dark-panelled hallway of old oil paintings and a display of full suits of polished armour. He entered the room on the right and walked up to the polished and carved wood bar. He sat on a stool and looked around at the low beams and ancient fireplace and sensed a feeling of familiarity.

He ordered drinks and sandwiches to take outside but while he waited he made his way to the washrooms. He gazed up a dark staircase where a huge bull mastiff dog reclined at the top landing. And then his eyes were drawn to a large oil painting of King Charles II. How could he explain it, but gazing at the image of that dark sardonic face evoked deep emotional feelings within himself. The dog stood in a protective stance when he lingered, so he shrugged it off and continued down the hallway. By the time he returned to the bar, their food and drinks were ready.

Bev was sitting with her face to the sun when he joined her, as though she hadn't a care in the world. She opened her eyes and greeted him with a smile.

"Mmm, that looks so good!" She took a swig of her ale and a bite of the roast beef sandwich with pure pleasure.

"You must come inside later and have a look around this place. It's amazing." Ted said nothing about the painting or how it made him feel. He sat and thoroughly enjoyed his lunch. They did go inside and toured the dining room, exclaiming of the colourful walls and decor. Ancient dark oak furniture, and relics of a past age were accented by a colour scheme of dark rose, burgundy and purple walls. It boasted a carvery of roast beef or lamb and six vegetables each Sunday. Bev made a mental note to return for the meal in the future.

After leaving the Inn they continued to walk the public footpath. It wound through woodland with welcoming shade as the afternoon grew hotter. Off the path to their right sat a stone structure Bev had never seen before. Ted explained that it was the remains of an old kiln, no longer in use since the industrial age.

They continued on walking through a park and then the path became fairly steep as it wound to the water. They had reached the harbour at Brixham, much to their delight. Moored there was a replica of the *Golden Hind*, an ancient ship which was a novel tourist attraction. They took photos. They bought fries liberally salted and vinegar sprinkled from a vendor to nibble as they walked the maritime village. And then when thoroughly tired out, they caught the bus back to Paignton. It had been a perfect day.

Two weeks had just flown by. They found that they liked Paignton and the Torbay area. But Ted was anxious to live in Sherborne so they made plans to leave. They were confident that the hotel would continue to run as it always had.

Sherborne

Sherborne, that most beautiful town. The sun shone down on market day and there was a buzz of activity near the old conduit at the lower part of Cheap Street. Bev and Ted wandered about amongst the laden stalls and made a few purchases; artisan bread, farmhouse cheese and a variety of fresh vegetables to take back to their small self-catering cottage on the outskirts of town. Since their last visit, a large supermarket had been built in the lower part of the town which supplied everything, but it was nice to get the farm fresh products.

They had registered with an estate agent to find a long-let flat or cottage and within days a place had been found for them. It was a two-bedroom upper and lower cottage at the top of the town almost directly behind The George pub. It was ultra-modern, fully fitted and furnished very tastefully. It would be just right for as long as they wanted it and room if the kids wanted to come.

They spent the first week or so getting out and about, reacquainting themselves with places they had longed to see. A drive down the A352 took them to most of them; Cerne Abbas, Godmanstone and Dorchester.

This afternoon they sat outside in the garden of the Royal Oak pub in Cerne Abbas and shared a ploughman's lunch with cool ale. They had walked all through the small village, passing the parish church and the 'old pitch market' reputed to have been visited by George Washington and onward past the duck pond. It was just as they had remembered; the ducks swam from every direction hoping for a handout and they laughed at the antics. Through an ancient wooden gate, they passed into the graveyard and then into a field where sheep grazed on the rich grass. From there they found the footpath to the Cerne Giant, a huge figure of a naked man with an erect phallus which had been etched out on the chalk hillside. The figure stood out from the background of green grass. It was said to date back to ancient times of pagan worship and fertility rites. They climbed the path and stood to gaze down at the peaceful little village below.

On the way back they stopped again at the holy well of Saint Augustine where a spring bubbled up from the depths of the earth and had been flowing there for hundreds of years. Bev kneeled over its surface said a silent prayer, then cupped her hand in the water and drank. A feeling of utter peace settled over her and as Ted took her hand to help her stand, her eyes filled with tears. No words could be said to express her feelings so she just stood and held him close, not wanting to shatter the moment.

And now here they sat out in the garden of the Royal Oak pub and shared a Ploughman's plate and cool ale. They picked at the cheese and crusty rolls with silence still between them. Ted nodded to an elderly couple who were making their way to a table and took a swig of his ale. He finally broke the silence.

"Do you see that plant way up there on the side of the church?" He pointed. "Yes, I do see it, dear. It's amazing that a plant can grow in such a place so high up there on stone. A seed was probably dropped by a bird, but who would think it had enough soil to grow?"

"I don't know why it has come to me now but somewhere I've heard a saying that in time the very stones will give up their secrets, and that plant growing out of the stone wall reminds me of it," he mused as he lit a cigarette.

"I think that comes from the Bible, Ted; 'the stones will cry out', she replied. "Well, I hope that some old stones will cry out to me and tell me why in heaven's name I've been coming back to this place time and time again and for what reason," he laughed. "Of course, there is no denying that I love it here, but all joking aside, Bev, I really aim to find out this time around," he said with conviction. "I will have an open mind from here on in."

***

Ted sat in the town library where he could be found most days. It was quiet there at the very back of the building in amongst the shelves of historical reference books. He had open in front of him, *Stuart England.* He had gathered that Philip Canton had lived in that time period. He made notes about the civil war and country life during that time. He looked through archives. He also took books home and into the late hours each evening he poured over text until his brain hurt.

"If you don't mind me saying so, Ted, I think you're going about this the wrong way. I think you just have to relax and let the answer come to you as it will. If we review what you were led to believe, Sherborne was where he lived so perhaps his death is recorded in the abbey archives. There is obviously some connection with this town and Sandford Orcas too."

"True, true," he mused. "I've always had feelings of a connection with the abbey and the manor house, we should take another walk to Sandford Orcas, but first maybe we can talk to someone at the abbey."

After lunch that day they walked down Cheap Street and turned right near the Conduit and through a gate to the abbey grounds. It was a weekday and no service took place in the abbey. They pushed open the ancient door to quiet, cool space. The lofty height of the fan-vaulted ceiling was always a breath-catching sight, no matter how many times they had seen it. They walked slowly to the altar where a white-haired man seemed to be occupied. He looked up as they neared him. "Good morning folks, lovely morning. May I be of any help?"

"Good morning to you too, sir. We noticed that there are many souls interred here in the abbey, but not a graveyard surrounding it. Is there a crypt?"

"There is indeed," he replied. "But visitors are not allowed there. The fact is, it is rarely opened. I remember some years back, there was a heavy storm and the river Yeo overflowed and caused flooding of the abbey basement. At that time, the crypt was opened so that the water could be pumped out. It hasn't been opened since."

"How interesting," Ted replied. "But is there a record of those who are entombed in the crypt?"

"Why, yes there is. Why do you ask?"

"Well, I know from what I have read that the history of the abbey goes back a very long way to some of the early Wessex kings buried here, but I have interest in finding the resting place of a man around the 1650's or thereabouts."

"A long-lost relative of yours, perhaps?" he quipped.

At that statement, Ted gave Bev a sly wink. "Yes, you might say so. We are doing some research into my ancestry."

"That does not surprise me. We have had others making similar inquiries. I can search the records for you, but it will take some time."

"Oh, that would be wonderful. We would be most grateful." Ted wrote down his name and phone number on a paper torn from Bev's notebook as well as the names of Philip and Michael Canton.

The gentleman glanced at what Ted had written, placed it inside a book he held in his hand and replied... "It's not a very common name, have you ever wondered if there might be a relationship to the English physicist, John Canton?

He was famous for discovering Canton's phosphorous."

"Can't say I've ever heard of him. Thank you so much. I look forward to hearing from you." Ted shook his hand and then taking Bev's arm they left the abbey.

The phone rang one morning about two weeks later and Bev picked it up. "Yes, he is here, one moment please." She handed the phone to Ted. "Hello, Mr Piercy, I have news for you. There is indeed a record of three Canton tombs... James and wife, Mary, and Philip Canton. The latter was born 1627 and died 1695. But there is no record of a Michael Canton. Is that helpful?"

Ted was in a state of disbelief and took a few moments to answer.

"Err... I believe it's the information I've been searching for," he stammered. "Thank you so much for your help. I'll put an envelope in the donation box."

Bev could tell it was positive news by his facial expression of utter surprise and when he had hung up the phone...

"He's there, Bev, he's really there!" Ted was elated.

"Can you even begin to imagine how this makes me feel? Don't you see, I'm not crazy after all. It gives credibility to all I have been through, all *we* have been through, all that our children have been through all these years."

"Of course, I understand, Ted. I'm just as excited as you are at the good news." Ted grabbed her hand and danced her around the sitting room, absolutely joyous.

"This calls for a celebration. Will you join me for lunch at the Plume of Feathers, m'lady." He bowed at the waist and kissed her hand in a light-hearted display of chivalry.

"I'd love to, kind sir," Bev laughingly replied.

They walked hand in hand down Cheap Street to the sound of the abbey bells ringing out the noon hour. It was another sun-drenched day and they were filled with the feeling that it was good to be alive.

Ted pushed open the old oak door to the pub and gazed around. Bev followed. It took a few moments for his eyes to adjust from bright sunlight to the darker indoors. An image formulated. There near the fireplace, nonchalantly sat his brother smoking a long clay pipe. He nodded and then just disappeared. Ted chuckled to himself, *just typical*. He went up to the bar to order their meal.

Bev, blissfully unaware, crossed the room and sat in the very place his brother had vacated. She gazed around her at the low-beamed ceiling, the old oaken tables and chairs, and the ancient stone fireplace where many a fire had burned and tried to imagine what it would have been like in Philip Canton's time. It certainly would not be a place for women unless one was a bar wench, she mused. It was totally a man's world. Women were only chattels, having no voice, there only for the pleasure and service to men. *I would not have fit in at all.*

Ted arrived with their drinks and her reverie evaporated.

"Cheers, love!" He raised his glass and clinked it to hers. "Cheers!" she replied. Within minutes, steaming hot dinners were delivered to their table; sausages, mashed potato and gravy and a smidge of greens.

"Lovely!" Ted enthused and tucked into his with relish. Conversation was light and though neither spoke about the phone call, it was upper most in their minds as they sipped, chewed and swallowed their celebration meal.

***

That night they sat sipping cups of hot chocolate before bedtime. As Bev had expected, his mentor came through.

"And so you have found me out, have you?"

"It would seem so," she replied.

"Well, all will be revealed very soon now, my dear lady. Take care." Ted came back to himself, yawned and exclaimed how weary he was.

"It has been a most interesting and rewarding day, but I'm bone tired, let's off to bed, kid. Tomorrow it's to Sandford Orcas."

Discovering Trent

It mattered not how many times they had made the trip to Sandford Orcas, there was always a shared feeling of anticipation and excitement.

Ted and Bev set out midmorning for a drive to the hamlet. It was another sun blessed day with the scent of new mown hay on the breeze. The car windows were all open to capture the atmosphere as they rode along.

"I can't help it you know, Bev, I have butterflies in my stomach, I am just that excited." His eyes left the road for a moment to see her reaction and was rewarded with a smile.

"I feel the same, dear. It's as though we are long lost children returning home."

They had reached that part of the road where the old oak tree grew and Ted slowed the car to a crawl and then stopped beneath its overhanging branches for a closer look. "Such memories," remarked Bev and tears brimmed in her eyes as she remembered past times shared with their children in its shade. And then Ted drove onward until they had reached the village.

Everything appeared exactly the same. Bev looked at her watch as they approached the 'Mitre Inn'. "I'm afraid we're too early, Ted. As you know, opening time is not until eleven."

"Not to worry, we can stop in later. Let's swing by the manor house for a peek."

But as the manor house came into view and Ted slowed the car to pull over, Bev touched his hand where it gripped the steering wheel.

"I have a better idea, let's continue on, just explore? We can always come back here another time."

"Sounds good," he replied and drove on.

"There! There! She pointed to the age-worn sign TRENT 1¼

257

miles. "Turn there!"

Ted did as she had bid him and drove down the narrow hedgerow-flanked road. Large tree branches overhung it in places offering cool shade. It curved and dipped in places and at a rise on the left, a farm gate stood open. Ted slowed the car so they could get a view beyond the gate to fields of golden grain.

Then only moments later, they arrived at the tiny hamlet of Trent. On a rise to the left of the road stood the parish church of St. Andrew's, solemn in the summer heat. Directly opposite the church stood a pub, 'The Rose and Crown' where Ted pulled into the gravelled car park. Theirs was the only vehicle.

They stepped out into the sunshine to the spicy fragrance of dog roses. Bev picked one of the gorgeous blooms from a thorny hedge and sighed at the heavenly scent. Honeysuckle hung over the fence in a profusion of fragrant pink, and pale yellow clusters. Bee hum and bird song welcomed. Perched high atop the weather cock on the church steeple, a blackbird trilled its melodious hymn to the heavens. From somewhere beyond, its mate trilled in answer.

Ted could see that Bev was just as enrapt of the place as he was.

"What a beautiful place. What a beautiful day." She almost burst into song. "Isn't it just. Let's explore the church first," he suggested.

The pub door was open and an apron-clad woman was outside watering potted red geraniums. Ted walked over to let her know they would be stopping for lunch after a stroll, not just taking advantage of the car park.

They ambled along the cobbled pathway stopping to read the gravestones here and there poking out from the well-trimmed grass. In the Rectory garden an elderly lady wearing a straw hat was cutting pink roses which she placed in a wicker basket. She noticed the pair, waved and then called out to them.

"The church is open. Welcome!"

"Thank you!" Ted called back.

Suddenly, Bev had the uncanny feeling that she had been in this scene before. It was something about the warm summer day, the church, even the lady calling out to them. It all felt familiar as though this very moment in her life had been foretold in a long-forgotten dream.

She tripped along behind Ted as they entered the cool sanctuary. Ted moved forward up the centre aisle in his own reverie while she walked over to the ancient font. She ran her fingers over the elaborately carved cover tracing the figures. Then seeing a table laden with brochures, she picked one up and dug in her handbag for change and dropped it into the little box provided.

'St. Andrew's Church, Trent' the cream-coloured cover had a sketch of the parish church. She opened the pamphlet, scanned some of the key points then gazed around until she found the carved pew ends depicted there. There were symbols of birds, animals, flowers and 'the green man'. She caught up to Ted, now sitting in one of the pews and looked down at him.

"Look here, dear." She passed the booklet to him. "It says that Charles II hid in the manor house nearby."

There it was again, that strangely familiar feeling at the mention of that name. He couldn't explain it, he just sensed there was a connection. The atmosphere suddenly felt cooler, had dropped by degrees and he shivered.

"Sit with me, Bev. I have a strange feeling that I have been here before and there is definitely something monumental that has happened here in Trent."

Bev sat next to him and felt the chilly atmosphere, her arms felt prickly and broke out in goose bumps. It wasn't like her to be so *aware*. Ted could sense her reaction and put his arm around her shoulder.

"Let's get out of here," he whispered.

They hurried out into the warmth of the sun. A tortoiseshell cat had been sunning herself on one of the gravestones and came running to greet them. She purred and rubbed around Ted's legs so he crouched down to pet her.

"Hello, you," he laughingly greeted her. She had lightened his mood already. "She is almost the spitting image of Tess's *India*. Cats are so sensitive to our feelings; she probably knew we could use some cat love." Bev stroked her too.

And then as though she had heard someone calling, she raced to the back of the churchyard. Then stopping, she looked back as though to say 'follow me'.

Follow they did only to see her disappear through slats in a gate at the perimeter of the grounds. Bev leaned over the gate to see where she had gone only to catch a glimpse of her disappearing behind the stone wall of a huge house. It was only partially visible behind tall trees and hedges.

"This has to be the manor house, Ted," she squealed in excitement.

It was only a glimpse that Ted needed to confirm his 'knowing' this place. He froze where he stood. Bev hadn't noticed his reaction; she was deep in thought. How she longed to follow that cat, to see within the walls of that great house, to see how others lived, to see where the King had hidden. But her thoughts were rudely interrupted by the sound of car tyres on the gravelled driveway, someone was coming. She grabbed Ted by the arm and stepped away from the gate, unwilling to be caught invading the owner's privacy. She propelled Ted in the direction of the pub.

They entered to the smell of food. There is nothing like it to lift the spirit. They sat at a table near a back window with a view of grain fields and the rolling hills beyond. It would seem that the little hamlet was surrounded by farmland. Ted ordered from the barmaid and brought their drinks as well as menus to the table. He was so parched he almost drained his glass in one swallow. Bev scanned the menu then looked across at him; he looked better already.

"I'll have the deep fried scampi and salad," she chirped then got up to find the ladies' room.

By the time she returned, Ted was already in deep conversation with one of the local lads. She saw that he was a freckled, sunburned, redhead and wore a plaster cast on his right arm. Seeing her approach, he smiled, noting that she was eyeing his cast. "Hello there, I'm Rufus," and he extended his good hand.

What a fitting name, she thought, as she grasped his handshake.

"I'm Bev. Looks like you've had an injury?" Their food arrived and he lingered, Ted noted.

"Join us won't you, Rufus?"

"Err, thanks. I will." And he sat and explained about his injury in his rich Dorset accent. They ate, drank and listened.

"I'm a farmhand, yer see, lived 'ere all me life. A cow got 'erself caught up in some wire. I tried to free er and she bolted, yer see. Fell against me arm and broke it in two places. Can't work like this, yer see." They sympathized and then the conversation continued. Ted mentioned the manor house and Rufus responded.

"'Tis a quiet place, nice people live thar. The Squire is a good bloke, comes in 'ere often. I understand his wife's side of the family go back to the early days. Now Sandford Orcas manor house... that place ...I won't go near." And he proceeded to tell them that when he was a child about age five, his grandmother took him to a summer fete at the Sandford Orcas manor house. He remembered being scared out of his wits. He had heard growling, dragging and scraping sounds. He had never forgotten it.

"I'll go to Nether Compton, Sherborne, Yeovil, all other places but not there." Then he continued with another equally fascinating story about 'potato caves'. There were natural caves in the surrounding landscape. During the Second World War the farmers were ordered by the government to increase production to feed the population. There was an embargo on supply ships from Europe and North America, England had to feed herself. One particularly good potato harvest some of the farmers, ignoring gypsy folklore, stored sacks of potatoes in one of the larger caves. Strange things happened. Not only did some of the potato sacks go missing, but also a man. When he finally did appear some months later, it was as though he had aged to an old man. His hair had turned white and he could speak only in gibberish, unable to tell what he had seen or what had happened to him.

The gypsies had warned that the caves were openings into the underworld. They had had past experiences and avoided them like the plague.

Bev and Ted continued to eat their food, not questioning but nodding where appropriate. As though Rufus sensed they were finding the story hard to believe and maybe needed a back-up, he added,

"There's an old man who lives down Corton Denham way who still remembers. He was only a lad at the time."

They had finished their meal, their empty plates had been taken away and still they lingered until Ted gave Bev the eye as though to says 'time to go'.

"Well, it has been fascinating talking to you, Rufus, but we must be going." They stood up to leave. "Perhaps we'll see you again, take care of that arm," Bev said and Ted shook his hand and headed for the door.

"Bye, now!" he replied and looked as though he was about to follow, but did not. When they were in the car, Ted chuckled as he turned the ignition.

"What a story. What a lot of old bollocks," he laughed.

"I wouldn't laugh, Ted, you've always said yourself there was something mysterious about this part of the country. Maybe there is an underworld. Remember Wookey Hole and the story about all those skulls?"

"Mmm," he mused.

Though Bev said nothing further at the time, she thought she would love to go exploring for those caves.

Though they drove back to Sherborne by way of Sandford Orcas, they did not stop. Bev remembered she needed to shop for groceries and do a laundry. How mundane, she thought, after such a wonderful mysterious day.

There was a time when Ted would have laughed at doing household chores but while Bev was out shopping he threw a load of laundry in the washer. Then he tidied the sitting room but his mind was totally consumed with the excursion to Trent. He planned to share his feelings with Bev this evening.

Bev had prepared a meal of cold ham, new potatoes, peas, garden salad and topped it off with fresh strawberries and clotted cream. They talked about meeting Rufus and the potato caves but nothing else.

Following supper they had taken a stroll through the town looking in shop windows, then down past the abbey and ended up in the park. They loved this place of vast lawns cut through with pathways leading to a central band shelter. There were trees of every description, some of them ancient. The pathways were flanked by flowerbeds in colourful display of roses, daylilies and daisies.

They sat on a bench under an arbour of white roses and watched a small boy playing ball with his father.

"It's been a wonderful day," said Bev. "I didn't mention it at the time but it felt as though I had already been there in a dream, do you understand what I'm saying? There was just something so familiar about us walking up to that church, seeing the lady picking roses and calling to us and even following the cat.

"Well, that's just what I wanted to talk to you about." Then Ted proceeded to tell her: how he had felt at seeing the painting of Charles II in Churston Court Inn, how he had felt when she had read the information in the church pamphlet about the King hiding in Trent and how he had felt as he leaned over the gate to glimpse the manor house.

"Putting it in perspective, I have a feeling there is a connection and that something very sinister happened in that little village. I feel that the answer is almost in my grasp. It's all starting to come together."

Bev grasped his hand. "Wonderful dear. If you look back at the past times we've been here, have seen that sign while walking, riding, but never once turned down that road until today. It's as though this day had been set aside long ago to be the right day, at just the right time in your life for discovery."

"Perhaps you're right, Bev," he squeezed her hand, then pulled her to her feet. "Let's walk a while longer."

Winter 1998

A blast of bitter wind tossed icy rain at the window and it ran down the pane like slow tears. Bev shivered. She peered out the kitchen window into the garden where winter jasmine blossomed along the fence and felt a pang of longing. Winter, her least favourite season of the year was upon them.

Soon it would be Christmas, the first one away from the kids. She really missed them. It will be just the two of us she realized and felt the sting of tears starting in her eyes *Don't give in to sadness* she scolded herself, then began assembling the ingredients for a hearty soup. The cutting of vegetables was therapeutic she thought and the next best thing was music. She turned on the radio to the cheerful sound of Terry Wogan's voice and began to feel better already. Then the first chords of '*How Bizarre*' filled the room.

Ted was in the sitting room reading *The Daily Mail* and it was as though he was tuned in to her wave length.

"Let's give the kids a call this evening, Bev, see what they're up to?"

"Can do," she called from the kitchen. "I was just thinking the same thing."

***

The phone rang at 8:30 am. Tess was getting ready for work and answered it on the second ring.

"Hi Mama, great to hear your voice. We're all doing ok. Phil just got over a rotten cold though. You know what he's like when he's sick, so damn irritable. I made him stay home from work and he wasn't pleased. I made him a pot of chicken soup loaded with garlic too."

"Good for you dear, I taught you well." Bev praised.

Tess went on to tell her all her news and then talked to Ted for some time. "Alonzo says hello. Phil is anxious to talk so I'll pass the phone to him. Bye now, love you."

He talked to Bev first. "Hi, Mum, I really miss you." Bev could hear a quaver in his voice. They talked for a few minutes then...

"Can I talk to Dad now, Mum? Take care, love you." She passed Ted the phone. "Hello, Son. Wondering if there's a chance you might like to come here?"

"Well, that's what I wanted to talk to you about Dad," he laughed. "I've been saving my money and I'd like to come right after Christmas, not before as we have a party planned, you know."

"Mum and I will send you both gifts of money this year, enough for your air fare, and for Tess whenever she wants to come."

"Thank you so much, Dad. Tess will be pleased too. Bye, Dad, love you. Got to get ready for work now, see you soon." Ted could hear the smile in his voice.

They all felt so much better after that phone call. The kids started their day on a happier note. Bev and Ted ended their day, happier too.

***

Sherborne was decked out for Christmas. There were small live trees with clear fairy lights placed at intervals all up and down Cheap Street. A large tree with coloured lights stood in the town square. A nativity scene with live animals; a donkey, sheep and goats, was set up like a petting zoo for the children. All the shop windows were subtly and tastefully decorated. Nothing garish was permitted. It all looked like a Victorian scene.

One evening in the last days running up to Christmas, the shops were open late. Businesses offered warm mince pies and a glass of sherry to customers.

"What a lovely touch!" Bev enthused as they browsed the shops, nibbling mince pies and sipping sherry. Truth be told, they had finished buying gifts, but it was an experience 'not to miss'.

"This would never happen back home." Ted remarked.

As they walked home holding hands, the Abbey bells rang out carols into the cold crisp night. And were those snowflakes?

***

It was Christmas Eve carol service and the interior of the abbey glowed with candlelight. Tall pillar candles flanked the altar and every parishioner carried a lighted candle. As the organ belted out the first chords of 'Oh, come all ye faithful' and voices rose in praise, Bev could have wept with the beauty of it. "What a lovely service! What a lovely evening!" she sighed as they were leaving the abbey grounds. Ted squeezed her hand, he had enjoyed it too.

Bev had prepared a light snack for after the service and they sat near the Christmas tree nibbling assorted cheeses, crackers, paté and sipping sherry. They had placed gifts to each other beneath the tree and were as excited to open them as two children. But their best gift by far would be the arrival of their son on New Year's Day.

***

Tess peered out the window into the dizzying swirl of snowflakes and beyond to where her car was parked. It was literally buried in snow drifts. It had been snowing since Christmas and the local roads were almost impassable except to heavier vehicles. Even if her car was not snowed in it would be impossible for her to get Phil to the bus station let alone to the airport; it was more than a two-hour drive. She was only just getting over the upset of rescuing her old tabby cat from a snowdrift this morning. He had grown restless from having been cooped up indoors and seeing his chance dashing out when Alonzo opened the door in a swirl of wind. By the time he was rescued his little pink nose, ears and toes pads were bluish tinged with cold. It had really upset her.

It was the morning for his flight and he paced the room like a caged lion, he was almost in tears. His bags were packed and he had been ready for days.

266

"I'm going out, I'll see what I can do, Phil." She was dressed in her winter coat, scarf and boots and waded out through the snow drifts to her place of work. How strange that the words of a carol kept repeating in her mind: 'in the bleak midwinter, snow on snow on snow.' No one should be travelling in this weather.

She breathed a silent prayer for help, having faith that someone would come to their desperate situation. She pushed through the snow and cold and couldn't believe her luck, there was her boss's 4x4 parked outside and he was just getting into the cab. When he heard her plight, he responded.

"Certainly, I'll drive him to the bus station right now if he's ready. Hop in, Tess." She felt so very grateful. Phil was peering out the window and when he saw them drive up he grinned from ear to ear. And then there was a flurry of hasty hugs and goodbyes...

"Safe journey Phil, love you, Bro. Give Mum and Dad a hug for me."

"Will do, Sis, and thank you for everything. Take care. Bye now."

After he was safely out the door and on his way, Tess gave in to racking sobs. She would miss him, had no idea when she would see him or her parents again. How she hated goodbyes.

***

On New Year's Day Ted took the train to Heathrow to meet him. Bev decided that she would stay at home and prepare for his arrival. It was more important to have a welcome of warmth and food she thought. She busied herself cleaning and preparing the guest room; a bright yellow and blue duvet to match the curtains, a gift of a cosy robe which she laid out on the bed, a selection of favourite magazines, a little dish of chocolates on the bureau and extra hangers in the closet. She had thought of everything. Satisfied, she then busied herself in the kitchen preparing a hearty turkey soup; it was light but nourishing for the weary traveller.

Finally, at 8pm she heard the sneck of the gate latch and then their boisterous arrival at the door. Phil almost fell into her arms, he was that weary. She hugged him and studied his dear face, he looked rather gaunt and skinny too she thought. But nothing that some of Mum's home cooking and TLC wouldn't cure.

He had a look throughout the little cottage and Ted helped him with his luggage upstairs to his room. He was well pleased with what he saw.

"You've done yourselves proud with this place, Mum, Dad," he praised. "Do you mind if I have a nice hot bath, wash off the travel grime?"

Christmas tree lights and candlelight was a cheerful setting and he had gotten his second wind. They sat and talked long into the night until he just had to give in to sleep.

The following morning after a full English breakfast; sausages, bacon, grilled tomatoes, eggs and toast, he had a wander through the town with Ted. With a hint of woodsmoke to the chill air filling his lungs, he almost had to do a reality check, it seemed so surreal. Only a day ago, he had been pacing a room thousands of miles away and now he was really here walking side by side with his dear old dad. His next thoughts were about assembling his mountain bike. He had brought the custom made metallic blue machine with him and couldn't wait to be out and about riding some of the country lanes. His first destination would be Sandford Orcas, he thought.

"You really ought to see Trent, it's only just a little further and signposted so you can't miss it," Ted suggested.

Several days later he cycled the familiar road to Sandford Orcas, passing under the old oak tree. It was the first time he had been there in winter and was almost surprised to see the bare branches, though the ivy twining around the trunk remained green all year round. He looked up into the top most branches to an abandoned bird nest with a sense of sadness but he knew that the birds would be back in the spring. Just then he caught sight of a tiny robin and watched as it warbled a song. It was such a reassuring sound.

He stopped briefly at the manor house and then did a circle around the courtyard. Then taking Ted's suggestion, he continued on until he saw the sign for Trent. The road dipped and curved. It was a great one for testing his performance. He could see right through the bare intertwined branches of the hedgerows to the fields and hills beyond. In winter the countryside had a quality all its own and surprisingly, was quite green still.

He arrived at the little hamlet and seeing the 'Rose and Crown' he stopped, locked his bike and entered to the warm scene. There were only a few patrons, all seated at tables. He walked over to the bar where a slender barmaid had her back to him arranging glassware. She had seen the tall dark and handsome stranger ride up on his bike. It had made her heart flutter so she turned her back to appear preoccupied. Then turning, she looked into his dark eyes.

"Welcome. What will it be?"

He was quite taken off guard by her sensuous green gaze and posh accent but replied... 'I'll have a pint of Stella please, and a Stilton ploughman's."

As she pulled the beer, they continued to chat.

"We don't get many tourists this time of year, especially Canadian. But we've recently had a Canadian couple here who are staying in Sherborne."

"That would be my parents, I'm staying with them for a while."

Just then another patron approached the bar. Phil took his drink and retreated to the other side of the room to a table where he could sit and observe from a distance. By the way she had greeted the bloke left no doubt in his mind that they were an item.

She brought his meal to the table, it looked amazing; a huge wedge of blue Stilton cheese, large slices of artisan bread and butter, pickles and salad.

"Enjoy your meal. I'm Kate, by the way."

"I'm Phil. Nice to meet you, Kate." He noticed that the guy at the bar followed her every move. *Best leave that alone,* he laughed inwardly.

Having relished every morsel of the ploughman's, he left the pub with a wave to Kate and "thank you!"

He walked his bike up the cobbled path to the church opposite and leaned it up against a wall. He entered the silent slightly musty atmosphere of the ancient building. He didn't know why it was so, but ever since he was a small boy he loved seeing through these structures, seeing the effigies of the long dead, reading the words etched in stone. It was as though time stood still here. He glanced at his watch and could hardly believe he had spent an entire hour already. He wandered then out into the churchyard and all around the back, looked over a fence to the huge stone manor house. He got a sense of familiarity to the place though he knew he had never been there before. *How curious. I'll* definitely come back here again, maybe on a warm spring day though. *He shivered.*

***

After two weeks, Phil proclaimed one morning that he was well over jet lag, well rested and anxious to find work.

"I'd like to stay, Mum, but I've got to pay my own way. I need to find a job."

"Well, dear, you're welcome to stay as long as you like, you know we love having you. But if it's work you want, this week's *Blackmore Vale* is on the coffee table, take a look through the job postings."

No sooner had he searched the ads than he was out the door, CV in hand. When he returned an hour later he announced with excitement.

"I've been hired at the hotel. They want me to start this afternoon."

"Congratulations, Phil! But what about work clothes?" Bev wondered. "Brought my blacks and whites with me, I'm all prepared."

"Well done, Son, no flies on you," Ted laughed.

He was soon settled into a schedule of work. He liked the job and the people he worked with. But now days out would be limited to his days off.

On a February morning promising sunshine, they headed off to Glastonbury. Though they had been there on two previous visits, this would be special. They planned to climb the Tor.

Instead of taking the steep, more direct path to the top they decided to circle to the left and take a less travelled path through old growth trees and then upward. Mossy great limbs reached to the ground like long arms. Bev and Ted sat resting on one while Phil raced ahead to scale the summit. By the time they finally reached the top, he was standing in the archway of the tower with arms outstretched as though welcoming the power of the place. "Isn't it just amazing!" he called to them.

It was truly an amazing view, all 360 degrees of it; the Glastonbury Abbey ruins, the town centre, and the vast patchwork landscape beyond. It was breathtakingly beautiful. And yes, there was magic about the place. It had been a centre for worship back to pagan times when it was the temple of the Goddess.

Bev got out her camera and snapped a photo of him and then one with his father. It was a moment to remember.

After ascending the steep path to the base, they lingered for a while in the garden. Winter pansies and primroses were already in blossom and the daffodils were in bud. Bev and Ted sat resting on a bench. Phil crouched down to study the symbols on the chalice well cover. Then on his way to where they rested, he touched a tree branch and felt a tingling sensation in his fingers. It seemed as though even the trees had a powerful energy. It was difficult to comprehend but it made him feel peaceful, grounded and at one with the earth.

***

Bev heard his key in the lock. He had worked late that evening and was starving. He warmed up the meal she had left for him and ate while watching a TV programme. Then he made a hot drink to take to bed with him. It felt so good to lay down. He sipped his hot chocolate, read his magazine and it wasn't long before he turned out the light. He stretched out on his back and took a deep breath. He had heard the abbey bells toll the midnight hour, had heard the sound of patrons from the George Pub noisily straggling through the lane, so he knew he was still awake. Suddenly there was a loud smashing noise of breaking glass. Was it from downstairs? Outside? Or in his head? And then he felt himself being levitated from the bed. He panicked at the sensation of drifting upwards and then sideways and feared bumping into the bureau beside his bed. As that thought entered his mind, he felt his body abruptly fall back to the bed.

He lay there, afraid to move for some time. What on earth was happening to him? He sat on the side of his bed for a few moments then got up and crept downstairs, all was silent save for Ted's snoring.

"Mum, are you awake?" he whispered, outside their door. "Yes dear, I am, are you alright?" she whispered back.

"Can I talk to you for a minute?" She could hear the concern in his voice so she threw on her robe and met him at the door.

"Did you by any chance hear glass shattering?"

"No. But I did hear people talking in the lane, I really haven't been asleep yet."

"Not to worry, I was probably dreaming. Goodnight now, Mum." He wanted to tell her about his experience but thought better of it. He was no longer the child needing comfort from a nightmare. Only that was no nightmare.

The Answer

Spring had crept in very slowly with warmer nights and sunshine during the days and then one day everything was in blossom and in leaf, every shade of green. Farmers were already ploughing their fields perfuming the air with the rich earthy smell. Sheep and frisky new lambs dotted the hillsides.

A pair of blackbirds busily built a nest in a tree in the back garden and sang into the late night hours. That sound had the power to lift even the most down spirited. But the spring weather and birdsong had little effect on Ted. He had seemed downcast for days. The arrival of his son had preoccupied his mind for some time but now that Phil was working there was more time to dwell on other things. As many times as he had made the trip to Sandford Orcas and Trent, he was none the wiser. There was still no answer.

Phil was eager to get out and enjoy the spring weather, it was his day off. "Hey! Mum, Dad, how about letting me treat you to lunch at the Rose and Crown?" He wondered. "Their fish and chips is to die for."

"I'd like that," replied Ted.

"I'll second the motion," Bev piped up from the kitchen.

Ted suggested that Phil drive, he'd be happy just to sit back and relax. Bev scrambled into the back seat of the Rover. She enjoyed Phil's driving, he was cautious and never in a hurry. Unless another vehicle was behind him, he drove slowly enough for her to see everything. It mattered not how many times they had taken that road, there was always something worth seeing, she never tired of it. Into the village they rode and as they approached the Mitre Inn, Ted spoke up.

"As it's your treat, Phil, I'd like to stop for a drink here first. Might as well enjoy myself as I'm not driving."

"Great, Dad!" Phil swung the car into the parking lot. He was happy to see that Ted's mood had already lifted a bit.

They sat near the fireplace where a fire burned in the grate giving out welcoming warmth. They sipped their drinks. Bev listened to their conversation about the latest car models, a common interest, and the possibility of attending the London auto show this summer. She looked across at the two men in her life with a sense of pride and gratitude. Their son had brought so much joy into their lives. What a blessing he had been.

Having little interest in the subject of cars, her mind wandered back to more than twenty years previous. It was in this very place that his birth had been foretold. She had been very young then and unwilling to accept the foretelling of the future by a spirit. But his soothsaying of events had been proven correct over and over in their lives. She had a strong feeling that the close bond between father and son had been forged in the spirit, was predestined too. *Perhaps this very moment in time was also predestined,* she mused. But her reverie was interrupted by their laughter and announcement that they were starving for the promised fish and chips.

It was the first time they had been together in the Rose and Crown. Phil was instantly recognised by the barmaid and she flashed him a welcoming smile.

"I see you've brought your parents today," she commented as she pulled their beer. "Will you be having lunch?"

"Yes, we'll have two orders of cod and chips and one piece of fish for Mum. She says she has a small appetite but will scoff some of our chips," he laughed.

Bev and Ted selected a table. No sooner had they sat than Ted recognised the lad, Rufus, seated across the room, he no longer wore a cast. Simultaneously he recognised them and came to the table just as Phil arrived with their drinks. He was introduced.

"Nice to meet you Rufus, you must be the guy who told Mum and Dad about the potato caves? I'm really interested."

"Yes, well I won't go into that story again but there are still caves out there," he stated. "Don't know if you've heard of the carriage with horses and people that was swallowed up by the hillside here about. That happened sometime in the 17th century I think," Rufus stated candidly.

"How very interesting," said Phil, his imagination running rampant, he could have listened to more. But their meals had arrived and Rufus did not linger. "Got to run, nice to meet yer, Phil. See yer again sometime," this he directed to Ted and Bev and then he hastily left.

Phil dove into his crispy cod and with a mouthful... "Can you believe that?" he asked with an earnest expression.

"I'd believe anything about this place," Ted stated with conviction. "There's more to this place than you could ever imagine." Bev gave him a strange look, *are we on the brink of an answer?*

***

That evening they sat chatting about the day. Ted was seated on the couch and seemed distant, listening more than talking. Suddenly he clutched at his throat as though choking. Bev went to him in a flash but then realized that he was going into a trance state. He seemed to fight for the next breath.

"Oh, God! I can't breathe!" He writhed and moaned, she held his hand.

"He's in a trance, Phil, try not to be alarmed." But as Ted continued to struggle and wail... "I can't get any air. How can this happen to a King?" Phil reacted.

"Dad, Dad, wake up! Mum, snap him out of it," he demanded almost in tears. Bev shook his shoulders... "Ted, wake up!"

At this, he did come out of the trance. His eyes were now open and he seemed fully alert and aware of his surroundings.

"I'm okay. It's all okay. I know what happened. I now know the answer. Please Phil will you pour me two fingers of Scotch with ice and water and I'll tell you." Phil went to the kitchen, thankful that Ted seemed alright but he felt on the verge of a panic attack himself. He poured the requested drink, took a large swig from the bottle, then poured a drink for himself and one for Bev. By the sound of it they would all need more than one to hear God knows what. He took a deep breath and returned to the sitting room, passed the drinks and then sat by Ted.

They sat waiting for what seemed like an eternity and then Ted began...

"I remember everything. It was as though I was in another man's body, feeling the agony of his death throes from suffocation. It was a horrible death and I know now that it was the young King Charles II. He was in a very cramped cubby hole of a place in the Trent manor house. Though his death was accidental and known only to Philip and Michael Canton, they kept it a secret. With the help of a farmer who later hung himself in the archway, they buried the body in the cellar of the Sandford Orcas manor house. But that's not the worst of it."

"How is that possible?" Bev interjected. "History tells that King Charles II lived and reigned."

"That's just it, you see, he was an impostor. It was I (Michael Canton) in that lifetime who was that impostor, usurper, fraud, villain. Call it what you will."

"Oh, my God!" Bev gasped. "Now I see it, what all this has been about. Philip Canton needed you to acknowledge what had been done in that lifetime."

"Exactly! By owning what I had done, there can finally be atonement and my brother has done his work and can move on."

Phil interrupted at this point. "I think I believe you, Dad, but this is all a bit heavy for me. If you don't mind, I think I'll go out for a walk, get some fresh air."

"Of course, Son, I fully understand." After Phil left, Ted continued...

"It's just as well that he doesn't hear *this*. It could serve no purpose."

Bev listened intently. After all these years it was a relief to finally hear the truth, to have an answer to why their life had been such a roller coaster ride.

"In the realms of the afterlife, Philip, Michael and the young

Charles made a pact. King Charles by reincarnating as my son and growing up in a close bond of love between father and son would be paid the debt of a life owed him."

"You mean Phil?" Bev covered her mouth in disbelief. "Precisely!"

"Well, I can understand now why you didn't want him to hear."

"But that's not all... for the final retribution, I have got to tell the story. You know, old bones in the cellar, stones crying out. At this point, I can't imagine how. Who would ever believe it?" He leaned forward, cupping his face in his hands and let out a deep sigh. "I just feel so very tired, Bev."

"Of course you do, dear. It's getting late, let me help you up to bed. I'll get you a hot drink when you're tucked in, and sit with you."

When she knew that he was sleeping, she crept downstairs and sat waiting for Phil to return. She played over in her mind all that had been said and it all made sense to her, right down to the timing. She realized that Phil was now the same age that the young King would have been when he died. She felt that his presence here where it had all taken place was like a catalyst for the events of today. And then it occurred to her that Rufus, the young farmhand, might possibly be the reincarnated farmer who had aided them and then taken his life. He had spoken openly of his abhorrence for Sandford Orcas, hadn't he?

She allowed her imagination to travel down that murky path but was soon interrupted by the sound of the gate latch and Phil at the door. She got up and gave him a hug as he entered.

"Dad's okay. Don't worry, he's sound asleep now."

"I know I should be used to it by now, Mum, but that was powerful. I'm glad I don't have to work tomorrow, think I'll have a shower and sleep late."

"Goodnight, dear, love you. I'm glad you're here."

"Me too, Mum, goodnight."

***

Morning came and Ted sat at the table idly picking at his scrambled eggs.

"I feel bone weary today. I think I'll go back to bed," he announced.

"You do that if you like dear. Phil and I can go out for a drive, leave you in peace," she soothed. She appreciated how much was taken out of him after an episode and this was a particularly severe one. He'd likely be weary for days.

True to his word, Phil had slept late but as soon as he was with it, Bev suggested they go for a drive.

"Let's head out to Nether Compton, take a walk in the woods, see if we can find the caves," he suggested.

"That sounds exciting," Bev replied, grabbing her hat and coat. "Better wear boots."

It was a warm sunny day and the small hamlet was only a short drive away. Phil parked the car near the Parish church in a shady spot and they walked from there to a wood beyond. Save for the barking of a dog somewhere distant, all was peaceful. They followed a footpath in quiet companionship, the events of yesterday unmentioned. Soon he would forget about it like a bad dream. No point in dwelling on something so obscure.

The ground under foot was soft and muddy in some places, she was thankful they had worn boots. They entered the woods where sunlight filtered down through the green canopy. A grey squirrel scolded, ring-necked pigeons cooed high up in the branches and blackbirds sang out in clear notes.

They reached a place where steep banks rose up on their left and in some places there were shallow recesses in the stone. And then they found a small cave carved out in the bank. It was large enough to sit in and there was evidence that someone had. Discarded drinks cartons and crisp packets strewed the floor.

"Well this looks a bit like what we're searching for, but it's hardly as Rufus described." Phil took a closer look. "It only goes back about four feet."

They were distracted by the sound of rustling in the underbrush and then sharp barking as a golden retriever sprung out onto the path, greeting them with wagging tail.

"Oi, Lassie, come here!" her master commanded and then he made an appearance from the same direction, a middle-aged man with a ruddy face.

"Good morning to you. Sorry about that, she's just a pup and so excitable," he apologized.

"Good morning to you, sir," Phil spoke. "My Mum and I are looking for caves out here, we were told of them by a farmer from Trent. Do you know of any?"

"I've seen only a few, but none deeper than this," he pointed. "But if you go a bit further you'll see a bluebell wood, now that's really worth seeing."

"Oh, thank you," Bev chirped, the excitement in her voice. Soon the subtle spicy fragrance of bluebells wafted on the breeze. At the top of a small rise, they looked down into a vale entirely carpeted in blue as far as the eye could see.

"Oh, Phil!" She raced ahead like a school girl and into the profusion of ankle-high blossoms. Phil followed, laughing at her high spirits. She found a mossy log and sat amongst them, inhaling deeply the heady scent, it was a balm to her soul. She couldn't resist picking a fistful to enjoy at home.

"As much as I'd like to stay in this enchanted wood all day, we should really get back, dear. Don't want Dad to be on his own too long."

"For sure, Mum, would we really go inside a cave even if we found one?"

"No! But thank you for coming here with me today. You know, if I were to be struck blind tomorrow, I would remember this beautiful sight always."

"Oh, Mum, you really are something, you are." He hugged her. "Let's go."

***

They arrived home to find Ted dressed, sitting at the table and spooning a bowl of soup. He said he felt much better and looked it. Although Phil greeted him cheerily and told of their escapades, he was wary. Bev went to the kitchen and found a vase and proceeded to arrange her bluebell bouquet. Phil retreated to his room and came down moments later to announce...

"I think I'll make the most of the rest of my day off and take the train to Salisbury, have a look around."

"That sounds nice." Bev could see that he was ready to go out the door. "Have a nice time, Son." Ted looked over at him with a smile. "Just remember to check the time for the last train."

Bev cleared the dishes and went to the kitchen to make a pot of tea. No sooner had she prepared it than she heard the deep distinctive voice of his mentor.

"Beverley, please come sit," he commanded. She did as she was bid, it surprised her to hear his voice again.

"Listen well, my lady ...My brother has an assignment." He made finger motions. "I see his fingers moving on a device that allows words to appear on paper of which I am not familiar."

"Oh, that would be a keyboard as a typewriter or computer," she stammered. "Yes, he must record an account of what happened here. In so doing, his soul will finally be absolved and I will be allowed to leave this plane and move on to another life. My work here will be done." Bev listened intently. He continued ... "But failing this, I will take him."

She weighed the gravity of those words. She believed him. She knew that in a trance state, it would be so easy to slide down that slippery slope to death. She vowed then and there that she would do whatever it took to help him accomplish what he needed to do. And then his mentor was gone and with a few deep breaths, Ted was back in the present.

"Everything okay?"

"Yes, dear, it is." She attempted a smile.

Later that evening she broached the subject again with Ted.

"But I have no idea where to begin or how to put it into words."

"I will help you, Ted, we'll do it together, you're a good writer, it can be done," she said in all sincerity.

"If you say so, Bev. You're a real rock." He hugged her. "Let's go to bed." As they climbed the stairs together, they heard the abbey bells ring out the Westminster chimes as though in celebration.

Dreams

With the acknowledgement of his past life it was as though Ted had opened the floodgates to a bombardment of dreams. He sat bolt upright in bed. He was in a sweat and gasping for breath. In the dream he was in that enclosed space again and feeling again the awful suffocation of the dying King. It was following the dream that he came to the realization that the breathless episodes of the past must have originated from his deep-seated unconscious mind. He could still remember how he would wake from a dead sleep struggling to breathe but oblivious to the cause. Now he knew why.

That realized, the suffocation dream was never again repeated. But others would follow, allowing him to finally piece together the sinister story. He explained this to Bev, and was at first perplexed at her response.

"What you must do, Ted, is keep a dream journal. As soon as you wake from a significant dream, write it down. In that way, the details won't be lost...you know the way of dreams, they pass out of mind like vapour. I'll buy you a journal today, you can keep it on your bedside table," she suggested with enthusiasm.

"Well, if you say so, but I don't want you reading what I write. I'll share the writing with you when I feel ready, okay?"

"Agreed, love." She recalled his scrawl, she'd probably not be able to decipher half of it anyway. But it would be hard to resist peeking.

In a cosy stationery shop in Crewkerne, they found a great selection of journals and Ted picked out one that appealed to him. It was leather-bound with a little lock and key. Bev smiled at his selection, he really did want to keep his dreams to himself. They had wandered the little town looking in all the shop windows and ended up at the George Inn for lunch. Over the meal, they chatted about other days spent in Crewkerne with the children, of such pleasant memories.

Leaving, they drove down the A30 and on towards Chard, another of the lovely little Somerset towns. They were now in apple orchard country where the famous cider was made. Orchards stretched out in every direction. A sign at a farm gate caught Ted's interest... Cider for Sale. He stopped the car.

"I think we should buy a quart or two. Phil would enjoy it, don't you think?"

"Yes, he probably would, and you also, I expect," she smiled.

They received a warm welcome from the farmer's wife and were given a tour of the cider house. They were shown the old wooden cider press that squeezed the sweet juices from the apples. It sat idle, awaiting the autumn harvest of the apples at which time the process would begin again. Verses of a poem ...? written on the cider house wall, she explained was the wassailing song which dated back to pagan times. It was a custom to honour the apple trees to protect them from evil spirits for a bountiful harvest. Bev found this especially interesting and was told she was welcome to walk in the orchards if she liked.

She walked amongst the rows of trees hanging with the beautiful apples ripening in the summer heat. With the sun beating down on her back and the sound of bee hum, Bev was in her element. She could almost taste the apples. Reluctantly she returned to the cider house where Ted chatted to the farmer. She had seen fresh vegetables, eggs and homemade pies for sale so they bought some as well as 'scrumpy', the strong farmhouse cider and apple cider vinegar.

"Best be cautious, the cider is powerful," advised the lady.

"Thank you for everything, it has been such a pleasure," cooed Bev.

***

Phil welcomed a glass and held it up to the light, it had a natural cloudy appearance, gave off a wonderful fruity aroma and he swished it around his mouth. "Aah... high alcohol content aside, it's got to be good for you."

"Cheers!" said Ted. Bev tried a sip, but declined a glass, she really didn't like the taste. She poured herself a glass of sherry instead.

They tucked into the savoury steak and kidney pie she had bought. The crust was light and flaky with generous portions of steak, kidney and rich dark gravy served with whipped potatoes and green beans; it was delicious.

Well satisfied with drink and good food, Ted retired to bed early. Phil followed, he had had a busy day at work and he felt knackered.

Bev sat in the recliner with her feet up and her head back, eyes closed she enjoyed the moment to herself. She thought about the day, she had really enjoyed it. Tess came to mind. She missed her so much, wondered what she was doing. *I might just as well call her.* They chatted at length, she was doing fine, missed them all, weather was good. Bev went to bed, tired but happy.

***

Perhaps it was the effects of the cider but that night Ted had another vivid dream. He was in the Sandford Orcas manor house with his brother, Philip, and the King. They had filled their bellies with good food, had drank copious amounts of strong cider and talked with loosened tongues. They sat around a card table in candlelight playing at cards. Charles being quite drunk had uttered words that had shocked them into conspiring against him.

The dream was so real he could taste the tart cider, smell the beeswax candles, feel the card in his hand and see that it was the trump card, the ace of spades. The dream continued in detail.

When Ted awoke he reached for his journal, scribbled the key points and then quietly crept from the bed. He didn't want to disturb Bev, she claimed she got her best sleep after he was up. He tiptoed downstairs, it was best to have none disturb his train of thought. Over a cup of coffee, he sat at the dining room table and filled in all the details of the dream. As he wrote it down, he was surprised at how much he remembered, *captured by my pen.*

Over the course of several weeks, other dreams followed. In one he was huddled in a ship headed for France. In his dream he could hear the creak and groan of the ship, he could smell the salt air, feel the wind on his face, see the billowing sails that carried the vessel forward.

In another dream, he was at his coronation ceremony receiving the crown of England. He could feel the weight of the thing on his head, could smell the sickening sweet scent of anointing oil, could hear the bells chime out in jubilation and the roar of the throng as he left Westminster Abbey.

He dreamed about the horrors of the Black Death in the city. He saw himself and family fleeing to the West Country where they would be safe from the contagion. He could see the lavish soirees held there entertaining the elite of society. He saw an elderly lady crumple at his feet after whispering his true name. He heard the collective sigh of relief from the guests that it was not the plague that had felled her. He could feel his remorse at the news of her death.

In one of the last dreams, he could smell the acrid smoke as London burned. But this time he saw himself involved in fighting the spreading flames. He could hear the crackling of flames and falling timbers, the shouts of men and the cries of frightened women and children. He then saw the devastation that the fire had wreaked on the city.

Another night, Bev woke to him mumbling in his sleep. It was the murmuring of another woman's name that really got her attention. *Barbara,* he moaned. Then realizing that it was the name of the King's most favourite mistress, she turned over and fell back to sleep only to be awakened moments later by Ted's amorous advances. *This is all right.*

The last dream, the most vivid of all, was a scene of him on his deathbed. He was surrounded by black-robed physicians who squabbled over the best remedies to inflict on his worn-out frame. He saw as they cupped him, bled him and poured vile liquids down his throat as he spluttered and gasped for breath. Then it was as though he was floating somewhere above the scene looking down on his dying body. And then all he felt was peace.

***

The dreams had abated. Ted's journal was full. He sat reading over his notes, amazed at the story that had formulated from his dreams. It was shocking... incredulous. It was time to share it with Bev. He felt like a worn out husk this morning but there was a need to unburden his mind and put it all on the back burner until he was ready.

She listened with acute interest to every word of the testimony of betrayal. She did not interrupt to question or comment. Then she understood why he had been so troubled with the psychic.

"Now that my assignment here is complete, I really need to leave this place, Bev. Step back and view it all from a distance, get a better perspective."

"Well, there is no need for us to stay here. Let's go back to Paignton, enjoy the rest of the summer near the water. I'm certain we'd be welcome back to Edward House, you own it after all," she suggested with enthusiasm.

"Splendid idea, I'd love that. I'll give Sean a call to make arrangements." Phil was a bit surprised to say the least but took the news in his stride.

"Don't worry about me, you guys. I know for a fact I can take one of the staff rooms at the hotel. I'm sure they'd love to have me at their beck and call. I'll join you in Paignton a bit down the road. I'd love to see that area again."

Paignton

It was wonderful to be back in Paignton. Everything about it was so different from Sherborne that Ted felt more at ease than he had in months. The sea air was like a balm to his soul. He took great deep breaths of it.

Edward House was pleased to accommodate them in an en suite room with a view of the back garden. It was to be their home for the summer or for as long as they wished. Bev arranged a small table and chairs near the window. She thought it an ideal place to sit and write a letter or have a bite to eat.

She didn't want to be dependent on dining room service for all their meals so she had a small fridge, microwave, toaster and kettle delivered. She wanted to be able to make a cup of tea, throw together a sandwich, or make a light breakfast whenever they pleased. Ted went along with anything she wanted, there was no point in arguing even when she suggested that she would clean their room and do their laundry. She thought she would enjoy doing a bit of gardening as well. Nor was she averse to jumping in and helping out in the dining room if they needed help. Sean, the manager, appreciated her self-sufficient approach, it was quite refreshing.

They were soon settled in and then walked to the town centre for supplies. The shops had so much to offer, much more than she had found in Sherborne.

Their little room became a pleasant retreat. One afternoon when they returned from a shopping trip, they opened the door to discover a cat sprawled out asleep on the bed. The calico miss, had obviously found their open window and made herself at home. 'Snuggles' was her name, they were told.

"Don't let her become a nuisance," Sean advised. "We keep her to insure there are no mice around and we've never seen one yet."

Now into the high summer of July and in vacation mode, most days they could be found in the park below the hotel. Not far from the duck pond, beneath the shade of a huge chestnut tree they sat in deck chairs to suntan, read and while away the hours. Bev packed picnic lunches for the most part but it was only a short stroll to the beachside kiosk for ice cream or to the pub for a cold beer. They would take it in turn to walk on the sand. Bev was left in care of their belongings in quiet reflection while Ted strolled to the beach. Her mind wandered back to Sherborne and Phil; they hadn't talked to him for a few days, he always seemed to be working. Then her mind slid back to Ted's dreams and the Trent manor house. She was curious to know if it still had the priest's hole. She pulled her cell phone from her purse and dialled Phil's number.

"Hi, Phil, just thought I'd try you and there you are. How are you dear?"

"I'm great, Mum. I have a surprise for you ...I'm coming to Paignton next week, on Wednesday that is. I called up one of the major hotels in Torquay and they want me to start work there as soon as possible."

"That's wonderful, Phil. Your Dad will be so pleased, we miss you. Really look forward to Wednesday. Oh, by the way, next time you're in the Rose and Crown, ask the name of the squire of the manor house, will you?"

"Sure, I'm heading there for lunch today... but why?"

"Oh, just something I want to know... nothing important, only don't say anything to Dad. He's put all that out of his mind for now, just enjoying his vacation. See you soon, dear. Bye for now. Love you."

"Next Wednesday then, Mum. I look forward to seeing you both and of course Edward House. Love you too."

Ted had walked across the green to the seawall then down the steps to the beach. He removed his sandals and walked barefoot, loving the old familiar feel of the sand between his toes. His mind was only in the present moment and loving it. He was the child again, far from the cares of the world, gazing across the waves to where seagulls cried and wheeled against a background of still blue sky. He walked and walked and then, looking at his watch, was shocked to see how long he had been. Thinking that Bev would be wondering, he headed back, only stopping on the way to buy ice cream. It had already begun to melt and drip down his fingers when he presented her with the soft ice cream, a chocolate flake bar stuck in the centre.

"I was beginning to wonder... you'll be pleased to know that I talked to Phil and he's coming here on Wednesday, got a job in Torquay."

"Wonderful!" he exclaimed as he lowered himself to the deck chair.

***

Phil arrived as scheduled and they met him at the train station. They were as excited as though it had been years since they had been together instead of a month. He booked into one of the small downstairs rooms at Edward House and was anxious for a grand tour of the place. Sean was pleased to show him through and had to admit that the kitchen, though definitely functional, was outdated. Phil made a mental note that the dining room and the kitchen would be redone to state of the art when he inherited the place. That old cooker would be the first to go. It was hard to believe that it dated back to his great grandfather's time. He was generally pleased with Sean's management.

Within days he found a furnished flat in Torquay close to the hotel where he would work. And then, as he had days to spare, he relaxed at the beach.

Bev sat at the little table looking out into the back garden. Snuggles occupied the other chair in quiet company and fixed her amber stare at her then began a methodical grooming session. Bev had made a cup of tea and decided to write a letter to Tess. She could say so much more in a letter than in a phone call and they delighted in receiving her newsy letters.

That accomplished, she decided to write a letter to Trent manor house as well.

She first formulated a rough draft and when satisfied, she wrote the letter.

Dear Sir;

By way of the Rose and Crown pub, I was given your name as the present owner of the Trent manor house. I hope you will not find my unusual request too great an intrusion, but my husband and I are presently researching for a historical book based on the fugitive period of King Charles II.

It is well documented that the Trent manor was a place of refuge for him for about nineteen days following the battle of Worcester in September 1651.

In the book 'Trent in Dorset - The Biography of a Parish' by Ann Sandford, she states that Ann Wyndham persuaded the king to go to her privy chamber, presumably the priest's hiding place from the days of Thomas Cromwell.

Ronald Hutton in his book 'Charles II King of England, Scotland and Ireland' states that Moseley Hall was another place of refuge and the only one of Charles' hiding places to survive more or less intact.

Our interest centres on the 'hiding place' in Trent manor and we would very much like to learn if it is still in existence and if so a description of it i.e. size, location, etc. Once again, forgive me for this intrusion of your privacy but a reply would be greatly appreciated.

Sincerely yours, (Mrs) B. Piercy

Bev read it over thoroughly, she was happy with her work. She addressed the envelope, gathered up her letter to Tess as well and then headed out to the post office. It was a pleasant walk and she'd be back before the men returned.

To her surprise and delight, a letter of reply arrived about a week later. Bev's hands were shaking as she tore it open. In it he thanked her for the interest in Trent manor and praised them for their bravery in writing about the subject of Charles II, as many books had been written. He went on to write...

"The book '*Trent in Dorset*' is not much good, but you might like to refer to the following books: '*Boscobel or the miraculous preservation of King Charles II*' published by Mrs Ann Wyndham in 1725. '*The escape of Charles II*' by Richard Ollard, the well-known historian, published by Hodder & Stoughton in 1966. (I think Antonia Fraser has written an even more recent book.)

The hiding place still exists and is described and photographed in '*Secret hiding Places*' by Granville Squires, published by Stanley Paul Ltd. in 1933. It is a priest's hiding place and was not used by Charles II, who occupied an adjacent larger room. I expect you would be able to get all these books from the London library. I hope this information will be of some help to you in your research."

Bev read the letter over several times, she was delighted that the hiding place was still in existence. Ted was out for a stroll, picking up his morning newspaper when the letter had arrived. Bev put it in a safe place for now, she didn't want to bring up anything to infringe on his holiday mind set. All in good time.

***

It seemed that the summer was pushing forward with incredible speed. Phil had moved into his flat and worked long hours at the hotel as it was the peak season for tourists. On his days off, though, they managed to meet for lunch or go out somewhere further afield. One afternoon they picked him up in Torquay and headed out in the car for Dawlish, another Devon seaside town. They took the coastal road which had breathtaking views of the bay and the red sandstone cliffs. Dawlish was known for the beautiful black swans that graced the waterway through urban park gardens. They ambled lazily through the little town and ended up at the parish church of St. Gregory the Great. It was not the interior of the church that drew their interest, but the graveyard surrounding it. They walked about amongst the headstones where they encountered the strange phenomenon of large grass-covered mounds rising up around the stones. Ted kneeled down and pulled away some of the long grass to reveal soft earth beneath. It was as though something had pushed up the soil similar to mole hills only much larger, some as high as the headstones.

"It looks as if something is trying to escape from the burial sites," Bev exclaimed. "Usually you see sunken areas where the coffins tend to collapse inward after so many years."

"It's quite creepy, if you ask me," replied Phil, his imagination running wild. "Maybe it's some dreadful gaseous contagion from the bodies."

"Well, I wouldn't want to speculate, there's probably some very logical explanation," remarked Ted. But there was no one to ask, so for now it remained a mystery. They walked away totally puzzled.

***

A solar eclipse was predicted and the media was focused on the event for weeks prior. A solar eclipse occurs when the moon passes between the earth and the sun, totally obscuring the image of the sun and blocking all direct rays, turning day to darkness. One had not been seen in the U.K. since June 1927. It was predicted that the best view would be in the south of England especially Cornwall, so people from all over the country flocked south.

It was the morning of August 11th and Bev and Ted walked down to the train tracks below the hotel. A special run to Cornwall of the Orient Express had been put on and like many other train watchers, they wanted a glimpse. Finally, it came into view. Passengers who had paid dearly for the privilege sat in the dining car sipping champagne with an air of self-importance and waved regally to the train watchers snapping photos of that famous train. And then it was gone, disappearing around a bend in the tracks in a cloud of steam.

The eclipse was predicted to occur at 11:11 am and crowds gravitated towards the beach. A flotilla of boats crowded the bay, everyone hoping for a good view.

After seeing the train, Bev and Ted set out walking in the opposite direction from everyone, across a playing field and into the quiet of a bird sanctuary. It was as though they responded to the beat of a different drum. They wished no crowds and noise for such a rare happening. They sat on a bench near the duck pond and waited in silence. As the process of the moon's shadow began to cover the sun, they watched through breaks in the clouds with darkened lenses at the stages of progression. Over a period of about ten minutes it slowly became dark and the temperature dropped several degrees. Fooled by the sudden darkness, birds fell silent, ducks came out of the water and settled for a sleep. At the moment of total eclipse, they sat in awe. It was such an eerie feeling and Bev felt moved to tears. She could understand why people in the early ages who had no understanding of what was happening thought it was the end of the world.

Then as slowly as it had darkened, it became light again. "Wonderful!" they exclaimed in unison.

Though Phil was at work at the time, all staff and guests of the hotel gathered outside to view the eclipse. He marvelled at the thought that if he lived to see another, he would be a very old man indeed, for it would not occur for another seventy years.

***

It was the noise that drew them to the window on that clear September morning. Against a backdrop of bright blue sky, two magpies scolded harshly from a tree in the back garden. The object of their scorn sat on the stone wall just below. The cat, Snuggles, was up against a formidable force as they obviously felt threatened by her presence. She stood her ground in a defiant stance as the magpies took it in turn to dive low over her head. The birds kept up their raucous scolding and dive bombing. The cat ducked her head each time they flew at her until she had had enough and slunk sheepishly away in disgrace.

Magpies are beautiful birds with blue black and white markings and long slender tail feathers. Far back in history, superstition had marked them out as birds of omen with a little saying; 'one for sorrow, two for mirth.'

At the antics of this pair and at the expense of the cat, Ted and Bev had enjoyed a good laugh. Bev thought she'd include the little caper in her next letter to Tess as she could use a good laugh right now. They had learned recently that she had split up with Alonzo, moved to the island and was on her own again. She really missed them.

Phil felt that he was ready to go home anyway, but hearing that Tess was so alone, he felt compelled to return. He loved the island and knew he would have no problem finding work and a place to live. So by the time Thanksgiving rolled around, he was on his way home. Tess was delighted, she'd be there to meet him when he arrived.

Bev and Ted saw him off at the train station where he would begin his very long journey home. They said their goodbyes, and with smiles waved him off on the train. But as soon as the train turned the bend and out of sight, Bev broke down and wept, not caring who saw her. Ted, too, felt the emptiness of goodbye and held her close until her tears were spent, and with a voice deep with emotion, he soothed, "Don't worry, my love, I feel the same as you. Let's give Phil a chance to settle and then we can make plans to go back, if you're ready?"

"Oh, yes!" She smiled through her tears. "Let's drink to that and have some lunch out someplace nice."

"Churston Ferrers, perhaps?"

"Please. I've wanted to return there for the carvery, let's go."

They drove to the village in silence, each thinking of Phil, praying for his safe journey and also for Tess. They were so pleased that their children were close, had been since childhood. As children, Tess had been the bossy older sister, and Phil giving into her demands. But as teenagers, their personalities were more evenly and respectfully matched. Now as young adults they were the best of friends and Phil was protective of his sister.

They arrived at the inn. The wisteria-clad walls were long bare of blossoms, the leaves already beginning to turn colour with the cooler autumn nights. The oak door creaked as they pushed it open to the welcoming aroma of roasted meat.

Ted took her hand and led her down the hallway to the staircase.

"I want you to see something first." He pointed to the wall at the top of the landing where the oil painting of King Charles II hung. They stared up at the dark features and long curly black wig of the man who had duped everyone.

"It doesn't stir anything now like it did the first time I saw it, but you can appreciate that then I was only just getting clues about the past."

"Yes, I can see what you mean, love. Come now, we can talk over dinner."

They were shown to a table in a cosy corner of the dining room. They ordered drinks from the friendly waiter then sat taking in the purple walls and decor. Over drinks, Ted confessed that he had been busy researching material for his writing. Days that Bev thought he had gone to Torquay to see Phil, he had spent hours in the library taking notes and photocopying many pages. He sighed as he told her that coming to Paignton had been for the best. It had given him the room he needed to accept his past and with the acceptance came much relief and release. He assured her that he was ready to return home, ready to write the story to the best of his ability.

Bev told him about the letter she had written to the Trent manor house and of the reply she had received. They laughed at each other's' secrets. Their meals arrived and were as delicious as anticipated and were consumed with pleasure.

Later back in their room, Bev showed Ted the letter. He could well understand her curiosity about the hiding place, it was after all foremost in the truth about the young King.

"I find it interesting that he states that the King did not use the hiding place," he rubbed his forehead, "but we know better." He went to his suitcase and pulled out the reams of notes he had taken and placed them before her. He had even begun to write the first chapter in his bold printing.

"I think the story should begin with the execution of King Charles I, something gruesome to spark the reader's interest."

He read out what he had written and Bev could see it was already a good start. "I've noticed that the South Devon College offers a crash course in computer technology. Would you be interested in taking it with me?" he asked. Although Bev was a bit surprised at the suggestion, she agreed. Why not be ready for the new millennium with a knowledge of computers? It was an excellent idea.

***

Sunday morning and they received a call from Phil and Tess to say that he had arrived safely, excited but exhausted.

"We'll be back before Christmas," Ted announced. "Mum and I are going to take a course in computer skills so we can be in step with the new age."

"Excellent, Dad. Take care, talk soon."

"Come now Ted, or we will be late for the service," Bev reminded.

It was a pleasant walk to the ancient parish church. To the peal of bells, they entered the sanctuary to the murmurs of parishioners greeting one another and the shuffles of feet on flagstone as they took to the pews. Then the Vicar took his place behind the podium as the first notes from the organ belted out a hymn.

Bev whispered a prayer of gratitude for their children's wellbeing and opened her hymn book. "Praise God from who all blessings flow, praise him all creatures here below. Praise him above all heavenly hosts. Praise father, Son and Holy Ghost," voices in unison rang to the rafters.

Christmas 1999

The aroma of roasting turkey wafted through her home as Tess opened the oven to baste the holiday bird. She was delighted to be hosting Christmas dinner for her family. Phil and his girlfriend had arrived early and were already helping themselves to the nuts and veggie platter she had laid out on the coffee table. They sat near the Christmas tree sipping wine and laughing at the antics of the cats with a toy mouse. Alonzo had been invited too. They had parted amicably, he was still a good friend and she was pleased that he was coming.

But most of all she was delighted that her parents were back in time for Christmas. They were expected at any moment now.

No sooner had she finished basting the turkey than they were all at the door, with happy smiling faces and arms laden with gifts. There was the noisy chatter of 'Merry Christmas' greetings, hugs, the taking off of winter wear, the placing of gifts around the tree, the pouring of drinks, and all the joviality that made this time of year so special.

Bev joined Tess in the kitchen. She was so pleased to be near her lovely daughter again and so very proud of the amazing young woman she had become. She could see at glance that Tess had all the dinner preparations under control, but it was fun to hang out in the kitchen for girl talk. Bev noticed a display of very healthy looking African violets in every shade from pink to dark burgundy basking in the sunlight on the windowsill.

"You certainly seem to have a green thumb," she commented as she touched a deep purple petal. "That's a perfect spot for them."

"I started them all just from leaves of other people's plants, put them in potting soil to grow new plants, I love them," replied Tess.

"Well I'm amazed, dear. You know my mother, your grandmother, used to do the same thing, but you would have no way of knowing that would you, she died before you were born." But when

Tess went on to tell her that she felt her grandmother's presence and looked upon her as her guardian angel, it moved Bev to tears. So there they stood in the little kitchen, mother and daughter hugging and laughing until they were interrupted by Ted who had come to take his turn at basting the turkey.

Candlelight glowed as they all sat around the dining room table. Ted popped the cork of a champagne bottle and topped up everyone's glasses for a toast to a happy Christmas and coming new year. The carved golden roast turkey was passed from one to another, each taking a generous serving as well as the accompanying dishes; roast potatoes, yams, parsnips, sage and onion dressing, green beans, corn, rich brown gravy and not forgetting the cranberry sauce.

With light hearted conversation at first, the topic then turned to the year 2000.

The media focused on computers crashing as the clock turned past midnight, referred to as the millennium bug or Y2K. It seemed that they played on the fear factor. Scared people bought up extra stores just in case there was a problem and took money from bank accounts. The world depended so much on computers that in such an event one would not be able to purchase most things required for daily living; groceries, gasoline, medications. Only the little corner grocery stores would be able to operate, and then with cold hard cash.

"I saw a woman frantically loading her shopping cart with enough meat to feed an army, besides several turkeys" Tess piped in. "It's just crazy."

"I tend to agree, dear. I don't agree with hoarding but I'll probably take cash from the bank, just to be on the safe side, only cash will speak if it does happen," Ted replied.

Everyone around the table had some comment and as Bev listened she couldn't help but think that no matter what happened, they would always get through it, would always be there for each other. She realized that the traditions that celebrate the joys of home and family life was a mysterious glue holding people together in times of difficulty. Society was not as it was in her childhood, today it seemed to be changing at the speed of light.

Dinner had been consumed, the dishes cleared and everyone retired to the sitting room for the opening of gifts. Wearing a Santa hat, Ted passed a gift to each. All eyes were upon the one opening the gift and after much oohing and aahing, laughter and 'thank you so much' the next person opened theirs, so this went on for some time. They laughed at the cats playing with bows and wrapping paper, it was a jovial evening. Then they helped themselves to a groaning display of desserts; everything from chocolates to cheesecake. Following coffee, they left declaring what a lovely Christmas it had been.

***

It was the dawn of the new millennium. New Year's eve came and one minute past midnight there was not the global chaos that everyone had worried about. If one listened hard enough, a universal collective sigh of relief might be heard. Information technology was still intact; computers were working as usual. It was as though they had inexplicable intelligence apart from human touch, reminiscent of the computer HAL in the movie '2001 a space odyssey.'

Ted had purchased a personal computer and was anxious to get it set up now that the Y2K bug scare was over. He had much work to do.

The Five-Year Plan

For the first several months of the new year it seemed that almost every day Ted and Bev were out shopping to furnish their apartment. Then one day they looked about them and were satisfied that it was a comfortable dwelling place. They also had a new car, and a boat for Ted's fishing trips which he enjoyed when he was not in the writing mood. There was nothing else needed. Moreover, Bev had a good job in nursing and Ted was hard at his writing. Although by the time she arrived home late at night, he was already asleep, in the morning they would review what he had written. Bev had always had an interest in journalism and she gave him a few pointers about the work in progress, but generally speaking it was coming along nicely.

They sat down together and devised a five-year plan at the end of which time they would be well set and ready for retirement. Five years in the life of a child is quite different from that of one past middle age. Five years could age, could change health status, could change circumstances. Moreover, nothing could be counted on in these uncertain times.

They would always remember the early morning of September 11th, 2001 when a phone call from Tess alerted them to turn on the TV to the horrific happenings being televised. Who had even dreamed of the catastrophe that befell America on that fateful day and the subsequent war on terror and invasion of Afghanistan that followed. Living close to an airport, they could remember the silence of the air space over Canada and the U.S.A. when all planes were grounded for a two-day period. Everyone was fearful. Bev and Ted advised their children to carry their cell phones and they established a safe meeting place should there ever be an emergency, it was best to be prepared. But gradually as in all things, time diminished the upset and life ticked on as usual. The hours, the days, the months and the years passed, some happenings standing out as being special.

In the year 2003, Bev turned sixty, they celebrated their thirtieth wedding anniversary and their son married. Where had all those years gone?

***

Philip Canton had remained aloof. Bev thought at times she caught a flicker of a different light in Ted's eyes that might be he, but that was all. Perhaps it was that he was satisfied with the progress Ted was making with his writing. Whether or not Ted had contact, he never mentioned it.

One autumn evening after supper, Bev walked by the ocean. She loved this quiet time alone. The sun had lowered in the sky creating a wide golden path across the still water right to the horizon. In time, the sunset brightened the sky in shades of vermillion and scarlet. She looked back to the homes on the shore, to windows of gold reflecting the glow. She watched the sky changing to mauve with streaks of lemon yellow then pale violet then pale turquoise with a vapour trail from a plane blazing orange. The afterglow lingered until a sliver of a silver moon appeared, the evening star twinkled and trees became silhouetted against the backdrop of sky. In that still twilight, Bev walked back home. She knew Ted would be waiting with a glass of sherry and a good movie, she enjoyed their time together on her days off from work.

They sat in their recliners, feet elevated and sipped their drinks. Bev looked across at Ted, he seemed more relaxed and at ease than she had seen him in ages.

"How lucky we are to have all this comfort, how well we have done," she boasted. And then she went on to list all their assets, Ted nodding in agreement. Before she could add another comment, he put his drink down on the side table and began the tell-tale deep breathing that always preceded a visitation.

"You could lose it all you know," came the voice of his mentor. Before Bev could open her mouth to speak, he was gone. Ted sighed

300

deeply and was back in the present, seemingly unaware. Bev tried to act as normal and suggested they begin to watch the movie, but she felt quite shaken. What ever could he have meant? Was there to be another disaster in which they would lose their possessions?

She watched and waited week after week and month after month for something untoward to happen but everything ticked on a usual. The children were well and seemed happy, she was healthy, Ted was still writing.

Then one day Tess stopped by for a visit. Bev was in the kitchen making a pot of tea and Tess quietly approached. "Anything bothering Dad?" she whispered.

"Nothing that I know of, dear. Why do you ask?" Bev replied.

"I don't know, he just has that look about him again, you know what I mean." She made light of it and changed the subject. Bev hadn't noticed but she knew the children had always picked up on the psychic where she was unaware.

Bev did however notice that he seemed to be in an inexplicable dark mood the following day but she hadn't time to dwell on it. She was expected at work in fifteen minutes and had to be out the door. She planned to call him on her supper break. He bid her goodbye with his usual hug and peck on the cheek.

The next morning as she was tidying his workplace, she noticed that the trash bin was full to overflowing with shredded paper. She picked out a few pieces and called out... "Ted, what is all this shredded paper?" He came to where she stood and with a defiant look stated, "It's my manuscript. I'm not happy with it nor is someone else I gather." Bev could not have been more shocked than if she had been smacked in the face.

"I can't believe that you did that, Ted," she seethed. "After all the work you put into it, all the time I spent going over it, I hope you saved it all on file."

"Yes, yes, I did. I've just grown tired of it. I'll get back to it sometime in the future," he assured. There was nothing else she could say, no point in arguing, she just shook her head, picked up the bin and left the room. It was his assignment after all, not hers.

Unexpected changes began to happen. Bev was given notice at work that her position was being deleted in three months' time. They were cutting back on staff. She, as well as one other nurse because they were the last to join the team, were those chosen for the cut. She was devastated. It would mean she would lose all her benefits, health and dental as well as group life insurance. She felt let down. She had contributed so much to improve the workplace but it seemed no one was indispensable. She was welcome to continue working, but only on a casual basis, picking up hours that might be available. She was truly angry and it began to affect her health. She suffered a bout of stress-related chest pain and spent the next several weeks going for tests. She was fearful. Ted was upset.

All tests proved negative and she was advised to take things easy. Lying in bed with her morning coffee, Bev's thoughts turned back over the past months and it became crystal clear to her what Philip Canton had meant. She *had* lost a great deal, but she was determined that she would not lose her health as well.

All things now in perspective, a clear path remained for an early retirement. She knew Ted would agree as they didn't spend enough time together. She'd talk to him about it this very day. With that thought in mind, she felt better already.

Ted was delighted with the thought of Bev stopping work altogether. The thought of having his wife around each and every day was all he had hoped for. To plan one's life is one thing, but fate sometimes dictates how life will unfold. Perhaps losing her job was the best thing that could have happened to them.

They talked it over and came to the conclusion that although they had all they needed to be comfortable in retirement, if they stayed where they were, boredom would set in very soon.

"You know I really and truly want to spend my final days back in my home country, Bev," Ted said wistfully. "There is so much there that we have not yet explored, always some quaint little village to see, I can think of a hundred such places I'd like to visit."

"You don't have to twist my arm dear, you know I'd love to do just that, we can head for Paignton and Edward House to begin with."

So they made their plans and in the spring of 2006 they were on their way.

Retirement

It was as though Ted sensed that he would never return to Canada again and needed to gather close to his heart as many memories as possible before leaving.

"Before we fly, let's spend some time seeing some of the places where we spent our early years together, Bev," he casually announced at the breakfast table where he sat stirring his coffee and waited for her response.

"Why, I'd love to do that," she replied with enthusiasm. "Sounds like fun."

So several days before they were due to fly they left the island, taking the ferry to the mainland. They booked into a hotel near the airport and then headed out on a tour of their old haunts. They were disappointed to see that the club where they had first met was no longer there, in its place was a huge ethnic deli. A favourite restaurant that they had frequented had burnt down and another was in its place. So much had changed and grown that they could hardly recognize the area where they had bought their first home. Finally, they found the little house where they had spent the early years of their marriage and stopped outside for a look. It had an unkempt appearance, the trees and shrubs that they had planted almost obscuring the windows. Bev sighed with a pang of nostalgia for the memory of bringing home newborn Tess and her early months of life.

"I wonder what life would have been like for us if we had always lived here? When you think of all the places we have lived and experiences we've had, would you have traded it, Ted?"

"No, not for a minute. It's hard to imagine dear, but I'm happy we did not. I truly think we would have stagnated here, how boring it would have been," Ted replied. "I have talked to the children about this in the past and they are happy they had the experience of living in other countries. They're more knowledgeable of other cultures, more adaptable as adults."

"You're so right, dear. I'd not want to change a thing either and now we're off on yet another adventure. I'm really excited."

They continued on to another place they had lived, where they had brought home their newborn son. They drove by it for a peek, recalling that time of life. Bev thought of how busy she had been with two small children, how happy to have been a stay at home mum, always there for all their needs.

Then Ted drove by the apartment where they had lived some years later. He couldn't resist going up to the door and checking out the names of tenants living there and was shocked to see that some remained. Next they drove by the children's elementary school, the little shops they used to frequent and the high school where Tess had graduated from. It was all so very nostalgic, it brought unbidden tears. They looked at each other with shared emotion and then laughed it off and drove on.

"There's just one place left I want to visit, Bev." Ted pointed the car down a long drive to the cemetery where his parents were interred. It had been many years since he had been there and he had no idea if he would ever come again.

A lady was selling flowers in the car park so they purchased a bouquet of white carnations. Ted remembered the exact location of the markers and, taking Bev by the hand, he led the way. He located the flat stones in a shady spot near the pathway. He kneeled respectfully at the cold granite slabs and traced his father's name with his fingertips then placed the flowers. It was always hard to see names of loved ones carved in stone. Bev put a gentle hand on his shoulder ... "I'll give you some time on your own, dear." She could see that he needed that space so she walked away. Only when she saw him stand, did she return. She hugged him close and whispered in his ear.

"You were a good son, Ted. You were there for both of them at the end."

"I just wish they could have been buried in their native England, is all," he replied with emotion and then turned and taking Bev's hand, they walked away.

***

Tess joined them for the trip. She needed a holiday, hadn't been back to England in many years and really looked forward to it. There was an emotional farewell at the airport as Phil and Sonia saw them off. They promised to be there for Tess when she returned in three weeks' time.

It was a lovely Spring day when they arrived in Paignton and they were welcomed at Edward House like family. Tess was impressed. Ted was pleased to see that the place was in good shape and still being efficiently run by Sean. He was happy to say that the place was fully booked for the spring and summer months already.

"We were full over Christmas but we closed for two weeks in the new year and got away to Cyprus. With the porter on site we had some much needed repairs and painting done."

"It looks great, Guy, well done," Ted replied.

While Bev and Tess unpacked and settled, Ted chatted with Sean. Tess was anxious to see her surroundings and as Ted was still deep in conversation, she and Bev wandered out together. They strolled around to the back garden, where the flower beds were already displaying spring blossoms; daffodils, crocuses and clumps of snowdrops. A calico cat sunned herself on the garden wall. Bev recognised her immediately. "Why it's Snuggles. I never would have guessed she'd still be alive." The old cat stood and stretched then jumped from her perch and ran to greet them, her tail in the air. "She must recognise you, Mum. Cats have good memories." She rubbed around Bev' s ankles and they both made a fuss of her, petting and crooning until she'd had enough and ran off.

"Nice that they keep a cat on the premises," cat-lover Tess remarked.

"Let's take a walk to the park, dear. I'll just let Dad know where we're going and I'll grab our handbags while I'm at it."

"Sounds good, Mama. I'll wait here for you."

Moments later they were off down the little road behind the hotel and into the park. Under chestnut trees bursting with new buds, they wandered arm in arm, then past the bird sanctuary where ducks sunned and a pair of regal swans lazily glided across the still water of the pond. They continued across an expanse of lawn and onward to the seawall and then down to the beach. As they walked along the hard packed sand where the tide had retreated Bev stopped to pick up a shell that had caught her eye and passed it to her daughter.

"You know, I have spent many hours walking this stretch of beach in the past thinking of you so far away, and now here you are walking it with me."

"Although I've never been here before, Mum, it seems familiar, as though I may have seen it in a dream. Could you believe that?" she asked.

"In this life, my dear, anything is possible. Come, let's climb the stairs to the top. I want to show you the view from Roundham Park."

When they reached the top and Tess saw the view of Torquay in the distance and the expanse of deep blue sea, she exclaimed in awe,

"Wow! It's beautiful. Do you think you and Dad will stay here?"

"I believe we will stay awhile, have a good look around, see if it's where we would be happy to live. Time will tell and we'll have all the time in the world now that I'm not working. It will take some getting used to, though. I hope time will be on our side and Dad and I can spend many years of retirement together."

"I hope so too, Mum, but make sure you make time for yourself and do the things you've always wanted to do; watercolours, quilting, writing, as well as seeing all the places you've wanted to see," Tess said in all seriousness.

"I plan to dear. But speaking of doing things to bring happiness, I think you would be wise to take this time away, go off on your own to some of the places you'd like to visit, think about what would make you truly happy."

"Yes, I'll do that, but for the next while I'd like you and Dad to show me some of the sights, take me to places I've not yet been."

"Agreed. We would love to do that. Now come, let's stop for a bite to eat before we go back. I'm starving."

***

One of the first things Ted did was buy a car so in the days that followed the little blue Renault took them on excursions to some of the National Trust sites; stately homes, castles, abbeys and gardens. It was wonderful to see historic places preserved for the public to enjoy.

They visited Totnes and took in the market set up in the middle of the town. They watched Morris dancers, browsed through antique and book shops then had lunch in one of the many ancient pubs. There was a myriad of things to do, they were spoiled for choice.

They took her to Torquay, Teignmouth and Dawlish. Bev was insistent that they walk from the Dawlish town centre to the church of Saint Gregory to check whether the unusual mounds in the graveyard were still there. It had been six years since they had been there. As they walked, they discussed what they had seen at the time and Tess was fascinated. But when they entered the graveyard and looked around at the headstones, there was not a trace of the strange mounds of soft earth covered in long grass. The grass amongst the markers was neatly mown. It had become even more of a mystery; they knew they were not mistaken in what they had seen.

Another day they visited Buckfast Abbey. They walked about through the monastic physic gardens planted just as had been done for centuries to provide the healing herbs of early medicine. The plant beds were in perfect symmetry and flanked by fragrant rose arbours. Bev and Tess were interested in the signs amongst the plants explaining the healing properties of each; lavender to calm, comfrey to heal and knit bones, lemon balm to calm, mint to aid digestion and rosemary to soothe a headache. There was a huge variety of the fragrant plants. Tess had studied herbalism and was familiar with them all. It so happened that they were there at the perfect time of day and as they walked about the gardens the cadence of voices rose and fell as the monks began their chant. It was the Gregorian chant and though they understood not a word, the beautiful sound uplifted the soul. Bev felt the hot sting of tears beginning and could see that Tess was equally moved by it also.

The abbey was entirely self-sufficient; orchards, gardens,

beehives and farm animals. Many products were sold in the abbey shop. They browsed in the gift shop and came out with specialty treats of lavender honey and tonic wine made by the monks. Ted nibbled on lavender shortbread as they walked to the car.

"I don't know about you girls, but I'm ravenous. We'll head out to Dartmoor National park and I'll treat you to lunch when we find somewhere nice."

"Sounds wonderful, Dad. I'm hungry, too."

"And me," Bev piped in.

He pulled up at a wayside inn that looked as though it could have appeared in the movie '*Lorna Doone*' and some of the people within could have been the characters.

"I'll bet this place has at least one ghost," whispered Tess as they found an empty table. To her delight, there was a write up on the menu telling of the ghost of a prisoner who had escaped Dartmoor prison in the 18th century and died on the moors of exposure. It was said that he made an appearance sitting near the hearth warming his hands every year on the anniversary of his death.

But any further thought of ghosts was banished as bowls of steaming stew were placed before them, with large chunks of succulent lamb, baby onions, carrots in rich dark gravy and flaky pastry. Ted tucked in with gusto and the girls followed his example. The food was excellent and the people so interesting that there was no need of conversation.

Following the meal, they continued their drive over the open wild moors. The road could be seen in the distance winding, twisting and curving in directions for so many miles they could see where they'd be some time from now. Bev couldn't resist... *"The road was a ribbon of moonlight over the purple moor, and the highwayman came riding, riding up to the old inn-door,"* she quoted then burst out laughing.

"Mum, I've never known anyone like you. You always have a poem or a song for every situation, don't you?" Tess laughed. Ted laughed too.

"Well, it's true. There's a line of a poem or song to fit every occasion. The older you are the more you know."

Clear rushing streams tumbled over rocky beds and flowed into the river Dart then outward to the sea. Random outcroppings of huge stones dotted the gorse covered landscape and shaggy wild ponies freely grazed the open space.

Though it was a beautiful sunny day with hardly a cloud in sight it was not difficult to imagine how bleak it would be here in winter. Bev shivered at the thought. In the distance they could make out the huge forbidding grey structure of Dartmoor prison and at that point they turned around and headed back.

***

The following day Tess announced that she was heading off on her own to explore some of the lovely places she wanted to see again; Sherborne, Cerne Abbas and especially Glastonbury. She wanted to climb the Tor, to visit the Chalice well, to browse in the crystal and new age shops and check out the latest crop circle sightings. So with her packed bag over her shoulder and map in hand, she set off with enthusiasm to catch the train to Exeter.

Bev and Ted used this opportunity to check out the availability of any houses or flats to be let. They found to their disappointment that it was not as easy as they had anticipated. One flat that they thought to be perfect was on the market one day and gone the next. They continued to search in Paignton but one morning Ted announced that he didn't think he'd be happy settling there.

"If I see that silly man wearing the pink bunny ears down town one more time, I think I'll scream." Bev had burst out laughing. It was true. Seaside towns did tend to attract some of the strangest characters.

"Truth be told, Bev, I'd like to check out my birthplace, Margate and Cliftonville." She was a bit surprised but agreed.

"When Tess leaves to go back home, we'll go then, dear." He seemed happy that she had agreed.

No sooner was Tess back from her travels than she was packing again for her flight to Vancouver. It had been a much-needed holiday and she had enjoyed herself, felt more rested than she had in a long while.

"I have a feeling I'll be back again soon, Mum, Dad. Don't worry about me, okay?" She dreaded goodbyes.

"Just make sure you call and write, dear," Bev held in check her emotions. To ease the journey a little they drove her to Newton Abbot for the train to London. It would save her a transfer with all her heavy luggage. Before they could say anymore, the train was in the station and then it was hurried kisses and hugs and waving from the window.

Tess arranged herself at a table seat and took a deep shuddering breath and then slow unbidden tears rolled down her cheeks. She hoped none had noticed. But to her surprise, a lovely Greek family had watched her hurried goodbyes on the platform.

"We'll help you with your luggage, dear, when we reach London," said the smiling motherly woman in her broken accent.

"Oh, how kind. Thank you so much, I'd be very grateful for your help," she replied wiping the tears from her cheeks. And then a conversation ensued and the journey was made so much easier.

Bev and Ted had held their emotions in check for Tessa's sake but as soon as the train left the platform, Ted made a hurried escape to the gents to spare Bev his upset. She had wandered across to a park to wait for him and he found her gazing up into the thick pink blossoms of an ornamental cherry tree, weeping her heart out. They hugged and cried together.

"God, how I hate saying goodbye to our kids. I feel quite certain we'll see her back here sooner than you might think, though," remarked Ted.

"Oh, I do hope you're right, I'm already missing her," Bev sighed.

Full Circle

"Do we really have to leave so early in the morning?" Bev whined. "You know I'm not a morning person."

"Indeed we do. It's a very long drive from here to Margate," argued Ted.

But for getting up early the next morning she was rewarded with one of the most spectacular pink dawn skies she had ever seen. As the road took them up a high hill out of town, she looked back toward the sea to the slowly fading beauty. And then gradually the sun rose higher to a perfectly cloudless blue sky.

"See what you've been missing?" Ted remarked. There was no argument to offer. She had been used to working late and lying in bed until 8 every morning. Ted would bring her a cup of coffee, and then a refill. Leisurely sipping the brew undisturbed, she would be ready to surface about an hour later. On the other hand, he was an early riser and crept out to get his morning paper then quietly returned to make his own breakfast. How spoiled she had been, she thought to herself as she gazed out the window at the changing scenery. But the arrangement worked for them so why change the routine.

The journey was a long one to be sure and they were exhausted by the time they had pulled up outside the little B&B at Number 16 Surrey Road just in time for the evening meal. It was a surprise to Bev that Ted had booked their stay at the place which had been his childhood home. The owners had only recently purchased the place and it was obvious they were keen to make a good impression. Bev and Ted were shown to their room, the one with a front balcony where they had stayed so many years previously. The 1950s decor remained and for Ted it was like stepping back in time to his childhood. There was just enough time to freshen up before dinner was announced. Descending the staircase, they lingered at intervals taking in all the old pictures of a bygone era and for a fleeting moment Ted was back in his past. The aroma of roast beef wafted up from the kitchen and it was as though he heard an echo of his mother's voice calling him for supper.

The table was lain with white linen, good china, old silver, crystal glasswear and centred with a bowl of bright flowers. Ted couldn't remember his mother going to so much trouble for guests but the effect was very welcoming. Their host seated them and lit candles then did likewise for another couple who had just made an appearance. And then he graciously introduced everyone creating a friendly atmosphere for an evening meal.

The wine was poured and within moments their hostess arrived and placed before them servings of roast beef, Yorkshire puddings, crispy roast potatoes with rich gravy and a medley of vegetables.

Bev took a sip of her wine and with a smile raised her glass to Ted.

"To your homecoming dear," she whispered.

"Thank you, love, it does feel like home and tomorrow we'll explore to see if there might be a place for us here."

***

They woke up to another beautiful sunny day and the tantalizing smell of frying bacon and freshly brewed coffee. Following a leisurely full English breakfast, they headed out on foot to explore their surroundings. At the bottom of the road was the old George Hotel which was boarded up and due for demolition to be replaced with a block of flats. Ted couldn't resist having a peek through the hazy windows into the ballroom. "My parents spent a lot of time here, partying and dancing well into the night. I remember I must have been about eight years old and I woke in the night with an earache and called for mother. When she didn't come, I tapped on the Irish maid's door. She was obviously annoyed to have her sleep disturbed and mumbled that my parents were down the street at the George. I threw on my clothes, crept out and made my way to the place. Peering in the window just as I'm doing now, I saw my parents on the dance floor. My mother was quite put out when she was summoned to see me. She marched me home with a scolding and I can't recall what she did for the earache." Ted made light of it.

"You poor little boy, I can almost picture your freckled little face peering in at them through the window," Bev remarked and steered him away from the place. But as they walked, Ted continued to talk as though now that memories had surfaced, he needed to speak out. "Perhaps my parents party attitude was a post war thing. I know my father saw so many horrific things during the war and comrades dying right beside him that maybe he needed to celebrate that he had been spared. I remember them always going to dances, and any excuse justified a party even when I was in my teen years. Then when they learned that I could remember jokes and mime Al Jolson, I was front and centre performing for all their friends." He made light of it but Bev sensed an underlying acid in his tone. Her life and their children's lives had been so very different from what he had known.

They crossed over the road to the bowling green where Ted could remember his grandfather all dressed in white, playing at bowls. "So typically British," he remarked as they walked the perimeter of iron railings enclosing the grounds. Across the expanse of lawn, they strolled to the promenade and gazed out at the sea far below. The sight of the golden sand, with waves lapping and a light breeze scented with seaweed and ozone stirred such feelings of nostalgia in Ted that for a moment he felt like the boy again. He had so many memories.

They walked the entire length of the promenade, ending up at the old clock tower. Ted remarked that like so many things viewed as a child, it seemed so much taller then. In the Margate town centre they were impressed with the variety of shops found there and stopped at a newsagent's for snacks and a local paper. Then sitting on a bench in a little park they munched on crisps and gleaned the ads. To their delight they found there was a good choice of rental flats to follow up on. They continued their walk all along Northdown Road and as they walked, Ted pointed out places he remembered and gave little anecdotes from the past. A sign 'Taylor's Emporium & Used

Furniture' caught their interest and Bev was keen to look inside.

They pushed open the creaky door to a place that more resembled a museum than anything. The place was literally crammed with everything imaginable; old tarnished silver, vases and china of every description, an entire shelf of scissors and knives, old pictures, postcards, paintings and brass wear. An upstairs room was jam packed with old furniture; tall wardrobes, bedsteads, tables, chairs, bookcases and much more. One could spend hours in the place and not see it all.

There was a pervasive smell of old and Ted felt almost overcome with a feeling of sadness as if all the furniture held memories of people's past.

"Let's get out of here, Bev, it gives me the creeps," he whispered.

"I'm feeling the same," she agreed and they made a hasty retreat out the door and back into the sunlit street. The sight of the church of St. Paul stirred memories of attending services there mainly with his grandparents but his parents did attend special holiday services; Easter, harvest festival and Christmas. The door to the church stood open and so they took a moment to look inside. Choir practice was just beginning but they were met with welcoming smiles so they sat in a pew and listened as the first hymn was sung. 'Abide with me, fast falls the eventide…' It was all Bev needed to hear to feel the hot sting of tears behind her eyes. It had been such a long time since she had attended church and it made her realize that she was in need of spiritual sustenance. They sat through the singing of the hymn then quietly made their way out.

"That was lovely," Bev whispered, wiping the tears from her eyes. Ted squeezed her hand in agreement then diverted her attention to a little bakery.

"Let's pop in here for coffee, love." He led the way.

She could see by the variety of baked goods in the bay window that she'd be in for a treat; gateaux of every sort, iced buns, donuts, tarts and cookies.

"Oh, Eccles cakes!" Ted exclaimed in delight. "I haven't had those in years, you'd love one, Bev." They did look yummy; sugary dried fruit-filled pastries.

They sat at a table by the window enjoying the cakes and coffee talking about the ads for flats in the paper. One in particular stood out from all the others. Under a listing by an estate agent in Broadstairs was a flat in the Palm Bay area which was a favourable location.

"Let's check this one out, Bev. I'll call them right away, but how about more of the Eccles cakes to take for later?"

"Good plan," she agreed. They emerged from the shop with a box of the treats and in the alcove of an antique shop Ted got out his cell phone and rang the agent. He was given the address for a drive by and was told that a viewing could be arranged if they were interested. In that mindset, they walked back to the guest house to freshen up and then seek out the place.

Their kindly host got out his survey atlas and pointed out the street location for them. He was pleased to hear that they had an interest in making a home there and wished them luck in finding a place .

"Why it's only two streets from here," Ted exclaimed in surprise. "We could walk there but after all the walking we've done already today I think we best drive."

The place was a huge early Victorian building that had been converted to modern flats. On the same street and opposite were nice middle-class homes with well cared for gardens. It was in an excellent location very close to a medical clinic, and shopping district within walking distance. It was situated very near a wide expanse of green that Ted recognized immediately as where he remembered summer fairs had been held. From there it was only a stone's throw to the beach.

"I love the location, such wonderful places to walk and fewer people compared to Paignton," Bev enthused.

"I'm happy you think so, Bev, because I quite like it too. I'll ring the agents now. Maybe someone could show us the flat."
Within the half hour a lady arrived with keys and they were shown in. They were pleased with what they found and agreed to stop by the office the next day to do the necessary paperwork.

***

It was but a short drive to Broadstairs and as they drove down the High Street Bev recognised it at once. They had been there before many years previous with Ted's parents on her first trip to England.

"Oh look, Ted, there's the restaurant where the waitress dropped a plate of fish and chips in your lap. Do you remember?"

"Indeed I do," he laughed." And here's the estate agents."

When they came out the door some time later after completing all the paperwork, they were none the wiser about whether the flat would be theirs. They were informed they would get a call as soon as references were checked. So they had a wander through the little town. It was a lovely little seaside place where Charles Dickens had lived and wrote some of his best novels. Many of the buildings dated back to that era and earlier. It was a popular haunt for Londoners for weekends and holidays so tended to get very busy.

They strolled the promenade to the rose gardens and found a sun-warmed bench near a bed of yellow beauties. They sat with the fragrance wafting around them and gazed out at sea. Ted's phone rang, he answered it on the second ring.

"Oh great! And we can pick up the keys now? Wonderful!" He was beaming. "Yeah!" Bev yelped, she could have danced with joy. "Let's go."

With the keys in hand, they returned to Cliftonville in a hurry now to see the flat that would soon be home. Opening the main door, they followed the hallway to the staircase and climbed the many steps to the third floor.

"This will be good exercise taking these stairs on a daily basis" remarked Ted. Bev put the key in the door of number 6, turned the knob and opened it. Then looking through it, this time with a more measured approach, they assessed what would be needed before they could comfortably move in. In the meantime, they would continue to stay on at the guest house. Tomorrow they'd come back and take measurements for furnishings but for now, just to know it was theirs was enough. One last look and they closed and locked the door.

"Come, Bev, let's celebrate with a drink at Ye Old Charles Pub."

Descending the stairs, on the next landing they met an elderly gent on his way up. "You must be the new tenants across from me at Number 5" he wheezed. "I'm Nick, I've lived here for years so anything you need to know, just ask."

"Nice to meet you Nick. I'm Ted and this is my wife, Bev," he said with a handshake.

"We'll be moving in soon, so see you." As they continued their descent, they could hear him gasping all the way up to his door.

"I think a chair at each landing would be good, he could rest at intervals," whispered Bev, always concerned with the welfare of the elderly.

"Seems like a friendly old chap," remarked Ted. Bev smiled to herself. She knew without a doubt that he would strike up a friendship with old Nick, they could share stories and he was probably a wealth of information.

"Let's just take a drive to check out our surroundings, Bev. I have a place in mind to take you. It's not far from here and then we can walk."

They drove through the Palm Bay area along the expanse of green to a small side road and then parked the car. They took a little path across a natural meadow then down a fairly steep concrete grade to the soft golden sand of the beach at Botany Bay. It was a breathtakingly beautiful spot with the white chalk cliffs rising behind them. A great arched pillar of chalk was separate from the cliffs and stood sentinel in the hard cool sand where the incoming tide lapped gently at its base. Save for a couple walking a great distance away, they were alone. The sea was calm and deep blue with a mist on the far horizon and screeching seagulls glided overhead. Far out, several huge freighters were anchored awaiting guidance to the Thames' estuary.

"I used to play in this very spot," Ted declared, then took off his shoes and socks and proceeded to walk along the water's edge. Bev followed but was reluctant to get her feet wet. She pulled her camera from her purse and snapped a photo of him; a solitary figure, barefoot, trousers rolled up walking along deep in thought as the waves lapped at his ankles. *I never wanted to leave this place all those years ago.*

Full circle. I have come full circle. They say you can't go home again, but here I am and it feels right. Maybe I will die here.

Bev gave him his moment, she was also deep in thought. She gathered up a handful of sand and sifted it through her fingers. *It is beautiful here, so much wide open space and fresh air. I hope I'll be happy here. For Ted's sake, I will try my very best.*

Then she ran to catch up to him and they walked back hand in hand across the golden sand.

Cliftonville

The kitchen window was a bright sunny spot for a window box and Bev was indulging her passion for gardening with potting herbs. She had selected purple sage, rosemary, thyme, parsley and chives. The aroma of the fragrant plants assaulted her senses and for a moment she could have been in one of the many gardens of her past. As she worked, a line of the song 'Scarborough Fair' softly played in her mind... 'are you going to Scarborough fair? Parsley, sage, rosemary and thyme' ...It was amazing how one could associate a certain scent with a memory. When she smelled the parsley and chives it took her right down the road of memory to her childhood home and her mother asking her to pick those herbs for the potato salad. Now there was a thought... perhaps she would make a potato salad for supper.

She cleared up her mess, secured the box and then stood back to admire her creation. She was pleased with the effect and the assurance that every time she entered the kitchen she would be greeted with the uplifting scent of her herbs. She defied anyone saying that an apartment dweller could not enjoy gardening, every other window in the place displayed her handiwork. Jasmine, rose geranium and African violets graced the bedroom window ledges, whereas white rose and gardenia were on display in the sitting room and fern in the bathroom. She had placed bright red geraniums in the windows of the stairwells, tropical plants by the chairs she had strategically placed for old Nick to rest and outside along the wall to the parking area grew scarlet runner beans, marigolds, petunias and a climbing pink rose. It had taken them weeks to furnish the place to their liking and the plants just added the finishing touch.

They had finally got sorted out with a landline telephone and internet service and Ted was well pleased, he had been quite lost without his computer. He was sitting at the desk checking and answering his emails when Bev brought him a cup of tea. "Anything of interest?" she asked as she placed the cup at his elbow.

"One here from Phil and Sonia ...all is well and they have already started the process of getting a work visa for Sonia. They hope to come next spring."

"Wonderful. And Tess, anything from her?"

"Here, you sit and read."

Bev had tears in her eyes when she finished reading the emails. Tess was not getting on well with her boyfriend and all she could think about was returning to England. She missed them so much but couldn't make a move yet. Bev replied to her email immediately... "You're welcome anytime. dear, we will help with your airfare. Just say the word. We miss you, too."

***

The forecast was for a warm dry summer and there were so many places to explore. One of the first places Ted took her was to Reculver. A Roman fort had been there followed later by a royal residence of early kings. All that remained was the double towers of a medieval monastery which was a landmark to shipping. They walked around the base which was precariously close to the sea but protected by a sturdy seawall. Of interest was the fact that hundreds of years previous the structure had been some distance from the sea, proof that the coastline was ever changing. Ted laughingly recalled how on one of his many escapades as a lad he had taken the bus to Reculver unbeknown to his parents.

"It so happened that I was spotted by someone who knew my parents and he phoned them. I believe he drove me home. It was to the chalet without supper that day for certain."

"Good Lord, Ted, you really were a little hellion, weren't you? I can understand your parents' upset, but I think depriving you of supper was pretty harsh punishment. Can't imagine our kids ever doing such a thing."

"Well, I suppose being an only child made mischief easier, no one to tell on me," he chuckled. "Come, I want to show you the village of St. Nicholas at Wade."

The road took them through open countryside with vast fields of bright yellow rape plants, fields of blue flax and white blossoming potatoes. Farms dotted the landscape, some with grazing herds of cattle and in the distance the sparkling ever-present sea. A road sign ahead directed them to the tiny village and Ted made a right hand turn. They followed the road to the centre and parked the car near the parish church. It was the lunch hour so they gave in to their stomachs first and walked to the nearest pub. There were tables outside so Bev seated herself under an umbrella.

"What do you fancy love?" Ted enquired as he opened the oaken door. "Surprise me," she replied.

He appeared a short time later with glasses of cool draught beer and bags of onion-flavoured crisps and as he handed her a glass ... "I'm pretty sure I used to come here with my grandfather and I would sit outside with lemonade and a bag of crisps." As he opened the bag and took a crisp, he remarked... "In those days, crisps were unsalted but a little blue packet of salt was in the bag to sprinkle if you wanted."

"How quaint," Bev remarked. "Funny that you should remember that detail."

Within a short time, their meals were placed before them; pan-fried Whitstable oysters for Ted and crab cakes with garden salad for Bev.

"Thank you, love, good choice," and she dove in with gusto.

"I know you don't care for oysters but I love them. They came fresh today from just up the way in Whitstable. It's well known for sea food. We'll have to visit there, too, one day."

Following their meal, they walked through the village which was made up of two pubs, a post office, a small general store, an antique shop, the parish church and a community hall and that was about it. Few people were out and about, the reason they soon discovered was that a jumble sale was being held at the hall and it was crowded.

"Oh, I love a jumble sale, Ted. Let's have a peek. Never know what we might find." Bev was on her way through the door before he could respond. The place was a buzz of activity; old ladies pushing forward to grab at a pile of clothing and children snatching through boxes of toys, men gathered in a corner in conversation hesitant, to get involved in the melee. Ted escaped outside for a cigarette but it didn't stop Bev from diving in. She emerged with a grin bearing a bag of her purchases; wooden spoons, a jar of local honey, a cook book and a slab of rich iced chocolate cake from the bake table.

"That was so much fun," she laughed.

They put her bag in the car then leisurely strolled through the village. Bev stopped ever so often to smell roses and jasmine blooming in abundance, to admire the hollyhocks in a profusion of bright colours taller than she. Seldom did they pass a church without having a look inside and this parish church of St. Nicholas was no exception. There was usually a wealth of history to absorb. They entered the cool sanctuary and walked about studying the stained-glass windows and reading the epitaphs. As Ted paused to read a particularly ancient one, it occurred to him that he had not had contact with his mentor in a very long while, not in fact since his scathing critique about his writing. It had put him in such a foul mood he had shredded the entire copy of his manuscript and in that state of mind had deleted the file also. He had been untruthful to Bev about saving a file. Though he knew she would find him out at some time, he wasn't going to let that bother him now. As far as he was concerned, it mattered not if the story was ever told. It was as if his brother had stepped back, given him more space and waited, always waited.

He joined Bev who was interested in the ancient wooden stairs leading to a very small closed door. She had cautiously climbed up them and tried the door, but it was locked.

"Someone is coming, Bev, hurry down at once," Ted whispered.

A middle-aged woman bearing a bucket of fresh-cut flowers entered, she had come to arrange the floral displays for Sunday service. She nodded in their direction and went quietly about her task. But it was their cue to leave.

That evening as Ted sat watching TV, Bev entered the sitting room with a tea tray which she placed on the coffee table in front of him. She passed his tea and a slice of cake then sat across the room in her favourite chair.

"Ted, you know I've been wondering if you might start writing on your book again now that we're settled?"

Ted choked on his tea and spluttered and coughed so violently that she got up and whacked him on the back several times. "Are you okay now?"

"Yes. Yes, I am. Sorry about that, dear. Yes, perhaps I will start on it again, but with the nice summer weather we're having I think it's important we get out and enjoy our surroundings, so much to see and do. Winter might be a better time."

"That's true. I'm sure you'll know when the time is right," Bev replied then spoke no more on the subject. Ted took another sip of tea and stared at the TV, his brain not registering what his eyes were seeing but thinking how uncanny it was that she had brought up his writing. It was as though she had tapped into his thoughts of today.

***

It was Wednesday and another gorgeous sunny day. How lucky they were for the warm weather. Ted had suggested a drive to Sandwich. He couldn't remember having been before so they were in for another adventure. Aware that the main roads could be quite busy, he drove the quieter out of the way routes and they were rewarded with wonderful sights.

Apple orchards both sides of the road confirmed the adage that Kent county was 'the garden of England'. The trees hung with huge apples ripening in the summer heat and a hint of the aroma wafted through the open car windows as they drove along. At intervals they would come upon a farm or a roadside pub. They stopped at 'The Duck and Dog' in Plucks Gutter for a cool drink.

The gardens around the place were a horticulture showpiece of bright flowers; window boxes, hanging baskets, pots and beds overflowed with a profusion of colour. Not only did the gardens impress but also the path leading to the river Stour. Long drooping branches of willow trees almost touched the gently flowing water, and huge blue dragonflies skimmed the surface. The river was very narrow here but Ted explained to her that there were many tributaries some much wider and flowing through many places; Canterbury, Chillum, Fordwich and Sandwich all joining to empty into the sea at Pegwell Bay below Plucks Gutter. Bev was amused at the name and added it to her mental list of many other unusual names of places, pubs and houses in England.

"I'll remember this place, Ted. It's lovely here, we must come back again."

"I agree. We will for sure," he replied.

They drove into the medieval town of Sandwich and were delighted with what they found. It was market day. They leisurely strolled through looking at all the stalls. There were many choices; antiques, house ware, sausages, Turkish delight, clothing and fresh farm produce and much more.

"We can make our purchases on the way back, Ted. Let's walk for a while?"

"Fine with me, I'm hungry so let's have our picnic by the river."

They wandered down a tree-lined walkway to the lazily flowing river and sat on a park bench. The Stour was much wider here. As they ate the sandwiches they watched a young lad fishing from the river's edge. Small silver fish jumped here and there and then a bite on the fishing line. Pleased with his catch he reeled it in with a grin in their direction.

It was a lovely peaceful place and following lunch, they continued to walk the Butts as far as it went in one direction. At the end of the walkway they crossed a road to a bird sanctuary. The entrance was a worn wooden gate. Bev read aloud the plaque displayed on the gate. It stated that the large field to their left had been the site of hangings back in the day. Those who had been hanged had been buried in an upright position, not even in death allowed repose. Looking across at the lumpy surface of the field, now a wild flower meadow, she shuddered at the thought. But that was not the extent of it... the still green pond to their right had been the ducking pond for those accused of witchcraft. The poor souls were 'swum', hands crossed and tied to ankles and thrown in the water. If they floated they were said to be guilty and hanged; if they sunk and drowned it proved innocence. Either outcome doomed them to death.

She pushed open the gate and reverently stepped forward, Ted followed. Bev gazed into the still green depth of the pond imagining the horrific happenings of the past but her thoughts were interrupted by a flock of ducks waddling down the path towards them. It changed the mood entirely, one could not help but be amused by their antics. They had been conditioned that the arrival of people meant a handout. Small bags of grain could be purchased from a dispensing machine along the pathway. They laughed at the ducks as they impatiently waited while Bev put in her coin. Then the troop of quackers followed them along the path as she scattered the grain.

It was peaceful there amongst the trees. It was as though all the negative energy from the horrific sufferings that had occurred there in the past were atoned with the presence of nature, the wild flowers and birdlife. But that past should never be forgotten.

On the walk back they discovered a medieval hospital and stopped to read the plaque. Bev had always been interested in the history of medicine so it was a treat for her to see the well-preserved ancient building. She could almost imagine what the treatment of the sick would have been like; rudimentary care, no more than a place of refuge, bread and hot broth rationed out by the monks.

They continued their walk by the river where small boats were anchored and passengers were boarding a craft for a tour down the river.

"Now that would be a pleasant outing," exclaimed Ted.

"Yes, we could do that another time dear. I really want to get back to the market square before they pack up," she replied.

They wandered back through the town, window shopping as they went and arrived back at the market which was still a hive of activity. Bev made her purchases of fruit and vegetables then searched for Ted in a sea of heads. She spotted him at the French stall where he was talking to the vendor about the donkey sausage and nibbling a sample.

"You're brave," she whispered as she selected a box of Turkish Delight.

"It's quite nice really, but think I'll settle for the salami. Quarter pound, please."

Happy with their purchases they headed back to the car and home. Sandwich would become one of their favourite places to return to time and time again always on market Wednesdays.

***

The dog days of summer were upon them with day after day of clear blue skies and unrelenting heat. Ted called it the mad August sweat for people did seem more irritable when it was so hot. It was almost impossible to enjoy eating outdoors for mean wasps seemed to be everywhere. One could only feel sorry for those in the inner cities, those working in uniform and in any workplace that was not air conditioned. Frazzled mothers yelled at bored and cranky children and couldn't wait for them to be back in school. Bev witnessed a child having a tantrum in the middle of Tesco's and when the screaming became too intense, she made a hasty exit vowing to do her shopping at a quieter time of day.

The majority of families flocked to the Margate beach because of the proximity to the fast food kiosks and penny arcade. It was a colourful and noisy scene.

Bev and Ted preferred the quieter coves of golden sand beneath the chalk cliffs and spent the hottest part of the day relaxing there in deck chairs.

Ted stretched out his sun-tanned legs and sifted sand between his toes as he gazed out across the expanse of water to the misty horizon.

"You can't begin to imagine how happy I am to be back here, Bev. It's as though I've found a part of me that had been missing."

"I'm so pleased, dear, and I'm happy here too," she replied. And it was true. She was content to be retired and spend every day with him. Who knew how many years they would have together she thought. Best that they be happy ones.

Cliftonville Winter

A chill North East wind at the end of October announced that winter was upon them. Bev wrapped her fleecy jacket firmly over her hips and pulled on her red wool hat, she wasn't about to let a cold wind stop her from taking her daily walk near the beach.

"The sea can be pretty ferocious in wind like this, Bev, so be careful," Ted warned as he plugged in the kettle for tea.

"I'll be fine...got the cell phone with me." She pecked him on the cheek and let herself out the door. It was invigorating to step out in the wind. She walked briskly along the promenade slanting into the northeaster and peered over the railing to the furiously churning, boiling sea below. Huge wild waves crashed on the seawall sending up great plumes of briny spray. She leapt out of reach of a particularly large spray, laughing at herself as she did so. She could taste salt.

Bev had wanted Ted to join her, but he had declined, having woken up this morning feeling achy and out of sorts. She hoped he wasn't coming down with something. She realized, of course, that sometimes his achy feelings heralded a psychic influence. She felt dread at the prospect. With this thought in mind, she turned for home having been out already for over an hour.

The wind now at her back had the force to propel her forward, quickening her steps so that she arrived at the door much sooner than she thought possible. A blast of wind slammed the door behind her and she climbed the steps to their flat. It had been a good workout and she wasn't at all tired. I'm in pretty fair shape for an old girl, she thought.

Ted was huddled as close to the fireplace as he could get. He was feeling miserable and relieved to hear her come in. He couldn't bring himself to voice his concern but he worried when Bev was out on her own; whatever would he do if anything dreadful happened to her and he was left alone? It didn't bear thinking about. While she was out he had come to the realization that a powerful foreboding of something wrong with either of the children was the source of the ache to his very bones.

"Hi dear, glad you're home," he called. "Come join me for a drink to warm you." Bev hung up her hat and coat realizing that her hands were freezing in spite of the exercise; she'd have to remember to wear her gloves next time. She poured a schooner of sherry and joined him in the sitting room.

"You were right, the sea was wild but exciting. You would have enjoyed it. How are you feeling?"

"Sit dear, it's what I need to talk about. I have a sense that something is troubling either of the children. Such an uncomfortable sense that something is very wrong."

"Well, we best give them a phone call before they head off to work. It would be about 8:30 there. Try Phil first, he's bound to be up," she was concerned. Ted was rarely wrong about his intuition.

"Hi, Dad, nice to hear your voice."

"Likewise son, is everything okay with you?"

"Yes, I'm fine. Just upset is all. We didn't want you worrying being so far away and all so I've kept it from you. But now that we know Tess will be alright, I might just as well tell you ... her bastard boyfriend roughed her up in an argument and pushed her hard against a wall, hitting the back of her head. She had the sense to call 911 for an ambulance and the police got involved as they do. She went to hospital for a skull x-ray and observation overnight. Sonia and I sat with her. She's here with us now but very fragile. I think she would be embarrassed to talk to you right now, Dad, but maybe soon. It's been very hard to keep from going and beating the crap out of him, but most probably he's living in fear of an assault charge, the police want her to press charges."

"And so she should. I had a dreadful feeling that something was wrong." Ted briefed Bev quickly as she had such a worried look. "Well son, that is upsetting news, but in future never feel you have to keep anything from Mum and I. We are always here for you. Give Tess a hug for us and tell her to call when she feels up to it. Here's Mum, she's anxious to talk to you. Bye, for now, Phil and God bless. Our love to Sonia, too." He passed the phone to Bev.

She talked until Phil announced that he'd be late for work. "Tell Tess I'll write, hug her for me and you take care. Love you, darling, bye for now."

Bev was furious..." There was something about that bugger that I didn't like right from the get go and I've always had a pretty keen sense about people as you know, Ted. This is really upsetting." She was on the brink of tears but was able to channel her upset into a letter she sat down and wrote almost at once.

My dearest Tess,

Words cannot express how sorry I feel for you that this last upset has happened. You must surely realize now that you are caught up in a circle of abuse and must get off the merry-go-round. It takes the two of you to play the game and the equation of alcohol would only exacerbate the situation. You do or say something that triggers him to lash out verbally but when it has now accelerated to physical abuse, you must break the chain. You blame yourself that you upset him to that point, he asks your forgiveness, showers you with gifts, you kiss and make up only for it to happen again and again- until something even more dreadful happens. The police are very aware of this, they see it all the time. You have come to a crossroad in your life, Tess, and the path you take now determines your future. You can carry on down that path of destruction to your spirit if you choose, or you can make a drastic change and come away. He'll not follow it's too far away. Break the cycle and save yourself, start a new life. Dad and I will help you all we can. In time you will find new friends and someone who loves you the way you deserve. So there you go, I've said it. Choose life.

All my love, Mama

Bev read to Ted what she had written and with his approval, she sealed the letter. Then gulping down the last of her sherry to steel herself, she headed back out into the bitter wind to mail her letter and that accomplished, she felt a modicum of relief from the stress and upset of the situation. She prayed that Tess would heed her advice.

***

Within hours of receiving her mother's letter, Tess was already making plans to leave for England. It would give her satisfaction to hear his pleading voice begging her not to go. She knew full well that he would promise not to hurt her again and even though it was the first time he had physically abused her, she had tolerated verbal abuse on a number of occasions. The first she noticed was that he was rude to his mother in her presence and it had embarrassed her. She ignored the alarm bells going off in her head at the time but in reflection, abruptness with his mother should have been a warning to her. How blinded she had been to think he loved her. That was not love. Love was gentle and kind.

Over the next several days, Tess was in a flurry of activity preparing to leave. She went shopping and bought an extra-large suitcase. She purchased Christmas gifts for her parents as well as for Phil and Sonia. She bought herself a new wardrobe, perfume and jewellery. The spending spree had lifted her spirits.

She sat wrapping gifts to take with her and those to leave behind for Christmas morning. Then she packed boxes of all her possessions to be shipped when Phil and Sonia planned to follow in the spring.

The boyfriend did everything he could to make amends, to change her mind about leaving, but she held firm. On the day of her departure he even showed up in tears to bid her farewell. But the memory of his battering was fresh in her mind and moved her forward to her new life without a backward glance. He was not yet aware that she had dropped the charges against him, she thought she'd let him stew a while longer. She had been so lucky to be able to walk away with her head held high; so many other women in that situation weren't so blessed. She knew her mother was right, he would not follow, she would be free.

At Heathrow, Bev and Ted waited with anticipation at the arrivals' gate watching others greet their loved ones. This scene of happy reunions never failed to bring a lump to Bev's throat. The waiting seemed forever and then finally there she was with a grin from ear to ear, looking stylish in a new outfit and pushing her luggage cart which was overburdened with a huge blue suitcase as well as other bags. Through tears and laughter, they hugged and kissed her and exclaimed how great she looked and how good to see her.

It was a long drive back to Cliftonville so by the time they reached home it was late and they were all very tired. Tess admitted she had been able to sleep for an hour or two on the flight but after a light meal, unpacking and visiting, she was ready for a hot bath and to fall into bed.

It was great to see her parents and they had made her feel so loved and welcome. Nonetheless, she silently cried into her pillow from sheer exhaustion of all she had endured and also from the relief she felt at being saved. She fell into a deep sleep only to awake in the wee hours hungry and craving a coffee. Not wanting to wake her parents she crept out to the kitchen and closed the door. Bev had shown her where to find everything she needed so she made a cup of coffee with buttered toast. She turned the radio on low and listened to the latest British hit tunes as she sipped her coffee. Yes, she was happy to be back in England and coming to the East coast would be a whole new experience.

The very next day, Bev had her out on a forced march down the many steps to the seawall and the beach. They talked as they walked and she unburdened her soul to the listening ear of her mother. That and the bracing wind had a cleansing therapeutic effect and she was beginning to feel better already.

That evening, Bev presented her with a crochet hook and a basket of yarn in assorted tones of blues, greens and purples. When she wasn't able to sleep it helped her mind to keep her hands busy. Every stitch held a thought and by the time she was over jet lag she had crocheted an entire afghan which she called 'insomnia.'

Every morning she started the day with a brisk walk on the seawall and in only a week she had lost eight pounds. She was pleased with her trim figure and it gave her the confidence she would need to seek work. On that note, she was going to have to wait until after Christmas for an appointment to get her national insurance number, much to her dismay. But Bev and Ted assured her that it was for the best, it would give her time to acclimatize to her new way of life.

They treated her as though she was on holiday and took her to all their favourite haunts, markets, shopping areas and pubs. Soon she knew her way around and was then out and about on her own. In particular, she liked the town of Broadstairs and spent time familiarizing herself with all it had to offer. She submitted CV's to a few places of employment and was pleased with the response she received. She put it down to her enthusiasm and her accent.

***

December sea fog seemed to permeate right through their winter wear to their bones causing Bev and Tess to step up their pace as they walked the seawall.

"Say, Mum, I was wondering if Dad has taken up writing again? Only I didn't want to ask him."

"Well, not that I know of, dear. I don't like to badger him if he's not in the mood. He did say he might this winter." There was silence between them as they mounted the many stairs to the promenade and when they reached the top...

"Well, I have never mentioned this before, Mum, but do you remember when Dad shredded his manuscript?"

"I do indeed," Bev replied. Her interest was sparked.

"Well, I had written a short story, one I thought I might carry on to write a novel about and I showed Dad, as you know I value his opinion. He read it and then said to me, 'Now this is what I call good writing, not the clap trap sort of stuff that I've been trying to do.' I feel responsible somehow as it was right after that he shredded his writing."

"Really?" Bev was incredulous. "He said nothing about that, Tess. I just assumed he was in a psychic black mood. You can't be to blame. Did you write anymore?"

"No. I couldn't bring myself to, thinking that it was my fault he had quit. But I still have it. In fact, I have it with me if you'd like to read it, Mum?"

"I would love that, Tess. Best hurry now, it's starting to rain."

That evening when Bev was tucked up in her bed to read, Tess handed her two pages of double-spaced print and stood at the end of the bed awaiting her mother's response.

January 1999 Madrigal

My name is now Madrigal and I'm running for my life. I'm on the TransCanada Highway now just outside of Abbotsford and the snow is coming down hard. The windshield wipers doing double time and still not keeping up. The snowflakes, if I look up into them, are hypnotizing, dizzy dancing, and if I stare too hard I lose the road and think too much.

My intention is to make the 7 pm sailing to the Island, but at this rate I don't know. The snow now piling up fast on the highway and we are all down to a crawl. My car an '81 Oldsmobile, 'Daisy', baldy tires and tired brakes; the only thing keeping me from sliding and meeting the ditch is the sheer weight of her right now, packed tight with the last of all that I own, or care to, including three cats.

If I do not leave now I will not have a life, not one worth living anyway, and sometimes windows of opportunity open and shut in the space of a few days or a few hours. Armando awaits me in a motel outside of Victoria. It was imperative that we get him far enough away that no one would find him, and then I would return to gather our last remaining possessions. It was, after all, really him they were after. Timing is everything, and it was not lost on me the finely tuned manoeuvrings of a compassionate universe. Armando received a large payout from a medical annuity a week ago, just at the same time we heard news that winds of friendship had changed direction and not in our favour. We were not safe, he was wanted, we were suspect and under surveillance, and we needed to make some very different plans. How could Armando have known all those years ago that a motorcycle accident that left him with a shattered kneecap and a broken body would indeed save his skin on some future date?

The two lions, Gizmet and Wazan, now snarling and attacking each other in their carrier in the rear seat, crazy and mad on tranquillisers that were intended to knock them for six. Their voices slurry and drunk, hurling insults as well as claws. India in her own carrier (I could have done this differently I now realize) howling like a banshee in fear and pissing like a horse all over herself

What the hell did that vet give them anyway?

My blood pressure starting to rise now, my desire for a drink so intense that I'm starting to shake. There is a bottle of vodka somewhere in this mess, I know ...probably the trunk, but there is no way I'm stopping for it now.

Despite my fear of the unknown, there is something exciting about leaving everything behind. There is nothing calling my heart back, not now, not in this moment. Even people who love me there, those that remain, may believe that I am a softy, crying now as I drive away, tears of pain for the parting of ways. But my cheeks are dry, very dry. Dry with cold, dry because I need moisturizer, dry because there are no more tears to spare.

In the years to come, I cannot know it now, but I will cry for what was left behind. I'll cry for a life that cannot be recreated and lives only as a memory, the scene of a perfect crime that I cannot return to. The girl I was for so many years, she is still standing very quietly gazing out across the lake like a tree that has lost a few branches and many leaves. She will become a ghost to me that wakes me in the night and asks far too many questions, but for now I hardly miss her.

"That is so good, Tess. It immediately grasps my interest and I want there to be more." Bev smiled. "I can see where Dad was coming from, and you do have a gift, I've always known that. Never let anyone dissuade you from writing, it is such an amazing outlet for your emotions and one day you will write that novel."

"Thank you, Mum, you've always been so supportive and I really appreciate it. Though I wrote it years ago, it's uncanny how I wrote then almost a reflection of what I am going through now, leaving a life behind and starting fresh."

"How true. Thank you for sharing it with me, dear. Now put it in a safe place and; get yourself to bed. You look very tired."

***

A huge Christmas hamper compliments of Phil and Sonia arrived one morning in mid-December. It was packaged extravagantly in a large wicker basket stuffed with every imaginable delicacy; chocolates, cheeses, crackers of every sort, biscuits, pudding, wine and much more. Christmas hampers were a very British tradition and it was a delightful surprise to receive one.

In the days leading up to Christmas, Bev and Tess busied themselves baking and preparing for their Christmas Eve feast. The spicy aroma of fresh baked gingerbread wafted throughout the flat to where Ted sat reading the paper, anticipating a cup of tea and a sample he knew that Bev would bring him shortly. She waited on him hand and foot these days and he could not deny that he loved the attention.

"Cup o' tea dear?" Bev called. And then there it was before him, a cup of steaming sweet tea and a plate of gingerbread cookies.

"Tess and I are going out for a walk, there's a few things I need from Tescos."

"Take care, dear, and thank you, you're so good to me," he looked up with a smile and took a sip of the hot tea.

"Of course, I am," she smiled and kissed him on the forehead.

Ted had planned a surprise for the girls. He had booked dinner at the old Walpole hotel for Christmas Day. He would tell them Christmas morning before Bev had a chance to begin her preparations, the bird could wait until Boxing day. Not only was it within walking distance from home so he would not need to worry about having a drink and driving, but also as there was just the three of them he thought it would be fun to celebrate with other guests. Pubs and hotels all over the country were fully booked well in advance, it being a popular English way to celebrate the holiday. How well he remembered Christmas at his parents' guest house. He realized it must have been so much work for his mother but how he had enjoyed those festive times. His mind strayed back to then but was jolted back to the present by the girls' noisy return.

"There's the smell of snow in the air, Dad. Maybe we'll have a white Christmas. Wouldn't that be nice? You know it will be my first English Christmas since I was a child."

"It would indeed, just as long as it doesn't hang around too long," he answered."

"And, yes, I know you've not had an English Christmas since Catford days, so I've planned something extra special."

"Now I am curious," she replied with excited anticipation.

***

Christmas eve it snowed, transforming their surroundings to a winter wonderland. The blanket of snow gave a hushed and magical quality to the atmosphere and put them in a holiday spirit.

A fire crackled in the fireplace, frankincense scented candles glowed on the mantle and colourful lights adorned the tree. They sat opening gifts, picking at goodies and sipping drinks to the backup holiday music from a TV Christmas special. For the many years they had performed this ritual it was always so special. They wished only that Phil and Sonia were here and perhaps all going to plan, they would be together next Christmas.

When all the gifts had been opened, with thank yous and hugs exchanged, Bev sat neatly folding the wrapping paper as usual.

"Now, what is that surprise you promised, Dad?"

"Well, that I'm saving for the morning, you have to have something left for Christmas morning," he said with a twinkle in his eye.

Christmas day turned out to be all that Ted had anticipated. Bev was totally surprised and delighted that she would be free of the kitchen and Tess just loved dining out.

The snow scrunched under foot as they made their way to the hotel. "Let's just take a bit of a diversion girls. I want to see my old home."

The snow had made the little guest house look as festive as a Christmas card with coloured lights and snow clad evergreens. To their surprise, Ted walked up the path and rang the doorbell. Unbeknown to the girls, they were expected to drop by for a cup of Christmas cheer.

"Merry Christmas. Welcome!" chimed the proprietors in unison. They had done a wonderful job of 50s style decorating and to Ted it was like stepping back in time to his childhood. Little bubble glass cups of mulled wine were passed around to the guests and they helped themselves to an array of tasty treats arranged at the bar. Time passed quickly with pleasant conversation and they were soon saying goodbye.

It had continued to snow so that by the time they stepped out into the early winter darkness their footprints were already covered. Huge snowflakes swirled about them as they picked their way along the snow-covered pavement.

"That was so much fun," exclaimed Tess. "Thank you, Dad. We could see that you enjoyed yourself, too."

"Yes, it was fun, but kind of weird. A bit like stepping through a time warp."

"I loved it," said Bev, taking Ted's arm to keep from slipping.

Then approaching the Walpole, the pleasant sound of Christmas music wafted out into the night from the latticed front veranda, lavishly decorated with trees and lights. They were greeted at the door by the hostess and ushered through to a dining room dimly lit by candlelight, tables set with white linen, crystal and silverware. Many of the guests had arrived and were already seated and called out a greeting as they made their way to a table.

Soft Christmas music blended with the hum of many voices in conversation over a traditional meal of roast turkey and all the trimmings. Champagne bubbles caught the candlelight and sparkled in crystal flutes as they raised a toast to a "Merry Christmas!"

Bev wiped her lips with her napkin and smiled at Ted who had stifled a groan as a brandy-flamed pudding was placed before them. This was the truly traditional end to an English Christmas dinner and no matter how full, one had to partake. Served with rum sauce it was absolutely delicious.

They stepped out into a night of falling snow, the swirling flakes caught in the glow of lamplight gave a magical quality for which fun-loving Tess could not resist. She leaned down and scooped up a handful of snow and tossed it at Ted's back as he walked ahead of her, hand in hand with Bev. That first lobbed snowball seemed to spark the child within all of them and began a boisterous, giggling, laughing, frolic in the snow which put just the right note to the end of a perfect Christmas Day.

The Winter of His Life

In the winter of his life, Ted enjoyed one last memorable and enjoyable year. It was true that he appeared much older than his years. His hair was almost white now and he had a slight stoop to his shoulders as though carrying the weight of his psychic burden over all the years had aged him prematurely. He was no longer visited by his mentor who seemed to have lost all patience with him. He had also noticed of late that Bev no longer had the light of patience in her eyes. She no longer mentioned the book he had never got around to writing and of this he was glad. It was just too much of an undertaking and besides there always seemed too much else to be doing.

Tess had needed help to get settled in Broadstairs. He was so happy that she had found just the right job which she enjoyed and was making new friends. She was fortunate to find a place to live from which she could walk to work; a room in a huge Victorian home of a young couple with two children. They treated her like family. She was welcome to join them for meals or she had access to the kitchen and could make her own. The best part was that she was not alone.

He made sure that she was invited to join him and Bev on shopping expeditions, pub lunches and outings to all their favourite places. She would join them for meals, always enjoying her mother's cooking. Life was good and they looked forward to the arrival of Phil and Sonia, hoped they would settle nearby.

That spring day quickly arrived and they waited at Heathrow to meet them. It was a repeat of the day they had met Tess, waiting at the arrivals area for what seemed like ages. Then there they were with smiling faces that melted away all the months of separation. Ted hugged his son with tears in his eyes.

"Welcome, Son, so good to see you." And then they all took it in turn for hugs of welcome to them both.

Within days of their arrival, they announced that they would be heading to Cornwall to live. They had fallen in love with the place on an earlier holiday. They could not be dissuaded.

"Oh well, it will give us an excuse to visit the West Country, Bev," Ted exclaimed with enthusiasm, hoping that she would feel less disappointed with their choice.

"That's true," she said grudgingly. "But nothing like coming all this way only to be on the opposite side of the country from us. I'm certain it's Sonia's doing, I don't think she likes sharing our Phil."

"Now, that's no way to talk, dear. Let's just enjoy their company while they're still here. We'll all go to Dover tomorrow. You'd enjoy that wouldn't you?"

"Yes, I would. And now I must get supper ready. They'll be back from Broadstairs any moment," she stated with finality.

The following, day they all piled into the Volvo, Phil in the front with Ted and the girls in the back seat. Phil was not yet aware that Ted planned to give him the car so he was curious to know what he thought of it.

"This old girl rides pretty smoothly, Dad. It's spacious too."

"Well, it's yours if you want it, will save the worry of transportation for a while and it's reliable."

Sonia piped up from the back seat… "It's a far cry from our sports car back home but I suppose it will do. Saves us a car rental at least."

Bev rolled her eyes heavenward, nothing like looking a gift horse in the mouth she thought to herself. But her thoughts were interrupted by Tess's cell phone chirping every few minutes with text messages. She giggled as she read them.

"Someone sounds awfully persistent," remarked Bev. But just then they pulled into the car park and Tess gave her a look to stifle any further comment.

It was a beautiful sunny and mild April afternoon and the view across the channel was breathtaking. From the vantage point of the cliff path they enjoyed a panorama of the sea, Dover castle, the town below and the ferry terminal.

Bev and Tess hung back from the others, talking in low tones.

"I've met a really nice fella, Mum, and he keeps texting me from Spain. He's at his parents' villa for a week."

"How lovely, dear. I knew there would be someone out there for you. I'm pleased." Bev hugged her waist.

Ted and Phil were in conversation ahead of them, Sonia holding on to Phil's arm. She looked back over her shoulder...

"Now, what are you two whispering about that can't be shared with the rest of us?" she levelled.

"Oh, nothing, no one that you know," retorted Tess, wanting to keep her new found friendship to herself until she was ready to make it known. Just at the moment Sonia was looking back, she took a step precariously close to the cliff edge and Bev gasped in fear. Luckily she was holding Phil's arm.

"Keep to the path, you guys. It's a long fall to the bottom."

"It is indeed," remarked Ted and went on to tell them that the chalk cliffs were slowly, continuously eroding away and great chunks had been known to crumble away without warning. He mentioned the fact that in 2001, Beachy Head near Eastbourne in East Sussex, the highest of the chalk cliffs at over 500 ft., had after a winter of heavy rainfall, crumbled away. He also threw in the information that it was a notorious place for suicides over the years.

Bev added that the locals actually patrolled the area hoping to prevent anyone from carrying out such a mission. It was difficult to comprehend how one's life could be so out of control to choose death as a way out, especially in that manner. What a shock it would be to pass to the other side and realize what one had done.

Tess felt a wave of vertigo as she peered over the edge to the crashing sea below. "All this talk gives me the creeps," she moaned and was happy when Ted announced it was time to leave. He wanted to stop in Sandwich for lunch and show off a favourite haunt.

***

London heaved with tourists. The air was like an oven with an over-baked smell of people and petrol fumes and it was only the beginning of summer. Bev and Ted had taken the train from Margate to the city to meet Phil, Sonia and her parents who were on their first ever trip to England.

In retrospect, the kids had been lucky to find work and a place to live within weeks of arriving in Cornwall. But they had no more than settled in when her parents announced they would be coming for a visit. Bev and Ted wanted to see them before that day arrived so taking advantage of the fine spring weather, they had made the trip to Cornwall. It was true that they had visited Cornwall before, but never to Polperro, a tiny fishing village nestled on the picturesque coast. It felt as though they entered a green and magical place as they drove the steep and narrow road that snaked its way to the village.

They found the kids happily settled in a little cottage near the upper part of the village as though they had been there for years. They had received the shipment of their belongings and had already hung pictures, found a place for everything and made it a comfortable home. They were anxious to show Bev and Ted the village and to take them for a pub meal.

It was a beautiful place of whitewashed and pastel painted cottages, many of them hugging the steep hillside. There were dear little shops with pots and window boxes of flowers blooming in abundance and a little stream that flowed through and down to the sea. The street was far too narrow so cars had to be parked in the parking lot at the top of the town. Horse-drawn carts gave a ride for the faint-hearted people who were unwilling to walk the half mile to the harbour. They walked. Cornwall was a county steeped in old tradition and folklore, and many old timers did not consider it to be a part of England at all. True, it was like a no-man's land. Bev couldn't help but notice in one of the shop windows, a 'gollywog' doll, which had been considered to be politically incorrect and racist.

"You wouldn't see that in England," Bev pointed.

"No," said Phil. "And yet I remember as a child, seeing the little black image on jars of jam of a certain brand."

"But this is Cornwall," Ted remarked.

They arrived at the ancient pub with it's dark blue walls covered in seafaring objects and stepped into the low-ceiling room which smelled of good food and beer. The place boasted a menu featuring fresh seafood that was brought in by the local fishermen each day. They were spoiled for choice.

Soon savoury meals were put before them and they ate, talked, laughed and Phil regaled them with a ghost story about the very place they were in. Footsteps and slamming doors were heard when the place was empty save for the bartender ready to lock the place for the night. And another tale of a witch that had changed into a hare when she was being pursued by angry villagers.

"People are adamant that the stories are true," he added. "I find it very fascinating anyway. I have a book on folklore you might like to see."

"Well, I'm not one to dismiss their beliefs," Ted said and then changed the subject. "So, when do your parents arrive?" he directed to Sonia.

"In exactly three weeks, and they would love to meet up with you in London." That time had passed very quickly.

Now here they all were waving a welcome near the lions at Trafalgar Square. Bev and Ted fell in with their plans of lunch and a tour of the National Art Gallery all within walking distance of where they had met.

The pub they chose was already a hum of activity as they found places to sit. Phil went with Ted to the bar to order food and drinks doing his best to talk over the noise of patrons. "The art gallery is probably not your cup of tea Dad, but that's what they want to do, so I'm just falling in with their plans. I hope you and Mum are okay with that?"

"I'm just so glad to see you again, Son, it's okay," reassured Ted as he paid the bartender. Secretly, he preferred a stroll in St. James's Park away from all the hustle bustle, but following lunch they made their way to the gallery.

As they climbed the many steps to the gallery, Ted hung back from the others for a quick puff of his inhaler; the sultry air was getting to him. He wished now he hadn't come, there really wasn't much chance of having a good visit with his son anyway. He didn't have much interest in all those old paintings, he'd seen them all before. When he could tolerate it no longer, he pulled Bev aside.

"I really need to get out of here, I'm finding it difficult to breathe."

Bev wasted no time in catching up with the others to make their excuses.

"We'll come to the West Country and meet again before Sonia's parents have to return, dear," she hugged Phil who was looking quite concerned for his dad.

"I'll be okay when I get out of here, it's just too close," Ted reassured with a goodbye hug and they made their way to the train station.

Once in the first-class air-conditioned compartment, he began to feel better almost immediately. Bev watched him settle into reading his book and sip on a cool beer. She could relax now, he was okay. She sat gazing out the window at the scenery flashing by oblivious to the fact that Ted had taken his last ever trip to London.

True to their word, not more than two weeks later they were on their way to the West Country. Arrangements had been made to meet up with Phil, Sonia and her parents in Sherborne, but Ted wanted to first stop in Paignton, and stay one night at Edward House just to see that all was well with the running of the place. He was always in contact with Sean, the manager, but it didn't hurt to pop by unexpected to make sure he was still doing a good job.

Ted found he need not be concerned. They were welcomed like long lost friends to a well-run hotel with a good rating. Business was good, the books in order.

After settling in to their favourite room, they set out to explore all the old familiar places; a walk to the park and duck pond, the seawall to the pub and arcade and then to Roundham park for the view of Torquay. The contrast of white buildings and the blues of sea and sky was always a splendid panorama, one they never tired of. Bev wondered at times if they would have been happier staying here and now seeing it all again made her realize that yes, she would have been. But Ted was content in his childhood home and that was important.

The following morning, keeping to schedule to meet with the kids in Sherborne, they headed out early, always enjoying the rolling Devon countryside. Soon they crossed into Dorset, signposted as a reminder. The undulating hills were the verdant green of summer and the air had a quality all its own.

Ted relaxed at the wheel and felt a twinge of excitement at the prospect of seeing old Sherborne again. It had been ten years since they had left the place.

Also he was very pleased to be seeing his son again.

They pulled into the parking lot of the Sherborne hotel just before noon, being first to arrive. Within moments, Phil pulled up beside them and then it was meeting and greeting all over again. Bev thought Phil looked a little strained, probably from trying to entertain the in-laws she guessed. She knew that mother-in-law was not an easy person to please. But then he was his old cheery self after checking into their rooms and having lunch in the restaurant. He even enjoyed showing Sonia and her parents through the place, reminiscing about when he had worked there in the bygone years. None he had worked with then seemed to be there now.

After lunch they all headed out for the town, walking the old familiar streets of Sherborne and seeing it through the parents' eyes as though for the first time. Nothing had changed. The abbey bells still pealed out the time of day to the tune of the Westminster chimes, the shops still held their old world charm and people were as courteous as ever. Ted felt right at home.

They explored the town walking from the top of Cheap Street to the bottom, father-in-law snapping photos left, right and centre, hardly seeing anything except through the lens of his camera. Their final stop was the abbey. They had the place to themselves, save for the elderly guide who seemed to be busy putting hymn books back in place. He looked up and smiled a welcome. Sonia and her parents sped off up the centre aisle, taking it all in with minimal interest. Bev was aware that none professed to be at all religious. Apparently, they had been soured by an upbringing by parents who were religious fanatics, and that past had rubbed off on their daughter as well. But how could

344

anyone not be moved by that ancient structure of stone and marvellous stained glass built to the glory of God? She followed Ted and Phil into a quiet place where marble edifices marked the tombs of the long dead and read with them the epitaphs. Like her, they were always moved by the place. Suddenly, rumbling chords from the pipe organ resounded to the fan-vault ceiling, sending shivers up her spine. How fortunate that the organist had taken just that moment to practise. She laughed inwardly at how father-in-law jumped at the sudden unexpected belting out of the music and then took his leave of the place with his wife in tow. Sonia wandered over to Bev and the men to say she would be waiting outside with her parents. Bev, Ted and Phil waited until the last chord played and then slowly made their way out. They never failed to feel blessed and uplifted by the experience of the abbey.

That same evening, a ride to Sandford Orcas had been decided on so they made their way driving down the narrow road to the hamlet. Around the last corner, The Mitre Inn came into view and Ted felt butterflies in his stomach at the sight of it. So many years of memories. It was a homecoming. Bev also felt nostalgic.

The publican who seemed to recognise them called out a friendly greeting and then seated them at a long table in the back where the public bar had been back in the day when Ted and Bev had first seen the place in the summer of '76.

They enjoyed a sumptuous meal of curried prawns, rice, oven-roast chicken and green salads, home-baked breads all washed down with a good wine. There was a hum of pleasant conversation and laughter ringing to the rafters of that ancient place, stirring up the ghosts of those long dead. To Ted, the feeling was so tangible he announced that if everyone was up for it, a walk to the manor house would top off the evening. The decision was unanimous.

The scent of honeysuckle and rose wafted on the warm evening breeze and Bev was in her element. She pointed out various plants that she loved; foxglove, comfrey, dog daisy and borage hoping to find a common ground with mother-in-law who seemed more interested in what her husband was saying. Then the manor house and parish church came into view and that caught everyone's interest. They walked around the courtyard hoping for a tour of the manor, but they were too late for a viewing. A wander through the church and grounds proved to be a pleasant experience. Ted pointed out the little cottage opposite.

"Bev and I spent the summer of '76 staying in that cottage. It was a summer to remember." Bev agreed.

"You stayed there!" Sonia's mum exclaimed in amazement. "I can't imagine anyone wanting to stay here, there's nothing here. There are so many other lovely places."

"Well, it suited us!" Bev tersely stated. "It was one of the most pivotal times of our life. Beauty is in the eye of the beholder and we appreciate the antiquity of the place and its place in history." Ted gave her an approving look.

The following day they decided to visit Stourhead House and gardens. Bev and Ted had not been there before either so they looked forward to a pleasant walk about. It was said to be one of the best 18th century English gardens and they would not be disappointed for it was a beautiful warm day as well.

The grounds were laid out to accent the natural beauty of the countryside and a path around the still lake gave a view from every perspective. They gazed across at the beautiful structure mirrored in the lake, resembling a Greek temple, the Pantheon. They walked, talked, snacked on cookies Bev had brought along and peered in at the various grottos along the way. Ted kept up a good pace, resting only once to sit on a bench for a cigarette. Bev was surprised how well he had done as they had walked the perimeter of the lake.

After a well-deserved lunch in the tea room, it was time to part company with Phil and Sonia. They had to return to Cornwall that day, but Sonia's parents planned to stay for two more nights to be squired around the countryside by Ted and Bev before they returned to Cornwall for the remainder of their stay.

By the time they arrived back at the hotel, they were all feeling the effects of the long walk so the couples parted ways to do their own thing for the evening.

They would meet at breakfast in the morning. Ted was only too happy to retire to their room, put up his feet and watch TV. Bev, on the other hand, as soon as she had freshened up was off out for the town to pick up a few delis for an evening snack. She entered the doors of the huge Sainsbury's at the bottom of the town, took up a shopping basket and proceeded up the produce aisle. She was overwhelmed with the huge selection she found there but in the end selected ready-made cheese and pickle sandwiches, packs of soup mix, grapes and butter tarts. She paid at the till, once again amazed at how reasonable the price of food was in this country. With her purchases in a plastic bag, she headed out the door. She mused that all those years ago when she had first come to Sherborne, plastic bags were as scarce as hen's teeth, everyone seemed to carry a wicker basket for their shopping back then.

She headed back in the direction of the abbey, wanting to see once again the street where they had lived. And as she walked, all the experiences of that time came flooding back to her as though it were only yesterday. She would remind Ted when she got back. By the time she reached the hotel, she was very tired indeed. Ted looked more relaxed and was quite ready for the little meal she offered.

They sat with their steaming cups of soup and recalled the day's events, memories of earlier years and plans for the following day. They laughed and talked until it was quite late. With birds still singing and it getting dark, so late now that it was past the summer solstice, it didn't seem right to retire at the usual time.

In the morning, Ted and Bev had all but finished their breakfast when the in- laws finally made an appearance. They greeted them and remained seated, sipping their coffee while the couple made selections from the buffet table. Bev leaned in close to Ted's ear ..." Their body language suggests to me that they may have had a tiff," she whispered.

"Oh dear, I hope it doesn't put a damper on our day out," Ted whispered back.

But they were smiling when they sat with their food and interested in the day that Ted had planned for them.

"I believe you would enjoy Salisbury, it's well worth seeing as the cathedral has the tallest spire in all of England and the Magna Carta is on display there.

And there is so much to see along the way. We've not been there in some time so we will enjoy it also."

"We'll give you a tour of our favourite places," offered Bev.

Ted could always be counted on to convey enthusiasm and humour in any circumstance and the trip to Salisbury was pleasant. They had taken the familiar A352 road from Sherborne which had many places of interest along the way. Ted slid a disc of his favourite tunes into the CD player and enjoyed the drive.

The in-laws sat in the back seat holding hands, seeming totally immersed in the music. On the outskirts of the town they took advantage of the park and ride. It was a system whereby cars were safely parked and visitors were bussed to the town centre.

They boarded the bus, the men sat together opposite the women. Mother-in- law took the window seat and gazed out at her unfamiliar surroundings, making an occasional comment. How strange thought Bev, that we don't really have much to say to each other even though my son is married to her daughter. Bev told her of how she had become interested in Salisbury after reading the book 'Sarum'. She said she had not heard of it and left it at that. Then there seemed to be silence between them as they listened to the men's conversation. Bev was glad when they arrived at the town centre, she would be happy for Ted to be the tour guide for the day. She knew how he loved showing off his England.

Bev enjoyed the day immensely. She was so pleased to see all the lovely places she remembered; the cathedral, the market square, the duck pond and water meadows and the New Inn. Having lunch there once again sitting in the back garden with good food and a view of the spire just put a cap on her day.

By the time they returned to Sherborne, it was near closing time for the hotel restaurant, so they went directly to their rooms to freshen up. Once in the room with the door closed behind them, Ted exhaled a deep sigh.

"That was hard work keeping those two entertained, but did you enjoy your day?"

"I did indeed," Bev replied. "I'm sorry I left it all up to you. I agree they are not the easiest people to please, but at least they thanked you and said they enjoyed the day."

At dinner, father-in-law announced that they would be retiring early as they planned to catch the 10 am train from Sherborne to Cornwall the next day. Ted assured them that he and Bev would be up early too and would drive them to the station. They would be heading home for Kent right after seeing them off.

At the train station next morning, they bid them goodbye with handshake and hugs. There could have no way of knowing it then, but it would be the last time they'd see Ted.

Once more that summer, they made the trip to the Cornwall. The kids had bought a new car and had no place to park the Volvo so Ted decided they would travel by train and drive it back. It had been very wet for a few weeks that summer and from the train windows was a clear view of the flooded fields along the way. Any low lying land was transformed into ponds were waterfowl gathered. The farmers were truly at the mercy of the weather.

Bev thought of Tess away in Spain with her boyfriend for the summer and felt a pang of missing her. She had phoned a few times, and sent them colourful postcards. Bev had brought them along to show Phil.

He was at the train station to greet them with hugs, as jovial as always.

"Sonia is at work so it's just the three of us this evening, I want to treat you to dinner at the Crumple Horn pub, it's so close we can walk."

"How lovely dear, we'd enjoy that," replied Bev.

"Sounds wonderful," Ted seconded as he passed their suitcase for the boot.

It was very nearly Phil's birthday so they gave him his presents. Birthdays had always been a very special time and it was lovely to be able to spend such quality time without Sonia's input for a change. But that was not to last.

The next morning, they all went out to explore the countryside and found themselves late in the afternoon on Bodmin moor and starving. Ted pulled in at a very old pub. They climbed the steps and entered a door that was so low that one had to bend otherwise bump the head, and the beams of the ceiling were likewise. They sat perusing the menus. It always seemed to take Sonia a long time to choose and Ted noticed that she was taking her time as usual.

"Have what you like kids, the treat is on us."

"Well, in that case I'll have..." and she went on to order a full meal. "We can have snacks this evening."

Bev gave Ted a meaningful nudge under the table and steered the conversation to Tess and her stay in Spain.

"Well, I should be jealous, but I'm not," said Sonia ... "Because my parents have promised us a few days in Paris next spring as a way of saying thank you for having them. I really look forward to that."

"That's wonderful!" Ted replied. "I hope that means you'll come see us as the channel crossing terminal in Ashford is so close?"

"We'll see," she replied with a snip to her voice.

"We will indeed, Dad, even if we have to take extra time off, "Phil confirmed. The next day the kids had to work and they were homeward bound for Kent.

Bev missed her own bed but it didn't prevent her from suggesting that they stay one night in Sherborne to break the journey. Ted was always eager to make the stop. He loved the welcoming atmosphere of the Sherborne hotel, loved the Dorset air, and loved that he could relax and breathe easier.

"It's just as well, Bev. I feel I'm coming down with a cold."

Bev plied him with cups of steaming tea and paracetamol and after a good sleep, he felt much better and quite able to make the journey. How good it felt to be home. No matter how anxious one is to get away, there is no place like it. Bev felt as if she had been away for a week instead of three days.

As Ted turned the key in the door, she checked the mailbox and to her delight, a letter from Tess which she read out loud as soon as they made a cup of tea.

Hello Ma and Pa!

Finally, I have a chance to sit down and write to you. I hope this letter finds you well and enjoying your British summer. We have been busy almost every day since we got here. Lucas' sister, Deb, and her husband, Andy, are really nice and her daughter, Claire, has a husband and little boy of about 10 months. It is very helpful to have them around as they have all been here about three years and know all there is to know about the place.

The Spanish people are very friendly and helpful. But Spain is not a first world country as we are used to and there is a major culture shock to be sure. The urbanizations are oases among the really grotty areas- so when you venture out you see a lot of poverty (though I think since the EU it is way better). Garbage! And graffiti on very run-down buildings. The villas are completely opposite, very beautiful architecture, swimming pools, palm trees and beautiful flowers. The playas (beaches) are lovely- though some are dirtier than others. The Mediterranean Sea is like a bathtub- but very refreshing when its 42°C out. I try to stay away from the noon day sun but have been swimming as late as 9:30pm and it's still so hot even then! Lots of mosquitos! Wouldn't have thought so, but it's true and (big). Have been eaten alive as usual. Could really make big business out of North American style screen doors and windows here. I've seen a few cockroaches (Las Cucarachas) but only flying across the floor in the night so fast you'd think you had just dreamed it.

I'm having an amazing experience just being here but the HEAT really takes some getting used to. There is no relief even at night so ice packs are my true friend. It is the hottest time of the year so I shouldn't base all of it on that. Living here for good?... I'd have to deeply consider it. I can see how there are so many things about the UK I would miss. But in the true Piercy style I know I will pine for Spain when I finally have to leave her. No regrets right now anyway.

We may not stay long in Villa Allegria as she is a bit small and not air conditioned, no cross drafts, etc. There are nicer places we could get for about 600 Euros per month, 3-4 bedrooms, 2 bathrooms, pool, etc. in an Urbanization.

We plan to go to Madrid maybe next week (5 hrs drive from here) so will stay overnight. Can check out both Spanish and Canadian embassies to see where I stand as far as working and staying longer than October.

It's really nice to hang out the laundry upstairs on the rooftop solarium sundeck and have it bone dry in 10 mins. No Lie. But my laundry has basically consisted of my bathing suits and towels. You can tell who the true Spanish people are because they are the ones walking down the streets in jeans and long sleeved shirt while I'm fading in my bikini and seriously hoping I could just be naked.

The shopping areas are mainly large mercados (supermarkets) and have everything you need, also air-conditioned - now there is a word I cling to. Everything is labelled in Spanish but it's amazing how quickly you pick it up and understand it. I think it is by far easier than French. Except for the time I bought tartar sauce thinking it was salad dressing. Oops! We bought a whole buggy load of food for 40 Euros. Groceries are way cheap, but eating out at restaurants can get a bit pricy. The local places where the Spanish eat are good food and good prices but you can get caught up in the tourist traps and regret it. Hope to venture out to Benidorm and to Murcia soon to see a bit more of Old Spain - the churches, the vineyards and orchards. It is very urban, modern and big in this area. Obvious that much of it the British have built as their playground.

So strange to see the size of the roads here, so wide compared to Broadstairs! Ha ha!

The brand new hospital is just up the road and the pharmacy (la farmicia) is a short walk up by the English newsagent and the supermarket.

My favourite short walk lately is to the pool (la piscine) I don't wear nearly as much makeup or jewellery anymore- Why! Because I'm too damn hot to care. Please write back soon. Take care of each other and give my love to Phil and Sonia.

Love Tess

"It sounds like she's having fun, but God I wish she'd come home. I miss her," Ted sighed. "I can't help worrying about her."
"Me too, dear, it's a good experience for her but it sounds like the heat might drive them home."

***

They need not have fretted, for by the end of August Tess was home in time to still enjoy an English summer.

Autumn of His Last Year

Bev could hardly believe that it was the beginning of September already. It seemed that summer had gone in the blink of the eye. September was her most favourite month of the year; the time when children were returning to school and the days were still pleasantly warm but with cooler nights and also the abundance of local produce. She was busy in the kitchen sterilizing jars for her apricot jam. She could hear Ted rooting around in the hall closet for something.

"Where is that box of old photos, Bev?" his muffled voice came from behind the closet door. "Oh, never mind, I've found them."

She finished pouring the hot jam into jars, cleaned up the kitchen then sauntered into the sitting room where Ted was sifting through old photos from his childhood. He held out one for her to see; a large black and white photo taken circa 1950s of a large group of people assembled in an auditorium. Ted pointed to a child sitting on the floor in the foreground dressed in a dormouse costume.

She recognised his cheeky smiling face.

"That was so much fun. Look at the people in the background wearing the huge Mardi Gras type heads. One of them was my father, I think he was the policeman." There were seven in all; a policeman, a nurse, a butcher, etc. all with outlandish oversized clownish egg head masks towering well above all the others in the group. "I'm going to show Sami and his wife this photo." Sami was his East Indian newsagent where Ted went every morning of the week for his *Daily Mail* and cigarettes. They had told him this morning that the annual parade was to take place on Saturday and would end up with a huge fete on the green, and Ted didn't want to miss it.

"I'd like to see that parade on Saturday, Bev, it will be just like the old days," he said with enthusiasm.

On the morning of that day Bev busied herself making a potato salad. She sliced thick slabs of cold ham and chicken to accompany a green salad and pickle and plated it all for the fridge. It would be much easier to have it all prepared once the parade was finished. Ted sorted out the folding deckchairs while she made a flask of coffee to take along. The parade was to start at noon.

"I want to get a good spot right on the corner of our street for a good view." So long before that time, they selected a vantage point and sat waiting. More and more people arrived and they felt themselves lucky to have such a good spot. Soon the distant sound of drums from a marching band could be heard. As well as starting at the Margate clock tower which was some distance away, some of the parade route was also uphill. Finally after what seemed ages, the first of the parade was in sight. There were children on decorated bicycles, then colourful floats carrying brightly costumed people passed by and a bevy of decorated dogs and ponies. And then there, at the end of the parade, Ted spotted the big heads bobbing above the rest, there were only two. He felt deflated and disappointed as they were no way near as he had remembered them.

"To think we sat here for all this long to see that!" he remarked with a disgruntled growl and got up folding his deck chair with a snap and headed off home, his shoulders slumped. Bev followed, trying to keep up with his pace.

"I'm so sorry you were disappointed, dear. You know things always seem so much more memorable as a child. Never mind, I've got a lovely meal ready for you at home," she coddled, hugging his waist.

***

The autumn days seemed to pass ever so quickly as there was always some place to go or something to be doing. How could anyone think that being retired meant having time on your hands. It seemed to Bev as though time sped up as she got older, and she remembered that as a child, summer holidays seemed to be endless. Ted seemed his usual contented self. He was always game for an outing to one of the many

354

beautiful hidden places of Kent. They always seemed to end up at some dear little village or another enjoying either a pub lunch or a picnic.

It was one such outing they had planned this morning so Bev gave Tess a call to see if she would like to join them. Her company was always welcome.

"Hi, Mum, I was just about to phone you. You'll not believe this, but I got a call last night from my friend Ben from back home. He called to extend his condolences as he had heard that Dad had died. I was truly shocked but I assured him that it was not true, that Dad was quite well. He wouldn't say who he heard it from, but isn't that weird?"

"Really… how… really," Bev stammered. "I find that hard to believe. I think we should keep it to ourselves though, not tell Dad. I feel certain it would disturb him no end. As it is, he's down at the car at this moment checking the oil before we head off. Do you want to join us, dear? We're going for a drive to Broad Oak farm for some produce and then for a walk in the woods, have a pub lunch somewhere," Bev enthused.

"I'd love to, Mum, pick me up okay? I'm ready whenever you are, see you soon."

Bev got off the phone feeling rather uneasy. Wherever could a rumour like that have come from? It was totally incomprehensible. She thought about it for a while, and it gave her an uneasy feeling of foreboding.

It was a gorgeous day though, one that was still warm enough to be summer but the air quality was different. There was a hint of ripened fruit and the musty smell of fallen leaves. Ted had chosen to sit in a deckchair with a cigarette near the car while Bev and Tess wandered down a woodland path under a canopy of golden leaves. They talked about the phone call again, both agreeing that it was uncanny and hoped it was not a premonition. Tess changed the subject by pointing out a wild herb growing near the path, she was interested in seeing some of the herbs in their natural surroundings that she used medicinally.

They almost stepped on it. A black adder there on the path in front of them. Neither had ever seen such a snake before. It did not appear to be disturbed by their presence and took it's time before slithering away into the underbrush. "I think they can bite," said Bev as she watched it slowly move away. Tess agreed. But a thought surfaced from somewhere in her mind. Was the sighting of the elusive black adder a bad omen? *I'll just keep that thought to myself. Mum has already had one shock today.*

"We best be turning back, Tess. Dad will be wondering where we are."

***

Sunlight filtered through the bedroom window, waking Bev early on that special October day. Moments earlier, she had heard the key turning in the lock as Ted left the flat to pick up his morning paper. She got up and made herself a coffee, there could be no lingering in bed this morning. It was Ted's birthday and she wanted to have a nice breakfast ready when he returned.

When she heard him laboriously climbing the stairs she greeted him at the door with the aroma of bacon wafting out into the hallway.

"Happy birthday, darling! I've made you a lovely breakfast," she said with a smile and planted a kiss on his cheek.

"What a lovely surprise, dear. Are you going to join me this morning then?"

"Yes, but I'll pass on the cooked breakfast."

She sat opposite with her chin cupped in her hand watching him tuck into his eggs and ham. It amused her to see him slather butter on his toast and then heap it with marmalade just as he had done all his life. Some habits last a lifetime she mused.

"Thank you, I really enjoyed that, and gifts too?" She passed him a pile of wrapped gifts.

"That gift from Phil arrived a few days ago and Tess will stop by this evening with hers. How would you like to spend the day, dear?"

"Well, I'd love to have a look through the Aviation Museum.

They have many of the war planes on display and then I'd like to have lunch at the pub in St. Peter," he said as he tore away at the wrapping paper, grinning with pleasure with each gift he opened. He especially liked the Zippo lighter with the ace of spades design, the significance of it not being lost on him. "Thank you, I love it."

On this special day in the place of his birth, the weather could not have been finer had it been ordered. The sky was a clear blue with warm sunshine and fresh salty sea air. Following the tour through the museum they drove to the tiny village of St. Peter just on the outskirts of Broadstairs. It was another of their favourite haunts.

They lingered over a meal of scampi and chips, then afterwards were drawn like a magnet to the St. Peter's churchyard. It was one of the most interesting places they had found, well wooded with many of the ancient headstones almost entirely hidden by overgrowth. They rambled the gravelled pathways, stopping at intervals to read some of the headstones, then finding an old weathered wooden bench they sat with their faces to the sun. Ted shielded his eyes for a moment to gaze across at one of the many stone angels. Over a family plot she stood, a towering sentinel with her wings extended, hands clasped before her and sightless downcast eyes.

"Say, Bev, have you ever thought where you'd like to be laid to rest when the time comes?" he mentioned candidly. Bev followed his gaze across the graveyard. They hadn't talked much about death before; it was ironic that he should broach the subject in view of the phone call Tess had received.

"I haven't really thought about it before... but... I think I would like my ashes interred next to my parents' graves back home, but with nothing as ostentatious as that stone angel over there, lovely as she is. What about you, dear?"

"I think I'd like mine to be at sea. There's something nice about thinking I'd become one with the sea. Will you do that for me, should I go first?"

"Of course, Ted. But enough of this talk. I'm sure we'll both be tottering on together till ripe old age." She grabbed his hand and pulled him to his feet and kissed him. "We should be going, I still have a few preparations for dinner and Tess will arrive as soon as she is finished work.

Tess bounded in the door only moments before dinner was ready to be served, bearing an armload of wrapped gifts and a rich chocolate cake, Ted's favourite. Then later that evening, Phil phoned. "Happy birthday, Dad. I hope you had a great day, I've been thinking of you all day at work."

"Thank you, Son, and for your great gift, too. Yes, I've had a wonderful day, very spoiled. Say...I've been wondering if you and Sonia could get away for a few days? Maybe meet in Sherborne?"

"Well, funny you should say that, Dad. I've been thinking the same. We get three days off together next week, let's do that." They talked at length and then Bev and Tess took turns for a chat with him. The phone was passed back to Ted.

"Thanks for calling, Son. By the way, I checked online and the Sandford Orcas manor house is open for tours until the end of the month. Care to see it again?"

"Love to, Dad, and I'm certain Sonia would too. Bye, now."

***

Three loud raps of the iron knocker and they stood back and waited for what seemed ages and were about to turn and leave when the great oak door finally creaked open. The tall angular grey-haired Squire of the manor graciously welcomed them into his quiet abode. After pocketing the admission fee, he led the way through the lower rooms; the dining room, the dark panelled sitting room and kept up a commentary as though rehearsed. Some rooms though, he avoided, namely the kitchen and his private living quarters.

He proudly pointed out the ornately-framed Gainsborough portraits of his long dead ancestors and shared a bit of family history. The faces seemed to stare down at the intruders of their domain. He then led them to the staircase.

As they ascended the stairs, Ted hung back from the others. He had felt a need to see this place once again and bravely challenged himself to feel anything out of the ordinary. The hushed, dark bedrooms were viewed first. He felt nothing. Next the games room and a walk around the ancient card table. He touched a pictogram of the ace of spades in passing and felt nothing. Lastly, the tiny room over the archway, this one they had not seen before.

They peered out through the small leaded window into the courtyard below. It was from this window that the ghostly visage of a bearded man had been picked up on a tourists photo. Ted felt nothing out of the ordinary. They retraced their steps back through the rooms for another lingering look then descended the staircase to the lower floor and the great sitting room.

They thanked the squire and filed out of the building into the walled manicured gardens. They walked a distance away and then looked back at the Tudor manor, beautiful and benign in autumn sunshine in spite of the fact that it was reputed to be the most haunted house in Britain.

"This is a truly lovely place," remarked Phil. "And I suppose I will be drawn to this area for the rest of my life," he sighed.

God forbid, not you too, Son. He had had a powerful magnetic need to return again and again for more years than he cared to remember. Perhaps it had just been his imagination that he had had a past connection here in this sequestered place. But today I feel nothing.

It was Ted's last visit to Sandford Orcas.

Christmas 2007

Ted could not remember having celebrated Christmas twice, but that was to be the case this year. "If the kids can't come to us then we we'll just have to go to them," he said to Bev after hearing from Phil that they wouldn't be able to come to Kent. It was unfortunate that Tess could not get the time off work to join them, but she had her gifts ready to send along. He sat with his cup of tea watching Bev wrap gifts. He had done his shopping early and had the packages stowed under his bed. Bev had finished all her traditional baking; a large fruit cake, her prize shortbread with red and green cherries, ginger cookies as well as a batch of chocolate fudge, Phil's favourite. She boxed it with the Turkish Delight purchased at the public market in Sandwich. They had enjoyed that outing, it being even more special this time of year.

About a week before Christmas they made the trip to Cornwall once again, breaking the journey by staying overnight in Sherborne. The weather was pleasant and road conditions excellent for the journey the next day to the kids.

They arrived late in the afternoon and no sooner had they unpacked than they were all walking to the 'Crumple Horn' for supper. The old pub was decorated for Christmas, a fire burned in the fireplace and there was a hum of happy people. Over delicious meals and beer, they talked and laughed and celebrated being together. Phil got up and snapped a picture of his parents both flushed and smiling. He was so pleased to see them so happy.

The following morning, as though it were Christmas day already, Phil fried up a hearty breakfast of bacon, eggs, grilled tomatoes, baked beans and toast.

"Eat up, everyone, we'll have snacks this afternoon, but dinner will be fairly late as the turkey is huge," he laughed. "We won't be cooking another come Christmas day but I'm sure we'll have plenty left over."

"You can also make a hearty soup," Bev chimed in. She never failed to make a broth from turkey bones, it seemed to be just what was needed after all the overindulgence of the season. Following breakfast and tidying of the kitchen, preparations for stuffing the bird began. Sonia made the dressing, Bev pared vegetables, Phil made a salad and Ted snapped photos. Once the turkey was in the oven they bundled up for a bracing walk to the harbour.

It was truly a beautiful spot. It was no wonder so many artists came here to paint the scenery; there seemed to be a special quality to the light that enhanced the cloud formations, the sea and rolling hills, still green even though it was winter. Fishing boats bobbed out in the deep with screeching gulls hovering near, a sure sign of fish. They would soon be coming in with the catch of the day. Walking next to his son, Ted felt quite well, breathing in the briny air.

"Are you happy here, Son?" he whispered.

"Yes. For now. But not sure for how long," Phil confessed.

"Only I had really hoped you would settle in Kent. Maybe in time you will."

And then their conversation was interrupted by Sonia..."Let's stop in at the pub to warm up near the fire and have a drink." It was a welcome break to give Ted the strength for the uphill walk to the cottage.

By the time they arrived at the cottage door, they could already smell the aroma of roasting turkey. But it would not be ready until much later. Sonia soon had plates of savoury bits and bites for them to pick on. While the turkey roasted they sat near the Christmas tree, nibbled the snacks, sipped on drinks and opened gifts. One gift that delighted Ted was a DVD of Billy Connelly, the Scot comedian. Phil slid it in the player and they roared with laughter, especially Ted, at the comedian's antics and rather crude jokes. It delighted Phil to see his father so enjoying himself and he would remember those moments, always.

Dinner was finally served; turkey done to perfection, stuffing, roast vegetables with rich gravy and salad. They ate, they talked, they laughed.

"Funny how it takes hours to prepare a Christmas dinner, and less than an hour to eat it," remarked Phil as he scraped the plates for the dishwasher .

"But well worth all the effort. That was delicious," Ted replied .

Sadly, the following day Bev and Ted had to begin the long journey home and the kids to return to work. They helped them to their car with their luggage and all the gifts they had received plus gifts for Tess. In separate cars they drove out of the village and to a pub for lunch, only prolonging the inevitable goodbyes. Again the glasses were raised to 'a happy season' meals were consumed and then it was time to go. In the parking lot standing near their cars, they hugged with farewell kisses and handshake.

"Cheerio, Son, thank you for a lovely time," said Ted as he hugged him close. "Bye, Dad, have a safe journey and let us know when you are home."

"We plan to break our journey by staying in Sherborne tonight," said Bev. "We always enjoy that no matter how many times we do it, and thank you for the turkey sandwiches; we'll enjoy those later."

With nothing more they could say without getting misty, Ted pulled the car out of the parking lot and they waved back as the tyres crunched on gravel signalling their departure.

Phil raised his hand in farewell, unaware that it would be the very last time he would see his father.

***

Standing outside the Sherborne hotel that evening, Ted breathed in the cold Dorset air, lit a cigarette and as he watched the exhaled smoke waft away, he thought about the many times they had been there before. It had been at least thirty years since their first visit. He thought about the elusive quest he had been on then and for the many more years after. *And where did it get me? Have I wasted my life? Will I ever write that story?* he questioned.

His mentor lingered near and waited. It was almost time.

The following morning they headed out of the town early. The sun, a red orb was just peeping over the heavily frosted hills and cast a rosy glow on the winter scene. They sang along to Christmas carols on the radio. They talked about the things they had to do when they got home. They talked about Tess and how happy she was with her new love. They talked of their visit with the kids.

"Do you think our boy is happy, dear?" Bev asked cautiously.

"Well, now that you mention it, I have my doubts. It's just their body language and little remarks to him when she thinks we don't hear her. I don't know, it's up to them to sort it out. Don't you be worrying about it, Bev."

"Oh, but I do. It's a mother's privilege to worry." She tried to make light of a subject that troubled them both.

By supper time they were home. How wonderful it felt. They still had Christmas proper to celebrate and it looked very much as though it would be a green one after all. It began to rain in earnest as they unpacked the car.

***

Tess arrived Christmas Eve, bearing gifts and a large bouquet of sparkly red and white carnations. "Merry Christmas, you two!" She hugged them in turn. "But don't get too close, I've got the start of a rotten cold." She busied herself putting the flowers in a vase and her gifts under the tree then she joined Bev in the kitchen to stir the gravy. She was eager to hear all about their stay in Cornwall. Bev opened the oven door to check the turkey.

"So, Mum, how's my bro getting on? Is he happy there?"

"Dad and I wonder, but you'll never hear him say otherwise even if he wasn't. You should know that. I do wish they would move nearer, that's a long way for Daddy to drive though he doesn't complain. I know it wears him out."

"Is he okay, Mum? Only I noticed he had a bit of a look about his eyes ...Oh, of course, you stopped in Sherborne ...it figures."

"This bird is done, let's get dinner on the table," Bev changed the subject.

Ted cracked open a bottle of 'bubbly,' and they gathered around the table for a another roast turkey dinner. Bev was of a mind that she would serve it again cold with salads on Christmas Day then they could get out for a drive instead of being tied to the kitchen. They pulled Christmas crackers, read out the silly jokes donned the bright-coloured paper hats, laughed, talked and ate until they groaned. Bev noticed that Ted had eaten well. *He seems OK to me,* she thought.

"That was lovely, Mum, thank you. Now is there anything on the box?" she asked as she cleared the table.

"Well, the usual," answered Ted. "But I have a very funny DVD I know you'd enjoy. It's a gift from Phil."

Tess had a sense of humour just like her father and she laughed unsuppressed along with him. Bev laughed to see them laughing then busied herself in the kitchen putting the finishing touch on the trifle for dessert.

Christmas day was green but grey. Rain clouds shrouded the coast. But after a hearty breakfast and gift opening they headed out in the car for a drive to St. Peters. It was very mild with misty rain and dreary leaden sky that might have put a damper on the day had it not been for their destination. As they pulled into the already full parking lot the rain was seriously lashing at the windscreen.

They ran laughing to the pub door and pushed it open to a warm and jolly scene. There was standing room only but then Tess saw that a table near the Christmas tree was being vacated and she made a dash to claim it. It just would not do for her parents to be standing in this crowd. Once they were seated ..."I'll get the drinks, I know what you like," and she pushed her way to the bar.

They raised their glasses once again to a Merry Christmas and Happy New Year then became part of the noisy boisterous crowd. Later when Bev went to the ladies, Tess had a heart to heart with her Dad.

"I'm really happy now, Dad. You and Mum have been so helpful at getting me settled. I've finally met the right man for me and we have great plans for the future. I dream of living in Spain with him, but when? I don't yet know."

Ted reached for her hand and held it across the table. "I am so happy for you dear, and I'm glad you have a dream. As for me, I have no more dreams." It was such a final statement that at first Tess was at a loss for a reply, and at that moment she caught a look in his eyes that dismayed her. "Oh, Dad," she said as she squeezed his hand. And on that note their conversation ended as Bev returned. She retrieved her coat from the back of her chair making it obvious that she was ready to go. "Time to go if you'd like dinner, you two."

For the remains of the day Tess thought about what her father had said, it was just so unlike him. But hey, it was Christmas. We must celebrate.

Boxing day after breakfast, Tess packed up her gifts and bits and they drove her back to Broadstairs. It was still raining. "No need to get out of the car, I can manage. Thank you so much for everything Mum, Dad, I love you," she said as she pushed the car door closed with her knee and then stood on the pavement waving as they pulled away. Bev blew her a kiss, Ted waved back.

It was the last time she would see her father.

***

They had seen the new year in quietly. Tess had invited them to a party but they had gratefully declined. On the eleventh day of Christmas, Bev was feeling out of sorts. She had a scratchy tickle in her throat and felt she was coming down with a cold. Feeling unwell or not, Bev decided to take down the Christmas decorations while Ted was out washing the car. She got out the Christmas box and began to remove all the ornaments from the tree. With each one she lovingly wrapped she thought about Christmases past and where they might be this time next year. She thought of the words of a carol 'and next year we all will be together, if the fates allow...' and for some reason it made her feel sad.

She hurriedly finished packing them all away before Ted came in for his cup of tea. As she dusted the coffee table, she lifted the vase of red and white carnations and there lay a fine black satin ribbon about eight inches in length, it looked very much like a book marker ... *how strange, where could it have come from?* Neither Ted nor Tess could shed light on the mystery.

Ted suggested that they get out for a drive, maybe stop at the farmer's market on the outskirts of Cliftonville. Their store of fresh vegetables was depleted so Bev agreed. As they rode along, she covered her nose and mouth with her scarf, hoping to keep her germs to herself. They arrived at the farm and while Ted talked with the farmer and stroked his dog, Bev selected the produce. She filled her basket with russet potatoes, winter pears, apples and broccoli. The effort seemed to wear her out and she began to chill.

By the time they reached their door, she was shaking with cold and wasted no time in getting into her bed.

"Please, Ted, get me a hot water bottle," she said through chattering teeth. She felt so ill. Her throat was sore, her head ached, she was nauseous and in the full grip of rigor as her body temperature rose to 104 degrees. Ted stood at the foot of her bed with such a stricken look on his face. His wife was never ill.

"Oh, please, dear, could you go out and get me some ginger ale?" she moaned." I need to drink and it may settle my stomach."

Ted wasted no time. But by the time he had purchased the ginger ale, returned home and climbed the stairs to the flat, he was gasping for breath. He soon had a glass of ginger ale over ice at her bedside. "There you are, love, that will help," he soothed as he laid a hand on her fevered brow.

"Thank you, dear, I'll be okay, please don't worry. Fix yourself a bite to eat."

Sometime in the middle of the night her fever broke and by the morning of the twelfth day of Christmas, though feeling shaky she was able to get up. Ted was still asleep. She made him a cup of tea and lightly touched his shoulder to wake him.

"Good morning, dear, cup of tea for you." He woke up with a shock to see her standing at his bedside. "You're better," he said, taking the cup with a smile.

"Yes, can't keep this old girl down," she smiled.

After breakfast, Ted went out to get his paper although much later than usual. He always got one for old Nick, their neighbor, on a Sunday and placed it by his door. Nick heard him and opened his door, "Good morning, mate, thank you. You alright?"

"I'm okay, but Bev is sick. I'm just hoping not to get what she has."

"Give her my regards," he said in closing the door.

Though Bev felt shaky and stayed in her housecoat all day, she still made the effort to carry on regardless. She was in the kitchen paring the pears for stewing and overheard Ted's conversation on the phone first with Phil and then Tess.

"I don't know what I'd do without Mum. I gave up trying to find things for my supper last night and ended up having toast and marmalade and Guinness."

Poor dear, she thought. I'll make him a proper supper. I know he'd enjoy salmon cakes with broccoli and cheese sauce.

Bev retired right after clearing away the supper dishes. "I'm going to bed to read, dear." Ted was watching his Sunday evening run of *Heartbeat.*

"I hope you have a good sleep love, and thank you again for that lovely supper." He blew her a kiss.

In the night, she heard Ted coughing. Her throat felt scratchy so she got up to make a cup of tea. She took him a cup and they sat on the edge of his bed sipping their tea. "I hope you're not getting sick too." She rubbed his shoulders.

"That feels wonderful, Bev. Think I'm ready to go back to sleep now."

"Good night, love," she said as she turned off his bedside lamp.

At six in the morning, she heard him rapping on the wall to get her attention. Moments later, he was gone. Taken. DEAD. She was sick but he was dead.

On the Shore

Come home! The year has left you old.

Leave those grey stones; wrap close the shawl, around you for the night is cold.

Come home! He will not hear you call.

No sign awaits you here but the beat of tides upon the strand.

The crag's gaunt shadow with gull's feet imprinted on the sand,

and spars and sea-weed strewn

under the pale moon.

Come home! He will not hear you call, only the night winds answer as they fall along the shore

and evermore.

Only the sea shells

on the grey stones singing, and the white foam-bells

of the North Sea ringing.

E.J Pratt

Saying Goodbye

Many months had passed since the initial shock, the disbelief, the tears, the funeral and the mourning for Ted's passing. Each had grieved in their own way. Bev mourned for the sheer absence of his presence, for the loss of his daily companionship, his laughter and his tender love.

Phil mourned for the loss of a loving father who had always been there for him through all the years of his life. He found himself at times reaching for the phone to ask a question or advice and then would be hit with the fact that his father was no longer there. It left him feeling gutted and empty afresh.

Tess for the most part bottled up her emotions, trying to remain strong for her mother. She felt guilt for the times she had argued with her father, they had often disagreed on many things. But then she would look back to their conversation in the pub at St. Peters realizing that almost her final words to him were said with love, and her tears flowed with release.

Now it was time to say goodbye to all that. Phil and Sonia said goodbye to Cornwall and moved up to Kent just in time to take the little holiday to Paris. It had been just the break they needed.

Tess waved goodbye, leaving for a holiday to Greece; there she relaxed in the warm sunshine, waded in the clear water of the Mediterranean, picked up seashells and healed.

Bev had declined the offer to join her, she didn't feel ready to travel just yet. She was beginning to feel quite comfortable with her own company. She walked a great deal; the beach, coastal paths, woodland, meadows, graveyards: always thinking, always planning. What she really needed was a peaceful place to grow a garden and write. That place she felt would be back on native soil. She knew for a fact that she would miss England when she left, would miss all the haunts she had found with Ted.

The summer passed serenely with many pleasant outings with her children; Canterbury, Whitstable, London and places more local but equally as nice.

In the autumn, Phil and Sonia made plans to return home. Sonia's work visa was due to expire and she missed her parents; had never been away from them for so long. On the day of their leaving while the taxi waited, Phil hugged his sister and mother in turn. "Please don't be sad, Mum, it's all part of the puzzle and the pieces are fitting into place, you'll see." Bev and Tess stood on the pavement outside and waved goodbye as they rode off in the taxi, destination Heathrow and home. When they were out of sight, Bev and Tess hugged each other and cried.

"Oh, God. How I hate goodbyes," whispered Tess.

"Me too, dear, but I'm sure it won't be long before we see the boy again. Come, let's walk to the Old Charles for lunch," she soothed.

Over drinks and lunch they chatted. Tess confessed that she had already discussed with her boyfriend the possibility of leaving England. He wasn't ready for a lasting commitment and could visit. "Well then, that should leave the way clear," said Bev with relief.

***

Bev scanned the tide table in the local paper seeking a date for a high tide at Botany Bay. She had not forgotten the promise she had made to Ted about giving up his ashes to the sea. She wanted to time it precisely so that the ashes would be carried out on the ebbing tide.

The time was right. On a warm September afternoon, Bev and Tess walked side by side across the Palm Bay green. Cradled in her arms she carried the surprisingly heavy urn along the path to Botany Bay. The beach was deserted save for a man and his dog in the distance. The dry golden sand was warm beneath their feet. At the water's edge, having selected a beautiful scallop shell, Bev scooped a shallow trench in the sand into which she poured the granular ashes. They cried sitting side by side on the warm sand and waited. Slowly,

slowly the water lapped nearer and nearer and they waited until it had completely covered the spot. In an offering of blessing, a light offshore breeze played with a tendril of aromatic smoke from an incense stick and carried it across the deep blue sea. White carnations, dried rose petals, lavender and herbs were strewn in the water and with tears running down her cheeks, Bev quoted the very poignant lines from the poem, *Crossing the Bar,* by Tennyson.

"Goodbye, Dad," whispered Tess between sobs.

They waited until the tide was at its highest and the white carnations could be seen bobbing as white specks far out at sea before they turned to leave.

"Come, Tess, darling, there is nothing here for us now. Let's plan to go home."

"Yes, Mama. Carpe diem (seize the day). Life is just too short!"

Epilogue

Ten years later; Edward House, Paignton, in Devon England.

It was a mild April morning and Phil stood in the kitchen of Edward House surveying the work that had been done to refurbish it. With the exception of the new gas cooker, it was complete and he was satisfied. The dining room had been remodelled to perfection and he was anxious for everything to be finished before Easter when his restaurant; the orangery was due to open. It had been his dream for many years to have his own restaurant and it would soon become reality, thanks to his inheritance. He felt elation as well as a measure of sadness that his father and sister could not see it happen. He knew they would have been pleased.

Since leaving England, he had returned twice before. His first trip had been after the death of his dear sister, Tess, killed in a fatal accident only three years after the loss of his father. Glastonbury had given him the spiritual peace he needed to heal. He had climbed the Tor daily and was uplifted at the sight of the wide expanse of England's green and pleasant countryside. It had given him the serenity and healing that he so needed. He had walked the road from Sherborne to Sanford Orcas also remembering times he had been there. He had always felt a special bond to that tiny hamlet.

The second visit had been after his divorce and he had brought his new love to introduce her to all his favourite haunts. She would be joining him later. His mother also promised she would come but for now needed to remain until her final book launch and signing. She had kept her vow to write the story and it was well received. Tess had also written a book which was published posthumously thus fulfilling a lifetime dream.

He sat on the new marble counter top leafing through the glossy pages of the current *Country Life* magazine, waiting for the workers to remove the old cooker to make way for the new. There was page after page of elite properties for sale. He could not believe his eyes, the Sandford Orcas manor house for sale? And why not ... many great homes of historic interest came on the market these days, the cost of upkeep unaffordable. How very interesting he thought, and then the workers had hoisted the heavy cast iron cooker from its site and were moving it out the door. *Under the flagstone.* Something compelled him to slide off the countertop and move across the room to where it had been. He picked up a crowbar and put all his strength into levering up the flagstone. He leaned down and picked up a small leather drawstring pouch that was so covered in a thick layer of dust it could have gone unnoticed. His hands were shaking as he opened it and shook out the contents into his palm. DIAMONDS, many of them in every shape and size glittered in a shaft of sunlight from the skylight. He could scarcely believe his eyes, but there they were and they were his. I saw this in a dream all those years ago. As a small boy in a shop in Brighton, a saleslady had placed cut glass stones in his hand and that night he had dreamed of this moment. The dream had never left him. In that moment Phil went through degrees of awe and disbelief and it came to him in a flash; the realization that he was meant to buy the Sandford Orcas manor house.

There was an overwhelming feeling of the presence of others in that room that day. He could almost hear his father saying *be happy my son, the final piece of the puzzle is in place.* The spirits of his father, his sister and Philip Canton stood by, looked upon him and were satisfied. Atonement had finally been granted.

***

One year later.

The premise of his mother's book had created such a sensation of media hype and speculation about the credibility of the story that it had prompted a team of archaeologists intrigued with the possibility of truth, to excavate the cellar floor of the manor house under the watchful eye of the new owner. To their astonishment, skeletal remains were found beneath a flagstone in the cellar.

They were painstakingly excavated and sent to Oxford University for anthropological and genetic analysis. It was concluded that bones were of a male, possibly in his early twenties and carbon dated to the mid-17th century. A DNA sample had been taken also and awaited a match of any possible descendants. They had also proposed an investigation of the outer wall of the Sherbourne Abbey, possibly removing the lighter hued stone to see if a parchment had been hidden. The story had sparked global interest, for if this was indeed the skeleton of King Charles II, history would definitely have to be rewritten.